The Vineyard

The Vineyard

MICHAEL HURLEY

RAGBAGGER PRESS

CHARLESTON

In Memory of my Mother

Also by Michael Hurley

The Prodigal

Once Upon a Gypsy Moon

Letters from the Woods

The
Vineyard

CHAPTER 1

Drowning seemed like the best option or, for that matter, the only option. Being an inveterate planner of all things, even the means and manner of her own death, Charlotte Harris had explored for a full year the various ways she might best do herself in. Every possibility always came back to the water and to this place. But now that she was finally here and making her final crossing to the island, the greenish-gray waves pushing ahead of the ferry across Vineyard Sound seemed too gentle—incapable, almost, of the kind of violence necessary to end a life.

The water off the coast of New England was warming, that year. This was no small consolation to anyone planning to drown in it. It was one thing to be staring at the maw of death and fighting for breath. Quite another to be freezing while doing so.

Not that the water was *warm,* mind you. It was merely *warmer* that year than most years, when wading in any higher than the knees was a test of moral character for all but two—maybe three—short weeks in July. Some believed the recent temperature change was nature's final reckoning for the sins of global warming. Some said it was just a temporary anomaly in the northward track of the Gulf Stream, which had wandered from its usual mid-Atlantic course, bound for northern Europe, to pass closer to the Vineyard that year.

There was at least one immediate repercussion of the

changing weather. Some may have thought it a trivial matter involving a trivial species, but it was quite a catastrophe to others. The warmer water had driven away the pink popcorn shrimp that were a staple of the New England fishery. This was the beloved variety caught off Cape Cod and in the Bay of Maine far offshore and to the north. They had swum off in search of chillier temperatures in the Labrador Current, or so everyone surmised. As a result, fishermen all across the Northeast found their nets, along with their wallets, coming up empty.

Except for one man. His name was Enoch, which didn't much matter, because almost no one knew his name or referred to him as anything other than "the fisherman." That seemed more polite than calling him the poacher, which some people thought he certainly was. In the oddest and most unexpected of ways, he would change Charlotte's life forever. But she did not know that, or him, yet. In fact, she scarcely could have imagined anyone like him.

An hour after driving her crumbling Fiat onto the ferry and buying a cup of coffee—black, no sugar—Charlotte stood at the railing of the ferry, transfixed. She was staring up at the spray that misted and disappeared into the heat of a blue, summer sky. In front of her, a man and a woman with two small boys and a bag of bread had captured the interest of a flock of seagulls suspended in midair beside the upper deck. The children stared at the birds and the birds stared back, as if they might be contemplating a change of places. The humans were leaning, longing for the sea and adventure. The birds feinted toward the ship, longing for rest and food. Each side hesitated in fear of being swindled by the middleman and ending up with nothing. For the price of a bag of bread, both parties were almost ready to make the switch.

Charlotte would have taken the offer.

She had done her homework, starting as soon as the invitation came from an old college pal, Eudora Delano, who never went by any name but Dory, to join her for the summer at her house on the Vineyard. Having Dory nearby would ensure that Charlotte would be missed, that a search would get underway and then be called off, and that she would be declared lost at sea for the sake of her grieving relatives, who would all say they *never saw it coming*.

Charlotte already knew how it would go—not quickly, but eventually and imperceptibly. She would walk out slowly into the sea until the riptide took her and the ocean floor subsided beneath her feet into the abyss. When fatigue made it impossible to tread water any longer and her head slipped beneath the waves, the immutable pharyngeal reflex, which keeps the windpipe safely shut against any suicidal will to the contrary, would resist opening until the gray curtain of anoxia slowly closed in around the edges of her mind. At last her limbs would cease to move, and the descent into a watery oblivion would come peacefully, unknowingly, painlessly.

Somewhere on the south side of the island would likely be the best place to do it, she thought. It was isolated and would be deserted late at night. No beach walkers. No teenagers screwing in the dunes. There she could be certain her body would be swept out to sea unseen with the current, which was an important part of her end game. More than death, she feared becoming the star of a silent, postmortem horror movie—her swollen, disgusting corpse ghosting ashore amid screams from wading children.

No, the Atlantic would forever hide Charlotte Harris along with the ashes in the tiny pewter urn now resting on the passenger seat of her car. It was the first time

Meredith had gotten to ride up front.

Only the sea was far and wide enough to cover the grief of losing a daughter, a marriage, and a life that once had seemed to rise continually skyward, like a zephyr. She was more certain of her plan now than ever. Her resolve stiffened with each roll of the ferry bow as it pointed toward the island.

The numbers 1183-2 were tattooed in a two-inch, bright blue line that descended down the top of her left forearm—the same effective method the Nazis had used to identify prisoners at Auschwitz. The numbers were a self-imposed badge of shame for Charlotte, as indelible as her sin. They comprised the paragraph and section number of a single line of the Code of Canon Laws of the Catholic Church:

The local ordinary can permit children whom the parents intended to baptize but who died before baptism to be given ecclesiastical funerals.

She had read and researched and deconstructed and analyzed and wrestled with that line in dozens of letters to dozens of apparatchiks of Catholic officialdom. Despite all her pleading, their rigid indifference had not softened in the least. *The local ordinary can permit,* the law said. What the ordinary can permit he can also refuse. And so he did.

The local ordinary was the auxiliary bishop of Boston, who was—in Charlotte's estimation—rather ordinary indeed, in the most ordinary understanding of the term. He was, to her if not to a great many others, a hypocrite and a buffoon. It did not please the ordinary to "permit" her child, *her Meredith,* to be given the rite of Christian burial in the Church.

Charlotte, who was raised in the mysticism and ritual of the traditional Church, had married Mark—a charming, polite, and very bright young man who was raised in a similar family from the same parish. In their second year of marriage and his third year of medical school, he abruptly announced he had become an atheist and took the unusual, further step of having his named removed from the rolls of the Church.

When Meredith was born, Charlotte and Mark argued and fought bitterly over the question of baptism. "She's my child, too," Mark would say, and of course she was. But Charlotte believed Meredith was also God's child. It was a bitter and bizarre, ecclesiastical sort of custody battle in which Charlotte was the mediator between two fathers. To make peace, she had ultimately agreed that neither she nor her husband would choose, so that Meredith might someday make her own choice. She had every confidence that her daughter would one day choose her mother's church. She never dreamed the choice would be taken from her.

Scattered memories of her own catechism, two decades ago, returned in disconnected threads weaving though Charlotte's mind as the ferry rolled along, just as they had every day for the past three years. She had been taught, like millions of others, that the souls of unbaptized babies languished in limbo—described as a kind of anteroom of purgatory—crying for their mothers. It was the reason Catholic grandmothers were forever throwing tap water and mumbling prayers at their grandchildren—something Charlotte's own mother never did, in deference to her daughter's wishes. "The time will come soon enough," Charlotte would say. Besides, it was ridiculous to think that a just God could ever perpetrate such heinous cruelty. Yet whenever she stood within the soaring cathedrals of God's power on Earth and heard the princes of the Church say it was so, her own dissent seemed so very small. What power did a mother's love have against that? Only the power of martyrdom and commiseration. If Meredith could not be with her one day in heaven, Charlotte would keep watch with her outside its gates.

Put out into the deep. That had been the Great Commission to the disciples, and the irony of that command now strangely pleased her. In the deep, she would give up her life and salvation to gain death and peace. In the place beyond the veil of this world, she would find her daughter and join her for all eternity. She believed this with all her heart and soul. The weight of ten generations of faithful obedience, including six priests on her mother's side and four nuns on her father's side, not to mention twelve years of Catholic schooling, had done quite a number on Charlotte Harris.

The pleated sundress she had chosen for "the occasion," as she primly regarded her own death, was neatly pressed and folded in the valise stowed in the trunk of her car. It was her only luggage. On the ferry, the tiny Fiat was dwarfed by the enormous SUVs and minivans parked all around it. They needed to be big enough to land platoons of parents, children, dogs, and bicycles, and all the assorted materiel of summer for the annual assault on Martha's Vineyard by the armies of New England. There was one couple, however, who looked out of place.

They were young—very young. The girl had a deep green tattoo across the small of her back that appeared and disappeared as her halter top rode up above her jeans. She was clinging like a wet dishtowel to the boy, who was better-looking than the girl, and as tall, lean, and hard as a light pole. Charlotte was thirty-two. She guessed the boy's age and did the mental math. There was at least ten years' difference between them, maybe more. A thread of imagination flashed briefly in her mind, then vanished. *Five years ago, she might have . . .*

The girl was busy administering something more like an otolaryngeal exam than a kiss. Whenever the boy broke the suction to gasp for air, he would attempt a few words before the treatment resumed. He was clearly anxious or excited about something and eager to discuss it, but the girl was determined to stifle any conversation with foreplay.

Charlotte overheard the boy finally burp out a few words about a justice of the peace, money, and a hotel. *Unbelievable,* she thought. They were two stupid kids— only babies—but they were getting married. The combined, crushing weight of painful memory and bitter regret came rushing toward her, and instead of the boy and the girl standing there, Charlotte saw Mark and herself.

In that moment, an inexplicable, irresistible impulse overtook Charlotte. She walked directly toward the couple and pushed the girl out of the way. The girl tripped over a tie-down and fell backwards onto the deck. Charlotte hadn't intended to be so rough, but she didn't bother to help the girl up, either. The boy, who remained upright, seemed dumbfounded and grateful for the oxygen. Stepping quickly into position with a predatory confidence that surprised even herself, Charlotte placed her mouth on the boy's neck and began to move her way up. When she reached his ear, she whispered three words in the deepest Lauren Bacall voice she could summon.

"Think about it."

The girl, still lying on the ferry deck, watched Charlotte just long enough for fear to turn to astonishment and then anger. She rose and rebounded with a right hook delivered with the kind of athleticism that comes only from frequent practice.

Charlotte was quicker, but only just. When she ducked, the girl's punch hit the boy squarely in the teeth. Amid the ensuing spattering of blood, the girl screaming and wringing her hand in pain, and the rush of startled onlookers trying to intervene, Charlotte escaped to the lounge unseen and found a seat hidden behind a magazine rack. Her work was done.

With any luck, she thought, she had given the boy a second chance. Boys being boys, though, she doubted he would take it. It would be his own damn fault if he didn't, and if that were the case, the words she had just spoken would haunt him forever. It was the kind of thing, along with saying whatever she damn well pleased to everyone, that Charlotte now felt free to do.

In the outer pocket of Charlotte's purse was a folded envelope with the address to Dory's house she had hurriedly scrawled in unreadable script while listening to Dory's convoluted directions. Dory's idea of their summer together was hastily contrived. It was to be three months of lying around an historic and stunning garden home in Edgartown in various stages of intoxication and sloth, interrupted by regular sorties to the beach, antique shops, art galleries, and restaurants. To Dory, this was heaven. She had no idea how far away heaven seemed to her friend.

It wasn't fair to do this to Dory, she knew. Coming to her best friend's house just long enough to have dinner, grab a quick shower, and commit suicide was abysmally rude behavior for a guest—in addition to all the other horrible things one might say about such a plan. But Charlotte had thought that part out, too. If she killed herself in her apartment in the city, people might not find her for days—weeks, even. There would be a stench by the time they did, which was silly to be concerned about if you're going to be dead, but she hated the thought of it, nonetheless. If she came to the Vineyard or any random beach on her own and walked straight into the sea, there would be no place to leave a note where anyone might look. No one would know where she had gone or have a reason to miss her when she didn't come back.

Yes, Dory's invitation to come to the Vineyard for the summer had provided Charlotte with the perfect cover. Dory would be there to find the note and search for her when she didn't come home. Dory would alert the authorities. They would soon find the abandoned car and make the declaration of death by drowning. Charlotte's parents would be notified promptly. Grieving would have a definite beginning and ending. There would be closure for everyone. Everything would be tidied away.

Charlotte had never been to Dory's house before, but she had seen pictures over the years. She and Dory had kept up with each other since their senior year at Smith through Facebook semaphore from opposite sides of the sea—Charlotte in Boston and Dory on the island. Every year Dory would travel south with her mother to their Palm Beach estate for the winter months, like a well-bred family of geese.

Dory was rich. Stunningly rich. Although she thought of herself as someone just like everyone else, there was no one quite like Dory. She lived her life as though everything were possible. No objective was beyond her ability to shape reality to her ends. So, when Charlotte had unburdened herself of the story of her failed marriage over martinis during one of Dory's excursions to Boston, Eudora Delano's Search and Rescue Service had snapped into action.

Dory decided that Charlotte must stay with her on the Vineyard until she got over losing her child to cancer, as if that were even possible, and got over losing her husband to the contagion of indifference that followed, as if that were even necessary.

Charlotte hadn't been able to touch her husband or let him touch her since the funeral, three years ago, without succumbing to waves of nausea. In those years they had drifted apart. He had begun staying late at work in Manhattan, while Charlotte, volunteering tirelessly in the hospice charity that had cared for Meredith, barely noticed he was gone. Rumors came from friends of an affair with a nurse or an underling or an intern or someone—it didn't much matter to Charlotte. She didn't know the truth and didn't care to know. Their life together no longer had a purpose after Meredith's death, and by the time they both found the courage to bring into the open what been lingering in the shadows, the memory of why they had ever married in the first place seemed to evaporate like the thread of a dream, beyond recall. In its place a silence and a numbness lingered that neither well-meaning friends nor well-paid therapists had been able to penetrate.

Dory had a plan to change all that. With her trademark overconfidence and well-born naiveté, she believed her goal could be accomplished in the course of a magical, wonderful summer, as if Charlotte were Sandra Dee coping with the problems of Gidget.

The creaking Fiat had been a gift from worried friends in Boston who said they *never* used it and insisted vehemently that Charlotte take it, as a symbol of their love and sympathy. It rumbled slowly across the crushed stone of the driveway of the empty house. It was as charming as she had expected. Of course it would be. It looked just as Dory had described it in her martini-infused campaign speech to get her to come there. Three bedrooms and two baths in an 1847 white clapboard colonial just off Water Street, with a view across the harbor to Chappaquiddick.

June was warming with the advent of July. A riot of pink and white roses had overtaken the fence along the sidewalk. Blooms of buxom, lush, neon-blue hydrangeas crowded the walkway to the front door.

Dory would get in that evening, late, once her flight landed on the Vineyard from a quick trip to New York. Dory was forever making quick trips. The surly bonds of gravity and money held no sway over her lifestyle. She did as she pleased, and it pleased her to give her friends some taste of the same freedom. That was the credo of her social class. Of them to whom much had been given, endless summer parties were expected.

On the kitchen counter was a note in Dory's distinctively cheerful script. *Welcome to Shangri-La!* Martha's Vineyard wasn't remotely a mystical, enchanted valley of the Himalayas, but Charlotte was certain it would become just that if Dory intended to make it so. In typical Dory fashion, after the greeting came a list of instructions—about where to unpack, where to store her clothes, where to shower (outdoors—"It's a Vineyard thing," Dory insisted in a parenthetical, underlining the words and adding a smiley face).

A list of groceries Dory hoped Charlotte would have time to pick up for the week was paper-clipped to a crisp hundred-dollar bill lying on the counter. Charlotte read the grocery list carefully, puzzling out the meaning of what she was expected to buy from Dory's blue-inked stream of consciousness. At the bottom, there was something scribbled about a "fisherman" and a "hunk," it not being clear whether she was referring to a hunk of fish or the fisherman himself. This appeared to be followed by some other illegible word, running off the side of the envelope, beneath which were the words, "two pounds," "blue Jeep," and "Chappaquiddick."

From this cryptic message, Charlotte concluded, she was intended to take the ferry to Chappaquiddick Island to purchase something of importance, two pounds of it, from a mysterious person who might or might not be a fisherman and standing near a blue Jeep. She hoped in the worst way it was not a kilo of cocaine or some such thing.

Dory wanted all these items to serve for dinner that evening, which in Dory's vernacular could occur anywhere from midnight to just before breakfast. Charlotte found a sheet of paper and a pen in a drawer and, recopying the shopping list in her own handwriting, stuffed the page into the envelope with the address she would need to recall to find her way home.

Chappaquiddick is just a stone's throw across the harbor from the island of Martha's Vineyard. The cramped ferry ride is over in a matter of minutes and repeated constantly, back and forth, throughout the day. Once traveling along Chappaquiddick's pastoral and almost completely unoccupied back roads, it was easy for Charlotte to spot the location Dory had only obliquely described in her note. Parked beside a dirt road was an ancient Jeep Wagoneer. It was covered haphazardly in sky-blue paint in what obviously had been a failed effort to hide the rust pocks along the lower half of the body. About fifty yards down this road, on the side of a bridge just before the beach, someone had hung a hand-drawn, cardboard sign on which the words "Ted's Car Wash" were streaked from rain and barely legible.

Leaning calmly on the tailgate of the Jeep, seemingly with nothing to do that day but wait for Charlotte to arrive, was a man. Lean but not muscular, of average height, he had sandy-brown hair and a fair, tanned complexion. He was not bad-looking, although he certainly was not what Charlotte would have called a "hunk," if that's what Dory was getting at. He was thirtyish, Charlotte guessed. He had a two-day stubble and wore jeans, no shoes, and a blue tee shirt with a tear in the midriff on the right side. A seasonal drifter, she thought. He was easier on the eyes than most. She could see coolers on the tailgate of the Jeep behind him, and nets.

"Can I help you, ma'am?"

The man's accent was distinctively Southern but strangely so—not like the accents she had heard in the Deep South of Georgia and Alabama. He wasn't smiling, but his expression was calmly inviting and put her completely at ease. She felt a strange impulse to take his question literally and beg for his help in lifting the weight of the woe that was crushing her. She might have done just that had her fingers fidgeting in her pockets not found her shopping list.

"Two pounds," she said, and nothing more, as if these were the code words of a secret greeting. *Two pounds of what?* she feared he would ask.

The man turned to open a white cooler behind him and retrieve a bag of chilled, glistening, enormous, grey shrimp that looked to be a great deal heavier than two pounds. From another cooler he shoveled a scoop of ice into the bag, tied it tight, and handed it to her. She waited to hear the price, and the man waited for something else—what, she had no idea. After a moment of awkward silence, she finally spoke.

"Will thirty dollars be all right?"

It was not an overly generous offer, but as the man had said nothing about price and it wouldn't do simply to take the shrimp and run, she felt the need to name a number. These were jumbo shrimp—the really big ones, like the kind they caught down in the Gulf of Mexico—not the tiny variety she was used to seeing in seafood markets in New England, back when shrimp could be had at all. She rarely cooked anymore but vaguely recalled the price of a bagful of jumbo Gulf shrimp at something around ten dollars a pound. She had offered the man fifteen, but even at that price, there was a problem.

"I'm terribly sorry," she said, "but I'm just now realizing I came here to pick up some things for dinner without anything other than this hundred-dollar bill and a credit card. I don't know what I was thinking."

It wasn't like her not to think of such things in advance, but she'd been in something of a daze most of that day. She started to hand the bag of shrimp back when he held up his hand to refuse her.

"What else do you need?" he asked, as he reached out to take the folded shopping list she held in her hand. As he read it to himself, she saw his expression change. Apparently he disapproved of Dory's choice of vegetables and wine to accompany the shrimp, she thought. It was several moments later before Charlotte realized he was no longer reading from the page but staring intently into her eyes.

"You'll want to do it off Gay Head," he said, somberly. Gay Head was a beach on the southeastern tip of the island.

"*Do what?*" she asked.

"The tide everywhere else runs in an eddy. It will draw your body back into shore eventually. Off Gay Head, the tidal current sweeps straight out to sea. It's a much better place to do it, trust me."

Her face went red-hot with fear and embarrassment. Her hand shot down into her other pants pocket. Dory's shopping list was still there. She had handed him the suicide note she planned to leave on the nightstand late that night, when she could slip away unseen.

It had been written in anger, one week earlier, on the same day a letter on official diocesan stationary had arrived from Boston. In the letter, the auxiliary bishop explained his "tender sorrow" in affirming the decision of Father Bernard, pastor of Our Lady of the Seas

Catholic Church, in Worcester, to refuse a Catholic burial for Meredith. Though named after one of the beloved saints of the Church, Meredith had not been baptized into their company and now, through the combined cruelty of cancer and official Christendom, she never would be.

Charlotte, mortified, tore the paper from the fisherman's hands. She could think of nothing else to do in that moment but turn and run. When she did, his hand slipped around her elbow to pull her back.

"It will be all right, Charlotte."

Upset as she was, she wondered for a moment how he knew her name before remembering she had signed the note. Escaping his gentle grasp, she fled to her car, shrimp tightly clenched in hand, and didn't stop until she was back in the driveway of Dory's house.

Dory had returned home by the time Charlotte arrived. Her champagne Range Rover was in the driveway, easily identified by the "Save the Sea Turtle" bumper sticker right above the unmistakably pink Vineyard Vines logo of a spouting whale. Charlotte was peering closer, trying to make out what the turtle in the sticker was supposed to be saying, when Dory's head popped out of the passenger window.

"*Charlie!*" Dory screamed in that annoyingly excited, baby-doll voice she reserved for greetings that called for the nickname she had given Charlotte in college. Both of Dory's arms shot out through the open car window as if she were, in fact, a baby doll whose string had just been pulled to make her say and do that very thing.

Dory Delano's family were *those* Delanos, as in *the* Delanos. They were pillars of polite New England society, going back to the whaling days. According to family legend, Herman Melville ran to sea to escape the wrath of Dory's great-great-grandfather after a missionary spinster aunt, who took more than a passing interest in Melville's salvation, had turned up in the family way. They found no record of the child, but Dory liked to say that her distant aunt had given birth to a great white whale. Scandals live long and die hard in New England, and every generation of the Delanos since the Melville affair had strived to live that one down. It still came up now and then, if only because the Ahab and harpoon jokes were irresistible at parties. Dory loved the whole idea of it. Her mother despised the very idea of it.

"Dory!" Charlotte replied, noticeably more startled than pleased. She hurriedly smoothed her hair and checked the skin under her eyes for tears. It had been a difficult thirty minutes since she left the fisherman. Dory climbed headfirst out of the side of the Rover, like a six-year-old. "Damn door's stuck again—stupid Brits. They can't engineer anything but dry gin." She tumbled out onto the ground, feet first, smiling widely. It was the way she always smiled. Dory did nothing in half measures. It was all or nothing at all—with everything.

Charlotte, who usually *did* do things in half measures, managed a smile back. Her old friend was here, they were on a beautiful island, standing in the stupendous garden of a beautiful house, and it was summer in New England. *Who wouldn't be happy?* she thought. Only someone who was planning to commit suicide that very night, of course. Charlotte's face revealed nothing, but she could no longer push that nearing reality out of her thoughts, even for a moment. She was tied to it like an anchor stuck in the mud, and the tide around her was rising.

"I just got back from the hunk—the fisherman, I mean," Charlotte said, now laughing a little at her own expense. "Here's the shrimp."

"Thanks. You're a sweetheart to pick that up for me. He's usually gone by dark, and I wasn't sure when I'd be back. So you agree he's a hunk, then? Kinda dreamy, isn't he, in a wild boy sort of way?"

"Um, no. I mean, I just bought shrimp from the guy—or rather, I should say, he gave it to me. He seemed nice. What, are you *doing* him or something?" The question surprised Charlotte even as she asked it. She was characteristically not so uncouth, or curious.

Dory ignored the question and began to unload the wine, which gave the question even greater importance in Charlotte's mind.

"He *gave* you the shrimp? Didn't you see the money I left?"

Charlotte explained about the money, but Dory was already racing ahead. She took Charlotte's disinterest in the fisherman as a worrisome sign needing her attention. She had been encouraging Charlotte to date since shortly after her divorce was final—even setting her up with a friend once in Newport—but, with Charlotte, men had been a tough sell. This summer would change that, if Dory had anything to say about the matter.

Not that Charlotte wasn't attractive. On the contrary, she was what Dory imagined would be every sixteen-year-old boy's sexy librarian fantasy. Nerdy, leggy, with mousy-brown hair always tied back and glasses that covered too much of her face. A favorite white cotton cardigan over a knit top covered "society boobs," as Dory had once described them. "You know, little Jackie-O breasts," Dory had tried to explain. (Charlotte didn't know.) "Small enough for you to wear fashionable clothes and big enough for men to want you to take them off."

Dory walked ahead of Charlotte and opened a door off the foyer. "Bring your stuff inside. Let me show you your room. It's my favorite."

It was a stunning home, done in the tastefully austere—yet classic—New England cottage style approved by Mrs. Delano, who presided over the even more palatial and stunning family home that sat on eighteen acres of undeveloped sound frontage on the north side of Edgartown. That kind of lot hadn't been for sale on the island since the Indian days, when Captain Augustine Visgoth Delano had purchased it— from the Indians. Dory's little bungalow in town, eighteen-hundred square feet in three stories, was built to house the family's less familiar and less welcome guests, of whom Dory herself was now one.

"Welcome to Edgartown's version of the Lincoln bedroom." Dory was as exultant about the house as she was ambivalent about the wealth and title and family name that had built it. "In fact," she continued, "we call it 'Grant's tomb,' because my family made President Grant spend the night here in town instead of at the family's estate when he came to the Vineyard. My great-great-great-grandmother hated Grant, or so everyone believes. It was a test of her character not to rescind the invitation once she heard of it, and in the end I think she would have done exactly that if her husband hadn't intervened." Dory smoothed the bed distractedly with one hand, as if she were caressing a child. "He rather liked Grant because he was a soldier, and disliked Lincoln because he was a lawyer." Lawyers were despised generally as a class. Too striving. Too self-serving. Too conspicuous in their prosperity. The Delano Way was to give conspicuously and prosper secretly.

Charlotte plopped down on the patchwork quilt that covered the high, four-poster bed. Carefully embroidered ringlets of berries and flowers rambled across the fabric. Made by prim ladies at Edgartown tea parties, she imagined, whiling away the long winter hours behind frosted windowpanes in serene comfort. The whole ethos of a bygone era was still present in the Delano house like the scent of perfume. It was all so exquisite. Quite so. It seemed to Charlotte as if nothing uncouth, no ill wind, could ever penetrate such a fortress of gentility.

Except she had penetrated it, she thought, and the thought broke her reverie. Charlotte Harris, the soon-to-be-suicider, had entered the quaint scene like a dark cloud. She imagined the papers speculating about what her last night on Earth must have been like, spent in the other-worldly elegance of the Grant bedroom. The Delanos were sure to be mortified—not grief-stricken for her, but mortified for poor, dead Ulysses. What a shame, they would say, that his Edgartown memorial had been brought so low by such infamy as this.

But it wouldn't be a proper suicide without a proper bath. Even in the abyss of a depression far deeper than the ocean that would soon swallow her, Charlotte had her scruples.

She opened her suitcase and laid out her clothes for the evening. There would be dinner at home—shrimp, as apparently Dory had in mind—and then. And then.

The bathroom was no less magnificently austere and refined than the rest of the room. A claw-foot tub squatted on the white tile floor. A Jacuzzi would have been so very gauche. This was the Grand Hotel, not the Flamingo, she thought. Blue toile curtains covered the windows.

She placed her hand on the ancient tub faucet, turning it first one way then the other to no effect. *Righty tighty, lefty loosey*—she never could be certain what that damn rhyme meant, no matter how many times her ex-husband had recited it to her, patronizingly, in moments just like this one.

Nothing happened. No water, no sound. A few more minutes spent contorting her body underneath and around the plumbing for a clue to its operation began to make her feel self-conscious. Plumbing repair was probably not the sort of thing sweating, naked women did in houses like this one, she thought. More likely they peered coyly from behind cracked doors, whispering pleas for help. So she did exactly that.

"Dory, the tub—what's the secret?"

Dory was passing in the hallway below with an armload of wine unloaded from the car. Apparently it was going to be one of *those* nights. Chicks and Chardonnay and the methodical cataloging and scoring of old loves and forgotten flames, year by year, glass by glass, ass by ass. Charlotte was certain she wasn't up for that and equally certain that Dory didn't care.

"Oh, Sweetie—my fault! I meant to tell you, in the summer we only use the downstairs tub and the shower outside. Outdoor showers are trademark Vineyard. You'll love it."

Dory set down the wine, bounded up the steps, reached through the crack in the door, and took Charlotte's hand. Charlotte followed, clutching the bath towel she had not tied down for travel before being taken in tow. She jerked along behind in short, pigeon-toed steps to keep everything in place.

There was a wooden shower stall, three-sided, at the far end of the backyard. Where a door should have been, some libertine (Dory, who else?) had decided that a high, thinning hedge of glossy abelia on the property line provided all the privacy needed. The fallen blossoms covered the grass in a delicate pattern of white and green and filled the air with a scent like oranges. Erected rather incongruously about six feet away was a deck with a wooden bench and towel rack, clearly conveying the intention that the bather should disrobe there and promenade *en plein air* to the stall, which Dory—all instructions having been clearly given—now left Charlotte to do.

Dory was a free spirit, a granola girl, a *bon vivant*. Charlotte was not. Charlotte, even in the throes of a suicidal depression, remained a Pop-Tart kind of girl, a wear-jammies-to-bed girl, and a woman firmly tethered to the moral and social conventions of the middle class, which certainly did not include gallivanting about naked in one's backyard.

When Dory was satisfactorily out of sight, Charlotte emerged from her towel and immediately regretted the decision. The fading light in the garden was still bright enough to give the goosepimply, white skin of her birdy legs an unwanted luminescence. She felt indisposed, a plucked hen, forced to adapt along with the other campers to the *new normal* of an open shower. She only then realized that she had come outside without any supplies. There was a petrified bar of Ivory in the soap dish and a nearly empty bottle of conditioner on the floor of the stall. These would have to do.

The shower was fitted with a pancake-sized shower faucet head that produced a wonderful spray reminiscent of a tropical waterfall, which the deep green, glossy abelia growing all around made seem actually plausible, even in Massachusetts. Charlotte let her guard down, at last, and breathed in the moist, citrus verbena of summer.

She was still a young woman, at thirty-two. Dory was the same age, but they were very different in almost every other way. Charlotte was quiet, gentle, and petite but well-formed, with soft brown eyes. The thin, short layer of hair on her arms, invisible every other season of the year, turned a yellowy blonde atop her tanned skin in the summertime, giving her the appearance of an adorable and shy, furry mouse.

Dory, by comparison, was not quiet or gentle or mouse-like in any way. She was five-foot-eight, with natural blonde hair given to the occasional streak of strawberry, and the strong, athletic physique of her Dutch ancestors. She and Charlotte once had sworn to carry on a Dorian Gray kind of competition to see which of them, by age forty, could better carry off the old lie, "You haven't aged a day since college." It was a friendly but secretly serious competition until it ended with Charlotte's marriage. To ensure fair judging, they had occasionally gone to bars together, sitting far apart and pretending not to know each other to see who could score more attempted pick-ups over the course of an evening. Sitting apart was important because they knew from experience that the halo effect of the hotter prospect would skew the results for any lesser creature basking in her glow.

After five years of this competition, Dory was mortifyingly ahead at one hundred thirty-four attempts to Charlotte's ten, and Charlotte had lied about two of hers. Dory had magnanimously insisted they stop counting years ago, but they had both maintained a mental record of the final vote totals down to the last precinct.

Charlotte explained Dory's uncommon success as having everything to do with her uncommon figure and nothing to do with being prettier or wittier or more charming. She never said this, of course, but it felt better to think it. Dory would be eighty-six, Charlotte imagined, and virile young men would still be longing to climb her, like Kilimanjaro.

Charlotte, on the other hand, was a magnet for arty, thin, effete, brooding, Byronesque New Yorkers who talked endlessly of themselves and their unheralded screenplays. They did not pick women up as much as they pined to be picked up by them, and this also, she reasoned, accounted for the lopsided score. Such men also invariably suffered from stage fright in bed, making the whole competition a joyless Sudoku game for Charlotte that she finally decided to end by marrying one of them.

Lingering there in the shower, Charlotte was contemplating her own form by mental comparison to Dory's, watching ribbons of hot water racing down each breast and ski-jumping off her nipples into the air. Two years of steady nursing after Meredith was born, remarkably, had not altered her figure for the worse. But she guessed it wouldn't be much longer before gravity and time were given their due and the ski jump became an Olympic downhill speed run. Never having to live with droopy boobs, she thought macabrely, was just another advantage of a premature death.

Studying herself in this morbid fashion, Charlotte noticed out of the corner of her eye a thin red light in the distance, through the leaves of the abelia. She recalled it had been flickering before she entered the shower, and it flickered still. It blinked on and brightened for one or two seconds, then faded and blinked off, like a revolving beacon. She was certain it was a channel buoy far out in the harbor.

She was mistaken.

CHAPTER 2

Back in Grant's tomb, wrapped in an enormous, plush towel, Charlotte imagined for a moment that life like this might just be *worth living for.* She smoothed the quilt with her hand. Her left foot stretched out on the bed while the other one dangled, only just touching the cool surface of the hardwood floor. It occurred to her then that she was in a pose for the high hurdles. *Indeed.*

If the only pleasures left were the smell of clean linen in a warm room, the reassuring firmness and permanence of hardwood floors and plaster walls, and the earthy delight of standing naked in an outdoor shower with her face held up to a soft, warm rain, she could have lived for that. Were it not for her grief and her guilt, she could have lived for a lot less than that.

But Charlotte's mind always circled back to the image of tiny Meredith—her unforgotten little waif of a child—wandering alone, in darkness, in the Valley of the Dead. She imagined her crying for her mother, and the breasts that had weaned her years ago still fairly ached to respond to that call.

According to Church teaching as Charlotte understood it, unbaptized babies and suiciders had a shared destiny—not hell, but *limbo,* a place for all those sullied by the unwashed stain of Original Sin. Sister Beatrice, she of boundless girth and authority, had relentlessly assured all the girls in St. Cecilia's 1993 confirmation class of this. In Charlotte's vivid imagination, limbo was a kind of vestibule of purgatory: a place of eternal sadness, but without the extreme sufferings of the damned in hell.

Limbo. The word rolled around in Charlotte's mind, circling the drain longer than usual. She thought of the time Meredith had triumphed in the contest of the same name at the skating rink party for her fourth birthday. The little girl had not a rigid bone in her little whisper of a body, as a result of which she could slither under a limbo bar, however low.

For Charlotte, suicide for the chance to spend eternity comforting her child wasn't a hard choice. At every Christmas Eve, watching little children singing at midnight Mass, she would look at one of them and think, *Who here would value her own life more highly than this child's?* The choice was simple, not heroic. The child always wins. You feed the child, protect the child, comfort the child, no matter what. It is the one, unfailing rule of civilization. It was a rule she felt she had somehow broken in the case of her own child, and now the universe was out of balance. There was no great strife in her world, no great hardship—just a hollow banality met with confidence that whatever fate awaited her on the other side of the grave surely would offer one of two things: either the ignorance of oblivion or an eternity of shared sorrow. If it were the latter, she believed she would find Meredith there—the one person on Earth with whom she had forged a true, eternal bond—and the two of them would face eternity together, come what may.

She decided she would wait no longer. The shower had definitely been worth it—and somehow important, as a kind of pre-inhumation ritual. But spending the next forty-five minutes drying her hair and putting on makeup made no sense at all. She would go as planned, but sooner. Not later, when Dory was in bed, but now.

She opened the door to her room quietly. She could hear pots and pans clanging in the kitchen as Dory prepared the shrimp. A distinctive popping sound signaled the opening of the first bottle of wine. Dinner would not be served for another half hour. Charlotte would be long gone by then.

It was already late. She tiptoed quietly down the stairs and out the door, softly pressing the latch behind her. The sundress, she now realized as she was wearing it, had perhaps not been a good choice. It was sweltering during the day on the Vineyard but quite cool at night, and a chill ran up her legs all the way to her neck as soon as she stepped into the open air.

The stillness of night amplified every incongruent noise—the rhythmic grinding of her steps on gravel, the opening and closing of the car door. It was a conspicuous time to be starting a car in that neighborhood. Dory would surely hear, wonder, and worry, but not enough, and not in time.

In a few minutes, Charlotte was stealing glances at a map spread out on the passenger seat, barely visible in the dome light, as she hurtled down the thin ribbon of highway toward Gay Head. The tiny car could not break sixty, but in the darkness the trees seemed to rush by at great speed.

The urn of Meredith's ashes rested on the floor of the car on the passenger side. It was a gray, joyless thing—so unlike the happy cherub it contained. Charlotte glanced at it once and then again, as if to make sure Meredith was going along with the plan.

She found the beach road with difficulty. It was marked only by a sign featuring an oddly fierce, red rooster telling passersby that fresh eggs were for sale at a nearby farmhouse. A narrow, sandy spur that seemed more path than road disappeared off to the left between two flowering bushes that all but concealed the entrance. She took it and was immediately enveloped in a darkness even deeper than before.

The road to hell may be paved with good intentions, but the path to purgatory was not paved at all. Ruts and potholes pushed and bullied Charlotte as she ran that gauntlet. What a fitting anticlimax it would be, she thought, to break an axle and become stranded along the way to one's own suicide—a live woman and a dead car stuck together on a murderous road. It would be untoward to wash a dead body out to sea while leaving a dead car in the middle of the road. A minute passed while she concocted a story for the ensuing road assistance. *I had an urge to go skinny-dipping,* was all that came to her. Dory would accept this unquestioningly, though not likely without some petulance for not being asked to come along.

But the axle did not break, and the steep descent eased to a gentler grade where the path spread out toward the beach. The car creaked to a stop, creaked again to release its occupant, and creaked a third time at the shutting of the door. Short as Charlotte's life expectancy was, the car wasn't much longer for the world.

She stepped out into the water's edge in a chilling onshore breeze. There was nothing before her but the bright moon on high and the dark sea below, met in this place at this appointed hour to demand that she choose at last the victor between them.

All the minutes of all the hours of all the days, every morsel of bread, every swallow of wine, every blessing and every blasphemy, every kiss and curse, every morning and evening, all the moments that had touched her and those now utterly forgotten, came at last to this moment. Whatever had been the banality or the brilliance of her life would now be made indelibly so.

There was a kind of larcenous elation in that—like graduation forced upon the undeserving truant as merely a more expedient form of expulsion, with less paperwork.

She was done. No matter how badly she had fouled things up before, after that night the score could never get any worse, at least insofar as it concerned her. The final tally would be fixed for all eternity. All her life's failed strivings and struggles would now be *enough*. It seemed almost strange that no one was there to hand out a final grade, but of course there wouldn't be. She was dropping the class.

The unexpected warmth of the water surprised her even before she realized she had begun to wade out into it. It covered her ankles, then her thighs, and made the raw night air seem more rude by comparison on the parts of her that were yet unimmersed. If her own baptism as an infant had been, by all reports, a freezing, wet shower endured with screaming and terror, this means of undoing the sacrament by immersion was markedly more pleasant. The warm water was far more welcoming than the cold air and earth she was leaving behind, and not at all the hypothermic ordeal for which she had braced herself, now, for months. *O Death, where is thy sting?*

Then she remembered. It was the Gulf Stream. That explained the warmth. She remembered hearing someone say in passing—in a store on the mainland, or perhaps on the ferry—that the stream had drifted closer to the island that summer than usual. The whole damn world was turning upside down. It had snowed that same year in Jerusalem.

When the water was up to her chest, the waves

rolling out to sea began to hold sway over her. At last her feet lifted off from Earth, not in the ascension of her soul to heaven, as Sister Beatrice had so often prayed, but in what would become the descent of her body to the abyss. Charlotte gripped the urn tightly in the crook of her right arm while using her left to scull and keep her head above water.

That was the plan.

Charlotte was quite certain she was destined for purgatory, no matter what. There had been quite a few too many trysts with quite a few too many married men—not to mention one married woman—for her to kindle much hope of heaven, which was exactly why Meredith's sentence seemed so unjust. Meredith's only sin was original and therefore derivative; Charlotte's sins, on the other hand, showed real creativity and initiative. Suicide was entirely unnecessary to ruin her chances for heaven. She was certain her chances had been ruined quite effectively as it was.

As the plan would go, she would put God to *the test* forbidden to Moses. She would say a prayer in this, her hour of need—the same prayer Sister Beatrice had taught the entire class (fraudulently, they all suspected) would *never ever go unanswered*. If it should be God's will that her life be spared, he would answer it and come spare it himself. If not—well, it was all on him. After all, Christ saved Peter from the waves in a storm on the Sea of Galilee. Saving her on a tony beach near Aquinnah would require a miracle of far less effort. The sea was quite calm, there was no wind to speak of, and it wasn't even raining. So she began . . .

Hail Mary, full of grace . . .

One permanent mark of a Catholic grade school education was the ability to recite the Hail Mary mindlessly—a skill ingrained by hours of repetition in uncountable rosaries. In this way Charlotte had once permitted herself a kind of existential recess from the tedious reality of middle school, allowing her mind to wander even as that tender invocation fell unerringly from her lips alongside her kneeling, pleated, kilted peers, who did the same. They taunted and insulted and teased each other in pantomimes of the eyes while their collective prayer droned on. And, when Sister was not looking, they snatched and grabbed and pinched whatever was within an arm's length to make someone falter.

Blessed art thou amongst women . . .

There was no point in tattle-telling. Sister punished accusers and victims alike. It was the universal system of Catholic school justice.

And blessed is the fruit of thy womb, Jesus . . .

Charlotte was playing the ultimate game of *Gotcha Last* with God. It was now or, quite literally, never for the Man Upstairs to get his last digs in. She had upped the ante and called his bluff. Her object was not to live but rather to create an interval of her own helplessness in which God would decide whether she should die. It was an interval that did not exist between the pulling of a trigger and the firing of a bullet but that lingered between swimming and drowning. If he wanted to make something more out of her life—to spare her—it would be up to him. If not, her blood would be on his hands. She had, after all, said *the prayer.*

She had recruited no less an ally than the Queen of Heaven to be by her side at this, the final showdown. She didn't actually expect God to show up, but that didn't mean she was letting him off the hook. Wherever she was headed—purgatory, limbo, or someplace in between—she would be going with leverage to demand to be closer to wherever Meredith was. Let God try to wheedle his way out of this one, she thought.

She didn't know just how many Hail Marys she had said, or how long she had been treading water, when she noticed that the lights from houses near the beach had disappeared beneath even the lowest trough of the long, rolling waves that were carrying her out to sea. It was dark, of course, and had been when she started, but the ocean darkness appeared to her a deeper sort of void. It was a darkness born not just of the absence of light, but the absence of hope, and the presence of loneliness. In fact, she had never felt so alone in all her life. The prayer she repeated seemed like a tether—a painter line of endless length that kept her connected to life without restraining her flight from it. With each word, the line peeled off more length to let her drift, all the while holding her close.

She guessed she was more than a mile from land. For the first time, she noticed an ache in her left arm, which had been constantly sculling beneath the surface to keep her afloat. The circular motion of that arm had become more labored and slow, as if the water were turning to molasses. Her strength was failing her. She carefully switched Meredith's urn to the bad arm and started sculling with the good one. Soon there would be no good one.

It was in that moment she came to her senses. She decided to return to shore and end the madness before her strength failed her, only to discover that the choice was no longer hers to make. The fisherman was right. The tides at Gay Head swept directly and swiftly out to sea, not along the shore. She had the will but no longer the way to propel herself—only the ability to keep her head above water for a little while longer. Life or death was, for the first time, a matter entirely out of her hands. She was terrified.

The sundress she wore had by now been proven, beyond a shadow of a doubt, a bad choice. Great billows of it were continually floating up around her neck, as if the dress had decided that if she weren't going to get the hell out of there, it would do so on its own. More annoying though was the way it caught her arm every sixth or seventh stroke and had to be pushed away. It was clear now that wherever she wound up, the dress would be flashing her naked remains to the world, as if to say, "Look at the poor fool. She didn't even have the sense to pick a proper outfit to die in. What idiot wears a sundress to a drowning?" And so she finally set it free, sinking beneath it and pushing the neckline above her head as she descended.

When it was off, she set it adrift. She was now a topless suicider. Imagining the wild stories that would surely accompany the discovery of her mermaid body— or her disembodied dress—preoccupied her thoughts with something other than death itself for a full five minutes. No longer hemmed in by clothing, her breasts achieved that buoyancy and lift known to the old women who swam at the YWCA near her apartment in Boston, their great flesh awakened by the water to a new vigor not seen since the last century. Charlotte's breasts now floated heavenward in hopeful anticipation of the end. She caught herself wondering if angels in heaven had perfect boobs to go along with the perfect rest of them, then wondered if such thoughts were the beginnings of delirium.

Holy Mary, Mother of God, pray for us sinners . . .

Most surprising of all was the moment when fear,

which had until then been closing around her like a vise, suddenly lifted and vanished. The sadness that had covered her life like a purple blanket since Meredith's death was also gone. *Perhaps this really might be a piece of cake after all,* she thought. Or, perhaps she was already gone and was experiencing a heavenly sort of anesthesia. That theory was rejected when a charlie horse gripped her right biceps. She simply couldn't move it.

Without her arm as an engine to keep her head above water, her mouth sputtered and slipped beneath the waves for the first time. The salt water stung her throat as she sucked and spit out sips of it before resurfacing. She did not want to die, but she was losing the means by which to live. A feeling of inevitability came over her as the last prayer came to an end.

Now and at the hour of our death. Amen.

Erupting of its own accord, a thin, raspy scream—unintelligible, as if from a dead language—exited her chest. A memory of Sister Beatrice suddenly pierced the confusion with rueful clarity. *And you did this to yourself, young lady. Remember that!*

"*Yes, Sister, I will remember,*" Charlotte thought. "*I will remember, for all eternity.*"

Unconsciously, she once again shifted the urn from her good arm to the palsied one, to free herself to swim. But the palsied arm did not respond, and the urn that contained the one companion—the one love she had left on this Earth—floated away across the abyss.

She screamed more clearly now—not the cry of a frail old woman, but a visceral, moaning rage that welled up from the lowest chamber of her being. Surely even the angels could hear it.

All was lost. Her thoughts were no longer of heaven or hell. Her mind was numb. She sank again entirely beneath the waves, as if a great weight had been bound to her lifeless legs. *This was the plan,* worked out so carefully, far in advance. Nature itself was tightening the noose. She would sink deeper and deeper until oxygen deprivation overcame the last of her reflexes, opened her throat to the sea, and lifted her soul to judgment.

But the body is a stubborn thing that cares nothing for plans or for grief or for melancholy or for judgment. The only imperative of the body is survival. Even when the mind wishes for death, the body will mutiny in favor of another breath, another heartbeat, another moment.

In the moment that was left to her, suspended beneath the waves, Charlotte felt her body uncontrollably spasm in a desperate effort to rise to the surface. The rebellion was almost enough—almost but not quite. Her hand grasped for the surface but remained inches below it, unable to reach any higher. Her muscles had met the limit of their ability to fight.

Indeed, this was the end. This was God's choice at last, not hers. Her eyes began to close on the final image of her life: her own, outstretched hand reaching for the moon and stars above the sea.

But it was not the final image. Before the darkness completely swallowed her, she saw a light—gauzy at first and flickering, above the surface. Then came a hand other than hers, descending beneath the water. It took ahold of her, stopped her descent, and pulled her upward. In her last, fleeting moment of consciousness, she saw the face of the fisherman.

It could have been a minute or an hour or five hours— she had no idea—before she realized where she was. The smell of sawn oak was her first inkling of conscious awareness. She was lying on the sole of a boat—a small skiff—rocking like a cockleshell on the open ocean. The sun had dried the seawater around her lips and made them sting. Her skin, wet and sticky with salt, had coated the wood with moisture that was now steaming up around her from the warmth of the morning. A slow rolling, then a clinking sound of something hard and heavy—metal on metal—prompted her at last to dare to open her eyes. Two oars were dovetailed and stowed inboard, like braces against her body. One of the oarlocks was knocking against the hull in a steady rhythm, like a clock.

But of course this was impossible, she thought. If it were midmorning, ten hours ago she had been swimming alone far out in the ocean. She felt her muscles ache beneath her as she tried and failed to roll over. She was utterly exhausted and as weak as a newborn foal.

She lifted herself slightly on one elbow. Through the thin slits of her eyes she scanned the horizon in the blazing sun. There was no sign of land. She had no idea where she was, how she got there, or how long she had been in that boat. Then, dimly, the memory of the saving hand returned, followed by the face of the man who had saved her from the darkness. It seemed impossible.

She was alone now. That too seemed impossible.

She had just seen him. He had just been there. Those two thoughts rolled back and forth in her mind as she drifted back to sleep.

CHAPTER 3

Trafalgar Wallace the Third, referred to by friend and foe alike as "Tripp," was not widely regarded as a good man or a bad man, as most people measure character. He was known as a practical man, which is a very different thing. He came from a long line of practical men who knew two things well enough that they didn't need or care to know much else: the proper way to invest the family's money and the proper way to spend it—or not spend it, preferably, while enjoying the things money could buy before grudgingly passing the remainder on to the next ungrateful generation. By this self-defeating credo, as the Wallace family tree spread and swelled in size across the centuries, the multiplying heirs were required to spend less of the family's money than those who came before them. This demanded a temperament they all distinctly lacked. As the latest Wallace heir, Tripp was doing on the ocean that day what he did best: squandering what was left of his inheritance.

Being a practical man meant practicing what needed to be done in order to do it well, and that was exactly what Tripp had in mind for the crew of *Victory* that morning. She was a sailing yacht, not a boat, and not just any sort of yacht. *Victory* was a forty-seven-foot custom Herreshoff yawl that had been in the Wallace family for four generations—since the days when yachts of that quality were designed and commissioned, not purchased, and could be constructed by throngs of idle

New England shipwrights ready and eager to build them at comparatively modest cost in the off-season. This was her eighty-seventh year plying the waters between Block Island Sound and the Vineyard. In that time, she had won the Vineyard Cup in fifty-three of eighty-seven contests, and Tripp meant to make the coming season's race the fifty-fourth. In the bright sun of that early morning, the teak coaming and rub rails shone a lustrous, deep auburn beneath the gleam of sixteen fresh coats of varnish. *Victory* looked like a grand piano that had gone to sea.

The high bluffs at Gay Head Beach made for predictable, steady winds—ideal for practicing the turns that would have to be made with mathematical timing in a race.

"Ready about! Five, four, three . . ."

The helmsman and crew stood together, coiled like a steel spring, ready to execute Tripp's command to force the great spade rudder through a mountain of rushing water and bring the bow through the wind. This would be the last tack before the downhill run to Edgartown and a much-anticipated breakfast of clam chowder and ale at the yacht club bar. There was no finer chowder anywhere on the island.

The moment the command "Helms alee!" should have been given passed with no word from Tripp, who stood motionless at the starboard rail, gazing out over the water. The crew of eight men, realizing something was the matter, looked up from their lines and winches.

It appeared at first to be a large piece of rough driftwood floating on the ocean. But as the hourglass shape of the stern came into better view, it was clear they were looking at a boat, drifting alone far out to sea. From that distance it appeared unmanned, and there was no one and no other vessel anywhere around it. It was too small a craft to be out there on its own.

Perhaps, they all thought, it was a tender that had slipped its davits. Whatever it was, it was Tripp's duty as captain to come to its aid. What no one dared utter was the dread fear that any drifting boat meant a lost seaman and the rueful duty of informing his family.

At Tripp's command, the crew expertly and instantly altered course for the derelict, and *Victory* closed the distance between them with the swiftness of a wild mare coming to the side of her foal. They were about to toss a grappling iron over her gunwales and bring her alongside when the form of a woman lying motionless on the sole of the boat came into view. Tripp, more startled than his crew by the sight, screamed the command. "Belay that!"

At the last instant, the crewman on the grappling iron altered his throw, and the iron fell just wide of the skiff into the sea. *Victory,* her sails and rudder now working at cross purposes, bobbed up and down as she waited beside the skiff that rocked like a baby's cradle on the waves rolling under her keel. Two or three seconds of confused disbelief passed in silence as all nine men gazed down at the lifeless form of the woman in the boat beneath them.

"Holy shit!" These words softly and slowly spoken by one of the dumbfounded crew broke the spell.

"Get a line and bring the boat alongside," snapped Tripp, now tabulating an entire list of unpleasant duties.

John Rose, a young Dubliner who was summering on the Vineyard for the racing season, leapt into the dory and steadied himself with hands on each gunwale. Anyone else jumping down from that height would have capsized, but Rose was as light and nimble as a cat. A second later, he had his finger on the woman's neck, looking for a pulse, and his ear cocked above her lips, straining to hear or feel a breath.

"Durgin!" Tripp bellowed to the ship's tactician in

the cockpit. "Get on the radio to the Coast Guard in Edgartown and tell them we've got a body." Carole Durgin disappeared like a wisp of smoke into the cabin, and immediately the crackle of noise from the ship's VHF transmitter could be heard on deck.

Tripp continued shouting at his crew. "Mark the time, take the coordinates, and record the location of death in the log." Tripp had the presence of mind to know that legalities of log-keeping in the reporting of a death at sea would not be overlooked by the local authorities.

"Belay that!" Rose shouted, his face now flushed. "She's alive!" The men looking over the rail stared at him and the sleeping woman in disbelief. In a thick Irish brogue, he thundered louder. "She's alive, goddammit! Help me get her on board!"

With this, Rose slipped one hand beneath the woman's neck and the other below her knees, then lifted her to the waiting arms of eight men who dropped to their bellies on deck to bring her gently over the rail. A moment later, the woman was lying on a settee in the main salon, her head on a pillow, her weary eyes beginning to open and focus.

"Roger that," came the voice of the Coast Guard radioman at the station in Edgartown, in response to the happy news that the castaway was alive and on her way to shore. A corpsman and an ambulance had been called to stand by at the yacht club pier.

Tripp studied the woman's face. She appeared, despite her obvious ordeal, tomboyishly beautiful. Wisps of matted, brown hair framed a sandy, suntanned face and swollen lips that looked like something out of a J. Crew summer-catalog shoot. He was content enough merely to look upon her and wait for her to volunteer the answers to a dozen obvious questions. What was her name? Where was she from? What was she doing there?

How had she gotten there? Why wasn't she dead?

Those same questions were swirling around in the thick, impenetrable fog that still shrouded Charlotte's mind. She was, after a sip of water, just lucid enough to make out the concerned and relieved faces of nine men staring down at her. Instinctively, she raised an arm to cover what she expected were her bare breasts, only to discover that she had inexplicably been placed back into the sundress she had removed and set adrift in the water the night before. It was already dry from the morning sun. Her next impulse was to reach for the urn of Meredith's ashes.

"Meredith?" Charlotte croaked through a dry, salt-burned throat and grasped for the missing urn like it were a lost infant. "Where's Meredith?" Rose didn't know she was speaking of a funeral urn and not a person.

"There was no one else in the boat with you, ma'am," Rose answered, with a sideways glance at Tripp. They all knew it would be a strange story, whenever she got around to telling it.

"Where is he?" Charlotte spoke again, as a tear streamed down her cheek.

"Where is who?" Tripp replied.

"The fisherman?" she answered, sniveling. "The man who saved me. Where did he go?"

Tripp didn't answer right away, as he and the men again exchanged uneasy glances. The woman was clearly delirious. She was ten miles out to sea when they found her, and they hadn't seen another vessel all morning.

Rose offered a helpful correction. "You mean another boat? Did you fall off a fishing boat?"

"No," Charlotte answered, growing more anxious. "He was in the boat with me. The fisherman. He came out in the boat and saved me. He was right there. Where is he? Where is the fisherman?"

"What fisherman?" Tripp asked. "I know most of the fishermen around the island. Who is it you're talking about, and we'll call him for you."

Of course, Charlotte didn't know. And she wasn't at all sure that what she thought she knew was real. But if anyone knew who the fisherman was, it would be the one who had first sent her to see him, the day before.

"Ask Dory," she said, before slipping back into the haze of sleep.

Tripp stiffened noticeably.

"Dory?" There was only one woman he knew by that name. "Dory Delano?" he asked. Charlotte didn't answer, but she didn't need to. Her mention of the Delano name caught the attention and turned the heads of several crew, who by now were busy making ready for port. It was the worst-kept secret on the island that six months ago Tripp Wallace had asked Dory Delano to marry him and that she still hadn't given him an answer. She would answer this question, though. He picked up his cell phone and hit the first number on speed dial.

"Dory, this is Tripp."

There was a pause on the other end of the line. Dory really didn't want to get into it with him again, after last weekend. It was too much, too soon, too cute, too junior high—too something, she wasn't sure. But whatever it was, she wasn't ready to go another round with Trafalgar Wallace that morning. Charlotte went missing from her room before dinner last night, and she was still gone that morning. Dory was in a general state of panic that didn't allow time for chatter with annoying men. He sensed she was winding up to brush him off, so he spoke quickly.

"You need to meet me in an hour at the yacht club. I found something that belongs to you."

CHAPTER 4

Dory didn't need another minute to collect her things. She hopped right in the back of the ambulance when Sheriff Tally offered her the chance. The rules usually prohibited anyone but immediate family from accompanying accident victims in county vehicles, but as usual the rules didn't apply to Dory's family. Besides, Dory was the only one who could tell the sheriff who the woman was, and that would be important once they arrived at the hospital.

The perishingly thin slip of a girl lying flat on her back on the stretcher seemed still undecided whether to cling to this world or drift off into the next. Her wan expression was immovable. She stared blankly heavenward, as if awaiting a judgment that might at any moment descend from on high and demolish her. She scarcely resembled the old friend Dory had welcomed to her home the night before.

Dory massaged the hand she held in hers and whispered worriedly, "Charlie, can you hear me?" But those red-rimmed eyes held their upward gaze, and no answer came from the sunburned lips that now appeared faintly blue beneath the oxygen mask.

A paramedic appeared at the open doors of the ambulance, ready to close them in for the five-minute ride. He seemed oddly hale and hearty compared with his cargo—an alien sea creature whose once-brilliant colors were quickly fading to gray outside its native environment.

"I'll need an ID for her if you can find one," he said.

Charlotte came with nothing, which wasn't unusual for her. She almost never carried a purse yet still looked young enough to be carded for alcohol wherever she went, and for that reason often stuffed a driver's license into a pocket somewhere. Her sundress, looking improbably neat and starched from the stiffening effect of dried sea salt, had two pockets in front. Dory reached inside one, then the other, looking for anything that might identify her friend to the world. In the second pocket she felt a piece of paper.

The paramedic waited impatiently for Dory to say something or hand whatever she had taken from Charlotte's pocket to him so he could get back to his clipboard and get underway.

"Ma'am?" he finally asked.

Dory would ordinarily have cringed at being *ma'am*ed by someone within flirting distance of her own age, but she was too busy reading words written in neat cursive.

I know those I leave behind will have many questions. They are the same questions I have asked myself these last two years, but I have given up on finding the answers in this world. What I seek is somewhere beyond, where my daughter is, where my happiness went the day she died . . .

The page was torn in half, revealing only the first part of the letter Charlotte had stuck in her pocket while getting dressed and which she had forgotten to leave on the nightstand, for Dory to find. A tear falling from Dory's cheek blurred the word *happiness* and made her stop reading long enough to blot the page with the cuff of her sleeve.

"Ma'am?" the paramedic insisted again, with a politeness that Dory suddenly found intolerable.

"Stop *ma'am*ing me, you idiot," she snapped. "Can't you see—" she started to say before the rear doors of the ambulance clicked shut.

The paramedic, no longer waiting for an answer, climbed into the medical bay and gave three raps on the wall to signal the driver. The siren overhead began a slow, whirring crescendo as the van pulled away. A thin glow from the interior lights illuminated the paper in Dory's hand only barely enough to reveal the words written on it.

It was nine hours before the sedatives they gave Charlotte wore off. Awakening, she saw a woman's face come slowly into focus at the edge of the bed. Dory had been there all day, waiting and hoping for the same answers Charlotte had nearly killed herself trying to find. Charlotte had more questions now than ever, beginning with the most obvious.

"Where am I?"

"Welcome back," Dory answered cheerfully, avoiding the question.

Charlotte didn't respond. Instead she turned her head, which seemed at first to resist the idea before flopping unevenly on her pillow like a melon rolling on the ground. This was the first time she had been awake, other than the few brief seconds after she was pulled onto the *Victory* that morning. She stared at the white, antiseptic walls mounted with handrails, then out the window.

A hospital, she thought. *I have failed even at failure.*

Dory began offering a succession of food, fluids, encouragement, advice, and remonstration, in that order. But Charlotte remained silent. That might have seemed a sort of ungrateful aloofness, given the circumstances, but it was only the outward face of inner shame. She knew she was *not well,* now—not just in fact, but in the eyes of everyone who mattered. What had been and still was her private anguish would now be swept up into a maelstrom of public pity, private gossip, and the unspoken, frightened loathing people feel around the terminally ill. Whether she was or wasn't *crazy* would no longer be even plausibly deniable, which meant that the issue would now either be endlessly brought up and analyzed or uncomfortably avoided and ignored to the point of absurdity, like pretending not to notice a horribly disfiguring injury. The point of a suicide, as with any theatrical grand exit is, after all, to *exit.* It serves no purpose to remain on the stage after one's lines are finished, staring stupidly at the audience until it is no longer possible for them to suspend disbelief in the absurdity of the story.

Seeing Charlotte gaze out the window, and sensing that conversation was not otherwise likely to begin soon, Dory came directly to the one question she most wanted to ask. It had to do with the piece of paper she had retrieved from Charlotte's sundress—the sundress the nurse had neatly folded, still crisp from its saltwater laundering, on the back of a chair beside the bed.

"I read this," Dory began, as if she were confronting a philandering lover with a bar bill from the Starlight Motel. She held the paper hesitantly out to Charlotte, who turned at last to see what it was.

Charlotte stared hazily in silence at the crumpled white scrap of paper, torn and shrunken to the size of a cocktail napkin. On it were recorded the words she had intended to be her last. She couldn't read them from where she was sitting, but Dory obviously had. They were written in damnably indelible ink that saltwater had only slightly blurred. It was then Charlotte realized she had not left the note on the nightstand in her room, as she had planned. It was in her pocket when she entered the water. Recalling what she had written as her final testament, she imagined the words sounded so childishly melodramatic now that they were so clearly un-final. A Looney Tunes sketch of a robust Daffy Duck, feigning death while sobbing his goodbyes to the cruel world, flickered in her mind. She had come back from the dead as a cartoon of her former self. It occurred to her that perhaps, fittingly, this *was* purgatory after all. It was that thought that prompted Charlotte to sit up anxiously in bed and look for Meredith.

"It's not here," Dory said. Charlotte had been talking out of her head in her sleep, off and on, about Meredith for hours. Dory knew she had brought the urn with her to the house. She had not found it when she searched Charlotte's room for clues to her whereabouts, and she knew it had not been with her in the skiff.

Charlotte sunk back into the bed as if an anvil had been slowly lowered onto her chest. It was a feeling of abject helplessness. Even Meredith's earthly remains were lost to her. Now the oblivion of this all-too-present world would stubbornly endure.

What Charlotte could not see were the words written on the back of the torn half of her note, in another shade of ink and in another hand. It wasn't a sentence, just a person's name and a place: "Father Vecchio, St. Joseph's."

"What is this about Father Tommy and St. Joseph's?" Dory finally asked Charlotte.

Charlotte rolled her melon head back over to look more closely at the paper and the words not written by her. She stared at them in silence.

"He was there," she finally said, weakly.

"Tommy? Father Tommy was there on the ocean with you?" Dory was pleading now, filling in words as if she were questioning a confused child.

"No," Charlotte answered after a long breath. The slightest tinge of annoyance in her voice made it clear she would soon be fully recovered.

Charlotte had no idea who Father Tommy was. She moistened her salt-swollen lips with her tongue before trying to say more. "The fisherman—your shrimp salesman—he was there. He saved me."

"He saved you? How?"

"He pulled me up. He pulled me into the boat."

"But you were found alone, Charlie, ten miles out to sea. There was no one in the boat but you."

Charlotte didn't answer—partly because she had no answer, but also because the answer didn't matter. She knew what she had experienced: the strong hand reaching down to her in the darkness, the kind face assuring her that she would be all right, the gentle embrace in which she fell asleep as she rocked on the waves. She remembered, too, the quiet peace she felt when she awakened the next morning to the cries of the men in the sailboat. The fisherman was gone, but there was no question it had been him. He had been there.

Dory eased out of the room quietly after Charlotte drifted back asleep. Tripp was waiting for her in the side hall, trying to make the smoke from his cigarette waft through an open window. He was standing next to Sheriff Tally, who was doing the same. When Dory walked up, both men hurriedly butted out their lights, like two boys caught smoking in the bathroom.

"So, what's her story?" Tripp began, preemptively.

That was the sheriff's question to ask, but Tripp liked to assume the position of authority when he could, and the sheriff seemed in no hurry to take over. He had already taken Tripp's statement about the woman he had brought in that morning: she was alone and sleeping peacefully when they found her, drifting ten miles out at sea in a small wooden skiff with no food or water or supplies, and no explanation other than something about a man who had "saved" her. But the chief and Tripp both knew that was impossible. They had checked at both marinas on that side of the island. There had been no report of another boat leaving that morning with a dinghy in tow. Not even an Olympic swimmer could have made it ten miles back to shore against an outgoing tide off Gay Head that morning.

An attempted suicide, which this certainly appeared to be, would require a full investigation and report, but Dory didn't want Charlotte subjected to the third degree in her condition. The sheriff had agreed to wait until she woke up and Dory had a chance to speak to her. Realizing she didn't know anything more about Charlotte's story than they did, Dory began by changing the subject. She smiled at the chief, then looked disapprovingly at Tripp.

"I see you've been hanging around Smoke. When did you go back to cigarettes again?"

Tripp's face spread into a crooked smirk. Dory was a smart one. That's why he liked her. Tripp was not especially smart. He was six-foot-two, darkly handsome, and just barely graduated from Williams. There were dozens of tall, well-bred, beautiful women from good families all over the cape who would have jumped feet-first into his gene pool. The fact that Dory showed no interest in doing the same kept him off guard. He wondered if she saw the things in him he disliked most about himself. Thinking she might made him want to change, even if change didn't come easily. That was what made Dory such an interesting quarry—that and her money.

"Smoke sends his love, Dory."

"I'll bet he does," Dory answered. Her eyes darted away.

The sheriff was impatient. "What's this all about,

Dory? I understand this woman is a friend of yours."

"Yes, sheriff, and I'm sorry that I don't have more to tell you, but it seems she just went for a walk and decided to hop in a boat down by the beach."

"By the beach? On Gay Head? Six miles from town?" he asked incredulously.

"Yes, I suppose. She had no idea about the tides, and I'm afraid I had given her a little too much to drink before dinner. She fell asleep soon after she started and woke up in the middle of the ocean. Quite a story, don't you think?"

It was quite a story—and a lie, of course—but it needed telling. Whatever compelled Charlotte to try to kill herself—or whatever it was she was trying to do last night—wasn't going to be helped by a lot of prying questions from a prickly, fast-talking Boston Irish cop like Sheriff Tally.

Tripp and Dory walked out of the hospital together, later that morning. "It's nice to see you, too," Tripp began again, making a point of pretending to continue the conversation they had started earlier.

Dory spun around on her heels and faced him, but the pithy comeback she had in mind just then flew right out of her head. Tripp was what all her friends would describe as drop-dead gorgeous, which she had always thought was such a ridiculous way of describing any man. He was much taller than Dory even when she wore heels—a welcome and rare quality among the men who had shown an interest in her over the years. He was athletic and trim without being muscular. Premature graying and a chiseled jaw gave him a patrician appearance that belied his boyish personality. All this made him distracting, if not a little unsettling to women who didn't know him well. Dory knew him too well.

No sooner had Dory missed her cue to open her mouth to speak than he rushed in and planted a kiss there instead. It kept her off balance. The nerves in her stomach twirled and darted upward like a flock of startled birds. Missing her moment to say something witty or scathing, Dory rested her head on Tripp's shoulder instead. That way he couldn't see her eyes, and she didn't mind letting him hold her.

"I've missed you," he whispered softly, sounding as if they were already a couple. They weren't.

"I'm surprised," she answered, still nestled on his shoulder. "I didn't think the biscotti bakers at Williams gave you a chance to miss anyone."

It was an unfair punch. She lately felt herself at a loss for words around Tripp, and not because he dazzled her. It was rather much the opposite. She flirted with him now and then, mostly out of boredom, but he wasn't really on her radar screen. They had something of a history, and that was partly the problem—a history that went all the way back. As children, Tripp and Dory had been inseparable summer friends who could tell each other anything and usually did, which led to a few bruised hearts and late-night sobbing phone calls in their teens. She used to give him sisterly kisses by the dozen, but in all those years he had flown only one unsuccessful sortie a few inches under the hem of her skirt before she started laughing and he turned back. He never tried again—even after she was old enough to wish he would—but he was always a friend. It had been ten years since the weekend that changed everything.

It was their freshman year of college. She went off to Smith and he went off to Williams, and that was supposed to be that. But right before they left, she could tell something deeper was tugging at him. He knew he would miss her, and for the first time he was willing to show it. In a panic about what he might say, she gave him a nervous peck on the check and flew away to her mother's car before he could say anything.

That fall he invited Dory up to Williams for a formal dance, and she had agreed to go, which was the ordinary thing for a Smith girl to do. He had also asked her to bring a friend to be the blind date for his roommate. The roommate's name was Lucius Tryon DeAngelo III, which was odd enough, but odder still was the story of how he got the nickname "Smoke."

One Friday afternoon, Lucius came back to the dorm carrying not one but three dime-bags of pot, which was overachieving even for Williams. He deadbolted himself in their room and refused to open the door to anyone. He started taking bong hits one after another, and before long the smoke was oozing out under the door into the hall, like a creeping pestilence. Tripp finally gave up trying to get him to open the door and crashed on someone else's couch. At precisely three o'clock in the morning, Lucius started blaring a song on their stereo through two huge speakers he had moved into the windowsill facing the quad. It was the seventies cult-rock classic, "The Low Spark of High-Heeled Boys," by Traffic—twelve minutes of ethereal sax and piano riffs over a hypnotic driving rhythm. It was the ultimate stoner song, being played on a continuous loop. The sax solo, wailing like an air-raid siren gone berserk, could be heard all the way to the dean's residence. Hundreds of kids woke up and went outside to see what was happening. Some were laughing and some were angry, but before long they were all belting out the chorus each time it came around. The smell of marijuana filled the air.

The campus police arrived an hour later, but they couldn't get past the deadbolt to open the room. It took another hour, six firemen, and one axe to break the door down. When they did, they found Lucius—clear-eyed and stone-cold sober, wearing a neatly pressed seersucker suit and a red bowtie, sitting quietly in a chair facing the door, a packed suitcase by his side. The police booked him for felony marijuana possession and disturbing the peace, then handcuffed him and led him out of the building. When he appeared outside, a crowd of thousands erupted in cheers and began chanting "Smoke! Smoke! Smoke!" The name stuck and stayed with him from that day forward.

Smoke was immediately expelled, which seemed to be his plan. His father paid his bail and got the charges reduced to a misdemeanor. The following Monday, Smoke started as a broker-in-training with his father's firm. He rose quickly, developing a preternatural sense and a sterling reputation for contrarian stock picks that paid big—really big. Before his twenty-second birthday, he boasted a net worth of sixty million dollars and his own personal SEC investigation, which went nowhere.

Smoke's legend grew along with the folklore about what really happened that night on the quad. Some said he had an out-of-body experience. Some said he achieved nirvana. Some said he met the devil. But the wilder the tale grew, the more every trust funder at Williams wanted to invest with him. Although he was no longer a student, Smoke remained a fixture at parties around campus, and "The Low Smoke of High-Heeled Boys" became the unofficial Williams anthem.

Dory came up for the formal with a friend named Margaret, whom she had asked to be Smoke's blind date. Smoke arrived by limousine wearing his trademark red tie. After a night of bad dancing and good drinking, they came back to Tripp's townhouse. Margaret followed Smoke immediately into one of the bedrooms and closed the door behind her. Tripp hemmed and hawed before saying an early goodnight. Dory could tell he was building up to say or ask something, but he didn't have Smoke's confidence, which Dory considered a good thing at the time. If he had tried to put some sort of slick move on her, they probably would have both burst out laughing again. Instead, he gave Dory some tomato juice. It was to ward off a hangover, he said.

While she dutifully obeyed his fatherly insistence to drink, he made a place for her to sleep on the couch. He handed her the soft and nappy Brooks Brothers shirt he had worn that night to wear as pajamas. *Such a gentleman,* she thought. It smelled of his cologne. She remembered dreaming he was making love to her as she fell asleep.

But the dream abruptly ended when she woke up the next morning and discovered she was no longer wearing the shirt—or anything. She was still on the couch but lying on top of Smoke, who was also undressed and curled around her like a snake. He was oddly wide awake and sober when she looked down at him. He said nothing. Not even "good morning." He just smiled that oily smile of his, with saccharine-sweet breath that made her suddenly want to retch.

She had no memory of how he got there. Margaret was long gone, and Tripp was nowhere to be found. Dory wasn't bruised or hurt, and she didn't fail to notice that she was *on top* of Smoke and holding him as tightly as he was holding her. She wanted to scream but couldn't get her bearings. Disgusting and improbable as it seemed to her then, she couldn't escape the worry that she might have somehow initiated whatever happened. There had already been other nameless morning-men in her past, but none of them spiked the creep-o-meter quite like Smoke. But still, she thought, he didn't belong there. Where was Margaret? And where was Tripp?

The clock on the wall said it was already nine in the morning. She stood up smartly and started to demand that Smoke explain what he was doing there, but before she could speak she felt the answer run down the top of her thigh.

Dory grabbed her clothes and stumbled into the bathroom to clean herself up. She had no memory of what had happened for the past eight hours. She felt violated and angry, but there wasn't a mark on her. She found Tripp's shirt neatly hung up on the back of the door. She couldn't stop wondering why she and Smoke were holding each other like newlyweds when she woke up. Incredible as it sounded, she couldn't banish the thought that she had just cheated on her date and made love to his friend.

She stared at the disheveled, baggy-eyed girl in the mirror with self-loathing. It was a while before she could bring herself to come out, but when she did, Smoke was still lying in the same place—now dressed, but still revolting. He seemed to be enjoying her obvious discomfort and decided to make it worse by saying nothing. Instead, he just stared at her as she picked up her purse and left.

She wished she could have come up with something witty, biting, or blasé to say to regain the upper hand, but she couldn't. There was a quality about the man— more particularly the vacancy in his eyes—that made her acutely ill at ease.

Dory went in search of a strong cup of black coffee at a corner shop she had noticed on the way in. She didn't expect to find Tripp sitting there. Some girl was feeding him like a mother bird, crouched in his lap and framing his upward gaping mouth with her hands as she deposited bits of biscotti from her lips into his. It was actually quite disgusting but so strangely tender that she stood there staring for a moment before deciding to interrupt them.

Tripp erupted as if hot coffee had been spilled on his lap when he saw Dory. The girl was catapulted backwards when he did, and nearly landed on her ass.

"Dory, this is Nora from history class," he said, as they untangled themselves. Nora-from-history-class hurriedly completed the introduction before making some sideways excuse that enabled her to scurry away.

Another nest, another mouth to feed, Dory thought.

Tripp stayed standing, smiling broadly now at Dory. It seemed utterly to elude him that she might be even a little jealous.

"You were sound asleep on the couch when I peeked in around six," he said, "and there was no sign of Smoke or Margaret, so . . ."

No sign? Dory thought. It was a relief. Time to regroup and rethink things. There was no need to correct his error and nothing to confess. It would only hurt him. Better to move on and change the subject. That was her best effort at logic.

"Where did you sleep last night?" she finally asked, partly hoping he might give her a clue to the mystery of the naked, smiling Smoke.

"In my room down the hall." He pretended for her sake that he didn't remember telling her that the last time he saw her. "I was wide awake at dawn, so I came in to get my running gear, did a few miles on the track, then stopped in here."

Tripp had always been an annoyingly early riser. It was a habit he acquired in long-distance sailboat racing. He had come in to get his running gear, which meant that if he saw no sign of Smoke, he didn't see them lying together on the couch.

As she was ruminating the logic or illogic of it all, Dory noticed Tripp looking at her as if she might not be altogether well. It wasn't like her to forget their conversations. She decided to change the subject, slapping both hands gently on his knees.

"Well, then. Is Miss Biscotti Boobs modern history or ancient history?"

She didn't care much about the other girl—in fact, she didn't care at all, which she found surprising. But as long as she could safely play the jilted girlfriend, that was her best move. She knew not to push it too hard.

"Don't be jealous, Dory."

"Jealous?" She laughed. "You flatter yourself, Tripper. I'm just amazed at your capacity for attracting every stray bitch on campus before breakfast."

Bitch was a bit harsh and gave too much away. She regretted the word as soon as it slipped from her lips. Tripp's face softened into a sad smile that said "I can see I've hurt you and I'm sorry," and that made her want to drop the subject altogether, right then. She did so with a wave of her hand that meant her last comment should be stricken from the record. They had coffee and ate biscotti from a plate. They laughed about his epileptiform dance moves from the night before. It had all been great fun. Until . . .

Dory didn't tell Tripp about waking up with Smoke, or just how far and wrong things had gone. She didn't say anything for all the usual, practical, if idiotic reasons women don't speak up about such things. There might have been violence between the two men if she had. She didn't want to put Tripp in a position to defend her honor, which he certainly would do. Smoke would claim consent or—worse—that she had initiated the whole affair, led him by the hand, pinned him down. She was *on top* of him, after all, and in her own mind she still could find no explanation for that little bit of bizarreness.

Her mother would think first of the scandal and gossip—all things her family had taught Dory scrupulously to avoid. And because it was possible to avoid those things, not because it was wise or just, she did. But she didn't forget. And she acquired a keen radar sense of whenever Smoke was around.

CHAPTER 5

They arrived home from the hospital in the midafternoon. The stillness of that hour, the warmth of the sun through the window sheers in the upstairs bedroom, and a feeling that the house she had so willingly abandoned the night before was now a secure fortress against the armies at war for her soul, made sleep not only possible but irresistible for Charlotte.

Dory wasn't much of a cook, but she was an indefatigable friend, and those skills were fungible at the most basic level. There would be no going out for dinner, tonight. Friendship with Charlotte now demanded some nurturing comfort food of the sort friends were expected to conjure up whenever the world turned gray. Macaroni and cheese. Grilled cheese sandwiches with cream of tomato soup. Meatloaf. Everything capable of making life seem good and right and full of hope again.

In the refrigerator, top shelf, was the rest of the shrimp she had boiled last night—at least two pounds of it—still luscious, bulbous, enormous, and pink. Nothing at the moment seemed possibly more comforting. *The Joy of Cooking* provided the answer: Shrimp Newburg, page 390.

The knock at the door was unexpected. Turner's impending arrival had completely slipped Dory's mind with the day's unexpected events. She did her best to hide that fact and to seem completely delighted when she opened the door to find her standing there, two enormous suitcases at her side. Turner Graham was the third roommate in the triple shared with Dory and Charlotte in Jordan House at Smith. She too had vowed to stay in touch after graduation and had mostly kept that promise. It seemed impossible that ten years had passed since then.

"My God, it's you!" Dory exclaimed with a wide smile and a completely genuine feeling of surprise.

"Yes, I'm afraid it is," Turner answered. She shambled unevenly through the doorway in high heels, wobbling under the force of Dory's half hug and the weight of the luggage.

"A day early, I know," she continued, beating Dory to her next line, "but when I tell you why, you'll understand."

Charlotte, pulled back from the precipice of sleep by loud and unexpectedly cheerful conversation, was now fully awake. She recognized the voice. Turner was the newest arrival for the summer reunion but someone whom Charlotte had not expected to live long enough to see again. *So much for that plan.* Now that she was here, Charlotte had no idea what to say. *Hi! I nearly offed myself last night. How was your trip?* Turner wasn't caught up on current events. She wouldn't understand if Charlotte did what she truly wanted to do, which was to say nothing, ignore everyone, and sleep for days.

"Charlotte!" Turner shrieked when her old roommate appeared silently in the hallway. Charlotte braced herself for another vigorous hug.

"Hi, Turner. It's great to see you." Charlotte's demeanor could not have more clearly contradicted her words if she had been wearing a black hood and leg irons.

"Wow, sweetie. It's been so long." Turner eyed her suspiciously. "You look worn out—I mean, you look fabulous as ever. My God, you're thin as a teenager. But you seem exhausted. Everything okay?"

Dory tried to wave Turner off, but Turner was looking the wrong way.

"Never better." Charlotte was in no mood to explain. Dory gave her a pitying smile and rubbed Charlotte's upper arm briskly in an odd, grandmotherly sort of way.

"God, I am famished!" Turner moved on, not missing a beat. She inhaled an olive from the sideboard as she passed by and spit the pit into her hand from a distance, as if she didn't give a damn what the present company thought about her manners, which was positively true and positively why she loved being there.

"There was nothing edible at the airport, and I didn't have time to stop."

"My dear, are we running from the authorities again?" Dory added "again" for effect, but the rest of the question she asked not entirely facetiously.

"Well, not the authorities, but running, yes."

"Oh, God, it's another man," Dory groaned, rolling her eyes and lamenting that she had been even remotely close. Turner Graham was what men used to call "a dish." She was old-school pretty, and that came with the usual privileges of membership. She had wavy, jet-black hair that she wore long, and she enjoyed flipping it back all at once, with a flourish. Everyone told her she looked like Ava Gardner or Rita Hayworth, and though she was usually not crass or drunk enough to say so, as a matter of fact she thoroughly agreed with both comparisons. She liked the attention of men and had always gotten a lot of it, usually without much trying. That's how she married an up-and-coming bank executive she had only just met in Las Vegas, and that's also how she divorced him a year later after having an affair with his very married boss. Her husband wanted to keep his job, and his boss wanted to keep things quiet, so Turner walked away from the affair and the marriage with a large lump-sum payment and forty thousand dollars a year in alimony for ten years. "Not bad for my first time in Vegas," she would say with a hearty laugh, never noticing how people cringed.

Turner wasn't into guilt and had no desire to lead what stuffier people considered a well-examined life. She wanted to live a good life, preferably without examining a damn thing. And for the most part, that's exactly what she did.

She used the divorce settlement for a down payment on an historic house in a quaint and uppity neighborhood in Morristown, New Jersey. That house had been her pride and joy. Buying it seemed like a good idea at the time, as did the adjustable-rate mortgage.

The alimony payments amounted to much less than what most of the ex-wives she met in Morristown had received, but they had all been married much longer. "Dollar for dollar, year for year," Turner would calculate, she had come out ahead.

Divorce had afforded her a near-perfect life, with but one persistent imperfection: the alimony was temporary and had finally run out six months ago. Her part-time job as a receptionist in a doctor's office wasn't going to pay the bills, which was part of what had brought her to her present difficulty.

"Yes, if you must know—not that you're surprised, I realize—a man is the reason I'm here two days early."

"Do tell," Dory answered, shooting a hidden smile at Charlotte to enlist her eagerness for the tale. Turner always told the best stories, no matter how gruesome or sad.

"I will, but my God, first tell me where you got this shrimp," Turner moaned, her mouth now full with a bite of Dory's Newburg. "Are you flying it in from the Gulf? Are we that obviously decadent now, Eudora, you filthy-rich bitch?"

"I will tell you, a desperately poor bitch though you are," Dory replied, "even though you'll never believe it, but I asked my question first."

Charlotte looked on in bewildered silence, only mildly interested in Turner's man-tale, but now keenly interested in what Dory had to say about the fisherman. He had, after all, just saved her life. She was sure of it, impossible as it seemed.

"Very well," Turner complied with great satisfaction. She loved going first in everything. "Where to begin? Of course, you remember the blog?"

God help me, Dory thought, choosing not to answer. Everyone remembered the blog, if only through Turner's viral infiltration of Facebook pages and email lists to assemble a social daisy-chain of followers, including several dozen of Dory's mortified friends. An army of ten thousand, they were all hostages to Turner's perambulations. *Followers*—not readers or fans—was the perfect aphorism where Turner was concerned. She didn't want to be merely read or admired. She wanted to be *followed.*

But she *was* followed, which Dory could not begrudge her, even if the reason had nothing to do with the quality of her writing. Every post featured photos of Turner, *the dish,* smiling and gaily cavorting alongside columns of her prose about nothing in particular. Her white tank top, no bra, was *de rigeur,* as was the fact that each scene appeared to be sunny and delightful while Turner, within it, appeared to be either freezing or delighted or both. The women read and watched in disbelief, with scandalized admiration. The men—

dozens of them from all over the world—were eager to become Turner's "friends." Every year, one or two of them tired of waiting for friendship to bloom and decided to meet her in person, usually unannounced.

"His name is Sir Robert Babbage," Turner said, beginning her narrative.

"Sir Robert *Bullshit*, you mean," Dory piped up. "Another phony lord?"

"Well, yes and no—I don't know anything about him, honestly, but it doesn't matter. He's from Sydney—"

"As in Australia?"

"Yes, and he's seventy-nine—"

Dory grasped her temples as if her head were about to explode. "Please stop, Turner. Just stop. We're eating here, for chrissakes."

"Which is ancient I realize," Turner continued, unfazed, "but it was really just harmless fun at first."

"At first? At *first*? You mean there's more?"

"He complimented a post of mine on the blog, and—"

"God almighty, Turner!" Dory was shaking her head in feigned disgust. She had run through the same ritual with her friend before, always with the same result. "How many times do I have to tell you—as if you didn't already know? It's your ass they pine for, not your writing. Your stupid ASS," she added with emphasis that was hardly necessary, "not your stupid BLOG."

"It *is so* the blog. It's a damn good blog—the Huff Post even said so. Anyway—long story short—"

"Too late for that." Dory was piling on, now.

"I didn't know any readers from Australia, so I complimented him back. I like engaging with my readers."

"I'll bet they feel the same."

Charlotte watched her former roommates with

horrible fascination. They were like two aging champions in a match volley at Wimbledon, each refusing to concede the point. She had forgotten all about the fisherman.

"He sent a photo of himself with his smiling, grown daughter, which I took to be just a way of putting his guns on the table and proving he was safe to let in the door."

"At seventy-nine, Turner, men don't have guns anymore."

"The point is—"

Turner paused to refill her wine glass for the fourth time and swallow another enormous bite of the Newburg.

"The point is, he asked for my mailing address—"

"Oh, God. You didn't—"

"I did, but it wasn't for him to come in person."

"Let me guess. He just wanted to send flowers."

"No, but close. He owns a tea plantation in India where they grow the most heavenly Darjeeling."

"Oh, God, not the tea again," Dory wailed, clearly relishing that she held the righteous upper hand. "Turner! You almost went into renal failure in our sophomore year from all the tea you drank during finals!"

"But this tea from India was exquisite," Turner pleaded. "I mean a cut above. I became addicted to the stuff."

"Of course you did. He was probably lacing it with opium."

"Don't be ridiculous," Turner snapped. "You know how I *adore* tea."

Turner had become overfond of the word *adore*. She pronounced it with a flourish of faux sophistication. It was spot-on Lovey Howell from *Gilligan's Island*—unintentionally so.

"He started sending me bags of it every month. I was swimming in tea. I would, of course, have to thank him, and he would, of course, write back and send more. Anyway, I think he must have felt we were developing some sort of a romantic connection."

"He's seventy-nine. What connection could he possibly—"

"Oh, don't be naïve. You know damn well what men are capable of."

"Yes, Turner," Dory sighed. "You have taught me that."

"So—do you want to hear the reason why I'm here early or not?" Turner complained.

Dory relaxed, took a bite of the Newburg, and with her mouth full, warbled, "You're here because I love you. What other reason do you need?" But clearly Turner wanted to get this off her chest, so Dory smiled sweetly and listened.

"He emailed me last night to say he was arriving at JFK and wanted to come by my house—"

"Let's see, that would be the same house where you sleep alone in your bed at night, at the same address you stupidly gave out to a man you've never met, who contacted you over the Internet after looking at photos of you braless in a tank top."

The words rolled off Dory's tongue with relish she could not resist, then immediately regretted. A hurt look lingered on Turner's face. She just stared at Dory, and the conversation sank into silence.

"Turner, I'm really sorry . . ." Dory finally began, softly.

The dam broke, and a tear raced down Turner's cheek. Her mouth quivered to speak.

"You're such an asshole sometimes, Dory."

"I know, I—"

"You think everyone has a life like this? With family

and friends and money constantly swirling around you, that you just can reach out and grab one whenever you want?"

Turner was unloading both barrels, now, and Dory had sense enough to stay low.

"You're right. I'm all alone, and I'm lonely! You win, Dory, so *fuck you*." The tears came more quickly now, along with a moan that sounded more painful than sad. The tone of her voice had changed. Gone was the glib ladies' luncheon banter. Her words were low and guttural. She forced out each one like a knife pulled from her gut.

"I like the attention of men, okay? Is that so awful? I need a man to help me, and you're damn right I want a man to make me feel loved and pretty. I don't like being alone. I can't be alone. And *yes*, goddammit, I flaunt what little I still have to make men interested in me, so I don't have to be alone. And you want to know whether I feel stupid that what I wind up with is a seventy-nine-year-old guy? Well, guess what? I do. You win."

Turner's voice began to crack, and she strained to form words in between the cries.

"I came here early to get away from him. So I wouldn't be there and have to tell him no. So I could just avoid it. I turned off the comments to my blog so no one could ask me where I had gone, and I wouldn't have to answer. I wanted a little peace for a while. Is that too much to ask for? I know my life is such a *fucking* mess, but I don't need the perfect people of the world to shove it in my face!"

That was all the speech she could manage. It was all tears and sobs after that. Charlotte reached across the table and held Turner's hands, deciding to intervene before someone drove a Spaulding to the cerebellum.

Dory, apologizing and desperate to make amends, got up and rushed around the side of the table toward

Turner. All three women stood, knocking over chairs, crouching and holding and leaning together in a slowly shifting, crying heap that finally descended to the floor beside the table. Sobs came from Dory and Turner in antiphonic measure. Charlotte, the woman who didn't just feel like dying but had actually tried to do so not twenty-four hours before, rubbed the backs of both women in rhythmic circular motions as if she had her own life completely together. She didn't even notice the comforting sounds she made weren't real words. That was the same way she had comforted Meredith as a baby.

In a minute or two, the din of sniffling and weeping and bleating dwindled to a few comfortably spaced clucks and grunts as noses and eyes were wiped and smiles broke out. Turner's mascara had run just enough to make her look like a linebacker in eye black, which Dory smeared off with saliva licked onto her hand. It was gross, but it was a good kind of gross.

There would, of course, be no attempt by anyone to clarify or analyze or rehash the previous five minutes. Everything that needed to be said was already said, or understood to be simply beyond the power of words to explain. An angry, purple thunderhead that needed to break and empty its torrents upon the earth had now done so. It would move out to sea where it would not be missed and never called to mind until it rolled around again.

Turner reached above them, her unseen hand darting about the table in search of something. "Where is it?" she said in frustration.

"Where is what?" Dory asked, thickly, through a suddenly stuffed-up nose.

"That dish of yours, the shrimp thing."

"Oh, the Newburg!"

Dory rose onto her knees, grasped the giant earthen

bowl and serving spoon from the table, and placed them in the middle of the three women on the floor. Turner immediately inhaled another mouthful and passed the spoon to Charlotte, who did the same.

"What the hell is this stuff, Dory? You didn't make this, did you?"

"I did. It's Shrimp Newburg."

"My God, I've never tasted anything like it. It's like big globs of white, creamy steak."

"I just followed the recipe."

"No," Turner insisted, shaking her head to signify what her mouth was too full to say, then swallowing like a snake. "I don't mean the recipe—which is good, don't get me wrong—but where did you get shrimp like this? These are, I don't know, turbo shrimp or something."

"I got them," Charlotte piped up, then added, with a sense of mystery, "from the fisherman." Her only real words of the last fifteen minutes.

Turner looked quizzically at Charlotte for a moment. "The fisherman? You say it like he's the only one. I mean, this is Cape Cod. You can't swing a cat up here without hitting a fisherman. Who is this guy?"

Dory started to explain, wanting to save Charlotte the embarrassment of saying something like, "the fisherman who appeared out of nowhere and kept me from drowning myself," but Turner wasn't done.

"Wait a minute. You mean you bought jumbo shrimp like this off the boat somewhere up here? There are no shrimp in New England this year."

Charlotte looked at Dory. This was her part of the mystery to explain. She was the one who had sent Charlotte to pick up the shrimp in the first place.

Dory began. "Well, funny you should ask, because everyone up here has the same question, but nobody knows the answer. A woman I know, Millicent Davis, showed up at a luncheon last month with a plate of these shrimp she said a guy she'd never seen before was selling out of a blue Jeep by the highway. Everyone in town has been trying to find the guy ever since."

"Find the guy? Is he hiding or something?" Turner asked.

"Well, he's off the grid, that's for sure. He's selling without a permit, but no one knows where he operates out of or really how he's doing it. A shrimp boat isn't an easy thing to hide around here. Besides, if there were shrimp in New England this season, everyone would be catching them, but I've only heard about this one guy."

"Don't you think he's just bringing it up from the Gulf?" Turner suggested.

"Well, if he is, he's bringing it up every day fresh with no trucks, no refrigeration, and no warehouse. That's a hell of a delivery system. And besides—"

"And besides, he saved me," Charlotte blurted out.

A look of remorse passed over Dory's face when she heard those words, and the conversation abruptly stopped. It was the face of a mother staring at a child's overturned bowl of spaghetti—neither anger nor surprise, just weariness. There was no help for it. Charlotte's suicide attempt would now have to be explained.

"Saved you from what?" Turner insisted.

"Turner, maybe not now," Dory sought to intervene. But Charlotte had something to say.

"Saved me from myself, I suppose," Charlotte answered. "All I remember is his hand reaching down for me, and pulling me up. I never saw him after that, but he took Meredith."

"He took *Meredith?* Your daughter? But honey, Meredith—" *Meredith is dead,* Turner started to say, but realized she didn't like the sound of it.

Charlotte's impulse to explain quickly waned. In the silence, Turner leaned slightly to look more closely at

Charlotte, worried she might be unwell. Dory pantomimed spastically for Turner to drop the subject, using wide finger slashes across her throat that Turner observed with growing worry.

"You slit your *throat*?"

"What?" Charlotte asked, hazily returning to the conversation.

Dory's arm shot out for the empty bowl of Newburg on the floor. Grabbing it, she sprang to her feet between her two friends and quickly changed the subject.

"Of course not, Turner, you goose! She's sitting right next to you. Does she look like she slit her throat? Besides, you both have totally licked the bowl clean. I'm tired, so is Charlotte, and we're all heading to bed. That's enough for one night."

Turner's bewilderment remained. It was only nine thirty. But Dory continued her hidden pantomimes, now scooping the air with both arms, trying to tell Turner to get her ass up off the floor.

The first floor of the house was being renovated that summer. Hardwood floors warped by decades of alternatingly humid and frigid salt air had to be ripped up and replaced, which meant that Turner and Charlotte would have to share the only remaining bedroom upstairs, the one Charlotte had left the night before. It was a proper nineteenth-century Yankee home, built in an era when middle-class merchants and whalers could afford homes on the Vineyard. That meant that it was designed with a sturdy and modest utilitarian tastefulness and not an ounce of vanity. There were no cavernous, oversized bathrooms, and the bedrooms were barely large enough to accommodate a full-sized bed frame. People in those days didn't linger in bedrooms or bathrooms. They lingered in their labor.

Bunking in the same narrow bed with Charlotte reminded Turner of summer camp. It didn't matter that they hadn't seen each other in years. They were old friends if not good friends anymore. Being alone with friends away from home in a small room in the dark made conversation inevitable and the telling of secrets irresistible. Even so, Charlotte did try to resist, if only because she knew where conversation of any kind must be headed. She said goodnight aloud so as to punctuate the end of the waking day and announce her departure for the world of sleep and dreams, only to lie there breathing uneasily, wide awake, in an excruciating silence that fooled no one and was finally broken by Turner's simple, two-word question.

"What happened?"

The question was spoken without need of context or predicate, because the context and predicate were already pressing in close around them in a dense, hot cloud of unspoken worry and concern.

Charlotte didn't answer for perhaps a minute, as she searched for some grounded, sensible, explicable place from which her answer could safely embark. But there was none. So she decided to leap, not looking and not knowing where the answer might lead.

"I decided to kill myself."

Dory's throat-slashing pantomime again came to mind for Turner, who still missed its meaning.

"My God, why?"

"Why does anyone try to kill herself? Because it seems pointless to go on."

And there, in the darkness of that proper bedroom in that proper house, Charlotte spent the next hour explaining all that had transpired to lead her to the depths of despair. When again Turner asked the question, "But why suicide?" Charlotte explained and reaffirmed her decision to follow her child into whatever vestibule of hell God had, in his indifference, reserved for them both.

Turner pondered Charlotte's story in silence, as if every word were taking its time passing through layered filters of reason and emotion to a place where its essence could be understood. At length, she asked the obvious next question in the form of a statement.

"But, you didn't drown."

It was an obvious point, the explanation for which Charlotte had omitted because she didn't fully understand it herself. The reason Charlotte didn't drown was a mystery, and at the center of that mystery was the fisherman.

"At dinner," Turner prompted her, "you said he saved you. You were talking about this fisherman."

"Yes," Charlotte answered.

"How did he save you?"

Charlotte paused a long time before answering. There were two questions she had asked herself over and over again since that morning. One was *how,* and the other was *why.*

How should have been easier. She was there when it happened, after all, but what she thought she knew and had seen made no sense. It was dangerous, she knew, to speak the words she would say out loud, because hers was the kind of testimony that changed things. Change could be dangerous. But to remain cloistered in silence was the loneliest kind of insanity. She needed to speak those words aloud to be certain that she and the world around her were still real.

"I remember I was losing the ability to keep my head above water—which, you know, was the point of what I was doing. Still, when it started to happen, and it was clear I wasn't going to be able to save myself—that this was really going to be it, the end—I started to panic. It was so dark out there—a kind of darkness so deep it's like something you can feel all around you. Even the stars disappeared. I could not see my own hand. It was as if I had already vanished from the face of the Earth. It was about then that my mind began to race like crazy, and I could feel my body beginning to fight what was happening—but fighting was pointless. That's how I planned it. The tide had taken me, I was exhausted, and I was far from shore. But it's one thing to plan something like that and a very different thing to be in the middle of it, while it's happening."

"Oh my God." It was all Turner could say. It was the only thought in her head.

"It was right then—like out of nowhere—that this little boat shows up. I can see the light from under the water, coming closer. A man is in the boat, leaning over the side to take my hand, and I'm not thinking of anything but trying to reach him, but at the same time I realize he's the same man who had sold me the shrimp. It was him. I'm sure of it. I remember this feeling of incredible peace when his hand held mine, as if all the struggle and the fear of that moment and all the worry of all the moments of my life until then simply vanished. None of it mattered anymore.

"I only vaguely remember him pulling me aboard. I remember lying there in his arms, looking up at him. I was no longer cold or afraid or tired, but he told me to close my eyes and sleep. That's what I suppose I did, because it was the middle of the morning when they found me."

"Who found you?"

"Dory's friend Tripp, on the yacht he was racing off the cape at Gay Head."

"How did you find this fisherman in the first place— you know, when he gave you the shrimp?"

73

"Dory told me where to go."

"*Dory* told you where to go?"

Charlotte had no idea why Dory knew this, except that Dory was clued into almost anything of importance that went on in the Vineyard—if not personally, then through the network of friends and busybodies who knew her or her family.

"So . . . ?" Turner was waiting.

"So, what?"

"So what about the fisherman?"

"I don't know anything else about him. He was gone when I woke up."

"Gone? Gone where?"

"I don't know."

"But you said you were ten miles out in the ocean. Did you drift closer to shore?"

"No, from what Tripp said I would have washed up in North Africa in another month or so."

"So . . . ?" Turner was waiting again.

"I know what you're asking, Turner, and I want to know the answer just as much as you do."

Turner began to sense the gravity of what had occurred—at least in Charlotte's mind. She finally asked a more pointed question.

"You have no idea where he went? None at all? Was there another boat? I mean, he couldn't have walked on water."

"There was no other boat. It was just him and me, and then he was gone."

Turner went exactly nowhere without her laptop and an air card that she could use to access and update her blog wherever she was. She got both of them out that night after she was certain Charlotte was fast asleep. There, illuminated in the ghostly white light of her computer screen, she began to write a blog entry under the headline: "Mysterious Vineyard Savior Walks on Water."

It was a plausible if unverified version of the story Charlotte had just told her. Turner hadn't written anything for the blog in a month, and she felt exhilarated to be writing something again—especially something so deliciously weird. Her words about the daring rescue flowed, although she carefully omitted the reason why Charlotte had been there in the first place.

When Turner was satisfied that she had written it well, she hit the button for "publish" and collapsed back in bed beside Charlotte, who was by then deeply asleep. It was four in the morning.

At nine o'clock, Dory set the table for a lazy, Saturday morning breakfast, fearing that both of her houseguests would be too lazy to eat it. But then Turner appeared, yet only half awake. The breakfast table in the kitchen was bathed in sunlight, and Turner was drawn to its warmth in the chilly air of a June morning.

It didn't truly warm up on the Vineyard until the fourth of July, and then only for a fleeting few weeks before fall jealously shooed the sunbeams away. Chowder was the number-one selling dish in restaurants, and the reason was simple enough: it allowed frozen tourists a chance to wrap their hands around something hot and steaming.

But the hydrangeas under Dory's kitchen windowsill insisted it was summer. Their blousy, bright blue and pink blossoms were so ebullient and filled with the energy of sunny afternoons that it was impossible to resist their spell, no matter what the weather.

Still groggy with sleep, Turner coughed out two words.

"Coffee, black."

"Yes, your ladyship," Dory answered primly, and not entirely facetiously. "Can I get you something to eat?"

Turner smiled wryly and said nothing, partly to acknowledge the resumption of hostilities in their ongoing battle of wits, and partly to assure Dory that she intended to come out on top in the end.

Turner took the lead. "The fisherman, Dory. I'm fascinated by this man. How did you know where to send Charlotte to find him?"

"It's all very mysterious. Like I said, he's operating outside the law here on the island, which is pissing some important people off, but so far he has stayed a step ahead of the fisheries police, the health department, and everyone else who would like to have a stern word with him."

"How does he do it?"

"It's secret, and if I tell you, you have to promise to keep it."

"My my, Dory, you've become quite the rebel. What will Mother say?"

Dory glared at her.

Turner drew her finger across her lips like a zipper and poked her cheek, punctuating with a period her promise to shut up.

"He sells his catch out of an ancient Jeep Wagoneer. I don't even know how he got it up here, it's so full of rust and holes. But the body's been painted over in pale blue. It's actually rather pretty.

"At first there was a sign by the road that said, 'Shrimp at the blue Jeep.' If you saw the sign, you went down the road another half mile, and there he would be, with coolers on his tailgate. But once the law came after him, the sign disappeared."

"How do you find him, then?"

"Blue paint. He must have a few buckets left over from what he used on the Jeep because that's what he uses for a sign now. He paints an X with that blue paint on a tree close to the road. The mark means that he'll be there at sundown. He never comes to the same place twice, and he never stays long because he usually sells out in less than half an hour. He strips off the tree bark with the paint slash before he leaves, so there's no trace he was there."

"So then, what are you doing? Roaming the island looking for blue paint? And I thought *my* social life was in the toilet!"

"Not only me. There's a group of us around the island who keep an eye out during our comings and goings. It's not every day, but when one of us sees the mark, we tell the others, and whoever needs seafood that day goes and gets it."

"My God, Dory, it's like you've joined the fishmonger's mob."

"You tasted the shrimp, Turner. You'd do the same."

"Damn right I would. That was amazing. But I still don't get it. What are jumbo Gulf shrimp doing on the Grand Banks, and if this guy's catching them, why isn't everybody catching them?"

"Don't know. Don't care."

"When's the next delivery?"

"Don't know that, either." Dory unceremoniously plopped an enormous golden omelet onto Turner's plate.

"What do I look like, a lumberjack?" Turner asked.

"From the way you tore into that shrimp last night, I'd say so."

The omelet was exactly what Turner wanted, even if she didn't care to give Dory the satisfaction of hearing her say so. Dory was a gracious host. Turner knew this, and she appreciated the kindness Dory was showing her. A summer in the Vineyard was well beyond Turner's means, and it would be a welcome respite from the troubles in her life. Turner knew, before long—when enough of the sea had washed over her—she would become a more gracious guest. In the meantime, her prickliness and touchiness helped her avoid acknowledging the obvious, which was that Dory's life was infinitely more fabulous than hers.

"So, I was reading your blog yesterday," Dory began. "Since when did you become a 'Bennett & Donald author'?" Bennett & Donald was the largest publishing house in the world. Having them publish your first book was like having lunch with the pope and dinner with the devil. The air didn't get any rarer. It was a title that Turner had added to her moniker on the blog two months ago, and it was a question Dory had been eager to ask ever since Turner showed up.

Turner decided to take another huge bite of the omelet to bide her time before answering. Dory filled in the gap.

"Have you written a book I don't know about?" Dory was being politely false. She knew that had Turner Graham written a book, much less sold it to the largest publisher on Earth, everyone in Turner's world would have been made acutely aware of every detail by now.

"Not exactly," Turner answered. The look on her face meant she knew there was no way to make what she had to say sound all right. She was trapped there in Dory's web, a sunny breakfast nook cleverly woven with cheddar omelets and fresh raspberries, and there would be no escape.

"Then exactly what do you mean?"

"Well," Turner paused, still swallowing and still looking for an escape route, "I met this man through the blog. He works at Bennett & Donald in New York."

"How fabulous! My friend's mother knows all the editors at Bennett & Donald. What's his name?"

"Stephen, but he's not an editor—not exactly."

"Oh?"

"He works on the loading dock, actually . . ."

With those words, Dory's mind turned to the task of stifling any hint of laughter, while an encouraging and interested smile remained hung on her face like a shop sign, saying "be back soon." Turner continued to extol Loading Dock Man's many virtues.

". . . and gorgeous, and smart, and funny . . ."

"How old?"

"Our age, you know."

"How old?" Dory was relentless.

"Forty-five."

"Turner, you're thirty-two."

"That's around my age. Dory, for God's sake."

"I'd say working on the loading dock at Bennett & Donald at forty-five, *actually*, is not being an editor at Bennett & Donald, *exactly*. Tell me he's not married."

Dory, without even trying, knew exactly where and at what moment to insert the pin to pop Turner's joy, though in this case she took no pleasure in doing so.

Turner paused again and let go a decidedly teenaged sigh.

"Yes, he's married—to a shrew who doesn't love him."

The safety harness flew off. Dory could stand it no longer. "I swear to God, Turner! Is there some sort of Web filter that lets only middle-aged married men view your blog? And don't you know that every married man is married to a shrew he thinks should adore him more? So what is it then, an affair?"

"Dory—it's not what you think."

"No, Turner, I'm sure it's not. People in affairs don't think—they feel. They live in a magical world ruled by

King and Queen Libido. The affair is never what the people in it think it is, because there is no thinking going on whatsoever."

Turner was done arguing, but Dory was still curious.

"Rewind for me. You met him through the blog—how?"

"He commented on something I'd written, and then he sent me a photo of himself and invited me for an all-expenses-paid trip to the city. He was charming and witty and a gentleman, and while you may be tripping over men like that up here in La-La-Land, they're pretty damn scarce in New Jersey."

All expenses paid were the key words, here. Turner was a beautiful woman, there was no denying. Any number of men over the years had paid her expenses and then some for the favor of her attention. But she never saw the arrangement for the age-old bargain it was, or if she did, she never let on. She reeled them in gradually and sorted them all out on the blog until she decided to accept someone's offer for a fabulous trip someplace where they could meet. They would have explosive, forbidden sex, after which they would "fall in love" and plot their escape together. This lasted until the money stopped flowing or the jilted wife's lawyers showed up—whichever came first. Then, she would move on to the next man in line who thought she was strangely beautiful and witty and *way too talented* to be writing just a blog. Some were sincere, and some were using her, but to be certain, she was using every one of them. In the end, she really didn't give a damn what it all said about her or them. The virtual blog world she invented for herself distracted her from the depressing reality of the world she actually lived in.

"So, okay," Dory continued as she cleared the dishes to the sink. "What does Loading Dock Man have to do—"

"Don't call him Loading Dock Man."

"Fine. What does LDM have to do with you being a Bennett & Donald author? They don't exactly pass book contracts out with the packing peanuts, you know."

"You're such an *ass*, Dory! He's got friends in the editorial department, okay?"

"Friends?"

"He wasn't always working a loading dock. He's got a brain. He comes from a good family. His dad was a doctor, and he got into Middlebury. He was a star on the tennis team before he got kicked out for his grades."

"A towering intellect, no doubt."

"He's one of those free spirits who don't need other people to stamp their ticket and tell them they're okay. He's content doing what he's doing, which is more than a lot of people can say about their jobs. He's in amazing shape—"

"Right—don't forget that part."

"And every executive in the building is lining up to play squash and racquetball with him."

"So, okay then, the entire Bennett & Donald editorial department has a crush on Loading Dock Man. What have they offered *you*?"

"Nothing—yet. But Stephen thinks I've got a great angle on my life story for a memoir—you know, my divorce, yada yada—"

"You know, Turner, people tell me—actual *Bennett & Donald* authors tell me—that the 'yada-yada' is the hard part."

"He keeps pushing me to finish, and when I do he's going to present it to one of the guys he works with."

"Works *for*, you mean, Turner."

"Whatever. How many agents do you know who would kill just to get a Bennett & Donald editor to *look* at one of their writers' books? You, of all people, should know that business runs on connections, and the publishing business is no different."

"When do I get to read the Yada-Yada Memoir?"

"I haven't written it yet."

"Of course not. You're too busy with LDM."

"I may just write it right here, in this house, this summer, and your lovely home will become so famous as the place where Turner Graham's memoir was written, you'll have to turn it into a tea parlor and sell tickets. How will that suit you?"

"Would suit me fine. If I'm going to be putting up an honest-to-God *Bennett & Donald author* all summer, I might as well get something out of it."

Just then, Charlotte appeared, wearing a giant, cotton nightshirt she had stolen from Dory's room. She hadn't packed for a long stay, and nightshirts were one of the many things she needed but didn't have. She trudged on the cold hardwoods in tiny, clipped steps owing to over-sized slippers (also Dory's). She looked as if she had either been sleeping for days or hadn't slept in days. Dory handed her a cup of black coffee, extra cream and sugar. Charlotte would have preferred just black, but she accepted it wordlessly.

"Good morning, sunshine," Dory offered, cheerfully.

Charlotte replied unintelligibly.

"What brings you downstairs at the crack of noon?" Turner asked.

"Your damn laptop, as a matter of fact," Charlotte answered, casting a sullen, sidelong glance.

"My laptop?"

"It's been beeping incessantly for the last hour. Did you set an alarm or something?"

Turner excused herself to go upstairs to see what was the matter with her laptop, but she was quite sure there was no problem at all—at least not a mechanical one. She hadn't told Charlotte or Dory of the story she posted to her blog about Charlotte's ocean rescue, and she saw no reason to bring it up now. She knew exactly what the rapid beeping meant, and it was now matched by the beating of her heart.

Her blog was set to sound a bell tone every time someone liked or shared one of her posts. The bell tone meant the story was getting traction and going viral, which is what every blogger hopes will happen but which rarely ever does. She usually kept the laptop turned on so she could take encouragement whenever the odd, random *beep* would sound—usually few and far between.

What was happening now was something else altogether. When she walked into the bedroom, she could hear that the *beep* tone had melded into a continuous, rapid sort of Morse code. She assumed this meant the computer had crashed or was about to. She cursed under her breath and opened the blog post. Everything loaded properly and appeared to be working normally, except for one thing. There was an unusual number next to the hit counter for the blog post about Charlotte's rescue. Turner thought it said thirty thousand six hundred and something, which was absurd for any story of hers, much less one posted only a few hours ago. She unfolded her reading glasses to look more closely and make sure she wasn't mistaken. She was. By then it said forty thousand two hundred and something. The last two digits of the counter were spinning too quickly for her to read.

CHAPTER 6

Charlotte wasn't even close to being ready to leave the house when Dory announced she was about to be late for a doctor's appointment and began flying around the room. Dory hesitated at the idea of leaving Charlotte alone, but it was an appointment she couldn't miss. Turner spoke right up and promised to stick around, which was all Dory wanted. Someone needed to be with Charlotte at a time when, having lost first her daughter and now even the urn of her ashes, she had never been more alone.

Charlotte, for her part, kept insisting that Dory and Turner stop walking on eggshells. Her only plan for the day, she told them, was to go to St. Joseph's Church and spend some time in prayer and meditation. It was the kind of thing she had done for years and, lately, had done more frequently though with less satisfaction. Prayer made her feel connected to the world beyond this one, the one into which her daughter had disappeared. And even though her prayers were now mostly arguments, shouting at God kept her from shouting at everyone else.

Turner insisted she accompany Charlotte to the church but drew the line at going inside. Church wasn't Turner's thing—never had been. But there was a coffee shop across the street, and, most importantly, it had Wi-Fi. She would wait there for as long as Charlotte liked, and Charlotte couldn't argue with that. She liked Turner, and it was already doing her good to be around her and

Dory again. Life was no less miserable—in fact it was more so—but for the first time in a long time, her misery had company.

In her pocket, Charlotte carried the torn letter with the note she couldn't explain—the note that said, simply, "Father Vecchio, St. Joseph's." Dory might have explained to Charlotte that Tommy Vecchio was a former Vineyard bad boy who became a priest and had since returned to the island as the pastor of St. Joseph's in Edgartown. But Dory had other things on her mind that morning, and the paper contained only Father Vecchio's name and the name of the church where, after a three-minute walk, Charlotte and Turner arrived.

"I'll wait for you over there." Turner pointed to the coffee shop, flashing the overly encouraging, breezy smile of a mother shooing her child into the doctor's office, where the unseen tetanus needle awaits.

Father Tommy was a good friend of the Wallace family. He was a few years older than Dory and had worked as a counselor at the summer camp she attended as a girl, run by the Catholic parishes on the island. Dory's parents were not especially devout. They were, in fact, acutely private about their Catholicism in the overwhelmingly waspy circles of Vineyard society, but they nonetheless wanted Dory exposed to all the usual influences of the Church as a child.

Church camp wasn't anything like the sleepaway camps in Bar Harbor that Dory attended in the warmer months of July and August each year. The day camp on the Vineyard ran for just two weeks every June, right after school let out and before everyone went off on vacation. Every Catholic kid on the island—rich or poor, like it or not—showed up. The parents and the priests made sure of it.

Tommy Vecchio was one of the working-class kids who later became one the "fun" counselors. He could be counted on to look the other way when a bottle of booze appeared at the beach bonfires held each evening. He was also known for not looking the other way when those same bonfires devolved into games of strip poker and skinny-dipping among the kids whose parents were late picking them up. It was rumored that Ruth Palermo, who left the island abruptly in the middle of her junior year of high school to care for a sickly (and hitherto unheard of) aunt in Newport, had gotten pregnant by Tommy. A rather ugly, churchy sort of brouhaha had started to build from whispers about the matter. But no sooner had the rumors started to swell than it was announced that Tommy Vecchio had answered the call of Almighty God to study for the priesthood. And that was that. Everyone knew Tommy was a rounder before, but now he was God's rounder.

Dory once overheard someone at the yacht club summer social clucking something a bit too loudly about Tommy. It turned out to be her mother, standing in a tight knot of other Catholic mothers, all of whom had drunk three old-fashioneds too many, saying how "damn pleased" she was that the diocese was getting someone who "isn't gay or a Marxist or both."

"So Tommy may have gone in for a little too much gin and grab-ass when he was younger," her mother pontificated. "He's now a priest in a line going back two thousand years to St. Peter, who—let's face it—was no saint himself when he first took the job." She paused to swallow. "You know?"

They knew.

Little Tommy Vecchio might not have been trusted to pour wine at church spaghetti dinners without skimming off some extra for himself, but that was years ago. The man who came into the church that afternoon to greet the lone woman kneeling quietly in the rear pew was Father Thomas Vecchio, who, like every other priest, was considered a vicar of Christ on Earth, and who, like every other priest, had the power to turn wine into saving blood and bread to heavenly flesh. Given the scarcity of mortals who could do that, his earthly vices were easily overlooked.

"May I help you?" he asked.

Charlotte thought the question strangely superfluous, given that it was a priest's daily vocation to help anyone and everyone who came to this place in search of hope and forgiveness.

"I don't know, Father—maybe you can," Charlotte said, easing back into the pew where the priest had seated himself beside her. "It's a long story, and I'm not sure I believe it myself, so I don't know that I expect you to."

"Long stories are my specialty. Go right ahead."

He was so smooth-skinned, fair and pale in the face, with deep-set eyes and full, jet-black hair. In the darkness of the church, the glow of candles still lit from the noon mass made him seem almost luminous, like an angel. Like someone she could perhaps even trust— trust not to be cruel and unfeeling like the others. Maybe a priest of a younger, more sensitive generation was what she had needed all along. He seemed so eager to help, but she wondered what authority such a young man could bring to bear on a church that had been so unyielding to a mother's supplications for her child.

She handed him the piece of paper containing the note that had drawn her to that place. She told him of her marriage and divorce following Meredith's death, and of the cruelty of the bishop under whom Father Vecchio served, and of her longing and fear and guilt.

Father Vecchio looked at the paper, not at Charlotte,

as she spoke. He turned the paper over and over with his fingers, compulsively. Watching this as she spoke, at first she thought he was contemplating something until she realized he was only fidgeting.

His face showed no emotion—not empathy or pain or sadness. When she had finished all that she could reasonably explain about the inexplicable events of the last twenty-four hours, he said nothing for what seemed like minutes. Just as the silence was about to become unbearable, he stood up and looked as if he might have decided to abandon her to her madness. Then he said simply, "Come with me."

Together they walked down a long corridor into the parish offices, which were empty except for one woman sorting a stack of papers into a filing cabinet. She looked up and smiled at Charlotte as she passed, but the smile faded too quickly from the woman's face, as if she simply didn't have the capacity to sustain it any longer.

When Charlotte passed through the door into the priest's office, her breath suddenly left her. There, placed neatly on the corner of the desk, was Meredith's urn—untouched, unopened, and in the same condition she remembered when she last held it in her arms in the sea off Gay Head.

"For the past twenty-four hours, I have been trying to find out who Meredith Harris was," the priest said, "and why this urn of her ashes was left at our door. Now I know the answer to the first question."

"But, I don't understand … how …?" Charlotte traced her hands over the smooth metal surface as a tear made a path down her cheek.

"I'm afraid I can't help you with that. But now you're here, and you tell me you want to bury your unbaptized child in the rite of the Church."

"I do—well, I did, until the fourth or fifth person in the bishop's office told me it was impossible. I came here today only because the man who saved me—the fisherman I told you about—I think he's the one who put that piece of paper in my pocket with the church's name and address on it."

Father Vecchio looked at the paper still in his hand before placing it on the desk and pushing it away, as if it carried some sort of contagion. There was clearly something else on his mind.

"Come, Charlotte. Why don't you sit down with me on the sofa for a while."

The invitation to come closer was one that Charlotte welcomed. Since her earliest memory, she had held priests of the Church in something more than merely high regard. She had acquired a feeling of awe and admiration for their power to forgive and transform. It was a feeling not unlike the adulation of superstar athletes capable of feats of physical skill beyond what mere mortals could do.

It was something learned from her childhood. Her parents rarely entertained friends, but whenever the parish priest came for dinner, it was like the Rapture for her mother. It didn't matter whether he was expected or not. Priests were a kind of royalty, and their favor was a thing much to be desired among the laity. Charlotte remembered her spinster aunt Maureen was always at the rectory—cooking, cleaning, playing pinochle. One night at dinner, her father's raised eyebrow and veiled remark clearly implied—even to Charlotte, who was eleven and just awakening to the wider possibilities between men and women—that the priests' fondness for Maureen was something other than spiritual. She would never forget her mother's instantaneous dismissal of the idea—not because she thought her father was wrong, but because it didn't matter whether he was right. "Whatever Maureen is doing for the priests," her mother said, "she is doing for God." That line prompted a snickering blasphemy from her fourteen-year-old brother Jeremy that got him grounded for a month.

Charlotte came around the side of the desk and sat on the sofa. Father Vecchio looked into her eyes—not a glance, but a prolonged and deeply serious stare. "Tell me what you're feeling," he said with the utmost confidence, as if he had long ago deduced that this was what female parishioners in need most desperately wanted to hear—the thing their husbands, fathers, sons, and brothers didn't or couldn't say to them.

"Well," Charlotte began, "I suppose I'm feeling a little betrayed—by my Church, I mean." The priest's brow furrowed in a show of shared pain and deep concern. "I feel like I've always done the things I was supposed to do or meant to do or asked to do for my faith, except this one thing I failed to do for my daughter. But the mistake was mine, Father—not hers. She shouldn't be punished for my mistake. She was innocent."

The priest glanced perfunctorily at the urn on the corner of his desk, as if it were bad manners to speak of Meredith and not acknowledge her presence.

"I just don't understand how a just God, a loving God, how . . . a God who lost his own son, could, could . . ." Her words were taken by quiet sobs. Father Vecchio pulled her toward him. With her head nestled on his shoulder, he spoke to her.

"We can't have the God of our choosing, Charlotte. We have to accept God as he is—just as we might wish to change things about our earthly fathers but can't. We have to take them as they are given to us."

The analogy was not helpful. There were many things about her own father that Charlotte would have changed if she could—mainly his inattentiveness toward her mother. But a lack of mercy and concern for his children were not among his shortcomings. Those were qualities he had in natural abundance.

"What father," Charlotte stammered, her wet face still pressed against the priest's shoulder, "what father abandons a little child to be alone in the darkness?" The question, once so succinctly stated, both startled and empowered her. She lifted her head so as to speak directly and be better understood. "Tell me, what father does that?"

Father Vecchio squirmed. He was more comfortable playing the inquisitor than the witness. Finally, his face softened just slightly, and he began to speak in a slower, different tone.

"It may surprise you to know I have the same doubts, Charlotte. About God. About faith. About fidelity. I don't have all the answers. Maybe, though, we can help each other to find the things we are looking for."

"It's no mystery what I'm looking for or where it is." Charlotte was more composed now that the conversation had taken a turn toward directness. She sat up straight and edged away from the priest, to address him properly. "I'm a good Catholic, Father—or at least I was until yesterday. It's the only faith I have—the only faith I've ever known. I don't know any other way to . . . to navigate through the world of life and death and heaven and hell, if you know what I mean."

"Of course."

"All I want is a proper burial and the prayers of the Church for my little girl's soul. I came here today only because someone I don't know wrote a name and address on a piece of paper, and it led me to you. I have no idea what happens next."

The priest failed to answer, as though his mind had suddenly wandered off somewhere, forgetting that it was clearly his role to say what should happen next. If

Charlotte could have known his thoughts, she would have learned that he was unfolding a number of plans for what was about to happen. Instead, what came to her in that moment was the faintly weird realization that he was not lost in thought but was actually staring at her chest.

Reflexively, she glanced down at her blouse and raised a hand to attend to whatever button had popped open. She looked up again to see the priest's face reddening, which struck her as pathetically adolescent and almost humorous. Statistically speaking, every third man she met on the street took more than a passing survey of her figure. Some men were more brazen about it than others. She had long ago accepted that priests were susceptible to the same weakness as the rest of humanity. She tried to get past it with a weary, exasperated smile.

"Maybe," he suddenly erupted, remembering himself, "maybe we should meet again, for a period of discernment. It could help us understand what God has in store for us—why he brought us together, and where he is leading us." With those words, he took her hands and held them tenderly in his.

Charlotte looked at the urn of her daughter's ashes, still sitting on the corner of the desk where she had found them—still no closer to heaven. Her choice was clear.

"Yes. I would like that very much."

She was quietly, cautiously elated. She knew something about the doctrine of discernment. As it was applied in the post-Vatican II sense, it meant a period of prayer and contemplation before deciding to do something that was questionably permissible under Church teaching. A period of discernment could justify an action in the eyes of God, because God had been invited to the table, so to speak, in the decision-making process. Although Father Vecchio had not said it in so many words, Charlotte understood him to mean that after some perfunctory equivocating and hand wringing, he might consider defying the bishop.

She was mistaken.

CHAPTER 7

Sitting in a chair by an open window of the Early Oyster Café, Edgartown's hottest new coffee shop and bakery, Turner was immersed in a story in the local paper about Flaherty's Wharf, an old building just put on the market. Owned by the Wallace family, over the course of two centuries it had served alternately and at times simultaneously as a cannery, a tavern, and a house of ill repute. It was now an empty derelict of a building. Great lamentations had arisen from the historical society about what was to be done with it and the importance of preserving its nineteenth-century whaling character. Turner was daydreaming about whales and harpoons and raging seas when a nearby car horn nearly blasted her out of her chair. It was Dory, and she was clearly excited about something.

"Come on, get in!" she shouted from the curb, seated behind the wheel of a gleaming convertible Jaguar. *Of course, a Jaguar,* Turner thought.

Turner emerged from the café onto the sidewalk, newspaper flapping in one hand and purse dangling from the other. She intended only to tell Dory that she was still waiting on Charlotte, then return inside.

"Where is she?" Dory asked.

"In the church."

"Doing what?"

Turner resisted the impulse to say *God only knows,* which was probably the truth. Dory didn't wait for an answer.

"Never mind. Charlotte is more than a match for Tommy Vecchio, it's a short walk home, and she has a key to the house," Dory said. "Let's go."

"Tommy *who*?"

"No time. C'mon—get in."

Dory had gotten a call from a friend that the "sign" had been seen on a farm road near Aquinnah, on the western end of the island. She was appointed to go there and wait for the fisherman's expected arrival before sundown. She would purchase a cooler of illicit shrimp as the representative of the group who eagerly awaited their regular allotment. Dory thought this would be the perfect chance to show Turner who the fisherman was and to answer her own questions about him.

"Why do you keep calling him 'the fisherman'? Doesn't this dude have a name?" Turner asked.

"He doesn't say much."

"What? He can't speak?"

"He *can* speak, Turner. He just doesn't say much. The strong and silent type, I guess."

Turner thought about this for a while. She struggled to keep the breeze from knotting her hair as Dory ignored the speed limit. "Kind of refreshing, I suppose," Turner finally said. "Most of the men I know can't speak but try to anyway."

"I'm not going for the conversation—just the shrimp," Dory explained. "And a few answers."

The blue paint mark was not easy to find, but it usually wasn't. When Dory finally spotted it on the third pass down the road leading to Aquinnah, she pulled the car over into some tall weeds on the shoulder and waited.

"You know how you know someone comes from money?" Turner asked.

"How's that?"

"When they pull a brand-new, eighty-thousand-dollar Jaguar into a weed bank like it was a used VW bus."

"Shut up," Dory answered. "Just keep an eye out for the guy."

"Is he going to sneak up on us, kemosabe?"

"No. One minute he's not there. Then one minute you look, and there he is."

"Like that guy?" Turner said, pointing to a figure standing near an opening in the woods across the road, on the other side of the drainage ditch, about twenty yards away.

"That's him!" Dory exclaimed, then popped the trunk and hopped out of the car. She gave Turner one handle of a cooler half-filled with ice, then took the other. They hobbled along with it as fast as they could, like two soldiers running ammunition to a battlefield.

When they arrived where the fisherman was standing, Turner took the time to get a good look at him. To her he appeared to be mid-thirties, taller than average— about six feet—with reddish-blond hair and deeply tanned skin. He wore the kind of clothes that any ordinary fisherman on the island might wear: a faded blue tee shirt, faded green khaki trousers stained with mud, and cracked and faded brown leather boots. In fact, the only things about him that weren't faded and worn were his blue eyes, which were vivid and piercing and staring straight at Turner. She was no blushing ingénue or shrinking violet, but she found it deeply unsettling to look directly at him when she and Dory came closer.

The transaction occurred exactly as Dory said it would, as if they were back at Smith and nervously trying to buy drugs from someone in a bathroom stall. The fisherman, wordless, opened a cooler full of the gleaming, enormous shrimp and deposited several bags into Dory's cooler. Dory handed him a handful of bills, which he accepted silently.

Dory saw her chance. "I don't suppose you know me, but I'm Dory Delano, and I live on the island. I'm a friend of Charlotte Harris's. She bought shrimp from you on Chappaquiddick two nights ago. I think she was unable to pay, and you were very kind to let her have it anyway, so I put some extra cash in there for you . . . "

She let a beat pass for him to make the expected nod of the head or to smile. He did neither.

"You know, for the shrimp you gave her that other night, too."

Dory paused again, waiting for some affirmation or acknowledgement. None came. She wondered for a moment if the money had not been enough, but that clearly wasn't it. The cash she'd handed him was ridiculously enough—intended more as a reward for saving Charlotte's life than payment of a simple fishmonger's bill. But the fisherman looked at her with what could be described only as a respectful and attentive silence. Dory found him reassuring and disquieting in inexplicable, equal measures.

"She said that you . . . that you saved her somehow. I guess I just wanted to say thanks."

That was not all she wanted to say by a long shot. She wanted to ask him about many things—chiefly what happened that night with Charlotte, followed by who in the world he was and where he'd come from and how on God's earth he was coming up with buckets of the best shrimp she'd ever tasted when no one else in New England could catch the first morsel. But she stopped there because what she had said so far made her feel like a pimply sixteen-year-old trying to ask the cute new boy to prom.

Turner, for her part, was watching Dory lose her confidence completely in a way she'd never seen before, and that was a subject far more fascinating to her at the moment than the strange man selling shrimp who may or may not have had anything to do with Charlotte's late-night swimming lesson. Then, taking Dory's cue, she grabbed one handle of the cooler as Dory lifted her end. The two of them trudged off—Dory sheepishly and Turner incredulously, the heavy cooler swaying between them.

"Okay—question," Turner began, when they had gotten a few feet away. "Actually, about three hundred questions, but first, how do you know what to pay him if he does not speak?"

"I don't. I just keep paying him more each time and hope that it's enough."

"That was a chunk of bills you put in his hand."

"Five thousand dollars."

"I'd say you're crazy, except that I've eaten the shrimp this man is selling, and if I had that kind of money, I'd pay it too."

"It's not the money. He never asks. He gave us the first cooler-full for nothing. I've felt so guilty about it since then that, you know—and then there's what he did for Charlotte."

"Yeah, what he did for Charlotte—whatever in the hell that was. Why didn't you ask him about it—or at least thank him?"

"I don't know, Turner." Dory sounded exasperated, and she was—more with herself than Turner's questions. "I don't know if it's supposed to be this big secret of his or what, but he wasn't saying anything, so, you know, I just didn't. I don't know why."

Unseen, behind them, the fisherman did not leave the edge of the woods. He stood there watching them until they were halfway back to the car, when he finally spoke in a loud voice.

"Eudora!"

Dory dropped her end of the cooler and stood upright as though she had just taken an arrow in the back.

"Did he say something?" asked Turner.

"He said my name," Dory repeated.

"I heard that. What in the world? I thought this man never spoke."

"You wait here," Dory said. "I'll go."

"No—are you crazy? He's probably going to *rob* you."

"You wait here," Dory insisted, and Turner put her end of the cooler down in the road.

Dory walked, now more slowly, to the place where the fisherman was standing. Turner noticed he did not come to Dory but expected her to come up a muddy ditch bank to him. *What the hell,* she thought— summoning Dory Delano like a servant girl. And how did he know her full name?

In the waning light, Turner saw Dory reach the place where they had just bought the shrimp and stand there like an acolyte. The fisherman said something to her that she could not hear, and Dory did not answer. In a slow deliberate movement that Dory might easily have evaded, he came closer to her and placed a hand on each of her shoulders.

"Dory, you okay?" Turner shouted, now getting more nervous, but neither Dory nor the fisherman acted as if they'd heard her.

Then Turner saw the straps of Dory's sundress fall down along her arms as Dory stood there, motionless. Even when the dress slid to her feet, she made no effort to cover her nude form, as she faced the man before her.

"Mother *fucker!*" Turner shouted, as she began running toward her friend and instantly slipped in a patch of wet mud. She picked herself up and started running again, but before she spanned the distance between them, the fisherman placed his hands on Dory's bare breasts and leaned over as if to kiss her cheek. With this, Dory's body dropped lifelessly to the ground.

"*You son of a bitch! Get away from her!*" Turner screamed as she reached the top of the embankment. When she was in range, without breaking her stride, she let go a wide, roundhouse punch—the kind her father had once taught her how to throw against bales of hay—and connected with the fisherman's cheek. The ring on her finger opened a wide, red line beneath his eye.

The force of the punch knocked Turner off-balance, and she fell. Gathering her feet beneath her and bracing for attack, she looked up and saw the fisherman still standing there, the right side of his face bloodied.

"She will live," he said, then walked into the woods. Through the trees in the direction he had gone, on a narrow spur road, Turner could make out the pale blue color of a Jeep.

Transfixed by the strange occurrence, Turner for a moment forgot the body of the woman lying beside her. But when her senses returned, she looked at Dory and saw that she was unconscious.

"Oh, my God! Oh, my God! Dory!" she screamed, pressing her hands frantically along her friend's head, neck, and shoulders, as if she were molding a lifeless lump of clay. "Please! Please wake up, honey! Oh, God, Dory! Oh God! Oh God!"

CHAPTER 8

The pulse-oximeter hummed and chirped in a cheerful, reassuring rhythm above the hospital bed. It was the only thing in the room, animate or inanimate, that seemed to be working correctly. The window was stuck open two inches at the top, inviting in a caravan of flies. The fluorescent light above the bed flickered on and off.

Turner hadn't been right since the ambulance went wailing off without her, Dory unconscious in the back. They left Turner sitting there, numbly, behind the wheel of an unfamiliar Jaguar, stuck in the mud of a weed bank, to contemplate for the first time the mysteries of a standard transmission: the punitive, vindictive clutch; the needlessly powerful Jaguar engine. It had been a stupid place to park. Mud and grass flew through the air onto everything, including her, as she tried to get out of there. It had been a nerve-wracking, herky-jerky five-mile ride to the hospital.

Covered in dark chocolate drops of stinking marsh mud, Turner had presented herself at the admission desk as the rescuer of the woman who had been admitted to Room 219 several minutes earlier. After a period of suspicion that was entirely warranted, the clerk allowed her to go in.

Dory's heart had enough oxygen—ninety-four percent, ninety-two, ninety-one, ninety-six, according to the numbers flying across the monitor—even if there was no outward sign that she remained present in this world. Yet even comatose, she remained the maddeningly beautiful woman Turner alternately envied and pitied, loved and hated, adored and ignored, and always—however secretly—thoroughly admired.

"Are you the one who can tell me what happened here?" said a petite woman in a white coat who was standing in the doorway. The name "Elizabeth Madison, M.D." was embroidered in fancy blue script above the pocket.

"Will she be all right?" Turner replied.

Dr. Madison hesitated. She wanted to know more about what took place out on the road, but she ventured her best guess about Dory for the moment. "I think so. She doesn't appear to have any internal injuries, but her heart rate and other vitals indicate she may have gone into shock. I just don't know why."

"I'll tell you why," Turner began winding up to let go of her rage of the last two hours. "Because she was assaulted and groped by some lunatic out on a dirt road in Aquinnah, that's why, which is exactly what I told the EMS crew! So, you tell me: where the *hell* are the police?"

"I want to know exactly—" the doctor began, but Turner no longer needed any prompting.

"It all happened very fast. We were there to buy shrimp."

"Shrimp? Is this that fisherman guy I've heard about? Did she eat some raw shrimp?"

Turner marveled at how information traveled so quickly and so widely on what was no longer a sleepy, remote island.

"No, she didn't eat anything. But that's the dude she kept calling 'the fisherman,' whoever the hell he is. He pulled down her dress. He assaulted her. Dory just stood there like a statue. She must have been petrified. I started running for him right then. The creep put his hands on her breasts. It looked like he tried to kiss her neck or something, too, but that's when she fell. I got there a second later and hit him square in the jaw."

Turner raised her right hand to display her skinned knuckles as proof.

"Then he just walked off. I don't—"

At that moment, Turner was interrupted by a thin voice that came from behind her, but it was so soft it sounded as if it might have come from someplace else. "It's cancer," the voice said.

Turner and the doctor simultaneously glanced at the speaker above the headboard, as if they might have missed something broadcast over the intercom. Then Dory opened her eyes. Swallowing thickly and moistening her lips, she repeated herself.

"He said 'cancer.'"

"Dory, my God—Dory, where have you been?" Turner squealed. She bent down to kiss her friend's cheek and to smooth her hair like a child, forgetting the words just spoken. But Dory was still trying to make herself clear.

"He didn't . . . he didn't try to kiss me. He spoke to me. He held my, my breasts . . . like . . . like he was examining me, or something. When he touched me, he leaned in and whispered in my ear."

"What did he say?" Turner asked.

"He said, 'cancer.' That's all I remember. I must have blacked out. . . . I am so, so tired."

Dr. Madison's mouth remained slightly agape, inviting a pass from the conga line of flies circling the ceiling. Her eyes were fixed on Dory, while Turner looked back and forth quizzically between the two of them. Dory seemed to be drifting in and out of sleep.

Dr. Madison slowly stepped to the bedside and, without saying so much as a kind word, spent the next five minutes assessing the patient whom she assumed was now delirious. Eyes, heart rate and rhythm, blood pressure, respiration, and temperature were all normal. She called to the nurses' station over the intercom for stat labs, then finally spoke to Turner.

"Are you family?"

Turner, a master of the opportune lie, didn't hesitate. "Yes." She assumed that to the person who answered affirmatively, information would be given that Dory would later want to know.

"Would you please step outside with me for a moment?"

Outside Dory's hospital room, Dr. Madison, spoiling for a fight, squared off and faced Turner.

"I just saw your cousin earlier today in my office for a complaint of a lump in her breast. I examined her and did a scan. Everything was—is—completely normal. Is this some kind of a joke?"

Turner felt a long, slow chill roll up her spine and raise the hair on the back of her neck. Stranger still, her thoughts at that moment randomly turned to the taste— the delicious, irresistible taste—of the shrimp Dory had prepared for her the night before.

"Get an over-read," Turner said abruptly, still staring out into space. She had enough friends over the years with breast cancer to know what came next, when a doctor was unsure of a diagnosis. A second doctor reading a breast film sometimes noticed things that the first doctor missed.

Dr. Madison was now not only suspicious, but indignant.

"I don't take orders, Ms.—"

"Graham. Turner Graham." Turner's eyes were blazing. "And you'll take this order from me, goddammit, or I will chase you all the way to the medical board like a rabid dog."

Dr. Madison turned on her heel and abruptly walked

away, fearless of Turner's threat and, Turner suspected, justifiably so. It wasn't the first standoff with authority that didn't go exactly the way Turner had hoped. There was nothing worse than being dismissed. She knew the feeling from frequent past experience. She hated it.

All that was left for the moment was to sit at the bedside and stare while nurses drew one vial of blood after another and Dory gurgled sleepily through it all.

It was dinnertime—or would have been, if there were any dinner to be had—when the remote sound of some sort of kerfuffle up at the nurses' station came airily down the hall. Turner didn't pay any attention to it at first. It wasn't anything much. The footsteps of unseen nurses hurried a little faster; their voices were more deliberate, their whispering a bit more urgent. Turner was in no mood to care about the reason, but if she had cared, she would have guessed that someone who was supposed to be very much alive was now very dead or soon to be so. *Heads will roll,* she thought. But it wasn't that at all. It was something more dreadful to the heads in question.

Constance Delano's voice was unforgettable. It was like Katherine Hepburn's, with the same mixture of gravel and refinement.

"What I want to know, Dr. Ferguson," said the voice, *"is why in God's name* no one thought to call me sooner than six hours after my daughter collapsed and was rushed to the hospital—a hospital," she paused to emphasize, *"that bears my husband's name!"*

Turner got up and went to the doorway of the room. Mrs. Delano was walking briskly toward her, slinging recriminations as she came at a tall man in a white coat—the unfortunate Dr. Ferguson, Turner presumed.

He side-skipped to stay beside Mrs. Delano and maintain eye contact. At his elbow was Dr. Madison. Apologizing profusely, he glared at his colleague whenever Mrs. Delano looked away, with a glance that said, *heads will roll.*

The Delano Wing. The moniker at the entrance to the emergency room had completely escaped Turner's notice. *We are in* the *goddamn Delano Wing,* she thought, and the doctor had still dismissed her request for an over-read of Dory's mammogram as if Dory Delano were some sort of Medicaid hustler.

"Oh, Mrs. Delano," Dr. Madison interrupted, hoping finally to change the subject. "You'll be pleased to know your daughter's cousin Turner has been here the whole time. She was with Dory when it happened."

Turner felt her heart flutter. Posing as *Cousin* Turner had seemed like a good idea at the time. Now it seemed like something else. But if Turner was a smooth operator, Constance Delano was an oil slick five miles wide. She had the unflappable grace common to her class, which was not so long accustomed to money as to have forgotten the treachery it took to get it.

Mrs. Delano looked at Turner squarely for two beats, then at her daughter lying in the bed, then with greater interest at Turner, who obviously had the information that everyone desperately wanted. "Hello, Cousin Turner," she said, in a tone of utter veracity. "How good of you to be here in little Dory's hour of need. How is our girl?"

Turner began to fumble an answer, but Mrs. Delano interrupted.

"Dr. Madison, I'd like a moment alone with my family."

"Certainly," Dr. Madison said, and left.

When she was alone with Turner and with Dory, who was still sleeping like a baby, Mrs. Delano spoke in a decidedly different tone.

"All right, young lady. I don't know who you are, but unless you want me to have you thrown out of here on your *ass,* you'd better tell me what happened to my daughter." Turner did exactly that, leaving out no detail, while Doctors Madison and Ferguson hovered uneasily out of earshot beyond the door. Dory remained in blissful slumber, her chest rising and falling easily with each deep breath.

When Turner was finished with her tale, Mrs. Delano was subdued. After an inordinate period of silence, during which she stared quizzically at her daughter, she walked to the door and summoned both doctors into the room.

"This is what's going to happen, Ben," she began. "You're going to get Marty Sullivan in here tonight to read Dory's mammogram."

Turner struggled but could not resist a gloating look at Dr. Madison, who was keenly focused on the floor in front of her shoes.

"I'm afraid he's on vacation," Dr. Ferguson replied, sheepishly.

"Then get him off vacation. I don't care if you have to send the hospital's helicopter to do it. I don't care if you have to hoist him out of his goddamn yacht in his underpants—just get him here tonight. When I hear from Marty, I'll decide what happens next. Have I made myself clear?"

Of course she had. There was never anything the least bit unclear about Constance Delano. Hers was a world of absolutes, and she ruled it absolutely.

It took two hours, but Dr. Marty Sullivan arrived at the hospital as he was asked, which is what any old friend of the Delano family would do. It was almost expected, then, that he would differ with Dr. Madison's diagnosis. The lump was cancer, of course. Anything less would have been an affront to Constance Delano's authority.

Turner felt both vindicated and devastated. Mrs. Delano was stoic in the face of a challenge to be overcome, like all others she had faced. Dory awakened—cheerful, hungry, and seemingly the picture of health, just in time to hear the news explained by Dr. Sullivan.

After getting over the shock of seeing her mother and Turner in the same room, Dory handled the shock of her diagnosis quite well. She had suspected something was not right for months. That's why she had gone that very morning to see Dr. Madison about the lump in her left breast. Dr. Madison felt it too, but nothing suspicious appeared on the mammogram. An ultrasound likewise showed no sign of malignancy. She told Dory it was just a fibrous irregularity in her breast tissue—likely a benign cyst—and that she should cut out caffeine.

Dr. Sullivan had seen something else. It was a poorly defined mass, but experience told him it was cancer. A needle biopsy examined by the pathologist—another friend of the family who likewise had raced to the hospital that night at Constance Delano's call—confirmed the diagnosis within an hour: invasive lobular carcinoma.

Playing both the diplomat and the gracious victor, Dr. Sullivan began by reassuring Mrs. Delano that ten to fifteen percent of all breast cancers are missed on mammograms.

"I'm not relieved to hear that, Marty," Mrs. Delano snapped. "I'd like to think my money is buying better care than the bottom ten to fifteen percent."

Dr. Sullivan paused, as if to add something to his

defense of Dr. Madison, then thought better of it and held his tongue. She should have gone further, and everyone knew it. Madison left the room without a word. Dr. Ferguson remained behind, relieved that the A-team was finally in the game, and trying without success to cheer Mrs. Delano.

"The oncology group will need to consult, but what you are almost certainly looking at, Dory, is a radical left mastectomy. It's what I would recommend."

"That's not going to happen," Dory suddenly piped up, breaking her silence of the past half hour.

"Sweetheart," her mother intervened, with an unexpected tenderness, "I understand how you must feel, but—"

"It's not going to happen," Dory insisted, her face stiffening with resolve. "He didn't let Charlotte die. I don't believe he'll let me die, either."

Turner drew a deep breath. The prescience of the fisherman in detecting Dory's disease had escaped her until that moment. If what Dory said was true, he *knew the truth*, this strange, infuriating man. The questions circling Turner's thoughts all evening, chiefly wondering what kind of man has the audacity to pull down a woman's dress in public, grope her bare breasts, and whisper in her ear as she stands there, stupefied, were now subdued by other questions. What kind of man can feel disease in his hands? What was his purpose—to heal her? To frighten her? To woo her? To control her?

Mrs. Delano looked around the room from one face to the other, as though she had lost her place in whatever script they were all reading. "Who on Earth is this Charlotte?" she finally asked.

"That would be me," came a small voice from the hallway. Charlotte had arrived outside the door just in time to hear most of the story. "And all I can say, Dory, is that if you're banking on some poacher selling seafood by the seashore to cure your cancer, you're crazier than I am."

Mrs. Delano's expression registered an enthusiastic *amen* to the point made. She didn't know who this woman was, but she was the only one who seemed to be making any sense.

CHAPTER 9

Three women, now bound by the shared grief, elation, and terror of the past twenty-four hours, collapsed in random heaps among the sofas and chairs of the living room, just as the sun was coming up. It was a scene reminiscent of so many late nights during their years together in college, recreated now in a time and place so far removed from that age of innocence as to be unrecognizable.

The arguments and counterarguments, tears and shouting at the hospital, with Mrs. Delano, Dr. Ferguson, and Dr. Sullivan joining the fray, had lasted well into the night. Dory resisted them all—especially her mother, who regarded the fisherman as a common masher and her daughter's newfound belief in him as something like the faith of Appalachian snake handlers. Dr. Sullivan kept repeating the words "invasive lobular carcinoma" as if they were a magical incantation certain to break Dory's resolve. But they all failed to move her from her faith—or her fear, unclear as it was just what was driving her.

Charlotte did not believe—not yet, anyway. She wondered about many things, namely why the fisherman had sent her to that beach, why he bothered to rescue her after the fact but not to stop her in advance, why he took Meredith's urn to St. Joseph's and made sure she would go there, and—the one question she didn't dwell on because somehow it made her uneasy—how he found his way safely to shore without a boat and against the current so far out at sea, that night. But these remained only questions for Charlotte, not articles of faith. And the fisherman remained for her a homeless vagrant—strangely kind, perhaps even mystical, but nothing more.

The smell of sausages and coffee, rising in the heat of midmorning, awakened them one by one. Constance Delano's chief cook and generalissimo, a fastidious and fearsomely large German woman named Rutla, was in the kitchen. She had let herself in with a key given to her by Mrs. Delano along with orders to report there each morning until further notice.

"A spy sent by my mother," Dory groaned.

"An angel making us breakfast," Turner replied.

"God bless her," Charlotte added.

After wiping the sleep from her eyes and lifting herself upright onto a chair, Turner quickly resumed the previous night's hostilities.

"I understand your emotions, Dory, and I respect them. I just question your judgment in making decisions based on something so fleeting. This is no-fooling, big-girl cancer. It's not something you treat with kale smoothies and meditation."

"You didn't see or feel what I saw and felt, Turner," Dory answered.

"I was right there, remember?" Turner countered, angrily. "I saw what you saw. He didn't feel me up, thank God, but we had our moment, too. I connected with his jaw and drew blood. You and I witnessed the same thing, Dory."

As committed as Turner was to her argument, she was equally disturbed by it. *She did* witness the same thing, and yet Dory had come away from that experience completely changed, while Turner had not. She felt somehow cheated by that. But it was Dory who concerned her. Turner was truly frightened at what seemed likely to happen. She decided to play to her strength, and negotiate.

"I have a solution," she began.

"I'm not a problem you need to solve, Turner," Dory protested.

"Hear me out. If Long John Silver is the miracle worker you say he is, he ought to have nothing to hide. He should be willing to tell you so himself, not just grab you and whisper sweet nothings in your ear. So, we find him and we ask him. If he won't own up to what you believe he did for you, I don't see the point in carrying a torch for him to the grave. One week—he shows, he talks, and I'm a believer. If not, you start chemo and the workup for surgery."

Dory said nothing. *The workup for surgery.* Those words hung in her thoughts like a slow-moving, dark cloud. It didn't seem possible that it had come to this.

Turner refused to sit idly through Dory's reverie. She finally blurted out the obvious. "Damn you, Dory, it's your life!" The fear came through clearly in her voice.

Dory looked up at her friend, as if from a dream, and saw that Turner was weeping. Big tears tumbled down her cheeks. A second later, Charlotte began crying, too. They were more afraid of losing her than Dory was of losing them. It moved something in Dory, deep down, and she felt at last her resolve soften.

"All right, I agree."

The answer came like a dam breaking. The three of them huddled together on the floor, arms around each other, and, with laughter and tears and hugs, felt some of the tension of the last two days slip away. Dory had a new mission to save her own life; in Father Vecchio, Charlotte had found a tentative reason to hope; and

Turner had newfound power as the erstwhile Delano "cousin" who lorded over them both.

Dory wasn't done yet. "But you're wrong about him—both of you—and you should know that better than anyone, Charlotte."

Charlotte was wiping her runny nose and tears from her cheeks. She was smiling again—something neither she nor anyone else had expected to see in her so soon.

"You're looking chipper this morning, Charlie," Dory noticed. "Tell me, what did you find at St. Joseph's?"

"Meredith's urn."

"My God! It was there?" Dory was taken aback.

"Yes, Father Vecchio had it. The fisherman left it on the doorstep. I don't think Father knows it was him, but I knew it was him. He must have left it there without a word."

"His trademark," Turner added, mockingly.

"Yes, his trademark, Turner, to perform random acts of kindness and help the lost to become found," Dory protested. Dory was mildly discomfited, though, over Charlotte's sudden familiarity with "Father." "So, what did you and Tommy talk about?" she asked.

"I asked him to let me bury Meredith's urn in the church cemetery, here on the island."

"And . . ." Dory waited. "What did he say?"

"He wants to meet with me to talk about it."

"Talk about what—how deep to dig?" Turner chimed in.

Charlotte didn't respond. A concerned look came over Dory's face. "Yes, talk about what, Charlie?"

"It's a Catholic thing, I guess. They call it discernment. But I think it means he's considering going against the bishop and giving her the rites of Christian burial in the Church if he can discern that to be God's will."

"And just what difference will that make?" Turner asked. Turner was not raised in the Church, and it was clear she didn't get what was still troubling Charlotte about the whole business of being inside or outside the fold.

"It matters to Charlotte, Turner, so don't make fun," Dory scolded, then asked, "Do you really think he might do this for you? Defy the bishop and all?"

"He didn't say it in so many words, but I'm sure that's what he means."

"Means?" Dory asked.

"What he means by wanting to get together to talk about the Church's role," Charlotte explained.

"God, save me from holy rollers," Turner blurted out. "One of you follows a pope, and the other follows a poacher. It's all just too rich! Me, I'm following the money."

The look of concern had not left Dory's face.

"What was it like for you, meeting Tommy—I mean, Father Vecchio," Dory asked, cautiously.

Charlotte paused, staring blankly at her for a moment before answering. "Fine, I suppose. I was surprised to find Meredith's urn, but he wasn't surprised to see me. He'd been expecting someone to come for it. He's younger than all the priests at my parish on the mainland, that's for sure, and the first one I've met who seemed to have any sympathy for . . . my situation."

"So, the urn," Turner asked, "did you get it back?"

"No, I left it there. I figure it's safer in the church's keeping than mine, and if I'm lucky, I'll find a home for my baby girl beneath the elm trees in the parish cemetery."

"Seriously?" asked Dory.

"I'm hopeful, that's all. He at least wants to talk about it, and that's different from all the others."

"What's there to talk about? You mean he's asked

you to come back and discuss whether he's going to grant your request?"

Dory's tone made it clear something wasn't sitting well with her about Father Tommy. A look from Turner said the same thing.

"What's so unusual about that?" Charlotte replied. "Priests counsel parishioners all the time."

Dory drew her hand to her mouth, as if she were afraid of what might spill out of it if she didn't. "Just be smart about it, Charlotte. I know a thing or two about Tommy Vecchio. He may be a priest, but he's still a man."

"Noted," Charlotte answered. She was well aware of the danger Dory alluded to. She had felt it in the way the priest had looked at her. It wasn't unusual for men to look, but it was unusual the way *he* looked. It wasn't enough to keep Charlotte away—she felt firmly in control. But she also realized that Father Vecchio held the power in their relationship. Power she believed had been given to him by God.

Rutla called them all in to a late breakfast, which Dory ate ravenously. Charlotte went upstairs to change, and Dory kept on eating, which was unlike her, while Turner kept her company. When the last morsel was gone and after the third cup of coffee, they heard an impatient knock at the back door.

"Is the patient taking visitors?" a cheerful voice asked. It was Tripp.

Dory rolled her eyes with a look that said, "Not now."

Turner answered for her, flirtatiously. "Only handsome, devious, and charming ones."

"Can I get credit for one out of three?" Tripp answered.

"You're in, buster," Dory laughed. "Come give me a kiss."

Turner had last seen Tripp years ago, when he was Dory's date one New Year's Eve in New York. As he walked through the door, he seemed to Turner to be a couple decades out of date but still well-heeled, in a moth-eaten blue blazer and wrinkled rep tie. Combed hair—a rarity for him—meant he had some business to attend to that day.

Dory tiredly pushed herself up from the table to hug Tripp's neck while Rutla began frying more sausage, wanted or not. Turner accepted a perfunctory kiss from him, and he joined the girls at the table.

Despite his bantering, the expression on Tripp's face brought all of them down to earth. Mrs. Delano had already told him about the cancer. The story of Dory's assault by the fisherman, which had led to her diagnosis but now was also standing in the way of a cure, alternately annoyed and intrigued him. He had come that morning to change her mind about treatment, but the heaviness in his face lifted when he learned of Dory's bargain with Turner.

"One week," she told him, "and when you meet him, I bet he'll make you a believer," Dory said.

"I never knew you to be especially religious," Tripp replied, interrupted by a spasm of laughter from Turner at the enormity of the understatement.

"It's not religion. I felt something—something physical, visceral—when he touched me, when he spoke to me. It's not faith. It's experience."

"Yes, Dory dear." Turner was showing off for her new audience. "They used to call it the Jimi Hendrix Experience. What are you smoking?"

Tripp couldn't resist an eruption of laughter, which Turner eagerly echoed, until both of them looked back at Dory and saw the tears beginning. The facade of bravery was cracking, the surreal normalcy of the morning was ending, and the pent-up anger and fear of the past few hours came rushing in. A moment later, Dory was sobbing on the living room couch, with Turner and Tripp kneeling beside her and Rutla hovering around all of them, swinging a platter of medicinal sausages and biscuits like a thurible above their heads.

Dory said nothing for a long time—just tiny cries through the tears. Then came at last the words, long and slow, "I don't want to die," from a voice buried in the sofa cushions. "I'm so afraid, I'm so afraid . . ."

"Me too, Dory." Everyone but Dory turned toward the stairs. It was Charlotte, standing in a robe and bare feet. She had come down to see what all the commotion was about.

Charlotte recognized Tripp from the rescue aboard the *Victory,* though it took him a moment longer to recognize her.

"Hello," she said.

"You're looking much better," he answered, which was certainly true. "How are you feeling?"

Charlotte didn't answer. Her condition was not the concern at that moment. Instead, she went over to sit beside Dory. She leaned in and spoke softly to her as she stroked her hair.

"I know the feeling of wanting to run from something you can't change, Dory. I know exactly how it feels. But you can change this. This isn't the end. You're going to beat this—and you can, Dr. Sullivan said so. You just need to listen to him. I'm the last one to tell you not to have faith, but this fisherman— whoever he is—hasn't asked you to believe in anything, much less himself."

"Exactly," Tripp chimed in. "And I can tell you that if Smoke has his way, the guy will be off the island before the day's out."

"Why is that?" Dory asked.

"Because he's a poacher, he's selling without a license or health department inspections, and he's cutting local fishermen out of a lot of business. Everyone's income is off because all the customers are looking for a guy selling fresh jumbo shrimp by the roadside. Everyone from the sheriff to the town selectmen to the business chamber is trying to shut this dude down."

"Why is it any concern of Smoke's?" asked Dory.

"He gives all the local ships their operating credit. Three of them in Oak Bluffs folded this week because they couldn't cover their loans."

"That sounds like the Smoke we all know and love," Dory said with disgust.

"Speak of the devil," came a voice from the foyer. They all turned to see Smoke standing there. "I hope I'm not interrupting anything. Dory! So nice to see you up and about after the scare you gave us all yesterday."

"Smoke," Dory said, tiredly. "What are you doing here?" It was an uncharacteristically rude greeting for a visitor of the sick, but she doubted he had her health in mind, and in any event, she felt no need to be polite to him, of all people.

"I don't mean to intrude. I was just driving down the street and saw Tripp's car and thought I'd stop in to catch him. Tripp, may I speak to you privately for a moment?"

Tripp looked at Dory, who looked not at all surprised. Smoke was a man of business—first, foremost, and always—and rare was the meeting or conversation with him that did not involve some business purpose. The two men walked into the next room, where Smoke faced Tripp and began to speak earnestly.

"This thing with the fisherman and his roadside sales

is getting out of hand," Smoke began.

"How's that possible? He's harmless. This is just one guy and one boat, right?"

"He's not harmless," Smoke retorted. "Just ask the three boats I foreclosed on last week for nonpayment. These guys have seen their business in peak fishing season dwindle to nothing. The lobster have moved off. So have the cod. Everybody wants shrimp—whether they can get it or not. Just looking for this idiot's hash marks has become the island's hottest summer sport."

"So, you know all the town selectmen. Just send out the sheriff and shut him down."

"I would have long ago, if I could. No one knows anything about him. No one knows where he keeps his boat. He apparently fishes only at night, and he doesn't have a base of operations. Just the blue hash marks on the trees. But people love the mystery, and they'd rather look for him than buy from someone else."

Tripp shrugged. "I'll be damned. Robin Hood, right here in Martha's Vineyard."

"Robin Hood, my ass. The guy's raking in money hand over fist—my money. Speaking of which, Tripp, you and I need to sit down and talk about your trust."

The trust account that Tripp had come into when he turned twenty-five was now, eight years later, in critical condition. The feeble inflow of gains no longer matched the monthly hemorrhage of losses and distributions. For the past two years, his standard of living had been increasingly supplemented by credit extended from Smoke's brokerage firm against capital—namely the *Victory*, and more recently the old warehouse his family owned on the waterfront. Only by Smoke's friendship and forbearance had Tripp avoided bankruptcy, but the piper could at any time demand to be paid.

"I know, Smoke. I know." Tripp's hands fidgeted in his coat pockets, which contained nothing. "I've been meaning to talk with you about that, too. Maybe we could get lunch sometime next week."

Smoke was unmoved. Lunch would come, no doubt, at his expense. He studied Tripp's face for a moment, then took a breath, as if he'd decided to say something he wasn't sure should be mentioned.

"Have you thought about what I said—what marriage to Dory could mean for your finances?"

Tripp had thought about it, quite a lot. In fact, he'd thought about it to the point where his guilt made it difficult for him to look Dory in the eye.

Tripp was silent, which prompted Smoke to soften the question.

"I know this is an awful time for her—"

"It is, Smoke. You shouldn't—"

"And I realize her health is the most important consideration, but she needs to get over this ridiculous obsession with this fisherman, and—"

"How do you know about that?" Tripp asked. It was not the first time Smoke had come into knowledge of something so recent or hidden as to cause Tripp to marvel at his omniscience.

Smoke smiled grimly. "I know a great many things about a great many people, Tripp, but if you must know, I had coffee with Elizabeth Madison this morning. She's looking for financing to open her own practice on the island. Seems she's been let go from the group at the hospital. Pity. She's going to do very well after I get her set up, and they'll wish they had her back."

Tripp nodded as if he understood what was being said, which he didn't. Smoke's capacity to control and influence people and events was at once both marvelous and incomprehensible.

"You never struck me as the kind to marry for love, Tripp. Now's not the time to become a romantic. It could prove very expensive for you. I'll call you for lunch tomorrow."

With those words, Smoke turned toward the door and called out his goodbyes to Dory. Smiling strangely, he looked back at Tripp.

"Tell me, will you, if you hear any news of this fisherman. I'm eager to meet him myself."

After Tripp left, Dory began negotiations to furlough Rutla from her infirmary assignment. Turner went outside to shower, but first checked her blog on the laptop in her room. A surprised grin came over her face when she saw the post about Charlotte's rescue had risen to over eighty thousand hits, with most people finding it by searching the terms "fisherman" and "vineyard" and "miracle." What she could not see were the thirty thousand attempted comments and messages directed to her from readers of the blog, on which the comment feature remained disabled.

"Bennett & Donald author, indeed," she muttered to herself. But the pace of visits to her site had slowed in the last several hours. It was time to add fuel to the fire. So she began typing the headline that would form the next entry: "Mystery Vineyard Fisherman Diagnoses Cancer Using Only His Bare Hands," with the subheading: "Missed by Doctors." Dory and Charlotte knew nothing of Turner's online musings, nor of the strong winds that were coming.

CHAPTER 10

Despite the tumultuous beginning of the season and the clouds in Dory's future, June in Edgartown was as bright as ever, and the three friends took advantage of every minute of it. There were walks down Main Street on sunny afternoons carrying giant, round mounds of mint-chocolate-chip ice cream, teetering three-high and dribbling down onto sticky fingers before it was licked gone. There were steamed littleneck clams with butter sauce and fresh horseradish, served with gin and tonics on the porch of The Crew House, overlooking the harbor. And there was the good-looking, Italian waiter who worked there. It became Turner's mission to see how many times she could get him to use the word "Tanqueray" in a sentence because she liked the way he said it. There were lazy hours lying on the beach by the lighthouse and meandering hunts for the perfect cockleshell, and double-dog dares to go skinny-dipping after dark that always descended into fully clothed refusals, recriminations, and false accusations of prudery—the truth, however, being that none of them was eager to expose great white bellies bursting with clams and Tanqueray and mint-chocolate-chip ice cream.

Turner had had great hopes for their summer together, but those hopes had been punctured and partly deflated by the nearness of death. Yet, in the days after Charlotte's attempted suicide and Dory's diagnosis, none of that seemed to matter. It was hidden for a little while behind blue skies and soft, warm breezes.

The early evenings were spent in the kitchen performing mad experiments in haute cuisine—possible now that Rutla had been relieved of duty. When the smoke and smell finally banished them outdoors, they would stroll into town to get something to eat. Dory inhaled rare steaks and stout ales with the fervor of a Gloucester sailor. Turner sipped gin and nibbled salads. Charlotte seemed to subsist entirely on cakes and cosmopolitans, but she consumed them both in impressive quantities and seemed to be impervious to their effects. She remained a waif. In her ever-present ponytail, baggy shorts, and sweatshirts—the preferred uniform of depressives and camp counselors—she might have been mistaken for a teenager.

Everywhere in town there was unceasing talk of bootleg shrimp—who had it and where they got it and where the blue Jeep had last been sighted—but it was nigh impossible to get in anywhere before it was all gone or the health department had cited the bar or restaurant for serving it. Wherever they went for the evening, the three of them would sit and watch—trying to gauge the length of marriages; the numerical ranking of wives; the probability and proximity of divorces; and the mores, net worth, and sexual proclivities of each passerby among the local populace that had swollen to great proportions that year as every year, with the arrival of summer.

They walked all over the island and up and down its hedgerows, partly just to relax, partly also out of Dory's wish to remain unavailable for her mother's harangue about her cancer treatment, which had already been put off past the one week Dory originally bargained for. Neither Turner nor Charlotte said anything, at first. They knew Dory was struggling.

The three of them were inseparable, except during

those hours when Charlotte made her pilgrimage to the rectory for her counseling sessions with Father Vecchio. These grew more frequent and intensive with time and, by the end of the third week, had become a nightly occurrence. Although there was no news of a decision for a funeral mass and burial for Meredith, Charlotte went faithfully each day after the church offices closed to complete the process of discernment that promised to lead Father Vecchio toward the Mind of God on the matter. This gave her a hope to hang onto and a purpose for her life, however tenuous, that helped her move on through the day-to-day business of living. She laughed now and then. The deadening pall that had blocked out everything else in her world for so long began to subside. Her sadness for the loss of her child was unaltered in depth or degree, but it was buffered now by the hope that some resolution of her crisis of faith and her despair for her child's soul was near.

Father Vecchio and Charlotte had become close. She began to see him less as a priest and more as simply a man. He had confessed an already obvious romantic interest in her that she did not feel for him. But out of the odd mixture of pity and high regard for the burden of his vow of celibacy, she had permitted deep kisses and lingering hugs. Each night after their closing prayer, he would more reluctantly release his embrace, then trace his hands from her back around to the front of her blouse, where he would clasp her hands in his and press them into her cleavage as he prayed softly in her ear. One night he suddenly, gently cupped her breasts with his hands and began to pray for the "soul of the child who nursed at this bosom." It was so transparently lecherous yet so pathetic that Charlotte was too startled and embarrassed to refuse him. As he continued to grope her blouse after the prayer ended, she fixed her gaze over his shoulder toward Meredith's urn, which had remained on the corner of his desk, in a place of limbo all its own.

In the evenings, after her counseling sessions, Charlotte would come home, undress, wrap herself in a towel, and descend to the outdoor shower. She went more frequently and stayed longer as the days wore on. Looking up, eyes closed, she would let the warm water wash over her onto the slotted wooden floor. On one side, the one that was open to the hedges, the thin, red glow of light came as always each evening, flickering on and off from the direction of the harbor, a beacon warning of some unseen shoal.

It was Friday, the end of the third full week of their summer together. In that time they had never spoken of the cancer, or the chemotherapy that should have begun by now, or the inevitable mastectomy to make sure the disease didn't return. Dory's promise to confront the fisherman or seek treatment was already two weeks in breach. Mrs. Delano had given up trying to convince Dory and now had a psychiatrist and old family friend from Boston calling her almost daily to implore her to accept medical care.

Turner and Charlotte and Dory had privately agreed that, for a time, these subjects would be banished from their reverie and made to seem all but forgotten by three old friends who had come together for a summer of forgetfulness. Charlotte understood but questioned Dory's faith in the fisherman. Turner neither understood nor believed. She thought of this man and his lewd assault, and of the weird hope he somehow had imparted to her friend, and she seethed with resentment. "Cancer," she thought—something he had whispered in her ear as if to excuse the cheap feel he wanted, as if he were doing her a favor. Turner could not accept the absurdity and the looming tragedy of it all.

Yet, despite these concerns, there had been no talk of the fisherman among them for those three weeks. Dory had not tried to find him or confront him. That would have brought things to a head too soon for her. However, by the end of the third week, Turner had decided it was time for Dory to return to reality, and Charlotte agreed. They were sipping coffee at a tiny bookstore café in Vineyard Haven, chatting and distractedly, halfheartedly reading Annie Dillard, when Turner flat-out asked Dory whether she had heard of any sightings of the fisherman.

"As a matter of fact, I have," Dory answered, as if she were expecting the question at that very moment. "I got a text message from Millicent Davis this morning. A hash mark was spotted on the East Road heading out from Tisbury." She paused after saying this, as if to contemplate the meaning of what she would say next. "I thought we'd go there at sundown to try to find him and get this over with."

Tisbury was a hippie town, popular with natural foodies and vegans and hemp growers and potheads and free-range chicken farmers and goat herders and social refuseniks of all stripes. One who wasn't any of these things—a solitary, old black man hunched over the engine of a car beside a church graveyard, in a garage full of cars in various stages on their way to the grave—stood up from his work to watch Dory's Range Rover turn the corner from the main highway onto the East Road, just past town.

The hash mark was right where Dory's friend

Millicent had said it would be, and so (surprisingly) was a man in a dark-plaid flannel shirt and filthy blue jeans, standing behind a portable table stacked three-high with coolers.

It was not him.

There were already ten people there waiting to buy what the man was selling, which turned out to be shrimp, though much smaller in size than what they had seen before, and frozen solid. A brand-new Dodge van was parked on the embankment, its back doors open to reveal several more stacks of coolers. A middle-aged woman, sitting in a lawn chair beside the man, was handling the money along with a two-way radio. She spoke into the radio every few minutes to check in, and when she did, a voice on the other end gave her the "all clear." The pouch she held in her hands was overfilled with twenties and fifties. They were making a killing.

But it was not him.

Charlotte, Turner, and Dory stood in line together for half an hour as cars left and cars pulled up. Dory kept to the rear of the group until they reached the front of the line, when she stepped forward to ask where the fisherman was.

The man didn't answer at first but instead gave a sidelong glance at the woman working with him, who studied Dory more carefully.

"You're looking at a fisherman, ma'am," the man finally said. "What can I get you?"

"No, I mean the man in the blue Jeep, the man who's been selling shrimp around the island. You know—I'm sure you've heard of him, or you wouldn't have that blue hash mark on the tree behind you."

The woman who had been counting money leaned forward in her chair. "We work for him, ma'am. Business got to be too brisk, so he needed some help. That's what we're doing. We're helping the fisherman

128

you heard about. Now, what can we sell you, today, sweetheart?"

"Nothing," Turner answered. "We need to see your boss. It's very important. He . . . he did something for my friend, and we wanted to thank him."

Dory looked at Turner and, deciding her explanation of the inexplicable reason why they were there was as good as any, nodded her head in agreement.

"We just want to talk to him," Charlotte added.

The man and the woman were clearly uncomfortable. The woman stood up and, turning away, began to speak continuously into the radio. A few seconds later, she turned back to speak to her partner.

"Joe, we've got to get moving," she said, in a tone that indicated she was clearly in charge. Then she spoke to Dory. "Ma'am, we're very sorry, but we've got to close for the day. We'll be back as soon as we can. Just look for the hash mark."

There were protests and offers of higher prices from the crowd, but the man and woman loaded the last of the coolers and the table into the van and were gone in the other direction down the road within a minute.

Turner saw the look of regret and despair on Dory's face.

"I've been such a fool," Dory said. "I don't know what I was thinking—the shrimp guy's cure for cancer. What an idiot."

"You're not an idiot, Dory," Charlotte assured her. "I know what you felt when he touched you. I felt the same thing, I guess. . . . I just didn't know what it was. It's the feeling of human kindness, and if you haven't felt it before or often, when you do, it's like something—I don't know—like electric. It's a feeling of being alive and connected to another human being. And for some reason I don't understand any better than you do, he saved my life. I just . . . I just don't think you can put your faith in him, Dory. He's not a prophet or a miracle worker. He's just a kind man—"

"Who is obviously building a pretty incredible seafood distribution business," Turner added with disgust.

"And someone who, along the way," Charlotte continued, "did something meant to be kind that I think anyone else would see as very bizarre and, frankly, pretty creepy—"

"Creepy, for sure—the man groped you, Dory. He sexually assaulted you!" Turner chimed in. Charlotte glared at her to back off, then continued.

"I understand that for you it had a different meaning that we can't hope to understand and that Turner doesn't mean to judge you for—right, Turner?" Turner didn't answer. "I just don't want to lose you over it."

Dory was nodding her head to affirm every word that Charlotte was saying, and Turner could feel the clouds of the last three weeks begin to lift.

"I guess I was just terrified, and with what happened to Charlotte, then what he did to me—I don't know. I was probably ready to believe anything."

"Look, no harm no foul, right?" Turner said, taking Dory's hand and then Charlotte's and starting to lead them back to the car. "We just need to get you in to see Dr. Sullivan, and then we can form a plan. Whatever comes, Dory, we're with you. Right, Charlotte?"

"All the way," Charlotte replied.

The mood was deflated but easy in the car on the ride home. Coming to the state highway, Dory was thirsty and realized she hadn't drunk anything all afternoon. She asked Turner to pull into the station on the corner to let her get a soda from the machine.

"I wouldn't call it a station. Looks more like a graveyard for junk cars," Turner said.

"Yep," Charlotte concurred, "and this must be the

gravedigger."

Outside the passenger window, a man was slowly approaching the car with a shovel in his hand. It was the same man who had watched them come through town.

"Don't open the door," Turner whispered. "I don't like the way he's looking at us."

"Haven't you learned by now, Turner?" Dory answered. "The Vineyard is full of weird men and the women who love them. God bless them all."

Getting out of the car, Dory flashed a big smile that she hoped would prove the wisdom of the words she had just uttered. The man didn't smile back.

"Just looking to get a soda out of your machine, if you don't mind." Dory began digging in her purse. "Do you happen to have change for—"

"Don't need no change, ma'am," the old man answered. His hands were thickly creased from years of hard work. His skin was a burnt shade of dark brown. The clothes on his back fit him like a permanent shell grown around his body, and the deep muddy-blue color of the cloth could not be distinguished from the oil stains.

"No, really, I'm happy to pay," Dory continued.

"Don't take no change. Just push the button and get what you want."

"Why, you're very kind," Dory said, a little unsettled by his generosity. "I'm Dory Delano, and these are—"

"Oh, I know you, Miss Delano. No doubt 'bout that."

Dory felt the sweat form on her palms and realized that Turner and Charlotte were still in the car—perhaps wisely so. But then she saw the man's eyes soften, with an expression that seemed almost like pity. He reached out and took her hand, which fit like the hand of a little child in his, and folded it in his palm, as if to protect it. Then he spoke again.

"You're lookin' for the fisherman. You're lookin' for Enoch."

Dory blinked at first in surprise, then realized that streams of cars carrying people looking for the same thing must have come by this same spot.

"Yes, like everyone else, I suppose."

"No, not like everyone else. He touched you."

Dory felt a wave of panic wash over her. The man still held her hand in his. But as he began to explain, he released his grip and asked her to sit next to him on one of two five-gallon buckets that were pulled up under the shade of an oak tree in the sandy, unpaved lot. Dory could see Turner and Charlotte staring at her, with pie eyes, through the raised car windows. They got out and hurried to her when the man walked off toward the soda machine.

"What are you doing, *now*?" Turner demanded. "Do you know this guy?"

"No, but he knows the fisherman."

Turner scoffed. "Yeah, and probably Elvis, too."

A loud bang could be heard as each drink hit the bottom of the dispenser. The old man came back with three cold cans of grape Nehi.

"Only kind I've got left," he said. He handed the sodas to his guests, then tiredly dropped his frame onto the bucket and took out a cigarette. Dust swirled upward in circles in the still air around him.

While the three women took their first swallows, the old man lit his cigarette. After one long puff, he spoke.

"Name's Simon." He did not ask for Turner's or Charlotte's name, and they didn't volunteer the information. Dory was too shocked too speak, but Turner had questions.

"So, those people selling shrimp down the East Road—they left in an awful hurry. I guess they got word someone was coming to write them up. Are all of them working for this one man—I'm sure you've heard of him—that people call 'the fisherman'?"

"No, ma'am. They got no part of Enoch. Workin' for them*selves*, they are," the man said. "They's all over the island now—folks from Boston and New York—sellin' shrimp brought up from wholesalers in Carolina. I seen the trucks on the ferry. Tiny things. Froze solid. Thawed out and put in coolers like they's fresh. Ain't nothin' like the ones Enoch brings."

The man's accent was lyrical and strange.

"Who is Enoch?" Charlotte asked.

"Enoch's the one y'all lookin' for—the one they call 'the fisherman.' I call him Enoch, 'cause that's his name. He's my friend."

They were having obvious difficulty following Simon's words. The old man's face cracked into a sly grin.

"I s'pose you know I'm not from around here," he said, chuckling. "I'm a Lou-zee-anna man. Been up here workin' cars now three years. Old man who hired me owned this garage. He passed away—been one year this season. He let me stay in the room back of the office. After he died and the place went to the bank, I just figured here's where I'd stay. Just kept on workin' cars, and people kept on payin' me to do it—cash money. Ice machine works, but the soda machine over yonder ain't took money the whole time since the old man died. The soda truck fills it just the same every month. Ain't nobody said nothin' so here I is."

He led the three women into the shop, where in the back they could see a small cot, table, makeshift sink, and an ancient hotplate next to the garage restroom. There was no furniture but a broken couch, yet somehow it had a pleasant, welcoming feel. On an apple crate next to the bed were books—*The Travels of Marco Polo* and *The Autobiography of Benjamin Franklin*.

"You're a reader, I see," said Turner.

"No, not me, ma'am. Them's Enoch's books."

"Enoch?" Turner asked, turning over a dog-eared copy of Carlyle's *The French Revolution* in her hands. "He lives here?"

"No, ma'am," the man answered. "I lives here. Enoch first come here lookin' for ice. I give it to him free—ain't costing me nothin'—and he and I got to talkin'. He fills his coolers for the shrimp he catch. He used to stay with me sometimes, when the weather was bad, but he don't do that no more. He don't come around like he used to."

"Why not?"

"Not since the trucks started comin'."

"The trucks?"

"Those same folks you saw today—the ones who pretend to work for him. They don't got what but they can buy and sell. They don't have the soul of that boy. They don't have his gift. They's here for the money. He's here for you and for me, and to be lookin' for his daddy he ain't seen in a long time now."

Turner was honing in on the unusual, the aberrant circumstance becoming apparent in Simon's words, like a shark drawn to the strange motion of a wounded fish. She circled closer while Charlotte and Dory stayed silently at the periphery, remora drawn along by her ravenous interest.

"His gift? What exactly is his gift?" Turner asked.

Simon heard the question and now seemed to detach from their conversation. He didn't answer right away. His eyes drifted outward, toward the marsh beyond the road, and the corners of his mouth creased slightly in the beginning of a frown at some sadness, but whatever the object of his thoughts, it was something beyond his powers of description.

Finally, he spoke.

"He can bring things to hisself. They come to him just natural, like a magnet."

Turner cast an annoyed sidelong glance at Dory, who looked stricken by the man's words.

"What does he bring to himself?" Turner insisted.

"He brings the shrimp—the big, golden shrimp from way down deep. Ain't no one can find 'em, but he does. He brings you here to me, and me to you. And he brought life to that woman there," he said, pointing to Dory, "and to that woman there," pointing to Charlotte.

He paused, there, to focus his gaze more closely on Turner. "But you, ma'am, I don't know 'bout you." His face creased into a look of worry. Something unsettled him. "There's a darkness around you, ma'am. A powerful darkness I can't see through."

"I've heard enough," Turner said, straightening herself and stepping toward the door, but Charlotte and Dory remained transfixed by the man. Turner turned sharply back toward them.

"C'mon, Charlotte—Dory," she called. "You've got a date with Dr. Sullivan."

As they were leaving, the man appeared by the window of their car, running to catch them. Turner reluctantly stopped and rolled the window down only a crack. She was not afraid. She was angry.

"Don't come to look for him here," the man said.

"Why would we do that?" Turner asked. "It doesn't look like he's selling any more shrimp."

"Too dangerous now, with the sheriff and some fella named DeAngelo lookin' to arrest him."

"Smoke?" Dory said, in confusion. The man clearly didn't know him by that name and looked puzzled at her question.

"Never mind," Turner interrupted. "If we need to find the fisherman, we'll contact you."

CHAPTER 11

It was two days, at noon on a Tuesday, before Dr. Sullivan could clear his schedule for the battery of blood tests, biopsies, MRIs, poking and probing that preceded the start of treatment. Charlotte and Turner had both ignored Dory's angry insistence that she arrive alone for these sessions, which Dr. Sullivan had made clear would involve hours of waiting for new tests to begin and the results of earlier tests to come back. To avoid any further delay, he had already scheduled the first trial of chemotherapy to begin later that week. What was left unsaid, but which was understood by all, was that nothing but radical mastectomy—if even that—would halt it.

Dory pretended not to dread this day, but her face had been a pale picture of dread since her encounter with the people selling frozen shrimp on the road to Tisdale. Her hope had fallen, then. She couldn't bring herself to speak of the fisherman after that. What, exactly, Simon had meant in saying that the man he called Enoch had saved her life was unclear. It seemed he had saved her from a misdiagnosis of cancer, but from the furtive glances of the nurses working around her, it was just as clear he had not saved her from the disease. A cure, if it was to come, would come through surgery and chemotherapy. She awaited her trial in silence, never betraying her true thoughts on the subject.

It had been six hours since their arrival at the hospital. The three of them were sitting in the excessively mauve women's lounge on the third floor. Dory's mother stared at them sternly from a portrait on the wall. Each of them had spent the last hour pretending to read a disappointingly narrow selection of "women's interest" magazines about nothing of particular interest to any of them. Turner was straining to see what was going on outside the double doors at the other end of the room, where she had begun to notice a stream of men and women in lab coats coming from or going to the oncology department in increasing numbers. This surely did not bode well, but for what seemed like hours after the last test, no one had entered the waiting room to say anything.

"I have to pee," Turner finally said—lying—then got up and walked through the double doors in the opposite direction of the ladies room. Charlotte watched her go, suspecting something but saying nothing. Dory continued only to read, finally absorbed in an article about a Connecticut woman who had left career, home, and family to raise llamas in New Zealand. It seemed like a good idea to her at the time, so the story went.

"What's going on?" Turner demanded of anyone within earshot of the nurses' station. One nurse looked at her anxiously.

"You are . . . ?"

"Ms. Delano's next of kin." Her lies flowed like cheap wine.

The nurse said nothing to her. She picked up the phone on her desk, pushed a button, and spoke in a low voice to the person on the other end. A few minutes later, an ashen-faced man appeared at the desk.

"Ms. Graham—Martin Sullivan, I believe we met the night Dory was brought to the ER. Thank you for bringing Dory in today. We have been on tenterhooks since the initial finding. But today, I have some unexpected news. I would like to tell Dory and all of you, together, what we've found."

Turner felt her breath catch in her throat and her stomach tighten. She feared she would vomit. For the first time, she was truly petrified about what was going to happen to Dory. Trying to peek around the door to the waiting room without being seen, she saw Dory and Charlotte both watching her intently. A slow wave of her hand brought them hurrying toward her.

The three of them crowded into a small conference room with Dr. Sullivan, a nurse, and two other specialists whose introductions were drowned out in Dory's mind by noise of the fear that death was not only near, but nigh. Dr. Sullivan would want witnesses for the heavy news he was about to deliver, Dory assumed. He then began to speak, beginning exactly as she dreaded.

"I don't how to begin to say what I'm about to say, Dory . . . "

No one ever does, her thoughts shouted. *Just say it!*

"Except that I have some rather strange and baffling—but, it appears—truly wonderful news."

Wonderful news. Dory felt her heart skip at the jarring incongruity of those words. Turner and Charlotte listened, expressionless, as if lifted from the ground, their animation suspended with the pause in the doctor's voice.

"You have no cancer, Dory."

Dr. Sullivan let the words sink in for one or two beats, lest the central message be missed. It was missed—completely. Dory stared at him in bewilderment. Understanding had not broken through the defenses that surrounded her mind like a fortress. He began again.

"Every test has been run and rerun, and . . ." He looked down, shaking his head as if he were being called to give account for some error he preferred not to admit. "I'll be damned if I can find any evidence that you ever had cancer." He lifted his head slightly and peered at Dory from under his brow. "That's why I wanted to wait until I could speak to Dr. Russell and Dr. Bertrand. They're the best in their field. They looked at your original films and results and compared them to the ones we've done today. There was no mistake in the original diagnosis, Dory, but I don't . . . I don't . . ." Words were failing him, now. He was off the medical map on which he had navigated his whole career.

Dr. Russell tried to pick up where Dr. Sullivan left off. "We reread the entire evaluation not just once, Dory, but multiple times. You've been very patient, and I'm sure this has been an anxious time for you, but . . ." Again, another doctor stood before the abyss of ignorance and could find nothing coherent to say.

Dr. Bertrand was the next to try, and he succeeded in summoning the humility to say the three hardest words in all of medical science: We. Don't. Know.

"Dory, it's as clear as this and as murky as the deep blue sea: you had advanced invasive carcinoma three weeks ago—a serious, no-fooling diagnosis—and now you don't. You have no more cancer—not a trace, not a residue. Nothing. And the truth is, we don't have a clue why. It was there—we're sure of that—but it's not only gone, it's as if it was never there to begin with. Dr. Sullivan brought us in to make sure the original results were not misread. They weren't."

"So, what you're describing, then, is . . . what exactly?" Dory offered, tentatively. "A miracle?"

The doctors looked at each other as if they had been expecting this reaction. Their brows furrowed again in unison at their discomfort with the term. Again, Dr. Bertrand tried to help Dory comprehend the incomprehensible.

"If you're asking me how, medically, this could have happened, I simply have no explanation for you. What I can tell you, empirically, is that there have been rare, reported cases . . ."

He kept talking, but Dory was no longer listening. She was jumping and screaming and crying in the arms of her two friends. She knew a miracle when she saw one, even when no one else had the faith to admit it.

CHAPTER 12

Food and people were everywhere. Every cupboard had been opened. Every bowl was summoned to duty. Rutla was restored to command. The tiny shop in town that sold outlandishly decorated cupcakes had been cleaned out of every dollop for the affair. By six o'clock, Dory's wine cellar was so decimated that reinforcements were arriving steadily through the back door, carried from McIntyre's store on Main Street by a breathless clerk. The rather severe, unnamed man on the phone, who was Tripp, told the owner that the president had arrived on the island for the weekend unexpectedly, and that several more cases of their best stock were needed at once. This was only vaguely plausible, even for the Delanos, yet it had been spoken with such urgency and authority that dusty bottles of Chateau Lafite Rothschild that hadn't seen the sun since before Dory was born came rolling in like kegs of cheap beer.

It was Tripp's idea for an impromptu party to celebrate Dory's remarkable news, and once he put the word out, the merrymakers came running. Vineyard society rarely needed to be asked twice to a party. The occasion and the exact nature of Dory's good news were known only to a select few, but Tripp believed that the best reason for a party was no reason at all, and the crowd that was now spilling out from the dining room into the sidewalk beyond the garden clearly saw no reason to ask questions. Despite Dory's initial reluctance at the idea, she was now glowing with excitement. She saw life afresh, and among so many old friends and neighbors, it seemed the possibilities were endless.

The air was delicious with the smell of buttercream icing and vanilla cake; of garlic and olive oil and cumin and basil; of roasted cashews seasoned with sage and Old Bay; and the warm, doughy sharpness of Rutla's cheddar cheese biscuits. The intoxicating vapor of old wine mixed with new champagne swirled through and around all of it.

Dory's mother walked in as if she had never seen the place before, stopping to say hello to one old friend after another and barely making any progress through the crowd. Her face, when she finally saw Dory, had in memory never been so ebullient and filled with genuine affection. She embraced Dory warmly in the kitchen, leaning in and whispering, "I was so frightened all this time. I didn't know what to tell you."

Which meant, Dory understood, that her mother did not know how to speak of death. It was true. Of course, no one does. She had long been forgiven of that.

"I know, Mother," Dory answered, comforting her.

"Don't question grace, dear, or try to explain it. Just celebrate it."

Dory had not spoken of the fisherman or the idea of miracles with anyone. Few people in the room knew the story. But the enigma of her newfound health continued to confound her. Her thoughts turned again and again to the fisherman's touch, to his warm breath against her neck, and to the word "cancer." He spoke it like an incantation, not an exclamation. Had he healed her—saved her—just as he had saved Charlotte? If he had, why was the disease still present when she was diagnosed later that day? Only one thing was clear: what once was there was now gone. The absence of an explanation left a void in her mind into which every wild speculation now rushed in.

Turner wasn't waiting for explanations. She was too busy writing her own. She had long since had her fill of champagne and cake and now cradled a cup of hot coffee in her hands against the usual chill of the night air on the Vineyard. Over the edge of the desk in the darkness of her room, she peered at the glowing screen of her laptop. She had a story to tell, and oh, what a story it would be, of an unnamed woman in Martha's Vineyard whose terminal cancer was cured by the tender, trusting touch of an itinerant stranger—the same mysterious fisherman who days earlier appeared from nowhere to pull a drowning woman from the sea and then return unseen to shore by no vessel but God's grace. A man who asked for neither money nor fame for his efforts and answered to no one, who lived on the land and by the kindness of strangers, who had no place to lay his head. It was a story that simply demanded to be written, and Turner knew she was the only person in the world who could write it. When she had finished, at the blinking cursor she proudly typed her name, adding the title, "Bennett & Donald Author," and hit *publish*.

When she was done, she felt her eyes grow heavy and her muscles ache for a bath. The shower in the garden was still overrun with revelers, but the light in Dory's room was off, which meant that Dory's luxurious claw-foot tub was hers for the taking. She slipped out of her dress and into a bathrobe. Peeking first around the stairs to see that the coast was clear, she padded quickly in bare feet down to the first level.

The toilet in the bathroom off the kitchen was seeing heavy use from the guests, but the part of the house that included Dory's bedroom was quiet and dark. Closing the door softly behind her, she gave one turn of the switch on the porcelain table lamp to give the room a soft glow. Looking around, Turner was reminded again that Dory knew how to live well. However fiercely she begrudged her mother's influence, Dory's choice of surroundings screamed the Delano money and the Delano breeding. Her bedroom contained all the usual emblems of Yankee propriety: a four-poster canopy bed with a cross-stitched, upholstered sitting bench at the foot; stodgy Queen Anne's toile chairs; a Ben Franklin partner's desk, mahogany with inlaid leather; a Delft vase bursting with fresh hydrangea blossoms; and a brightly polished brass hatstand. It was tasteful, uncluttered, and classic. Not much more than the bed linens had changed in sixty years.

She turned on the water to the tub, which flowed hot from the ancient spigot in a single, steaming rivulet that was either all off or fully open, unimpeded by modern fittings, filters, and fixtures. Just pure water, solitude, and simple pleasure, which is exactly what Turner had in mind.

She slipped off the terry-cloth robe and hung it on the hatstand in the bedroom, then returned to see the water steaming in the tub. Her leg muscles yearned for the soothing heat, but missing were the expected bottle of bubble bath and a washcloth. Tiptoeing across the cold tiles, she noticed her figure in the cheval mirror and stopped, inevitably, for a critique. Her backside was still blessedly free of cellulite but widening, concernedly. Her legs had always been slender and well proportioned above delicate ankles, all of which remained so. Where she usually gained weight, around her hips, could be hidden easily enough in everything but mirrors. She considered her breasts to be not her strongest asset but still enough to hold up a strapless dress without spilling out of the top of it—a blessing, she surmised, of long-deferred childbirth. Standing before the mirror and turning from one side to another in half pirouettes, she imagined what she must look like walking down the beach. She was generally pleased with herself, all things considered.

The water filling the tub burbled less noisily as it rose close to the level needed for a satisfying soak, but the bubble bath remained nowhere to be seen. At the end of the bathroom, behind the door, was a tall cabinet that looked like a place Dory would likely store such things. Turner walked there and was reaching up on her tiptoes to the highest shelf when she heard the bathroom door open and shut and the sound of a man's voice. It was Tripp. He was hurriedly undoing the front of his trousers and saying something, seemingly directed at her.

Turner froze, relaxing only slightly a moment later after realizing he was only peeing, not peeping. Not that she was overly bashful about Tripp Wallace in particular. There had been one memorable sailing trip aboard his boat, going from the Vineyard to Nantucket and back again for the weekend, eight summers ago. Dory had asked her along at the last minute for moral support. Somewhere between two and three bottles of gin, Turner had joined the nude review of wives and girlfriends cajoled into sunbathing topless while they sat as ballast on the windward rail. Turner was certain she was the least memorable of the dozen or so women in that lineup, but there was quite a bit more of her in view, now.

She continued to stand there, motionless, not sure whether the polite thing to do was to interrupt or let him finish, as he fumbled inordinately with his belt and zipper to relieve his obvious distress, stepping in place from one foot to the other as he did this, as if the sensation of walking would override the more urgent sensation to urinate, which he clearly had been waiting a long time and wanted very badly to do. But he was continuing, with a drunken gregariousness, a conversation he clearly believed he was having with Dory. It seemed to Turner rather sweet and rather bizarre at the same time to be the recipient of this misdirected intimacy.

So she remained there, beside the cabinet with nothing but a bar of soap in her hand—chosen as a weapon of self-defense that she was now sure would be unnecessary. She considered the possibility that he might finish what he came to do and leave none the wiser that the woman in the corner was anyone other than Dory. As he babbled on and continued to labor with difficulty to try to withdraw himself, she found herself suddenly wishing she had shaved her legs.

"God, I thought I was going to burst waiting for the main bathroom to open," he was saying on one foot, then the other. "How many times do women have to pee in one night? I've been looking all over for you—I thought you'd left. Janie Mossberg's been asking questions about the buzz she's heard around the hospital. I was doing my best to fend her off, but—"

It was at this point in the non-conversation that Tripp finally turned his head to the left to speak directly to his audience and realized he had arrived in the wrong hall. By this time, he also finally grasped and extricated the thing he had been so urgently seeking. In his shock at seeing someone other than Dory standing there, he continued to turn not just his head but his shoulders and all that went with them from his intended target, at precisely the point of firing. The spray of urine went across the room in the direction of Turner, who screamed at being shot at in this manner. She quickly stepped to one side, ready to return fire with the bar of soap if it came to that. Tripp, seeing a naked woman he did not yet recognize trying to evade his fire at the other end of the bathroom, was mortified. But what had waited so long to begin could not be stopped. In a panic, he stuffed himself back inside his silk trousers. His trousers then began to bloom in a long, dark blot running down one leg, until out he came again, spraying and spattering about the room with undiminished force.

Turner completely forgot her nakedness and, while trying simultaneously not to laugh and to stay out of the line of fire, began to speak.

"Oh, my God! I'm so sorry! What can I . . . can I? Here . . . here, can I . . . help? Oh, my God!"

The words sounded ridiculous to her even as they left her lips. Tripp was not listening. He was still teetering from the effects of too much wine as he continued to wrestle with his trouser zipper. All the while, he kept spraying impressive arcs above and around the toilet bowl and the rest of the bathroom, like a jammed machine gun on the back of a runaway Jeep.

What number of bottles the man must have drunk to still be going all this while, there was no telling, but the floor beneath his feet was becoming slick. Still doing his step dance, he backed up to the edge of the tub, which stopped him at the level of the knees while the rest of his body continued its backward momentum. After a brief moment of equivocation, momentum won the battle, and he fell all the way in. A great wave sloshed up and over the side, catching Turner by surprise—again—and making the floor slicker still beneath her bare feet. She unwisely attempted to retreat. In the next instant her feet went skyward and her great white beamy backside came down hard on the tile.

There was a brief silence after the storm, and a momentary pain that was soon interrupted by the sound of Turner squeaking. She was holding in, for the most part, spasms of laughter that now wracked her body lying on the floor of the bathroom, except for the errant squeak and snort that forced its way out. Finally raising herself high enough to peer over the rim of the tub, tears streaming down her cheeks, she found Tripp resigned to a comfortable bath and the satisfaction of complete relief, aided by the effect of the warm water. She quickly tamped down another burst of laughter and composed herself enough to grasp his face in both her hands and kiss his cheek, barely getting out the words, "You poor man," before the laughter came again.

Tripp was not laughing but rather staring in understandable bewilderment. He had come just seconds ago on a routine mission to his girlfriend's private toilet and, finding the light on, expected to find her there. Yet he was now neck-deep in a tub of hot water and urine, fully clothed, being alternately kissed and pitied and laughed at by a naked woman he barely knew.

Sensibility soon returned, with practical necessity close on its heels. Turner remembered herself and went slipping and sliding toward the bathroom door. She retrieved the bathrobe along with a towel for her guest.

"Let me have your clothes and I'll run them through the dryer across the hall," she told him.

Tripp was only too happy to accept this solution. Turner stepped out, and a moment later a hand conveying trousers, shirt, socks, and underwear in a large wet clump came tentatively poking out from behind the barely opened door, where its owner stood crouching, unseen—a needless show of modesty bordering on prudery, Turner thought, given recent events.

She put her own clothes back on and tiptoed across the back hall to the laundry room. Judging from the din of conversation, the party was still going strong. As she crossed the hallway, she noticed that the light in the room upstairs was on, which meant that Charlotte was finally home from her counseling session at the church.

Turner had not used the new combination washer-dryer in the laundry room, as that was Rutla's domain when she came on weekends to clean. Turner thought of recruiting help from Charlotte, who often washed her own clothes, but she thought better of revealing Tripp's bathroom mishap to anyone unnecessarily. On top of the machine was a half-full basket of dirty clothes and an empty basket where clean clothes went to be folded. Inside the machine was a single blouse—light blue cotton, the kind that Charlotte had been wearing a lot since she got to the Vineyard. She said she liked the way it breathed.

Turner picked the blouse out of the machine and smelled it the way her mother used to do to see if it was clean or dirty.

That's when she knew. The smell was unmistakable, as was the moist stain on the button-down front she noticed a moment later. The blouse had been placed inside the machine, instead of in the basket, so that no one else would touch it before it was laundered along with the rest of the clothes.

So that no one would see.

Tripp's dignity was saved. Turner never said a word. He returned to the party wearing a slightly rumpled version of the shirt he had worn on his way to the bathroom and a clean if more fitted version of the same pants. No one noticed he had been gone—least of all Dory, who was busy making the rounds to speak to the many old friends who had come out for no other reason, insofar as they knew, than to inaugurate another summer on the Vineyard together.

Charlotte eventually descended from her room to help with the party cleanup. It was about midnight.

When the last guest left, the three friends converged in a pile beside the one remaining bottle of champagne and a block of sharp cheese in the kitchen. Dory cut off small corners of it at a time, in this way telling herself she wasn't eating very much of it, ignoring the fact that she'd been whittling away at that block for upwards of a half hour. It was now almost gone.

Turner embraced Dory for no reason other than to say she was glad she was alive and still her friend, and Charlotte joined in. Nothing was said for a full minute as they soaked in the incredible gift of their friendship and the place where they had come together to celebrate their love and memories of each other, and to make new ones. Eventually they made their way to the living room couch—a way station where they could summon the strength to head the rest of the way to bed.

"I trashed your bathroom, Dory," Turner said.

"What?"

"I trashed it bad—had a bubble bath in there about an hour ago and made a soupy mess of your floor. I'm so sorry. I tried to mop it up as best I could, but I'm afraid it's still a hazard. Be careful when you go in there."

Dory looked at her in a way that spoke of her continual wonder—which was genuine—that she would ever truly know or understand this odd and remarkable old friend, Turner Graham, but she of course didn't mind. "Whatever, Turner," she said. "Have a pool party in there if you like. Mi casa es tu casa."

"I'll try not to have any more water battles with myself next time."

Turner turned to Charlotte, the quiet one, who was pensively sipping her champagne while smiling at the thought of Turner playing in the tub.

"How'd it go with Father Vecchio tonight?" Dory asked. Turner was glad the question came from someone else. It was what she had been dying to ask ever since she'd found the blouse.

"Okay, I guess."

The lie was written across her face but apparent only to Turner, who knew the truth.

"It's been three weeks now," Dory continued. "He should be getting close to a decision about the funeral. I'm sure he wouldn't have gone all this long, if . . ."

Charlotte looked up at Dory with a tight-lipped smile. "I'm sure you're right. Very soon, now, I think he'll be able to make a decision and notify the bishop. Very soon."

"When's your next session?" Turner asked.

"Day after tomorrow."

"What time?"

"Why, you have plans?"

"No, just curious," Turner answered, covering.

"Six o'clock."

"After the office is closed, then?"

"Yes," Charlotte answered, becoming a little nervous and annoyed at the persistence of the inquiry. "He's respectful of my privacy, I suppose."

"How thoughtful of him," Turner replied, and forced a smile to her face.

CHAPTER 13

It was a Monday. The streets outside the church were quiet when Turner arrived at Father Vecchio's office in the rectory at six o'clock, the appointed time. Turner had told Dory of the blouse. It had been difficult to do—not because of the subject, but because telling her felt like a betrayal of a friend, and because she failed to tell the whole truth. The nude bathroom fiasco with Dory's on-again, off-again boyfriend, however innocent, seemed best omitted.

Upon hearing the story, Dory realized what she had long suspected: that a dear friend was being manipulated by her faith and her grief. She knew what had to be done. Turner—the stronger, bolder one between them and, importantly, the one whom Father Vecchio did not know—was chosen to take the lead. An emergency was elaborately fabricated that required Charlotte to drive Dory across the island to Vineyard Haven that afternoon, and Turner—knowing that Charlotte would be fearful of disappointing the priest—promised she would stop by to make her apologies for her. Dory and Turner had agreed that Turner would confront the priest about his abuse of Charlotte's trust and demand that he stop and tell her the truth about Meredith's funeral, which likely meant that there wouldn't be one. But Turner had quite a different sort of confrontation in mind.

The rectory was as dark as a dive bar when Turner arrived. Soft jazz was playing on the stereo. "Typical," she muttered to herself. The priest came out to greet her at the door with a drink in his hand, wearing street clothes. The look on his face went from surprise to disappointment to suspicion. She felt a visceral revulsion at his greasy piety and self-importance.

But she was not there to explore the flaws of Father Vecchio's character. She had a specific task to complete, and to do that she would need to stoop to enter the sordid, twisted world in which he lived. So Turner sought to put him at ease with a willing smile and the touch of her hand on his arm. She could see the excitement in his eyes.

"Father, I know you don't know me, but Charlotte is a dear friend, and she sent me to tell you that she's had an emergency and won't be able to make it tonight."

"Okay . . . well, sure . . . I understand. That's not a problem. Thank you for coming."

He would have closed the door but for her hand that remained on his forearm. He waited awkwardly for her to remove it so he could do just that. Instead, she stepped up to the threshold, closer.

"Father, I wondered if I might come in and visit with you for a while, if you have the time." She distractedly touched her hair and flipped it back.

The invasion was a fait d'accompli. He would have had to close the door on her head and arm to stop her now. He opened the door wider but did not yet seem to relax. He stood in the living room, stiffly, as he waited for this strange woman to explain herself. He seemed put off by her willfulness. He liked to be in complete control where women were concerned.

"May I have a drink with you?" Turner asked.

The priest's eyes softened. "Mine's a vodka Collins. Will that do?"

"Perfectly."

Turner eyed the room as he left for the bar. The only

seat was a sofa. He returned with a fresh drink for himself and one for her and asked her to sit with him. He waited for her to sit first, then seated himself at a safe distance from her. She repositioned herself in the middle of the sofa, closer, cornering him at one end. The anxiety returned to his eyes.

"So, how do you know Charlotte, Miss—?"

"Graham. Turner Graham—but please, call me Turner."

Her hand found its place again on the skin of his forearm, which she now grasped firmly, anchoring herself to him.

"Charlotte and I are old college friends. All of us who knew her were grief-stricken about her daughter, and all of us—her friends—are cradle Catholics too, so we know the terrible dilemma she was in. I just think it's so kind what you're doing for her, and so sensitive to her situation. There just aren't enough young, dynamic priests like you. When Charlotte told me she couldn't be here tonight, I wanted to come by and tell you myself."

As she continued the conversation, she shifted her hand from his arm to his knee, keeping eye contact the entire time. She thought she noticed his leg jump slightly—a reflexive impulse shooting along the nerve to his groin. He smiled nervously and took a long swallow of his drink. Turner felt the urge to chug her drink to help her get through this, but she could tell her plan was going to take some time, and she needed to stay way behind in the count to maintain her bearings. She lifted the glass to her lips and pretended to drink, but drank nothing. The priest took another long swallow and soon got up to refill his glass.

Turner was nothing if not a talker, and her skills were now put to good use. They talked about God and faith, about the state of the Church and what people like Father Vecchio were doing to save it, about why millions like her had left the Church over the hypocrisy of its leaders—and throughout it all, the hypocrisy of what was happening in that room at that moment was lost on Father Vecchio. Forcibly ejecting the words from her mouth, she spoke about how good it was to have someone like him to talk to—then, bringing the conversation deftly around to her ultimate point— someone to help her and others realize that priests are "just men, just like every other man, with the same weaknesses." She said this with earnest, wide eyes that made her feel like she was starring in a seventies porn film, but the cheesiness of it seemed only to enchant the priest.

He spoke mostly of himself and his own struggles with faith and celibacy, and she kept her hand on the same spot on his knee, occasionally rubbing it as he drank—his fifth vodka to her one, by the time the first hour passed. By the end of the second hour, they had covered all the worldly troubles of the Church and moved on to their respective childhoods and families. Turner's hand then traveled nonchalantly higher, from his knee to his thigh. She occasionally patted and rubbed him there in slow, circular motions. When he came back with his sixth vodka and her third, she decided it was time to move the conversation into new territory.

Turner reclined into the couch and let her head fall back on the cushion. She looked dreamily up at the priest as though she were simply enchanted by him. Her hand returned to rest on his thigh. Dory's lacy, push-up bra that her friend reserved to be worn only in ball gowns (which was to say, never), had been tightened to make 34B look like 34D, and was having its intended effect. She was spilling out of her scoop-necked top, and the priest's compulsive, furtive glances at her chest told her he noticed. He moved closer to her and stretched his arm behind her head, cradling it in his hand. She could feel his stare moving down her cleavage like a laser pointer.

"Does it get lonely for you here, Tommy?" she said, dropping the title "Father" for the first time.

"You have no idea. I'm sure it would bother me more if I had more time to dwell on it, but even in this small town, there's a steady stream of the bereaved, the sick, shut-ins, brides-to-be, people struggling with various addictions and depression, and they all want—they all need—my time. I don't very often get the chance to sit down with a woman like yourself and talk about my own feelings."

"I just want you to know, Tommy, I'm a good Catholic, but I'm not one of those who think priests are superhuman. I know you have the same needs as any other man."

His *needs*. It was all she could do to get the word out. She was speaking in clichés because the man himself was a cliché. Even though she wished she could think of something more nuanced and original to say, if only to keep herself from laughing, it was clear that nuance and originality were not in high demand with Tommy Vecchio. Her shtick was exactly what he expected from women and exactly what he wanted to hear. Turner Graham had, in the course of two hours, managed to become Father Tommy Vecchio's dream girl.

"And I want you to know," she continued impatiently to the point, "when I think of helping a priest, I know I'm helping the Church."

He nodded in affirmation.

"I also want you to know that Charlotte and I feel the same way about that—you know, about helping you—and since she couldn't be here tonight, I . . . I just want you to know I would be happy to—you know, help you myself. In fact, I'm kind of embarrassed—I don't know how to say this, and it's probably a sin, but—I really, really want to, and I hope you'll let me."

Something changed in his face just then. Something unsettled him. Something hadn't rung true. The cliché was too much even for Father Vecchio. He recoiled from her slightly as she finished speaking. She was wracking her brain to understand what it could be, when it suddenly dawned on her.

Charlotte hadn't been a willing victim.

Charlotte hadn't decided to "help" him. No sooner had Turner realized this, than the priest unwittingly admitted it.

"I'm not sure I can agree with you about Charlotte." He was chuckling, now, as if he were letting her in on a secret little joke about what a silly girl Charlotte was. Turner wanted to slap him. "I don't know what she's been telling you, but I don't think she shares your point of view. We have become close these last few weeks, but we . . . we quarreled the last time she was here, and she was very upset when she left that I wouldn't give her an answer about the rites for Meredith. I was going to tell her, tonight, the sad news that I haven't made any progress with the bishop. I don't see a way I can offer her what she seeks for her child's remains. But I guess I'm curious—what 'help' did Charlotte tell you she was giving me?"

Turner panicked inside while pretending to listen to the priest with attentive concern. She felt her heart race at the same time a dull sluggishness washed over her, Even though she was far behind him in the count, the effect of the alcohol was catching up with her. Thin dots of perspiration started to bead on her lip. She didn't answer right away because she wasn't sure what to say. A slight tension, an unspoken awkwardness, was now palpable.

He put his drink down. The plan was falling apart.

Turner feared she would soon be headed home, having accomplished nothing more than two hours of a drunken thigh massage of a narcissistic, delusional predator who should have been an easier mark for her than any of the legions of men she had known who would gladly have taken his place.

Turner could think of nothing to do but one thing—the only thing there was to do. She moved her hand from his thigh gently to his groin, which was already bulging, and began slowly stroking him while peering into his eyes. There was a faint hint of a willing smile on her face.

Physiology trumped psychology, as it usually does. The priest seemed to forget his inhibitions. Turner barely stifled a scream when he lunged for her, placing his open mouth on hers and sliding his hand inside the neckline of her blouse. He cupped her left breast and painfully tweaked her nipple between his thumb and forefinger. She winced in pain that he ignored while he shoved his free hand under her skirt and up her thigh. He grasped the hem of her underwear and began to pull. A sensation of nausea overtook her, and she stood up abruptly. The plan, if it was going to work at all, would have to work now.

"I'm pretty excited and flattered and, well, I'm also a little nervous!" Her laughter, now, was as false as the smile on her face. "I guess you know now I've been hoping for this all night."

"I was hoping that's how you felt," he said, with a congratulatory tone.

"So . . . I need to freshen up in the bathroom. Maybe you could get undressed and wait for me by . . . by the fireplace?"

"Fine, but let's move into the bedroom."

"No! No—I mean, it's so much more romantic out here, you know? The fireplace and everything?"

"But there's no fire."

Turner glanced disappointingly at the flowers sitting atop the andirons. *Damn details*, she thought.

"Right—I know. Why don't you make one while I get ready?"

She leaned in to kiss him softly, then whispered, "The idea of you tearing my clothes off in the living room, beside a crackling fire, really, really excites me. Will you do that for me? Will you, please?"

The "please" was more than he could withstand. "All right, Turner. As you like it." He spoke as if he were giving a child a much-wanted new toy. The self-satisfied smile on his face betrayed no inkling of what was to come.

From inside the bathroom, Turner could hear the sound of snapping twigs and logs dropping on the tile floor by the mantel, then the crumpling of newspaper. She felt herself hesitating. She wasn't sure she was prepared to do what she had planned to do. Even for Charlotte, who was as deserving of her loyalty as anyone, this seemed well above and beyond the call. But when she thought about what it would mean to do nothing—to simply run out of that infernal place and never come back, to let this predator win at his game— the clutch in her gut told her she had no choice.

She removed Dory's bra in the usual series of contortions until she pulled it out through her sleeve. Standing in the mirror, she tousled her hair and examined herself. She unbuttoned the top button of her blouse, but without Dory's push-up bra the cleavage was no more. In its place was only the slender, relaxed outline of her breasts and the darker shade of color at the dimples made by her nipples, visible through the sheer fabric. She reached up under her skirt, slid off her underwear, and stuffed it into her purse along with the bra. Next to the loaded gun. And the camera.

She had checked the battery of the tiny black camera five times already that day, and she checked it a sixth time, now. She checked again to make sure the dial was set to video, then attached the camera by the small clip on the back to the top rim of her black leather purse. She carefully pressed the "record" button, making sure the camera stayed in place. Everything worked as planned. An incriminating red light glowed on the back of the camera, invisible to anyone but her. From a few feet away, the camera looked like a decorative buckle. He would never know it was there until it was too late.

When she walked out of the bathroom, she could hear the quiet crackling of the fire still getting started. Beside it lay the priest, completely naked in a ridiculous, centerfold pose, facing her and sitting up on one elbow. He was not yet ready for her, but he was stroking himself anxiously to get there. She stopped to place her purse on the coffee table at the precise angle she imagined would capture everything, then stopped to stand just out of the camera's field of view, facing him. She forced a smile that she feared looked more like agony.

"I thought masturbation was a sin, Father Vecchio." She made sure to say his name, a little louder than necessary.

"Only for sinners, my love. Not for you and me."

"Can you make it harder for me? I like them really hard." She listened to her own words as if they were spoken by someone else. She worried he could hear the quaver that was now obvious in her voice, and see the tremor that was beginning in her right knee. She was completely terrified.

He was not. He was making it harder now, with steady, rhythmic strokes. "Can you help me?" he asked.

"That's what I'm here for," she said, and again forced a smile. *This is what whores must feel like, constantly faking it,* she thought. *I have become a prostitute.*

The fire started to catch on and began filling the room with light and heat. She knew she had to keep things moving as if she had every intention of going all the way. She remained where she was standing, a safe distance away from him, but took a deep breath and reached down with her right hand for the hem of her skirt. Twisting it, she lifted it slowly, deliberately upward, in an excruciating striptease. A minute passed before the skirt was high enough that she could feel the warmth of the fire on the skin of her exposed pelvis. All the while the priest kept pounding himself, harder and faster, almost out of control. He called her to come lie down with him, but she dared not move into the camera's field of view.

"Almost, Father Vecchio. I have something else I want to show you. Can you keep it hard for me a little longer?"

"Yes! Yes!" he laughed, maniacally.

With one free hand, she reached up, slowly undid the next two buttons on her blouse, then pulled back the fabric. Her left breast tumbled out. He moaned when he saw this and tried to slow down, to control himself, but it was too late. A thin stream of fluid shot out across the room toward her, landing close to her feet, followed by two smaller, shorter spurts, and then he was done.

It was an adolescent peep show, tailor-made for a juvenile man. Turner had gotten more than she expected and all she needed, but the priest seemed eager for more. He started to get up and come to her.

"All right, here I come," she reassured him. "Wait there while I get what we'll need from my purse."

She walked over to the purse that was steadily recording Father Vecchio's demise. She reached first for the gun, then thought better of the idea and put it back before he could see it. Vecchio was foremost a coward, and a weak, pathetic man, she told herself. She had been ready all along to display the gun—even to use it—but she now doubted any of that would be necessary. Instead, she pulled the camera from the side of her purse and conspicuously switched off the recording function, making sure he saw her do it. Then, displaying the camera openly in her hand, she turned squarely to face the priest.

"Now you listen to me, you *slimy, fucking son of a bitch.*"

Screaming crude profanity made her feel more powerful when she was under extreme stress, in moments like this one, when power was what she needed most. The priest's eyes widened, and he reached for his clothes. Turner's voice was rising. She buttoned her blouse as she spoke.

"I may not have come here tonight looking for hope and consolation, but *Charlotte did.* What kind of sick bastard preys upon a mother's grief? I'm not a Catholic, by the way, *asshole.* What kind of *sick church* tells people that babies aren't welcome in heaven? Who gave you the *fucking right* to speak for God, you *pompous jackass?*"

Turner felt herself shaking uncontrollably from anger fueled by a mixture of hatred and fear. The priest rightly feared what might come next. He had gotten back into his underwear and was now stumbling on one foot, trying to put his trousers on while keeping a safe distance. His eyes were fixed steadily on the camera in Turner's hand.

"God only knows why she put her faith in you or your sham of a religion, but *by God* you're going to make good on that faith, now, do you understand me?"

The priest acknowledged nothing, said nothing. He stared only at the camera.

"This is my card," she said loftily, pulling it from her purse and placing it on the table. It was crisp and new.

Turner Graham, Bennett & Donald Author.

"It has the Web address for my blog. Fifty thousand hits a day, *asshole!*" She was triumphant, now. "That's where your little whoopee video will be posted if you don't get the *goddammed bishop* and his minions over here to hold a funeral and a proper burial for Charlotte's baby in the church cemetery—with full honors—in one week's time."

"That won't be a problem," Father Vecchio eagerly interrupted, relieved that the terms of surrender were so reasonable.

"*The goddammed bishop himself,* do you understand me? Or I won't just post this on my blog, I will send a press release to every newsroom in New England to tell them about your unique approach to counseling the bereaved. I'll bet the other women you've 'helped,'" she said with dramatic air quotes, "will start coming out of the woodwork when I do. What do you think the final settlement will be, Father? Thirty million? Forty? No telling."

Her fear was subsiding, and in its place, her loathing of the man before her increased. He was more gullible and pliable than she expected. By the time she had finished her speech and made the threat as clearly as she could make it, the priest had finished dressing.

He looked almost normal, then. She looked more like the floozy in that scene, wearing no underwear and no bra under a sheer blouse, but there would be no opportunity for another costume change. If people on the street saw her leaving the rectory in that condition, they would just have to come to their own conclusions.

She tucked the camera deep into the recesses of her purse and stepped toward the door. Walking backwards, she kept a wary eye on the priest, who began walking slowly toward her to follow her out. Her hand found the door, and without looking, she turned the knob. It was locked. He was five feet away. A dead stare covered his face. Her fear returned and now erupted in her like a geyser.

"You'll need the key for the deadbolt," the priest said with pathological calmness. Then, hesitating as if to seek her permission, he added, "I'll have to open it for you," and slowly took the next step toward her.

Turner stepped aside as he passed beside her, keeping her eyes fixed closely on him and her hand firmly on her purse, which held the camera. He took the key from his pants pocket and placed it in the lock. When the door opened, she turned her head for only an instant to look down at the first step. As she did so, she felt her body violently jerked backwards by her right arm.

He had snatched her purse without pulling it cleanly from her shoulder, and the force had pulled her backwards toward him. They collapsed together onto the floor of the living room. She fell on top of him. Her face hit the carpet where a pungent odor of semen still hung in the air. A gash opened up beneath the priest's right eye where his head hit the corner of the coffee table on the way down. Blood seemed to fly everywhere, but most of it landed on Turner's blouse.

The camera had rolled out of her purse onto the floor in the fall. The priest, blinking to see through the blood now streaming from his forehead into his eyes, grasped the camera and started pulling himself up. Turner reached for the purse and the gun inside. Holding the pistol grip tightly in her hand, she climbed up the priest's back and pushed him back to the floor. Pulling his bloody hair with one hand, she used the other to shove the muzzle firmly under his chin.

He hadn't expected a gun. He quickly relaxed in submission. Turner stared down at him from above, hardly pinning him with her weight but controlling him nonetheless. She spoke now in a seething, trembling voice with her hand on the pistol grip shaking uncontrollably, poking the barrel repeatedly and painfully into the bone of his jaw and the soft spot under his chin.

"Tell me, Father, what circle of hell will you be headed to when I pull this trigger?"

CHAPTER 14

Dory screamed reflexively when she saw Turner. She noticed first the blood on her blouse, then the red scrape on the side of her face. Rutla came running when she heard the noise. Dory was immediately frantic. Her hands alternately clasped beneath Turner's chin and reached out for her shoulders.

"Oh, my God, Turner—don't tell me. Oh, no. Are you hurt? No? You're okay? Oh, God. Oh, God. Tell me you didn't . . ."

"What's all this?" asked Rutla, arriving behind Dory, speaking in her clipped German accent.

Turner sighed deeply, realizing for the first time as she stood on the steps of Dory's house how completely exhausted she felt. She craved a hot bath and thought of the tub in Dory's room. The image of Tripp standing dripping wet in a bath towel waiting for his clothes to dry came incongruously to mind, bringing the hint of a smile to her face that seemed hardly sane, under the circumstances.

"Yeah, well, you should see the other guy," Turner joked, returning to the present. This relieved the tension for Rutla but not for Dory. She feared that their plan to confront Father Vecchio had somehow gone horribly wrong.

All was well, Turner reassured her—better than either of them could have hoped. Turner got her bubble bath. The tension of the past three hours had drained the last ounce of energy from her muscles. She was drifting away on a cloud of steam and eucalyptus when Dory came in with two cups of tea prepared by Rutla (jasmine, with lemon) and sat down beside the tub. They laughed and cried, and laughed some more. Dory brought the bloody camera from Turner's purse, and they watched the video together. It made Turner shake to realize the genuine danger she had been in.

They turned it off before the end. It was enough to know they had him—*the bastard,* as they referred to him in unison—where they wanted him.

Calls came the next day from a law firm in Boston, "on behalf of the auxiliary bishop." Turner didn't return them. Instead she got up early, walked to the rectory— *the scene of the crime*—and taped a note to the front door. It said, simply, "Five more days."

Charlotte, they learned, had already decided the night before—after her last session with Father Vecchio—not to see him again. Turner and Dory were glad she had regained her conviction in herself, in the end. Her conviction in her Church and its priest had failed her. But when Charlotte learned, after a call from the church office, that Meredith's funeral would be planned for the coming Saturday, she was sanguine with joy. In the end this small measure of grace had come to her and to Meredith, and somehow, incalculably, the arithmetic of faith had worked itself out. Her burden was lifted. A debt she owed to her child would now be forgiven.

Dory and Turner never told her. On the day of the burial, the arrival of the bishop in full regalia for the funeral mass was a complete surprise to Charlotte. His presence was never explained, neither was the reason for the retinue of lawyers who came with him, nor the Church's decision to pay the full cost of the plot, burial, and headstone. Turner stood her ground. There was no settlement, no deal, nothing ever on the record—just a very real and dangerous threat to the assets of the Archdiocese of Boston. The lawyers held their fire, and the ceremony went forward as planned. The prayers for this little child of God brought tears to the eyes of every mourner but the bishop, who was stoic to the point of coldness, and Father Vecchio, who stood speechless, cowering beside him, looking determinedly downward at the earth beside the open grave.

As people gathered for the service, Dory saw Charlotte staring pensively at the gash in Father Vecchio's forehead, then at the scrape healing on Turner's cheek, then back at Father Vecchio. A quizzical look crossed her face, but if she had any suspicion about how those two injuries were connected to the long-awaited celebration now going forward, she never revealed it.

A woman came to the front of the church and took the pew behind Charlotte, Dory, and Turner. She introduced herself as Margaret. She was the church secretary Charlotte had met that first day in Father Vecchio's office. She patted Charlotte's shoulder and held her hand there as Charlotte wept quietly. Watching this, it occurred to Turner that Charlotte was now protected on all sides from the predator who had, in his own twisted way, made this day possible. None of the three women comforting Charlotte would have suffered Father Vecchio to come near her, all of them for the same reason.

Turner had insisted on a burial in the churchyard with a headstone, not in a columbarium above-ground from which Meredith's ashes might be at risk one day of being removed. Although Charlotte was still unaware of Turner's intercession for her with the priest, when the plan for an earthen burial was explained, she gladly agreed.

When the last prayers were said at the altar and the

small party gathered in the churchyard, the open maw of earth waiting to receive the remains of the tiny, helpless child was a jarring spectacle. It fell to Charlotte to release the first handful of soil. When she did, she collapsed at the edge of the grave as if to enter it herself. Her inconsolable sobs filled the air of the garden, spilling into the street nearby, and stopping every mother there, in her tracks. They knew that sound in a woman's voice could mean only one thing—only one kind of horrific loss. They all knew. Father Vecchio and the bishop looked away as they waited.

Dory and Turner, their faces already wet with tears, cried out in unison and dropped down on their knees in the fresh earth to hold their friend. It was as if the reality of losing her daughter had only just sunk in, and despite the joy she felt that Meredith's short life had the Church's blessing, that blessing seemed less valuable now. Charlotte was jealous that God should have her little girl, who was once and for so long unwanted by him. She was no longer sure that he deserved her. From that low posture, her face peering over the edge of the grave, it seemed as if Charlotte were again descending into the abyss, only to be pulled back again by those who loved her.

It was the Fourth of July—three days after the funeral—before Charlotte emerged from the unlit shadows of her room. Turner and Dory had kept constant alternate watches during that time, offering tea, sandwiches, and—when it seemed wanted—their silent companionship. In those days, as it would be for all the days to come, Charlotte navigated as best she could along the unknown heading by which a mother learns to say goodbye to a child. It was a voyage never to be completed, a landfall never to be achieved. All she could hope for, everyone knew, was to find some moments of peace along the way. Dory and Turner did their best to give her that.

The Fourth of July in New England is not a time for sadness, and the Edgartown parade—the biggest event of the season on the Vineyard—is not a spectacle for mourners. So it both surprised and elated Dory and Turner when Charlotte said she wanted to go.

Each year the parade so widely surpasses every other celebration elsewhere on the island that the entire population comes streaming into town to experience it. Bunting hangs from every picket fence. Roses and hydrangeas abound in their greatest glory. Tweedy old denizens, like the Delanos, are called upon to display their families' finest automobiles—in the case of the Delanos, a black Rolls Royce once owned by Queen Elizabeth—and wave from gilded windows like royalty as they pass down the parade route. The town fire department shines the old pump truck to a mirror finish and wheels it out by hand. The children revel in the shooting spray, and every heart swells at the sight of the young men who have pledged to walk through fire when the time comes to save the lives of those very revelers. Car dealers—there are two—roll by in antique roadsters and the latest new models. Flower shops, church floats, summer camps, town selectmen, and—eagerly awaited each year—a woman dressed as the Statue of Liberty performing a freeform ballet on roller skates, all stream by as hundreds of cheering locals and tourists stoop on the curb or sit on folding chairs, holding melting cones of ice cream on the only dependably sweltering day of the year.

The loudest cheers always come for the bulging old men marching stern-faced, in shrunken uniforms, behind the band. There are fewer of them every year, and those that remain are given a reception that grows more rousing with time. This is followed by moments of silence at the passing of the great wooden cross, carried every year by the Knights of Columbus of St. Joseph's Church. People step forward from the crowd to touch it. Some place notes and flowers upon it. This summer, the church processional was led by His Excellency, the auxiliary bishop, who apparently had decided to make a three-day stay of his trip to the island from the mainland for Meredith's funeral. Father Vecchio, who would have been a curious sight with the gash on his head, stayed home that year.

Charlotte stared pensively at the passing cross, then at the bishop. Her thoughts were a dense, gray cloud, impenetrable even to her. For reasons she could not have expressed, she refrained from bowing her head as the cross passed by, which did not pass unnoticed by Dory and Turner. Ever since Charlotte's breakdown at the funeral, they had posted themselves constantly at the ready to help her or to restrain her, as the need might be.

But as soon as His Excellency had passed, there came in his wake an irresistible retinue of clowns, wheeling in big shoes and orange hair on tiny tricycles. Their laughter and hooting horns brought a smile at last to Charlotte's face, and she remembered she was hungry. It would be ice cream or nothing. Some sweetness, at last.

They spent fully three hours that evening, sitting on the beach beside the inlet that leads directly to the sea, watching the light fade on the stone wall of the lighthouse. The fireworks were due to start soon, but a misting rain had begun to fall. Charlotte didn't care. She insisted that they stay, and by the time the fireworks began, all three of them were soaked but quite warm in the humid air.

The rain abated, but the clouds did not. An hour after

dark, the first explosions from the fireworks barge could be heard high in the sky, but no fireworks could be seen. They were exploding well above the dense cloud bank that hung low over the island. People on the beach waited for some sign of clearing, but there was none. Gradually they all left, and except for a few drunken teenagers dancing around a bonfire fifty yards away, Dory, Turner, and Charlotte were more or less alone. When at last Charlotte announced she was ready to end what had been the first good day in a great many days, they got up and spent the next five minutes laughing and smacking the sand off of each other's legs and backsides—with color commentary about the relative size of each. Then they started for home.

They dawdled most of the way, walking arm in arm through the streets of the town. It was one of the many charming things about Edgartown that walking arm in arm down the middle of tree-lined streets was not only possible but the most pleasant way to travel. It was for Turner and Dory a victory lap of sorts. They had at last given a little child her rest and brought her mother back from the dead, and now the sap of life was rising again in Charlotte. None of them said much of anything other than to remark at the ubiquitous, overachieving blush-pink roses and the bright blue exuberance of the hydrangeas, bursting above the fence rows and glowing even now, in the street lights.

The occasional bicyclist went squeaking by in the night, staying politely out of their way. Ice cream lickers, lovers young and old, and laughing children late for bed streamed slowly past on the sidewalks, succumbing here and there to the smells of fudge, fresh bread, and sweet cakes along with the panoply of delights put out in front of each tiny storefront.

At every little café, they noticed the signs. "We have Holy Jumbo shrimp." "The Fisherman's Gulf Shrimp—

Fresh." "Miracle Jumbo Shrimp Chowder." Simon was right. There wasn't a boat in New England, much less a skiff manned by one itinerant fisherman, that could have held all the Gulf shrimp being touted as freshly caught off the coast of the Vineyard for the first time in natural history. Everywhere in the harbors, the fishing boats sat idle—their owners going bankrupt, unable to sell the scarce cod and lobster at a worthwhile price, their crews unemployed and increasingly drunk. But the ferries had doubled their service to carry the seafood trucks that streamed in every day from New Jersey.

The tackiness of so much hucksterism in this little town, so dear to her, saddened Dory and bewildered Charlotte, who couldn't understand why anyone would think there was anything holy or miraculous about catching shrimp. Dory wasn't sure what she believed. She had no more confidence that what she once thought were "miracles" were any more genuine than these signs. Had the fisherman healed her or merely misdiagnosed her? Had he come out of nowhere and walked on water to save Charlotte, or was he just an incredible swimmer? She had no answers to these questions, nor the faith to supply them.

When they reached the corner of Summer Street, Dory noticed the unmistakable black limousine idling at the curb in front of her house. As they came closer, the back window lowered with an electric hum. It was her mother.

Constance's face had a look of defeat and relief, but a smile that said clearly she was glad to see her daughter. They had spoken only briefly at the party and once on the phone since Dr. Sullivan had given her the happy, bizarre news.

"Hello, Mother."

"Hello, darling. Hello, girls."

"Hi, Mrs. Delano," Turner and Charlotte chirped

together, sounding unavoidably twelve years old.

She reached out of the window rather feebly and beckoned Dory toward her. Caressing Dory's face with her hand, she spoke with uncharacteristic emotion.

"My sweet daughter. Do you know that I love you?"

"Of course, Mom." Dory's voice cracked. "Of course I do." Dory placed her hand on her mother's shoulder. How strangely frail she felt. She had not held her mother in so many years.

"I want to have a party for you girls and this fisherman fellow of yours," Mrs. Delano continued, holding Dory's arm. "I want to hold a celebration for my child and the man who saved her."

"He won't come, Mom. They're after him all over the island. No one sees the signs anymore—not the real ones, anyway. It's not safe. He won't come. He can't come."

"You ask him for me, won't you? This family has always honored its friends. You know that."

"Yes, Mom, we have." That was as dependable a truth as any Dory knew.

"Dr. Sullivan and the others at the hospital are falling all over themselves to come up with some scientific explanation for me that won't make them look like the silly geese they are. I don't care what anyone says, whatever the reason or cause, I will not let this kindness, this—this miracle if that's what you want to call it—go unacknowledged. Your father would not hear of it, rest his soul, and neither will I. Besides, it's high time we had another summer social. I realized at your party that there are entire families I haven't spent time with in years."

The Delano estate was enormous by the standards of any time or place, but on the Vineyard it was practically a nation state. The five hundred guests invited by Constance Delano would fit comfortably in the courtyard, which was filled with fountains and would be bright with luminaries hung in the trees for the party. Ten times that number could have fit on the entire grounds without running into each other. No one who was anyone in Vineyard society could bear not to attend. All would come. Turner begrudgingly agreed to go in search of the fisherman at Simon's garage the very next day, carrying an invitation to the party and an order for a great deal of shrimp.

Simon was surprised to see Turner, given the tenor of their last meeting. She was just as surprised to be there, after the remarks he made about her—"like he was some sort of damn palm reader," she had complained. If it weren't for Dory and her mother, she never would have agreed to go.

Simon welcomed her into what would have been the main office of the garage, right next to the storage room where he slept. Enoch, the fisherman, wasn't there. As Turner expected, Simon didn't know where he was or when he'd be back. Enoch was the Clark Kent of saviors, it seemed. But when Simon heard the party was to be held in the fisherman's honor, his interest was piqued.

"How many people gonna be there?" he asked.

"What difference does it make?"

"You want shrimp?"

"God, yes. That would be wonderful. People all over are desperate to eat what he has to offer."

"How many?"

"How many shrimp?"

"How many people."

"Oh, I don't know, exactly, but five hundred invitations have gone out."

Simon stared directly at her, expressionless, while his mind was obviously elsewhere. Then he finally spoke.

"You come by here, night of the party. I'll see what I can do."

And that was that—strange as it seemed. He gave her no assurances, no directions, no whereabouts. Before she left the room, she glanced again at the table where Carlyle's *The French Revolution* had lain on her previous visit. It was gone. In its place was a smaller book—older, with a dark green hardcover. She picked it up. The cover was stamped with words that had faded almost to invisibility with time. She opened the pages and tried to read the first lines, but could not. It was *The Imitation of Christ,* by Thomas á Kempis, in the original Latin.

CHAPTER 15

Tripp Wallace knew from experience to expect Dory Delano to be late, but this was beyond the usual truancy, even for her. He had been waiting in the yacht club bar for over an hour—closer to two— when she came blowing in like a sudden squall amid a deluge of apologies.

"I'm sorry, I'm sorry, I'm so sorry," she began, getting fully three sorrys out in the short time it took to walk from the entrance door to the edge of Tripp's seat, where her words fell to breezy, quick kisses and halfhearted hugs.

She was only half-serious about the apologies. She had not so much intended to be later than usual as she had unrepentantly resigned herself to the certainty that she would be. For a woman to be late to any function was *de rigeur* in the orbit of Vineyard society as in all polite society. No respectable woman arrived on time for anything, but most certainly not a single woman arriving for a date with a single man. Ever. It was verboten.

Being on time betrayed earnestness, effort, and planning, which almost always stemmed from a fear of failure or a need to succeed—both emotions that the old-moneyed elite tried hard not to show. This, of course, was a lie. The rich feared failure acutely and pursued success pathologically. But as much as Dory loathed, or pretended to loathe, the rules of Vineyard society, she moved carefully within them most of the time, and there was no clearer rule than that a single lady should *never* be on time when meeting a single gentleman.

However, being fully two hours late well exceeded the wide bounds of propriety and veered uncomfortably close to rudeness. As a result, Dory felt uneasy when she walked into the bar. Tripp's sad puppy-dog look didn't help her faltering confidence. But she thought a vodka tonic might.

From ten feet away, she called to the bartender, Manny, to pour her a double. Manny was an old friend of an old friend, in a bar full of old friends and people she had known longer than she could remember.

She had put Tripp off about going on this sailing date for as long as she politely could, precisely because it *was* a date and the first one they'd had in a long time. There had been coffees and dinners and drinks with friends and tennis doubles and lawn parties and church bazaars—all manner of oblique interaction effectively obscured by the camouflage of small talk with other people. But for the past two months, he had been pestering to take her sailing—alone—on *Victory* for the day. The entire day.

Everyone thought of the *Victory* as Tripp's grandfather's yacht, the reason being that Tripp and his father before him hadn't staked much of a claim in life for themselves apart from the family's money. Tripp, like his father, was merely a caretaker and not a very resourceful one at that. The *Victory* was one of the many things given to him—a beautiful remnant of a gilded age of splendor and plenty.

She could picture how the day would go in her mind. It would be an Ivy League orgy, which meant there would be more booze than food, all of it poured out against a backdrop as carefully staged as a Ralph Lauren ad. Tripp Wallace was inviting a girl out for a day of sailing, just the two of them, followed by—as he had carefully described it to her—a "romantic" evening watching the sun set over the sound, enjoying a dinner made for her, by him.

Apart from never being on time, other rules were equally clear. One was that a woman didn't walk into a date like that unless she were fully *in play*—meaning available for and at least amenable to a more serious relationship with the man in question. Dory didn't see herself as *in play*. Anyone else she would have easily and quickly turned down, but Tripp was different. He wasn't a good friend so much as he was as an old friend.

He had known her as a child making sandcastles on long, sunny afternoons. He had known her as a skulking, bored teenager, wandering through late mornings in smelly tee shirts with bedhead hairdos, bad breath, no makeup, and hairy legs. He had known her as a ridiculously self-important debutante. But despite more than a few opportunities, he had never *known* her, in the Biblical sense, and for that she had always regarded him as both a gentleman and an oddity. Their whole relationship over the two decades since puberty had seemed like one long and thoughtful game of chess. But time and events had now moved her pieces into a corner.

He had never pushed her, but he also had never entirely given up the pursuit. The energy between them teetered between the platonic and the romantic without moving decidedly or for very long in either direction. That gave him a certain unattainability in Dory's eyes that kept her a little confused. He was both devilishly handsome and utterly unthreatening, which was partly what made him—and this day—so unpredictable. She had always flown in an orbit safely above anything serious with Tripp. But she sensed—*worried* would have been too strong a word—that if she allowed herself to drift into his gravitational pull, there might be no coming back.

When Dory finally permitted Tripp to come up for air, he appeared to be in his usual good spirits. "Good thing we don't have to sail with the tide," he said, raising his glass from the bar in a halfhearted gesture at a toast, while smiling to make it clear that forgiveness was close at hand.

"I have no excuse." She knew that might be the only completely true thing she'd say all day, so she let the words ring a bit.

"Thanks to Rudolf Diesel and his wonderful invention, you don't need one. I sail when a lady is ready and not a moment sooner."

The old Wallace breeding never failed. He knew, instinctively, not to interrogate her on the reasons for her two-hour delay. He might be an absolute bastard on substance, but Tripp Wallace rarely faltered on form— or at least so it had always seemed to Dory, if not to those he deemed less worthy of his charm. Knowing when to let a woman have the upper hand was the surest sign of a gentleman, and gentility suited him well. Whatever befell Tripp Wallace in this life, he seemed to push through it with a combination of sunny optimism and good manners that formed an impenetrable kind of armor.

"But I must tell you," Tripp continued, "when my grandfather was helming the *Victory,* he and all his crew would have left without you an hour ago, and if you had been my grandmother—well, I'm sure I wouldn't be here today."

There it was, Dory thought. Not fifteen seconds in, and already a clear shot across her bow. She was officially in the running to be the successor to a long line of Wallace women who were given the choice to get on board or be left at the dock.

The *Victory* was a gorgeous yawl, and never was she more beautiful than this afternoon when Tripp escorted Dory to the gangway on the yacht club pier. Marked by a sign with the ship's name carved in gold leaf, it was the same pier where men in spats and women in hoop skirts had come aboard *Victory* for outings on the Vineyard during the Wilson administration. In fact, President Wilson had been one of her earliest passengers.

But today it would be just Tripp and Dory. Without a word, she knew to take her post amidships and cast off the spring line when the engine surged into forward and the old *grande dame* began slowly to pull away from the dock. She watched Tripp go through the paces he had repeated thousands of times before. The long, mahogany bowsprit jabbed aggressively through rays of sun and shadow that lay across the harbor channel. Tripp left the helm long enough to haul the main halyard, and effortlessly, swiftly, the gleaming mainsail shot skyward along the spruce mainmast. The giant, billowing headsail unfurled above the foredeck. The ship leaned hard and dug her shoulder into the waves in a fifteen-knot breeze. They were headed to weather and already making ten knots of speed as they passed the lighthouse at the inlet. They didn't make many boats like the *Victory,* and they sure as hell didn't make them anymore.

Sailing was part of the lifeblood of the Vineyard, and sailing with Tripp in that place on that day had a kind of ease and familiarity that felt like home to Dory. She knew every shoal and eddy around the entire island like few other people did. Tripp was one of the few.

Tripp had never done anything in life nearly so well as what he did at the helm of a boat, and that was at once Tripp's glory and downfall. Legends were made aboard great sailing yachts like *Victory,* but money was made elsewhere. And money was what Tripp needed most. She knew this was partly the point.

He had made a wheedling sort of proposal to her several months before—a halfhearted, tipsy, unworthy, "if-I-asked-would-you-say-yes" kind of non-proposal, rumors of which had somehow spread among their friends on the Vineyard as a real proposal that Tripp refused to repeat and that she was rudely refusing to answer. This suited Dory just fine. A real proposal would be insufferably dramatic and require the courtesy of a real answer she didn't care to give. But if a genuine proposal of marriage were coming, the sea was where Tripp Wallace would find his courage to make it. Dory only hoped she would find the courage to turn him down with kindness.

The water was cool, but the air was warm. The sun eventually vanquished the clouds, and the ocean turned to rolling fields of royal blue tossed with white diamonds of light. Dory relaxed and soaked it all in, her back against the cabin trunk and her feet stretched aft along the teak-and-holly bench in the cockpit. She pretended to sleep as she watched Tripp carefully through dark Wayfarers. Apart from a little weathering around the eyes that only enhanced his good looks, at thirty-three he was virtually unchanged from the boy she had always known. This was both remarkable and infuriating to her. She had lost count of the flaws that had accumulated on her own body, and a new discovery seemed to come every day. It was one reason why she was still wearing shorts and a turtleneck that morning. Tripp Wallace would be a handsome man for decades to come—and a continually eligible one if he chose to be—but from the way he kept looking at Dory through eyes squinting at the sun, it was clear he had another plan.

After what must have been a full hour of silence

punctuated only by the rhythmic plunging of the bow against the waves, he finally spoke.

"I don't think I could ever live anywhere else."

"Why would you?" Dory asked, then immediately regretted the question. She knew he didn't have the money to keep up his father's estate and the life it afforded him on the island. She didn't know how much longer he could hang on. In fact, she was amazed everything hadn't come crashing down around him already. She knew somehow that Smoke had a hand in helping Tripp defy gravity a little while longer, but no one doubted that gravity would eventually hold sway.

She decided to shift the subject. "I know what you mean, actually. But I guess I've always felt differently about this place."

"Oh? How so?" They were still being painfully polite, pretending not to remember their old familiarity.

"You know—the same old story. I've never been sure about taking my place after my mother in the great pantheon of dutiful Delano women on Martha's Vineyard."

"Oh, that, yes," he said in a tone teetering between boredom and exasperation. They had had this conversation before, and it was clear he wasn't eager to have it again.

Dory, seeing his face fall, sought to embellish and improve her point. "I know it sounds childish—poor little rich girl and all that—but I get a feeling of claustrophobia whenever I imagine myself living my mother's life."

"But it seems to me you are living your mother's life. You're living in the family house in Edgartown, spending the family money, and riding on the family name wherever you go. What is this grand protest that you imagine you are having?"

"Oh yes, well said, Trafalgar Cabot Wallace the

Third."

It was a cheap shot. Tripp still had his family name, but he didn't have his family's money, and he didn't have the kind of carte blanche in life, anymore, that Dory would always know.

He was right—*damn* right—and his words burned in her ears even as she laughed them off. *There was no protest. There was no grand plan.* There were the usual boards and fashionable directorships and fundraisers and "working groups" for this or that charitable foundation, and endless auxiliaries and so on and so forth, all of which streamed out before her like a magic carpet that promised to carry her into a well-regarded, blue-haired old age in New England. But there was almost nothing about Eudora Delano that was new or special or different from all the other well-heeled girls she had known in her life—almost, that is, except for one thing. Being still single at thirty-two made her odder by the hour and was the closest thing to a conscientious objection she could muster. But apart from that dubious triumph, she had been spinning her wheels since college—just like Turner, just like Charlotte, and just like the three of them had done all summer and would probably do the next summer and the summer after that.

She had long comforted herself that there were no easy answers to her "problem." It wasn't as if she could go get a job waiting tables and take away some struggling Falmouth girl's chance at a summer job, hustling tips from tourists that Dory could buy and sell by the boatload, just to show she had a common touch. It wasn't as if she could really "succeed" at business, either. Her family money and her family name ensured that anything she touched turned to gold, which meant she couldn't even be a proper failure. The children of old money lived in a world apart, capable neither of being self-made nor unmade. It was a comfortable way station in life, and few who were in it ever wanted to leave.

She started to explain all this to Tripp, who knew perfectly what she meant and needed no explanation.

"All that may be true," she began, "but none of it matters—none of it's permanent—unless and until I'm married and settled down and popping out little towheaded children in matching fleece. That's when the nail goes in the coffin, my boy. To the manner born, to the manner bred, to the manner buried."

"Good God, Dory. You sound like a bad rewrite of *Breakfast at Tiffany's,* only you actually can afford everything they're selling at Tiffany's, so the Holly Golightly routine won't work on me."

She let the money reference pass without comment. Money was the one thing that permeated everything in their world and the one subject no one ever discussed. But they were discussing it now, which meant they were sailing off the chart.

"I'd just like a little variety, for chrissakes," Dory protested. "I'd just like for once not to do the thing that everyone expects people like me to do. I'd like someone to look back and say, 'You know that Dory Delano, she, she . . .'"

"*She coulda been a con-ten-dah,*" he said with a wry grin, in a remarkably bad Brando impersonation.

"Tripp, you can pretend all day that you don't know exactly what I mean, but I know exactly that you do, so you're not getting my goat, and that's that."

A smile gathered slowly at the corners of his mouth. He stared far out to sea over the opposite rail. She loved sparring with him, but she knew it would cost her far more than a penny for his thoughts at that moment. They were well practiced in the same, exclusive game with the same unspoken rules that each of them knew perfectly. Merely knowing that they knew made for an intimacy and an ease that Dory understood she would find within a very small circle of men. She sometimes wondered if that were enough. She was wondering this again when he threw the helm over to starboard.

"We're going to heave-to," he said. The abrupt change of conversation and the onset of movement in the cockpit was a welcome interruption, as far as Dory was concerned. When the bow crossed to leeward, Dory reflexively tightened the windward sheet and Tripp pushed the tiller back to windward, perfectly balancing the helm on an even keel and bringing the boat nearly to a standstill—the preferred attitude for serving meals on board. She hadn't noticed, but the water in the lee of Cape Poge Lighthouse was almost calm and invitingly clear. They were three miles safely off the lee shore.

"What's for lunch, Captain? Or I suppose it's dinner, by now."

"You'll have to forgive me. It's frozen mahi filets trucked over from Falmouth. No one's catching anything this summer, and I'm afraid I don't have the same pull you have with this fisherman fellow."

Dory pretended to pout for only an instant before giving way to a wide grin. She had no pull with the fisherman that she knew of, but it suited her to have Tripp Wallace think she did. She planted a kiss on his cheek and got up to go below. He followed her down the companionway steps into the galley.

Dory had to admit it: watching a man fussing over her with dish towels and measuring spoons and garlic cloves and pots and spatulas was rare and delicious fun. Tripp handed her an overfull goblet of Sauterne. She lay against the backrest and reveled in the attention, which he divided between her and the pan on the stove.

At every opportunity, he refilled her glass with unfailing promptness. She held the alternately disappearing and reappearing wine in one hand while the other was compulsively twirling her hair. Her long, tanned legs were comfortably outstretched on the starboard settee of the main cabin. The cushions were a god-awful burnt-orange plaid, having not been reupholstered since the seventies. Women hadn't often been aboard *Victory* since Mrs. Wallace's death thirty years ago, and the dark, clubby interior was long overdue for an update. Dory knew Tripp was lucky just to *have* the boat. There was barely money for maintenance, and none for cosmetic improvements.

The galley stove was wheezing in loud protest after long disuse, but in time a steaming *pièce de résistance* came forth: mahi filets lightly sautéed in a mixture of sesame oil, black pepper, honey, and soy sauce, served over a bed of rice noodles, and drizzled with pan juices. She knew it was the very best he could do (on a boat or anywhere else), and it was tolerably good, at that.

When they finished lunch, they stayed below to talk in the cabin. The Sauterne was delicious. It was artfully paired with the mahi, and although after her third glass Dory found it harder to make mental notes in general, she made one to order a few bottles for her cellar when she got back to town.

Watching her swill the last of the third bottle of wine in circles at the bottom of her glass, Tripp was wishing he'd had the foresight to bring a fourth bottle, when Dory abruptly changed the subject back to the conversation they'd been having in the cockpit.

"So, what's your game, Tripp Wallace?" She felt cocky now, and confident, which usually meant she had no reason to be either. She also had a habit of using his first and last name when she had something funny or indignant to say. This was neither.

Tripp stared in bewilderment. "My game?"

Dory would have none of it. "You know damn well

what I'm talking about—the romantic cruise, the dinner, the wine. We haven't flirted like this since college. *Where are you bound*, my good captain, sir?"

She could feel herself falling into a dangerously low orbit, just as she had feared. The wine had slowed her propulsion to the point that hovering safely above matters of the heart would no longer be possible. A controlled, crash landing was now the best she could hope for.

"Eudora, dear, I've been flirting with you steadily since the fourth grade. You just haven't been flirting back, at least not so far. But hope springs eternal."

"Oh, and what if I decided to flirt back? What then?"

She noticed his lip ever so slightly tremble. He had until now been a vision of calm, but she could see, underneath, his nervousness was growing—as if the challenge frightened him. He wasn't drunk at all. He was scared. After smiling blankly to the point of awkwardness, he finally thought of something to say.

"I would consider myself a lucky man. A lucky man indeed."

Dory was just warming up and feeling in control, which was the surest sign she had let go of the wheel. "And what if I said you were just after me for my money?"

The quivering of his lip increased to the point where it was pointedly obvious, which only added to his embarrassment. He looked away, saying nothing.

The sucker punch had nailed him. A plastic, embarrassed smile lingered on his face. He said nothing at first. Like a flattened prizefighter using the count to regain his bearings, he waited a while before coming to his feet, then decided to throw in the towel.

"I . . . I would say that I didn't blame you one bit because I know that must be exactly what you think. How could you not? I may have a rich name, but it's no secret I'm as poor as a church mouse, and you can't pay the rent with a name. If it weren't for Smoke, well . . ." His words trailed off, never revealing exactly in what way his world would end without Smoke.

This humiliation was too excruciating for Dory to watch. She rose from her recumbent luxury on the burnt-orange plaid settee cushion and gently placed her glass in the sink with the dishes Tripp had hastily dumped there.

"Sometimes I can be a jackass," she said. "Will you forgive me?" With these words she melted into his lap, folded her arms behind his neck, and—surprising even herself with that uncharacteristically kittenish move—pressed her mouth softly into his. She was even more surprised when he immediately came up for air.

"No, no apologies are needed," he said, pulling back from her lips. "You know me, Dory, and you've known people like me all your life. I wouldn't know how to *be* anyone other than who I am. Outside a very narrow and rarefied world, filled with a small and cloistered group of people, I don't know how the world works or what my place in it is. I don't have a map, Dory, and I don't have a goddamn clue. It's terrifying. It's not like I can go get a job at an oyster bar somewhere, making mimosas for aging Connecticut divorcees. It's one thing to be incompetent, quite another to be an incompetent laughingstock."

"Do you see me laughing?" Dory asked, the wine now emboldening her exponentially.

"No. I see an old friend on a mission of mercy."

She stared at him determinedly, but not long enough to think better of what happened next. Removing both arms from his neck and balancing herself uneasily on his thighs, she reached down and pulled her top and bra over her head in one fluid motion.

"Now what do you see?"

It was, in a word, awful—saved only by the fact that it was over almost before it began. Even for Dory, who had never made a point of rating such things, it barely registered on the meter. To say it was a two on the scale of ten would be a generosity owed entirely to the novelty of it, not the ecstasy of it.

First there had been the awkward, head-banging struggle to enter *Victory's* cramped forward berth together, then single file, while attempting to undress each other and remain in the moment. This was a boat built in an era when women came aboard for ceremony and champagne, not to lie down, and certainly not to lie down while having sex. Her legs fit nowhere, her hips fit nowhere, her ass fit nowhere, and her flailing knees did bruising battle with every corner and knob.

She remembered, in passing, feeling grateful and then strangely curious as to how and why, exactly, he had a supply of condoms stored neatly in a rack above the berth, clearly in anticipation of just such a spontaneous and rare moment. But her curiosity was short-lived. No sooner had she unwrapped one and got it ready than he shrunk away beneath it. "Stage fright," he mumbled sheepishly. Reflexively, she excused and consoled him with undaunted affection. He would rally again after a few more minutes of this, only to retreat again in the few seconds of distraction it took her to try to sheath him. After three attempts, unwilling to admit defeat and intoxicated enough not to realize the risk of victory, she abandoned all prefatory efforts at the condom and worked her way on top of him before the moment passed a fourth time. She felt his very soft and receding presence inside her for what could not have been more than ten seconds before he moaned and exploded, more on her than in her. Already a gooey mess, she saw no point in her running to the head. She simply lay there in his arms, roused to wakefulness for the moment.

"You're rather goal-oriented," she said, immediately wishing to have it back. She was nowhere near an orgasm herself and likely never would have arrived there. It was unfair to punish him.

"I'm afraid the excitement was a bit much for me. It's not every day a beautiful woman drags me into the hold of my own ship and ravishes me."

"Oh, no? From the storehouse of prophylactics you have back here, buddy, I would think it was a regular occurrence."

His face reddened, and he stammered when he spoke. "That . . . that, yes—well, you can see what poor, poor use I make of them."

She decided to let the rubber mystery rest. Tripp Wallace had a minor reputation as a bit of a player, although her experience of the last fifteen minutes suggested it was undeserved. No matter. She had known him long enough, and she believed that, in the main, she knew him well enough not to be overly worried about the rougher, outer edges of his character.

Lying there in the veeberth, she gradually became more aware of the wonderfully cradle-like motion of the boat as it nodded rhythmically on long, rolling waves. The tide of wine was slowly ebbing, leaving exposed something that had been on her mind for a long time. It had been there, in fact, for fourteen years. She had wanted to say something to Tripp about it all that while, but she had never found the reason or the right moment. Now, in the aftermath of the intimacy they had finally shared, after all those years, she had found both.

The subject of her concern was the reason, she had long assumed, why Tripp had never wholeheartedly pursued her before. For her part, the casual disinterest she exhibited most of the time, until that day, was largely a front and a defensive measure. The truth was she felt guilty about something. It was something she might never have told him except for the nagging and growing feeling that he already knew and thought less of her because of it. The day's romantic events seemed to have changed all that, and she believed it was time to speak.

"Tripp." She called his name softly from the spot where her head rested on his shoulder. He didn't answer.

She pulled herself up to see his face. He was wide awake.

"Tripp, I need to tell you something, and then I want to ask you something."

He gave her a bewildered, lamb-to-the-slaughter stare. "Fire away."

"You remember that weekend for the formal at Williams, when Smoke came up and we all spent the night at your place? We came back late. I fell asleep on your couch."

His expression and the smooth tone of his voice did not waver. "I remember every moment with you, Dory, including that one."

"Did Smoke ever speak of it afterward?" She felt his body tense slightly beneath her. He was slow to answer, and when he spoke, his tone was more serious than before.

"No, no he didn't." It had to be a lie. Dory realized this when the obvious next question—*Why do you ask?*—never came.

She decided to come to the point. "Did . . . did you know that I slept with him that night?"

"Oh? How could I know that?" Again, the unchanged expression, the voice devoid of any note of surprise. He had posed a question to avoid an answer. They were circling each other like snakes.

"Well, I'm not sure . . . I'm not even sure that *I* know. I just remember waking up on top of him on the couch, and neither of us was wearing any clothes. I was pretty drunk, I guess, but . . ." She paused there, inexplicably.

Obligingly, he prompted her. "But what?"

"I knew I'd had sex that night with someone."

"How do you know if you don't remember?"

"Because it was running down my leg in the morning, just like it is right now."

It was an abrupt, hurried, and embarrassed answer to a stupid question that she couldn't resist zinging him for asking. As soon as she said it, she sought to reassure him.

"I was hoping it had been you—it would have been wonderful if it had been you. But you weren't there in the morning. Smoke was. He never said anything, which was all the weirdness I could stand, but weirder still was the look on his face. I knew it had been him, not you, but I didn't know what to say. I mean—all I know is that I woke up holding him close, like a lover, not an attacker, revolting as that sounds to say. I'm a little afraid of the man, to tell you the truth. Something about him. He's a weirdo."

She let the impact of her words settle for a moment, like a large rock tossed in a small pond, before she continued. "I know I had a lot to drink that night at the formal, and I just felt like I'd betrayed you, Tripp—that I had lied to you and made a fool of you, somehow. Even though we had never been together in that way, I think I wanted to be without really knowing it, and no matter what, I was your date. I should *never* have slept with your friend. I was just too afraid, all these years, to hurt you by telling you about something I was wasn't sure you knew. But the longer it went on, I came to resent you in a way, I guess, that you lorded this sin over me—even unwittingly."

She paused again, now waiting for the conversation naturally to fill in from his end, but there was only silence, punctuated by the faint warbling of a horn, five blasts in succession, likely from a tug leaving Edgartown Harbor far to the east.

"So, that's why I'm asking now, did you know?"

"What does it matter, Dory, after all these years?"

Again, a question answered with a question.

"It doesn't matter, unless you tell me it does, I suppose."

Tripp rolled over and sat up on one elbow—all the room the cramped cabin would afford him. He seemed resigned to the fact that he would have to answer her, and he clearly wanted to do so from a reinforced position. Again, he did not speak immediately. In his dark eyes and somber expression, a decision seemed to be grinding its way slowly to the fore. If he was in a contest with his better angels, victory was by no means certain for either side. Finally, he formed his words slowly, in the measured prose of a diplomatic cable.

"I know I loved you then. I know I love you now. I have always loved you and always will. Smoke is jealous of that affection, only because he's incapable of feeling it himself, and for that reason can't tolerate anyone's happiness, least of all mine. So, to answer your question—no, I didn't actually know, and no, I'm not surprised, and yes, I could have guessed, and no, I don't care."

She reached out and caressed his cheek, in a gesture of peace and forgiveness. A look of sadness hung about his face, and he dropped his eyes from hers. She didn't know it—she had no way of knowing—but that had been his one chance to tell her the truth that had haunted him for years and that haunted him still. Her question, in that moment, had been to him a flickering of light, a slim and fleeting hope of escape. He longed to seize it, but he could not. When he looked up at her again, there was new fire and defiance in his eyes.

"Eudora, who do you think Smoke is?"

It was a strange question. Her answer was stranger still. "Who he is, or what he is?"

If he would have answered—if he could have answered—she would never know, because at that precise moment the entire vessel shuddered hard and lurched forward, nose down, to a sudden stop. It was a familiar and sickening feeling to a sailor. They had run hard aground.

Tripp scrambled out on deck. "Oww, fuck!" He looked forward, across the bow, to the surf crashing beneath it onto the beach. "That's not possible! We were six miles from land, easy, and drifting seaward. There's no way we could have drifted ashore!"

Dory came running on deck behind him, utterly unaware for the moment that neither of them was wearing any clothes. She did not at first recognize where they were in relation to the island, looking shoreward from the sea.

"We forgot about the tide," she explained. "It's been coming in for the past four hours, and the wind has clocked to the north."

Tripp went forward to douse the headsail and throw out an anchor. Dory's attention was drawn to the figure of a person, perhaps two miles away, on a high bluff. The noise of a horn—five short blasts—came from the same location. Someone was attempting to signal a boat coming too close to shore that it was running into danger. Whoever it was must have been unable to tell that they were already aground.

Dory grabbed a pair of binoculars, the better to see

the person who had tried to warn them. She recognized her immediately. It was Rutla staring back at her, through her own pair of binoculars, and holding an air horn in her hand. Dory watched Rutla drop her binoculars to her waist in an expression of astonishment that the naked woman staring back at her from the deck was Dory.

The *Victory* had drifted ashore with the tide onto the beach at Eel Pond, not more than a mile from the Delano estate. "Gotta go," Dory shouted, heading swiftly down the companionway steps without waiting for an answer from the ridiculous man sliding back and forth on his bare bottom at the bow, trying to secure the anchor.

"Gotta go?" he shouted back at her, incredulously. "Wait! What the hell?"

"Yep, it's pumpkin time. I'm outta here, pal." Dory shouted more loudly, so he could hear her from where she had gone, behind the closed door to the head in the main cabin. Of course, there was no toilet paper to be found. She was looking for something to rub off the sticky, drying aftermath from the skin between her thighs and knees. When she opened the cabinet above the sink, a small brown prescription bottle tumbled out. According to the label, it was dispensed only the day before to one Wallace, Trafalgar, III, Viagra, 100 mg tablets, quantity: four. There was only one tablet left.

"In one day?" she wondered out loud. "Humph! Lot of good it did him."

She put the bottle carefully back and retrieved a hand towel from the shelf above. It was one more strange moment in a strange afternoon of the strangest summer of her life. Why Tripp had gone to the trouble of coming with "ammunition," she could easily imagine: he had been planning to *score*—or more likely, as she followed the logic of it, hoping to score and afraid he

196

might not. Either way, it was perversely flattering but more than a little creepy to think that he had gone to so much trouble—condoms, Viagra, Sauterne—to prepare for his conquest. It was a little worrisome but also too funny for her not to laugh, considering that only one of the three had actually worked.

She emerged from the companionway in short order, dressed and purse in hand. The boat was close enough to shore that if she timed it right, she could jump in and get wet only up to her knees.

"I can't believe it," now shouted Angry Naked Man. "You're leaving me here high and dry?"

"High, yes, but not exactly dry. Don't worry, Columbus. The tide is coming in. You'll be off the bar and sailing back to Edgartown in an hour. You'll be back in time to drown your sorrows over dinner at the club."

A look of panic came across his face, as if he saw an opportunity getting away. "Dory, look, I'm really sorry about this. I know this is such terrible form—"

"Nonsense." Her face softened. "I've had a wonderfully romantic day, Tripp." It was a lie, but a worthy lie.

"And now you've been the perfect gentleman and parked your yacht right at my doorstep. What more could a girl ask for?"

She climbed over the railing. *Victory* was so hard aground that it felt like she was standing on a concrete pier. She doubted he'd be off the bar before morning.

"Oh, well. Tootles!" She leaped, squealing, into the waist-deep surf, landing steadily on both feet, and proceeded to walk up the beach. She could see Rutla still standing in the same spot but no longer bothering to strain for a closer look.

It was almost time for dinner. She would be welcomed home, of course, and apart from a few discerning and disapproving looks, Rutla would reveal nothing of what she had seen for all eternity. That day was hardly the first time she had witnessed a member of the Delano family bare-assed on the beach, and it would almost certainly not be the last.

CHAPTER 16

Plans for Mrs. Delano's party were a welcome diversion for Dory and, for Turner and Charlotte, an insight to a way of life all but forgotten in the rest of the world. Constance Delano was a throwback—way back. Her house, her tastes, her manner—and, as a consequence, the lives of everyone who worked for her—were something out of F. Scott Fitzgerald. He had, naturally as one would expect, stayed at the Delano estate once for a week in the summer of 1923.

Rutla ruled over the party preparations like a tyrant, and they were running like clockwork. She had ten days in all to get ready. Late July would be hot but dry—the best time for an outdoor gala. Dory's mother had insisted that Dory and her friends stay at the house, ostensibly to help with the planning and preparation, but in reality this was Constance Delano's long-awaited opportunity to reconnect with the daughter who had drifted away from her and who, these last ten years, had remained mostly at arm's length.

They had their differences, Dory and her mother. But Dory's brush with death—whatever it was, or wasn't—had been a wake-up call for Mrs. Delano. She always gave Dory her space, and Dory had seemed to need quite a lot of it, but now she was drawing her back to her side and planned never to let her go.

An essential part of the plan, as far as Mrs. Delano was concerned, was Tripp Wallace. He was a Vineyard boy (all men were boys now, to Constance Delano), and the perfect match for Dory. It was no secret that his family's fortune was failing, but breeding and manners never fail, and he had both in spades. Dory's inheritance would amply supply a good life for them and generations of their children, if only her affection could open the way.

To aid love in the direction in which it should go was the bounden duty of every well-born mother on the Vineyard and none more so than Constance Delano. Tripp Wallace would be invited to the party and paired with Dory throughout the evening at every opportunity. In the meantime, despite Mrs. Delano's pretense that Dory was to be put to work planning a proper party to regale all of Vineyard society with the story of her remarkable healing, Rutla consigned her, as if she were convalescing, to a lawn chair beside the shimmering blue pool. This was nestled in a sloping, emerald lawn that ran all the way to the edge of the sea. Despite being in the open middle of everything, it was one of the most beautiful spots on the island.

Turner was only too happy to keep Dory company, and Charlotte—though not yet quite herself and unlikely ever to be so again—welcomed these weeks of peace and quiet. There were, after all, far worse ways to grieve for what was lost than sitting by a pool, being offered lemon cucumber dill sandwiches and tonics by doting servants.

It is a habit of those society women who imitate whenever possible the affectations of the French, to be blasé about their bodies, but it was not a habit that Dory had ever warmed to. She did not often enjoy the pool, but when she did, she was as well buttoned as a parson's daughter. Charlotte was mostly of the same mind, and, although she sometimes wished she were not, she saw no benefit in changing. Turner, however, who throughout her life had been drawn to every mannerism of wealth like a moth to the flame, wasted no time in enjoying the pool *au naturel.* This passed utterly unnoticed by Rutla, the German, and was suffered decorously by the grounds-keeping staff, who knew to suffer everything decorously. Dory and Charlotte endured the display in their swimsuits, smirking and eye rolling at this, yet another one of Turner's many and inevitable foibles, while mentally cataloging her every feature and flaw.

At the end of the day, after dinner, they would go down to the beach and walk the long expanse between jetties that demarcated the Delano property. In the middle was a pier that went far out into Eel Pond. When the tide was low, they would dig for clams and find them by the score. The groundskeepers would bring tin and wood and burlap and prepare a clambake until the aroma of roasting corn and steaming clams brought the entire household inexorably to the beach, where they would sit late into the night, warming themselves by the fire until it flickered into coals. When the tide in the pond was high, the three friends went skittering about in an antique Herreshoff twelve-and-a-half sloop. It had belonged to one of the Henry Cabot Lodges as a boy and had been passed down to the Delanos when the time came to teach Dory to sail. She spent her summers on it from the time she was ten and would head far out into the ocean. Now it sat mostly idle, waiting for the next child. It was a boat made to last, like everything in New England. Life there for the watermen was not easy. The working classes were built for hardship, and they built things accordingly.

The day of the party dawned to clear skies and calm

winds—what Constance Delano had been praying for. Turner spent a leisurely morning and afternoon getting herself ready, until she left herself too little time to keep her appointment with Simon. She went racing out the door at six o'clock. The party started in an hour. She had told Mrs. Delano that the appearance by the fisherman was by no means certain, but if he were coming she would find out "the night of." There was nothing to be done about it, and the party would go on regardless, so Mrs. Delano made peace with that plan.

Turner saw the blue flashing lights reflecting in the trees on the road just outside Tisbury. Even driving Charlotte's laggard of a car, she had been going fifty in a thirty-mile-per-hour zone. She cursed her luck in hitting a speed trap on this night of all nights and slammed on the brakes, hoping to slow down enough to avoid a ticket. But the police were not looking for her.

She parked the car and walked toward the men. Two officers were standing outside the garage, with Simon. Another man dressed in a white dinner jacket was with them. She had seen him somewhere before. She recognized him as she got closer. It was Smoke.

One of the officers sounded impatient. He was raising his voice at Simon, while the other one looked ready to arrest him.

"Harboring a fugitive," the officer shouted. "Operating a business without a permit, handling hazardous waste without a license, trespassing on bank property, maintaining an unlawful dwelling—I can keep listing the charges, and we can go down to the station to talk to the magistrate, or you can just tell us where your friend is."

Smoke looked serene, even laconic. Simon looked frantic. His eyes darted back and forth among his interrogators. When Turner walked up, he did not seem to recognize her.

"Ma'am, you'll need to step back from the suspect," one of the officers said.

"Suspect? Suspected of what?"

"She's all right, Howard," Smoke interrupted, and reached a hand around to touch Turner's shoulder.

"Hello, Turner. Looking forward to seeing you at the party. What brings you out here?"

"I came here to meet the fisherman."

"The fisherman" had already become enough of a cult figure on the island that those two words needed no explanation.

"That's funny," Smoke said, laughing, "so are these officers, but Simon here says he doesn't know the guy."

Turner looked at Simon. His eyes were now pleading with her, but she felt no pity. This was the man who had said her future was shrouded in shadow. Now his own future was looking pretty dark, and she found herself relishing the irony.

"The fisherman's name is Enoch, and this is his friend," Turner told the officers. "Simon, tell them you know Enoch."

"That's a lie!" Simon spit out the words. "I've never seen the man."

"But you do know him, Simon. You told me so."

She then turned to the officers. One was tall; the other was shorter than Turner. The taller officer was taking notes, but the shorter one was clearly in charge.

"What difference does it make, anyway?" she asked. "Whatever fishing regulations the guy has violated, he's done nothing worse than all the other poachers out there. You guys are not the fisheries police, so why the third degree?"

"We're not here on a fisheries matter, ma'am," the shorter officer replied.

Smoke decided to explain.

"There is credible evidence that this man they call the

fisherman is actually a dangerous sexual predator," he said calmly, as if he already had the whole story figured out. "He lures women to buy seafood from him for the purpose of assaulting them. We know what he did to Dory."

"To Dory—how?"

"The hospital informed me—I mean, the police. The hospital has a duty to report incidents of a sexual nature."

"But there were no charges filed. Why—"

"As you know, there rarely are in such cases. Victims often don't report the crime, out of shame or fear."

"Victims? What victim?"

"We understand from the history given to us by the doctors that you were a witness, Turner, and they were actually going to come question you, too. Now that you're here, why don't you tell these officers what you saw?"

Turner saw Simon begin to relax only slightly, now that the police's attention was turning toward her, but his eyes remained wide with fear. She paused, realizing that the truth would be exactly what Smoke wanted to hear, and that a lie might land her in jail.

"It was nothing," she said. "He touched her gently, and then she fainted."

"Touched her—where? How?" Smoke asked. The tall policeman kept taking notes.

"Is this your investigation, Smoke, or theirs?"

"Ours, ma'am," said the tall one. "But we need to know the details, as hard as it might be for you to give them."

Turner sensed a railroad job in the making, and she could already hear the train whistle blowing. There seemed to be no way out.

"It's not hard to tell at all," she lied. "He didn't hurt her. He just touched her—that's it. That's all! It was no

204

big deal." Another lie. It was a huge deal to Turner, at the time, and, but for Dory, she would have gone to the police herself.

"Touched her where, how?" the taller officer asked.

It was a question with no good answer, which made Turner angry. She hated being trapped. She resented it. Without thinking, she suddenly grabbed the taller officer's hands and pressed them to her breasts.

"Like this, you *idiot.*" He pulled his hands abruptly back as his face reddened with anger. He began to reach behind his back for handcuffs, but when Smoke touched his shoulder the officer looked up and, seeing Smoke shaking his head, seemed to think better of the idea.

"What you're describing—and demonstrating— would be an assault," the shorter one said.

"What are you all, the spin-the-bottle patrol?" Turner was taunting them both now, trying to change the subject. She knew that what the fisherman had done was, at least in legal terms, an assault. In fact, that's exactly how she saw it at the time. But for some reason she still didn't understand, that's not how Dory saw it then, and it wasn't how Dory saw it now. And what mattered to Turner was Dory—not these cops and their protocols, not the fisherman, and certainly not Smoke.

The officers ignored her question. The shorter one asked her again. "We'll need you to take us through what happened in detail, ma'am. We can do this here, or we can do it down at the station. Your choice."

Turner resigned to tell them what they wanted to hear.

"He slipped the straps of her dress off her shoulders and pushed the top of her dress down. Then he held her breasts in both hands for a moment and whispered something to her."

"My God," Smoke exclaimed. The insincerity of his

shock was as obvious as the faint smile beginning at the corners of his mouth. Turner glanced at Simon, who clearly wished he were anyplace but where he was at that moment.

"Was she wearing a bra?" the shorter officer asked, missing the look of incredulity on Turner's face.

"It's July in Martha's Vineyard," she answered, petulantly. "Is your wife wearing a bra under her sundress in this heat?"

The shorter one began to speak but stumbled on his words. Smoke seized the opportunity to jump back in.

"What did he whisper to her?"

"You'll have to ask her."

"Dory didn't tell you?" Smoke persisted, knowing Turner certainly would have asked.

"'Cancer.' All he said was 'cancer.'"

With this, Simon bolted from the huddle where the officers and Smoke were standing and began running for the marsh across the road.

"Stop!" the officers yelled in unison, and ran in pursuit. Smoke looked at Turner, as if she were to blame for the interruption, then took off after them.

Turner watched Simon. He was running like his life depended on it. His fear seemed ridiculous given that he wasn't even the man the police were looking for, but he ran as if he were.

The two officers and Smoke got far enough into the marsh to fill their shoes with water and watch Simon hopping from bank to bank, widening the gap between them. By the time they sloshed their way back to the cars, Turner was gone.

CHAPTER 17

The party was sure to be a bust, now. The expected appearance of the fisherman to take a bow for saving Constance Delano's only daughter was not advertised or even mentioned, publicly, but enough people knew of Constance's hope to present him to Vineyard society that it had created quite the buzz leading up to the event. As Turner returned from her bizarre encounter with Smoke, Simon, and the police, she dreaded breaking the news that the guest of honor would be absent.

Constance took the news with more bewilderment than disappointment. She was not used to people refusing her invitations—in fact, no one ever had—and it simply had never occurred to her that anyone she might ask to join her at the premier social event of summer in New England might actually take a pass. But Enoch, whoever he thought he was or was pretending to be, appeared to have done just that.

"Very well," Constance said, noticing the relief on Dory's face. "We don't need to announce anything about it, since nothing was ever said formally of his coming. But if people ask, I will tell them he healed my daughter, because that is what I believe, whether he shows up or not. I'm just disappointed we won't have the shrimp that everyone's raving about, to serve."

Constance was reminded by this thought that she had not given Rutla a direct order of any kind in almost twenty minutes, and she disappeared into the kitchen to remedy the omission.

"God, what a relief," Dory exhaled after her mother was gone.

"I know what you mean," Turner answered.

"No, you don't," Charlotte replied. "Both of us were about to be put on display like two aliens from outer space—living proof of the miracles wrought by the shrimp god. I felt ridiculous just imagining what I'd say. Now at least I can enjoy Dory's party in peace."

Turner was dreading what she had to tell Dory. She decided to get it over with.

"It's just as well he isn't coming, but if he had, I don't think anyone would be talking about you, Charlotte."

It was one of Turner's coy little prologues, and neither Dory nor Charlotte was in the mood for it. They stared at her blankly until she continued.

"They're trying to arrest him, Dory—because of you."

"Because of me? Why?"

"For sexual assault."

Dory's face seemed to light up with an electric charge when she heard this, and Turner moved quickly to quell the rage.

"It wasn't me, Dory. I didn't tell them. They already knew. I swear it."

People started arriving around seven o'clock. Rutla was spinning and spitting out orders like a Gatling gun, but despite the high level of anxiety in the kitchen, the staff circulating among the guests and attending the banquet table were a model of decorum. Everything was impeccably and beautifully arranged, except for a large empty place on the buffet table in front of which was a card containing the words "Fresh Vineyard Jumbo Shrimp," written in calligraphy.

Dory spotted Smoke circulating among the guests far across the lawn. He was in the stone sculpture garden planted in heirloom roses that he pretended to be admiring. He was eyeing the crowd for a sign of someone. Dory knew who he was looking for. He turned when he heard footsteps on the gravel walkway behind him, and smiled at her as if they were old friends, which they most certainly were not.

"I don't recall sending you an invitation, Smoke."

"Why, Dory! How wonderful to see you!"

"What are you doing here?"

"Well, I came to see you, of course—our miracle girl—at the invitation of your mother. I'm a friend to many old families on the Vineyard, you know, and the Delanos are one of them."

"Yeah, well, I'm not one of them. Turner told me what you're cooking up."

"Yes—Turner. Very bad form to slip away from the police when they haven't finished asking their questions. Makes a person look guilty as sin. But not to worry, Dory. They know you're the victim, here, and so do I."

"I'm not pressing charges, you asshole."

Dory's temper was making it impossible for Smoke to keep up even the appearance of gentility that he usually wore like a mask. He looked at Dory more critically, now. She was about to become an annoyance to him.

"The police don't need you to press charges, Dory. They need to find a man who is wanted for questioning in connection with a number of suspicious activities—and who also happens to be costing me a lot of goddammed money."

Dory knew Smoke well enough to know he didn't give a damn about anyone grabbing her boobs, and that given the opportunity and an alibi, he would do worse to her or any other woman who happened to be unlucky enough to cross his path. She also knew that he never invested his time or energy in something that didn't offer him an immediate and substantial return.

"What do you want, Smoke?"

The smile returned to Smoke's face.

"Well, right now I'm dying for some of that fresh Gulf shrimp. Do you have any?"

They both spotted Dory's mother waving with a great smile on her face and beckoning them toward her. Dory reluctantly took Smoke's arm. Tripp Wallace had arrived.

In her bare feet, carrying gold lamé slippers in one hand and lifting her dress with the other, Turner walked the beach spreading out from the Delano estate. She had wandered away from the main lawn, hoping to avoid everyone. Smoke's questioning of her still hung in the air, like a pall. Dory was, inexplicably, still mad at her, and Charlotte just wanted to be left alone so as to avoid anyone who might be coming to see the "suicide girl." The sun was dropping below the hill, and the entire bay of Eel Pond was cast for the moment in a golden glow. Turner walked out onto the pier to watch the sunlight shimmering on the water in the distance.

It was such a beautiful place, and the beautiful life she supposed Dory had lived there, growing up in the bosom of such a respectable, comfortable family, seemed so far beyond her grasp. Apart from the four years she spent on scholarship at Smith, respectability had eluded Turner her whole life. At times it seemed just near enough for her to believe she might actually attain it, but some miscalculation, some misjudgment—

usually in the form of the next wrong man—always intervened. Dory was right, she told herself as she looked far out to sea. She was no more a "Bennett & Donald author" than she was an astronaut. There wasn't a junior copy editor at Bennett & Donald who even knew her name.

It was nearly dark everywhere in the pond now, but far out beyond the inlet, in the open ocean, some light from the distant horizon remained. She saw there what first appeared to be a pod of dolphins until, moving closer and becoming clearer, it took on a different form. It was a man rowing a boat. The wooden prow lifted up slowly over the rolling waves then disappeared beneath them for several minutes of slow progress toward shore, until at last man and boat entered the darkness of the pond and disappeared altogether. After he was gone, Turner found herself wondering about the many people on the Vineyard whose lives depend on the economy of the sea and how much they must do every day merely to survive, while people in the paper economy—which described every one of the guests at the party she couldn't bring herself to attend—had time to swill champagne and make small talk. She was still wondering about this when she heard the quiet impact of wood on wood beneath the pier. Looking down at the water, she saw a man sitting in a boat. Beside him was a small basin, covered in burlap.

It was him.

He looked up at her as if he knew her. She certainly recognized him. After that day in Tisdale, when she hit him in the face, she could never have forgotten him.

He was the same—skin smooth and deeply tanned; arms and legs toned and athletic, but not especially muscular; a simple, dark tee shirt; no shoes. He seemed to fit perfectly into his skin. Despite the growing shadows, his blue eyes were iridescent with light. She did not find him particularly handsome, but his presence was somehow compelling. She couldn't take her eyes off him, and for the first time in a long time, she found herself at a loss for words.

"Simon sent me," the man finally said.

"You're Enoch, aren't you?" Turner asked, with utterly no purpose other than to say his name. She knew who he was.

"I am. And you are Turner."

There was a calm in his voice, and a certitude in his manner, that Turner found excruciating. She felt a strong impulse to run from him or toward him, but staying anywhere in between seemed intolerable.

He reached into the boat and lifted the basin covered in burlap and ice.

"Simon said you wanted shrimp."

Turner was jarred from her reverie.

"Why . . . why, yes. Yes! That's wonderful! I didn't think—we didn't think—you would be able to make it."

"He said you needed enough for five hundred. I'm sorry I couldn't bring you enough. The catches are starting to dwindle. I'm finding fewer in my nets every day."

"Oh," Turner sighed, not expecting this admission of vulnerability from the man her friend believed possessed unbounded power. "I'm sorry to hear that. I . . . I hope things get better for you." She sounded like a Hallmark card.

He did not make a move to step up onto the dock, and the reason was clear.

"I know you can't stay," she said. "I know they're looking for you—and now for Simon. It's not safe."

He neither agreed nor disagreed. The look in his eyes was more one of indifference to her point, but he remained in the boat.

Turner realized she had nothing with which to pay

him. "If you wait here, I can go to the house and get some money."

"No need. I will see you again," he said, as if it were more of a promise than a plan.

Turner thanked him and wished him well. Lifting the basin, she noticed that it was considerably lighter and contained far fewer shrimp than she had expected, but at least she would now make good on her promise to Dory's mother, and there was no small consolation in that.

Walking up the pier and trying to hold the basin far enough in front of her to avoid ruining her dress, Turner heard the "tock-tock" sound of the oars clicking in the locks of the fisherman's boat. She had a sudden impulse to look back, to see him again, and when she did, she found that he was exactly in the same place she had left him and was looking straight at her.

"Some people say . . ." she began, timidly, "some people say you are a predator."

He made no answer to this statement, nor did she expect one, because it was only half of what she had started to say.

"Other people say you are some sort of prophet, and that you have power. That God is on your side."

He stared at her silently, for a moment, then asked, "Who do you say I am?"

Turner couldn't remember why she didn't answer, and why she simply walked away. Perhaps, she thought, she didn't have an answer. Perhaps she was afraid of the answer she might give. But whatever the reason, she felt the impulse to leave, which is what she did. Five minutes later, with the long-awaited delivery of fresh shrimp, she walked into Rutla's kitchen like a conquering hero.

Upon examining the basin that Turner had brought up from the dock, Rutla discovered there were only about a hundred shrimp—far too few, but the fact that they were enormous in size compensated somewhat for their number. Once they were boiled and braised to a delicious pinkness, it was Rutla's genius to cut them into fifths and serve each section wrapped in bacon on top of a sliced, toasted baguette—enough for each guest to have just one.

Constance Delano was dizzy with excitement—a mood she had rarely been known to experience, much less display. She seized the microphone from the band and announced the arrival of the "shrimp from the fisherman" with all the giddiness of a prom queen. People rushed as politely as polite people normally do, to get into position.

Rutla's finished creations were proudly carried out into the party on large silver trays by waiters, who went forth two-by-two—one with shrimp, one with champagne. The crowd descended on each offering with equal enthusiasm, but being aware that the shrimp was the more precious commodity and in short supply, they began breaking their portions into twos and threes and fours or fives to make sure everyone around them got a taste, with the unexpected result that the waiters returned to the kitchen with seemingly more servings than when they went out. The champagne, however, was not so carefully dispensed. The Delano estate, which had long been known for its wine cellar and the most extensive collection of French champagne in all of New England, almost ran out that night. But by the time the feeding frenzy was over, everyone who was left standing was too giggling drunk to care.

Turner watched this spectacle with no small amount of pride. But as delighted as she was with herself for reeling in the much-sought-after fisherman and his catch for the party, she still knew almost no one there, and Dory and Charlotte had seemed to be elsewhere all evening. Her work was done. She began to sense the release of a great deal of tension, and with it she noticed she felt a little tired, even though it was just nine o'clock. One of the many niceties of being a guest at the Delano estate was the privacy afforded by so large a house, and for Turner that meant being able to shut herself in her room to read or write in complete solitude.

The screen of her laptop again gave off its welcome glow in the darkness, and this time the words flowed effortlessly. Sitting in front of the window in her room that overlooked the south lawn, Turner could hear the party guests milling about, the hum of their conversation more exuberant now than before. It was a pleasant white noise that posed no distraction from her task. She typed out a title, "The Feeding of the 500," spelled numerically to make it fit on one line, and began telling the story of what was, at that very moment, playing out on the grounds of the Delano estate. It was to be another thrilling miracle wrought by Enoch, the fisherman. The excitement of his unexpected arrival, and the filling goodness of that holy food, made for great prose, but not quite enough drama to suit Turner's sense of grandeur. As she was just about to click the button that said "publish," she moved the cursor again to the title and added another zero to the number. Then, she was done. Then, it was perfect, and up the story went into the ether, like a prayer.

Turner didn't remember going to bed, but the laptop still beside her on the bed meant she must have fallen asleep at the wheel. The room was dark all except for the dial of the clock radio, which read 11:00. There was almost no sound other than the distant laughter coming from the road. Partygoers were saying their last goodbyes at the gate. The lush, pastoral grounds around the main house appeared a deep sea-green in the starlight. Only the odd tiki lamp lingered still lit. Looking out the window at this strange world, Turner could see the main garden. She wondered whether Dory and Charlotte, whom she hadn't seen in hours, had convened there around an unfinished bottle of wine as the three of them had so often done in recent weeks, but they were not there. The only other light was the soft glow coming from the underwater lamps in the pool. The night was winding down.

In the still air of the room, Turner could smell stale champagne on her breath and something else, faintly, that was equally unwelcome. She tried to pinpoint the smell by trailing it with her nose around the room. But everywhere it smelled the same, until she realized it was coming from her. She pulled the midriff of her dress up to her face and took a long whiff.

Dead shrimp.

Some of the ice from the basin had gotten on her clothes, and with it the smell of shrimp—now neither fresh nor holy. It would mean another needless dry cleaning bill she could ill afford. In the closet behind her were at least a hundred dresses Mrs. Delano had bought for Dory that could not fit in the closets containing the other two hundred dresses Dory owned but never wore. Turner thought to leave the one she was wearing on the back of the door and take another—Mrs. Delano would never miss it—but the smell of low tide, fainter but still noticeable, remained on her skin. Only a bath would do.

She slipped her underwear off and shrugged into one of the plush terry-cloth robes that hung in every guest room of the Delano house. It was nicer than any hotel on the island with the exception of the shortage of bathrooms. Fresh water is scarce on a saltwater island,

and the means of getting it are scarcer still when the place was built two centuries ago, which explained why there were eight bedrooms but only one bathroom on the second floor.

She tiptoed her way barefoot down the hall. The sound of talking in the great room was clearer outside her room than in it. Female voices she didn't recognize were all atwitter about some subject Turner was only too happy to avoid. She didn't particularly mind being around the kind of society women who populated Dory's world, but keeping up with their expectations of how a young woman should converse and deport herself was like an Olympic sport. Turner was glad not to be engaged in that competition at that hour. She headed directly for the bathroom at the end of the hall.

The bathroom was never locked—there were only women in the house—but it was locked that night, and the sound of someone retching inside was unmistakably male.

"Are you all right in there?" Turner asked.

There was no verbal reply—only another upheaval of the poor creature's stomach. He didn't seem close to being done with the task at hand.

Finding her way to the downstairs bathroom at that moment would have required Turner to make an entrance in her bathrobe during the social event of the season among the high-born ladies of Martha's Vineyard whom she could hear chattering in the parlor. She thought not.

But outside the French doors at the other end of the first floor, in sight of no one, was the pool. All the tables had been folded and put away for the night. The area was almost completely dark and deserted. The warm water of the pool—heated even in the summertime—would offer enough of a bath to stop her from smelling like a dying squid.

Although the pool, deck, and surrounding gardens were empty, there were still a few too many partygoers mingling about for Turner's courage, even if they were a hundred yards away. This was just as well, she thought. There was no rush. The stars were out. It was an unusually warm evening for summer on the Vineyard, and Rutla, in her unfailing prescience, had left two champagne stands, a tray of glasses, and a platter of cheeses and French bread by the loungers for any revelers who might wander out by the pool after the buffet tables were cleared. It all belonged to Turner now.

The ice in the buckets had long since melted, but the Moet was still cool, and the cheese was sharp and firm. The salty tartness of it made her smack her lips and sip champagne to wash it down. She realized then that she hadn't eaten anything all night—even the manna she got from Enoch. Beside the fact that she was suddenly starving, it seemed a shame to let Rutla's thoughtful gesture go unrequited. She pulled the robe tighter around herself against a sudden chill in the air.

Turner enjoyed an entire bottle of Moet and most of the cheese before the first bite of bread, as she waited for the coast to be clear for a quick dip. When the first bottle was gone, she began taking little bird bites in between bigger gulps of champagne, until the second bottle was half empty and she no longer cared whether the coast was clear. The blue light shimmering in the pool began to call her name. She had to pee in the worst way.

She walked in slowly until she realized that the water was warmer than the air and let herself sink all the way in. She felt again the delicious profligacy of water swilling up, over, through, and around her legs, then her thighs, hips, and breasts. It was one of the most sensual, purest pleasures of life to her, and although she didn't own a penny of the luxury that everywhere surrounded her, she felt at that moment like the grand lady of the manor. Closing her eyes and releasing an underwater plume of urine, she let herself imagine that all of this decadence was hers—this place, this life, this feeling, and the money that made it all possible. It was an exquisite dream, and opening her eyes to look up at the night sky, it seemed impossible that it could not be real—that all of this was not, in fact, hers and hers alone.

The stars above were shimmering like sunlight on a black sea. One shot across the horizon just as she heard a familiar voice speaking to someone else, and the sound of footsteps.

It was Tripp Wallace. He was wearing a navy blazer with a white oxford shirt and faded, Nantucket red slacks. Whether it was the champagne, the hour, or both, Turner forgot for the moment that she was completely nude, alone, and utterly exposed in a swimming pool, and considered instead how devastatingly handsome this man was in a place so full of devastatingly handsome men. As he walked closer along the edge of the pool, she saw that he had removed his tie and unbuttoned the top three buttons of his shirt. His face looked haggard, and his hair was a mess.

She wasn't sure at first if he had seen her—not surprising since she was in up to her neck, quietly peeing the River Nile in the deep end. As he came closer, though, it was clear he was looking straight at her. She noticed him look up slightly and almost nod at something behind her, as if he were about to speak to someone else, but when he did speak, he was talking only to Turner.

"Let's see," he began, confidently. "If I remember this correctly, you should be naked, and I should be falling in."

She scrambled for something witty to say in reply. Tripp's opinion mattered to her. He was one of the rare men who made her feel unworthy, and in the weeks she'd been around him that summer—at least when he was sober—she found herself always trying to impress him with something pithy and sardonic or erudite to say—preferably using words like pithy and sardonic and erudite. But the champagne had muddled her mind. What came out of her mouth was much less pithy than she'd hoped.

"Um, you got the naked part right."

Words immediately regretted—not because they were suggestive, which she intended them to be, but because they were coarse. She might as well have yelled, "Come and get it!" But subtlety was not high on Tripp Wallace's list of priorities that night, and he kept coming her way.

As he got still closer—close enough for him to get the first inkling that she might not have been bluffing about the naked part—Turner began to think she wanted him to come even closer still.

It was crazy. He was her best friend's on-and-off-again boyfriend, though for what reason she never could understand. Dory was always railing on and on about how much she hated the world that Tripp Wallace came from and represented—the same one that her family practically invented on Martha's Vineyard. Dory was toying with him, but he still belonged to Dory, and it was the first rule of the playground that you don't steal your best friend's toys. Or was, until that night.

"Is that so?" he said to her, smiling and then veering around toward the steps leading to the shallow end like a shark who has just smelled blood in the water. He was no longer as drunk as he had been earlier that night, but she was not yet as drunk as she was going to be when all the champagne finally made its way through her system.

As she watched him take the first step down the stairs to the shallow end, she realized he was not going to remove his clothes. *What a macho, devil-may-care move,* she thought. If he was trying to make her feel irresistible, it was already working. This was not to be a reprise of their drunken bathtub rescue. That had been all in awkward fun and laughter. Neither of them was laughing, now. She felt her heart pounding. She was not afraid, but she knew she was being swept out to sea with the current and would have to swim with it before coming back ashore, miles away.

Every inch of her skin tingled in anticipation. She began to feel herself want him. Her thighs ached, she wanted him inside her so badly. He waded closer, reached out, and touched her hand. She did not trust herself to wait for the next banal thing she might say to him. Instead she pulled him toward her, took hold of the waist of his trousers, unzipped them, and grabbed expectantly.

Her surprise was total. She was ready for him to a point of readiness beyond all reason. She had been since the moment he walked into the pool. He, clearly, was not ready for her. Given the dramatic come-on and the whole power play of wading into the pool in his clothes, she expected him to ravish her. Yet, after several minutes of persistent rubbing, it was clear there was no genie in that particular bottle—at least not one who had any interest in coming out to see her.

The mighty wave of sexual anticipation that only moments ago had threatened deliciously to overwhelm her now receded meekly to the depths. Unwilling to let it go, she placed her arms around his shoulders and attacked his mouth with deep, wet kisses, at the same time pushing his trousers and shorts down to the bottom of the pool with her feet. Hugging his neck, she hoisted herself onto his hips and wrapped her legs around his waist as he stood tall in the deep end. She was a wide-open target, but he refused to fire. The softest part of him yielded and flattened and retreated under the writhing motion of her body.

He said nothing. She could not see his eyes. His face was forced to the side of hers by their embrace. She dared say nothing. She was not ashamed for him. He was, after all, *the* Tripp Wallace, of bacchanalian legend. She thought it unlikely that "the problem," whatever it might be, was on his end. It had to be her. Only moments ago she had felt the surging power of her own irresistibility. Now she had never felt so resistible in her life.

Hoping only to avoid eye contact for as long as possible, she pressed her breasts into the cool, wet fabric of his shirt. Her nipples were still hard as rivets. She held him tight for another few moments of silence until the lack of energy in his arms made it clear that she was the only one still holding on.

When he finally looked at her, he was neither ashamed nor disgusted. His eyes seemed lifeless. Bloodshot streaks around the corners, visible even in that soft light, were the only clues to the living person within.

"I've been drinking quite a lot tonight," he said, with an incongruous sobriety of speech. She was familiar with this particular alibi. Mixed with the smell of booze in his kisses, she had detected the faint odor of vomit.

"It's all right," she said, then realized he hadn't apologized for anything. He had merely made a statement.

There might have been, at least, the consolation prize of honest conversation with a naked man defrocked of his bravado. Turner was rather looking forward to this when it became clear that the encounter was over. He abruptly dropped her, placed both hands on the pool deck, and raised himself and his trousers out of the water with one swift singular motion more reminiscent of a swim team champion than a drunk.

"I'll get us something to drink," he said as he turned to walk away, carrying his wet trousers as he went.

"No—stay here—don't bother," she started to call out, but he never looked back.

In the moments that followed, she tried to muster something like indignation but quickly had to acknowledge that she was neither terribly surprised nor terribly disappointed. No wonder Dory never seemed overly keen about him, she thought.

Either the water had gotten warmer or she'd gotten cooler, but as she made her way to the shallow end by the stairs, she could scarcely tell the difference between where the water in the pool ended and the blood in her veins began. It was too deliciously comforting to leave just yet.

She laid her head back on the topmost ledge of the steps leading into the shallow end of the pool and let her legs float out in front of her. Her right hand instinctively found the soft, tender spot between her legs, and she began gently, almost distractedly, rubbing in a slow, circular motion that quickly grew more elliptical and focused. She didn't care if Tripp came back and found her like that. She forgot about Tripp and time and place as the welcome, familiar waves finally came rolling over her. Her eyes were closed, and though she'd never been able to climax quietly, she stifled her moaning just enough that night to keep Mrs. Delano and the Edgartown Flower Guild from running to her aid.

When the last spasm of electricity had run through her body, she lay there motionless, her eyes still closed, imagining the night sky and how she and Tripp, embracing each other beneath the stars, must have looked to the angels. Her mind raced with random, scattered thoughts. What drink would he make for her? Would he try to guess what she'd want or bring her some concoction she'd never had before? He drank gimlets, she knew. Had he been paying enough attention to her that summer to notice that she preferred cabernets and vodka tonics? What would be the first "real" thing he would say to her, and what would she say in reply?

Then, as quickly as they materialized, all of these thoughts vanished like ephemera. She now heard an equally unexpected but familiar voice speaking directly above her head.

"So show me again," the mouth in the strange, upside-down face above her was saying. "Is this how he touched her?"

Lying on her back, she saw Smoke's hands descending onto her bare breasts, which piled up beneath him like mounds of pudding on a buffet. He squeezed them and laughed. She screamed, jackknifed under the water, and popped back up in a fighter's stance—a rather ridiculous naked boxer.

"You bastard! Get away from me!" she yelled.

"That's exactly my plan, now that the show is over. My goodness, Turner. What a performance! I had no idea you were so talented."

"You *fucking* creep. What kind of weirdo are you? You wait till Tripp comes back. He's gonna kick your ass."

Smoke paused and smiled grimly at this. It was a look she might have mistaken for pity.

"Oh, I don't think he'll do that—come back, I mean. He got what he wanted, and so did I. I guess the question is, what do you want, Turner?" With that, he walked away.

She watched until he was gone, then quickly climbed

out of the pool and put her bathrobe back on. She waited about five minutes, shivering more from stress and fear than cold, not wanting to admit that Smoke was right but knowing from the first moment that he was. They had played her as a team, though Turner could not have known just how practiced they were.

In five minutes more, the lights in the parlor were out. Turner collected herself and left.

Turner entered the main part of the house again through the French doors. The clamor in the parlor was gone. There was only silence and the sound of the few remaining pots being washed by the bus staff in the kitchen. There was no one left in the main part of the house. Mrs. Delano must have gone to bed, but it was starting to bother Turner that she hadn't seen Dory or Charlotte in so long. Charlotte was not in her room, nor was Dory in hers. But as Turner walked back down the spiral staircase to the first floor to continue the search, she heard the sound of laughter. A light was shining underneath the door of an unused room at the far end of the hall. She went there to listen. The voices were Dory's and Charlotte's. She knocked gently and went in.

Turner couldn't recall the last time Dory had seemed this glad to see her. Even Charlotte, who had been more or less sour for weeks, was brimming. The room was strewn with magazines and dresses, and the two women were sitting on the floor cross-legged, like teenagers at a slumber party.

"My God, Turner! Where have you been?" Dory exclaimed.

"We've been looking for you all night," Charlotte added. "We couldn't find you at the party, and somebody said you were down at the beach. Did you hear? The fisherman mysteriously arrived and brought shrimp."

"Yes . . . yes, I heard that," Turner stammered. There was something very weird going on with her friends, but she couldn't put her finger on it.

"There was a ton of it," Charlotte continued. "People couldn't even finish it all. The wait staff had the rest. It was delicious, the way Rutla prepared it."

Dory was catching on.

"Turner—you don't know, do you?"

"Know what?"

"Jesus!" Charlotte exclaimed. "Were you not in the garden when Mrs. Delano made the announcement?"

"Announcement? No . . . no, I guess I wasn't. But I've been looking for the two of you all night. Why aren't you in your rooms?"

"Mother was using all the first-floor bedrooms for the guests' purses and coats, so we—Oh hell, Turner, it doesn't matter. Look!"

Dory held out her left hand. On her ring finger was an exquisite diamond, two carats at least, in an ornate, antique setting—platinum, Turner would later learn. An heirloom of the groom's family for six generations.

Turner felt her heart drop to her ankles. Tripp hadn't exactly been a fixture in Dory's life lately, but no other candidate for engagement was coming to mind. Turner didn't give a damn about Tripp—not after what had just happened, and not after what Smoke had just said—but she cared quite a lot about Dory. Still, it could not be him. Even Tripp Wallace would not propose to Dory Delano in one moment and try to nail her best friend in the next.

She stood there thinking well past the instant when she should have been leaping for Dory's joy.

"Oh my God, her face!" laughed Charlotte, noticing Turner's look of astonishment.

226

"Who?" was the only word Turner could expel with what little air remained in her lungs.

"Who?! Who? You goose, Turner! Tripp Wallace, who else?!" Charlotte exclaimed, incredulously. Dory was still extending her hand, as if she expected Turner might kiss it, in a show of respect.

That explanation did nothing to relieve the vacuum growing in Turner's lungs. With her last spoonful of air, she blurted out the next question.

"When?"

"Two hours ago," Dory answered. "We went racing around looking for you after Mother made the announcement, and when we couldn't find you, we came in here. Charlotte has been picking out dresses and colors ever since."

"I may hate marriage, but I adore weddings," Charlotte began. "It's all I can do to just—" She stopped to look at Turner.

Dory saw the tears in Turner's eyes and withdrew her hand.

"I don't think I've ever known a dearer friend," Dory said, pulling Turner by the hand down to sit next to her and cradling her head in her shoulder.

"But I thought . . . I thought you weren't sure about him," Turner sniffed. "I thought you were just friends."

"I know I've said I wasn't sure this was what I wanted. But when he asked me tonight, suddenly I realized it was all I ever wanted." Misunderstanding completely the reason for Turner's sudden emotion, Dory sought to reassure her friend. "But that doesn't have to change anything between us. We'll always be friends, we three—the very best—I would never do anything to jeopardize that."

"Tears of joy," Charlotte said, also trying to comfort Turner, "are the sweetest."

Turner did her best to smile and admire the ring

227

given by the man who had just made a naked pass at her not thirty minutes ago. She wanted to blurt out, "But I just tried to screw him in the pool and he just tried to let me," but she could not. She didn't have the heart to tell Dory the truth about her fiancé or the courage to admit that she had flagrantly violated the first rule of girlfriends everywhere. All she knew was that Tripp Wallace had been willing, if unable, to cheat on his fiancée not two hours after they were engaged. It was clear he didn't love Dory and never would. No one understood this better now than Turner, and no one was less able to do anything about it.

CHAPTER 18

It was now almost August. The summer seemed to be picking up speed to slingshot into fall. The July holiday from cooking, cleaning, and the general banality of daily life that Dory, Turner, and Charlotte had enjoyed while staying at the Delano estate was coming to an end. Constance Delano's grand gesture of the season was over. Her party had been a stunning success. She had nobly honored, albeit in absentia, the fisherman who she and others on the island believed had saved her daughter's life. She had served the dish that everyone on the island was dying to try. And she had capped the whole affair with the surprise engagement of the Delano heir to the scion of one of the island's oldest families. That the Wallaces were no longer a wealthy family was well known only to Constance and a few insiders, and by them generally ignored. On the Vineyard, the glow of a family's good name lingered much longer than the shine of its gold.

Now that her festival was over, Constance Delano returned to her busy and prickly former self, now busier and pricklier than ever. She had made it clear that the "girls," as she referred to Dory and her two summer guests, were underfoot, and she encouraged them to return to the house in town. The porter would deliver their things in the evening. Dory decided it would be an excellent afternoon for a long walk back into town. The three companions set out arm in arm across the lawn and down the long, gravel road that led out through the gate.

As they turned the corner of Summer and Winter streets, they could see a man standing in the distance, waiting for something or someone. He was outside a house. Their house. He was looking around, impatiently. Whatever the reason he was waiting, he had been there a long time.

It was also apparent that he didn't belong there. He lacked the casually distracted and unhurried demeanor of a tourist. He was not dressed in fine clothes or sporting clothes, which were the only two choices of what to wear in Martha's Vineyard in the summer. He was standing close to a truck parked at the curb, as if he feared someone might steal it right out from under his nose.

Dory and Charlotte said nothing about the man, but they both noticed Turner slowing down as she watched him very keenly. There was a new look of worry on her face.

"Do you know him?" Charlotte finally asked.

Turner did not answer. She hoped an answer might not yet be necessary. When they finally arrived at the house, the man turned toward the three of them but immediately focused his attention on Turner.

"About time you showed up," he said. A Brooklyn accent was unmistakable.

"What are you *doing* here?" Turner asked through clenched teeth. "I told you I couldn't see you again."

"I had to come."

Turner gave a sidelong glance at Dory and Charlotte, who were looking back and forth at Turner and the strange man.

Turner now lowered her voice, for emphasis.

"Where is *your wife?*"

"My wife left me."

"Smart girl," Turner immediately shot back.

That was when Dory knew it was him—the guy from Bennett & Donald. Loading Dock Man.

He was tall and broad-shouldered, good-looking, and nervous about something. Whatever had once been between him and Turner was now clearly over, at least as far as Turner was concerned. She started to walk past him.

"I have to talk to you," he said. "Privately."

"Say what you came to say. These are my friends. I have no secrets."

"Oh, really," he said, snidely, smiling. "Have you told them about the stories you've been writing in your blog—stories about them?"

"I didn't name any names," Turner protested. "They were just stories."

"Yeah, well not anymore, *Bennett & Donald Author*," he replied. There was going to be trouble, now. That was clear.

Turner's face flushed. He was calling her out in front of her friends, who knew nothing of the blog posts about one woman saved from drowning by a fisherman who walked on water, and another cured of breast cancer detected and then cured merely by the touch of the same man's hand, and another—posted just last night—about the feeding of the five thousand. She hadn't referred to them by name or to the name of the town where they lived—just the Vineyard. She had written the stories as mystical fiction, not fact. But fact and fiction had quickly merged into a phenomenon.

Dory and Charlotte now looked at Turner, expecting a denial or an explanation. The three went inside, leaving the man waiting on the doorstep. When the door closed behind them, Turner faced a withering gale of questions from her friends, who hadn't understood much of what the man was saying but didn't like what little they did. Turner put them off, stalling for time to figure out what had happened, and reassured them that Loading Dock Man, as bizarre as the situation seemed, was harmless and should be allowed in. She made halfhearted introductions. His name was Stephen. He smiled weakly before returning his attention to Turner.

"We need to talk, Turner," he said.

They went out to sit on the back porch while Dory and Charlotte, preparing lunch in the kitchen, kept looking out at them for some clue of what news this man from the loading dock at Bennett & Donald could possibly have come all this way to bring. When Turner reappeared at the back door to the kitchen a half hour later, he was gone, but it was clear from the determined expression on her face that she had not won whatever argument they were having.

"I need to explain," she began.

"That would be helpful," Dory answered. "Why don't you start by telling us what you wrote on the blog?"

"I wrote about us—about you, and Charlotte, and the incredible things that have been happening on this island this summer."

"It sounds more like you wrote something incredible," Charlotte said, petulantly. "Did you really write a blog post about me trying to commit suicide? My God, Turner! Are we friends at all? How the hell could you do that?"

"Yeah, Turner. How *could* you do that?" Dory chimed in. "Did you really write a blog post about my breast cancer?"

"I didn't do that," Turner answered, angrily, now raising her voice. "I never mentioned either of you in what I wrote. I made sure you were both unrecognizable, okay? What kind of fool do you think I am? The craziness on the Vineyard about this mysterious fisherman is just that—crazy! But if you're trying to tell me that all this doesn't make for a great story, you're wrong, and if you're asking me not to write about it, well, you don't get to make that call. But that's all it is—*a story.*"

"I don't agree, Turner—not at all," Dory answered. "We trusted you, and there are things between friends that are not meant for publication. But all that aside, I still don't get it. Why is this guy here, and why does he look like you just shot his dog?"

"The problem," Turner began, calming herself and taking a breath, "is that a few hundred thousand people out there don't think it's a story—they think it's real—and they've been contacting bookstores wanting to know when the book will come out."

"The book? What book?" Charlotte asked.

"The book by the Bennett & Donald author."

"What book, and what Bennett & Donald author?" Dory hissed, losing patience.

"Readers are calling it *The Book of Enoch*, and the Bennett & Donald author, that would be me."

"What the hell is *The Book of Enoch?*" Dory was shouting now.

"It's just the title I gave to a series of stories on my blog. People liked them, saw that I was a Bennett & Donald author, and—"

"But goddammit, Turner, you're no more a Bennett & Donald author than I am," Dory exploded. "You're having a *fucking affair* with a married man who works on the loading dock at Bennett & Donald."

"I am *not* having a *fucking affair*. I never slept with the guy, and I didn't know he was married."

"If you never slept with him, what difference does it make whether he's married?"

Turner didn't answer.

"They're all married, Turner. Goddamn, haven't you figured it out yet? Those guys following your blog?

233

News flash: the ones who are older than sixteen are *all married.* They're not interested in your writing. They're interested in getting laid."

"Yeah, well, a few hundred thousand of them are interested in my writing, now."

Dory was incredulous. "What are you talking about?"

Turner took another deep breath, hoping to regain her heading and finish what she had started to tell— what she needed to tell—both of them.

"Bennett & Donald already has two hundred fifty thousand advance orders for *The Book of Enoch.*"

"What?" Charlotte's eyes narrowed.

"But there *is no* book—just a couple blog posts," Dory insisted.

"You're right. I know that, and you know that, but the public doesn't know that. And this non-book is hotter than anything else in Bennett & Donald's catalog, right now. So I have a choice. There either is *going to be a book,* and I will sign a contract with Bennett & Donald for a one-million-dollar advance, or Stephen's going to lose his job, I'm going to be sued for using the Bennett & Donald name, and no other publisher will ever touch anything else I write."

There was silence for a long time, as the reality of what was happening started to sink in for Dory and Charlotte. All the while, Turner struggled to suppress her glee—first, that she was about to become a *bona fide* Bennett & Donald author, and secondly, that Bennett & Donald was going to pay her a million dollars for the privilege she had forced upon them.

CHAPTER 19

The radio interview wasn't scheduled to start until one o'clock that afternoon, but Turner had been pacing the floor of her hotel room since breakfast. She kept thinking, *There is no book*, and alternatively, *There must be a book*. She had fallen through the looking glass, but this rabbit hole was deeper and weirder than any she ever could have imagined.

Emile, her erstwhile "editor" from Bennett & Donald, met her that morning at the train station in Boston. He was Argentinian and at first glance seemed promisingly similar to other Argentinian men she knew, of which there were exactly two—both ski instructors in Aspen. He was urbane, athletic, and gorgeous with long black hair, but when he opened his mouth, he was disappointingly all Princeton and Park Avenue.

The dynamic was becoming increasingly clear: Turner and her "cockamamie story," as Stephen had described it, were a godsend to a publisher constantly in search of the Next Big Thing to sell to a shrinking readership. The world was eager, the market was ripe for a new theology of redemption, and Turner's stories about a strange fisherman on the Vineyard conveniently filled that void.

It was also immediately apparent that Emile was a smooth operator—as smooth as they came. It was his job to make sure that that this orphan writer, left in a basket on the Bennett & Donald loading dock, realized her full potential to lead the company out of the wilderness.

WRUS, "the Walrus," was the major talk-radio affiliate for all of New England. If a story was going to spread like wildfire in the grassroots of America, this was the best place to light the match.

In all the years Turner had listened to the station while coming and going around Boston, she never imagined the place was this small and bare-bones. Apart from the radio equipment, everything in the place could be had for fifty dollars at a flea market. A scruffy intern from BU met her at the front desk carrying a huge soda in one hand and smelling of pepperoni. Two even younger and scruffier-looking interns showed her where to sit and arranged her mic. When, by the clock on the wall, the show was due to start in five minutes, the host finally appeared on the scene. He was tall and thin with a goatee, wearing sandals and a coral guayabera that seemed to say he wished he were anyplace but there.

"Billy Drake." He smiled broadly and held out his hand. "So, this is the voice crying in the wilderness of Martha's Vineyard?"

"Nice to meet you," Turner stammered, caught off guard by the vigorous handshaking. "I'm very thankful for the—"

"Yes, absolutely," he interrupted, looking down at a clipboard in his hand. "Emile has told me all about you."

This was a surprise, considering Emile had spoken to her only once on the phone and met her for the first time two hours ago.

"This will be great," Drake continued, oblivious to the puzzled look on Turner's face. "Please, sit down."

He began to run through a checklist of what to expect once the person visible through the studio glass window—who was yet another child intern—flipped the switch for the "On Air" sign. Turner followed roughly half of what was said, concentrating mostly on leaning over far enough to reach her mic without tipping her chair over and crashing to the floor.

Drake and Emile were clearly well acquainted. They stepped outside the soundproofed studio, where Turner could see but not hear them talking. The smile disappeared from the host's face, and he was no longer talking but listening and nodding at what Emile had to say. Four minutes later they came back in, and the "On Air" sign lit up.

"So folks, today we have with us the woman you've all been talking about. That's right, Turner Graham, the writer of the blog *Jersey Gal*, is with us in the studio with the answers you've been waiting for about the mysterious stranger described in her forthcoming blockbuster from Bennett & Donald, *The Book of Enoch*. He summons the bounty of the ocean to his nets where other boats lie idle. He walks on water to save a woman drowning far out at sea. He cures deadly cancer with the touch of his hand. He feeds the multitudes with just a few morsels of food. Is he the true Messiah? Could two thousand years of history be wrong? When we come back, we'll explore these questions and take your calls to the woman who has seen it all with her own eyes, Turner Graham."

"Oh, shit!" Turner erupted into her still-dead mic.

The "On Air" sign switched off, but Turner's face remained a brilliant red. She slowly turned to Emile, trying to restrain herself from lunging at him.

"The true Messiah? Are you kidding me? Where the hell did that come from?"

"That was the sound of you becoming more famous than the pope."

The interview was a nightmare. Half the callers were screaming she was the Antichrist, while the other half were ready to anoint her a latter-day John the Baptist. Prying questions came about her love life, her sexual orientation, her family, work history, and finances. The easiest to answer were the callers who wanted to know whether she would donate the money made off the book to the poor. She told them she needed every bit of her fifteen-percent share to pay debts, but that Bennett & Donald was welcome to part with some of its eighty-five percent. Emile did not respond.

Through it all, Drake grinned and gloated like a circus barker, clearly enjoying the energy of the crowd on the other side of the phone lines. It would be his highest-rated show of the year. Emile remained seated close beside Turner, listening to her every word and signaling almost imperceptibly to Billy whenever he thought it was time to move on to the next caller. The interview lasted only thirty minutes, but to Turner it felt like hours.

There were eighteen radio interviews scheduled with as many stations over a single week. They were all divey operations in bad neighborhoods around Boston and New York and Philadelphia, each with some facsimile of Billy Drake. This was Bennett & Donald's strategy. The morning television news shows were screaming for Turner to appear, but Bennett & Donald wanted Turner to remain the hidden scribe of the prophet—the outcast, traveling the hustings and delivering her gospel to the gritty masses of talk radio.

The strategy worked better than anyone had dreamed, which was saying something, because Bennett & Donald was betting large. By the time Turner returned to Dory and Charlotte on the Vineyard, the controversy over *The Book of Enoch* had grown from a brushfire to an inferno.

CHAPTER 20

The road into Edgartown is always slow-going in the summer, even on the best of days, but today it was insufferable. Up ahead, blue lights flashed, directing traffic away from the center of town—away from the Delano guest house. When she finally got close enough to catch the attention of one of the cops standing in the intersection, Turner pulled the ball cap farther down over her eyes, lowered the window, and shouted, "Officer, what's the holdup?"

"You know—it's those protesters and celebrity hunters. They're blocking the main road in. You have to go around and come in from the north side."

"Protesters? Protesting what?"

"That idiot on the radio, Turner Graham."

She had not spoken to Dory or Charlotte during the week she had been gone. She couldn't bear to face them. Her last words had been indignant assurances that they would not be identified. But after the radio interviews, curiosity seekers had started streaming into town, asking questions and making connections. Most still didn't know that Dory and Charlotte were the two women described in the blog stories, but somehow they had discovered where Turner Graham was spending the summer, and several dozen of them filled the streets outside the house.

The crowd was divided into two camps. One was chanting, "BLA-sphe-my!" pointing at the others, and carrying signs conveying some form of the same message—that Turner Graham was a false prophet and the devil's handmaiden. The others were singing some verse together softly and carrying signs saying, "Turner Our Mother," calling her their guardian and guide and urging all to "follow the fisherman." Three policemen calmly stood watch at the fence around the house.

Turner got out of her car and walked, stupefied, down a side street. The noise of the crowd filled the air. Dory and Charlotte were nowhere to be seen. A black limousine was parked near the patrol cars. A man in a dark suit got out and walked toward her.

"Ms. Graham," he said quietly, then flashed a badge. "Jonah Barnes. Special Security. I'm here to get you safely to the Delano estate. We have a team set up there to protect you until this mess dies down. Please come with me."

This mess. It perfectly described what was going on all around her, what she had made of her life, and what she had done to the lives of her friends.

She entered the main hall of the Delano estate, pausing inside the doorway as if she'd never been there before. It was still midafternoon, but it was darker inside than she remembered. Then she saw that the lamps that were usually on had been turned off. No one was there to greet her.

As she moved through the foyer, a fleeting glimpse of the French doors leading to the patio brought a flashback of that night by the pool, and Tripp, and Smoke. It seemed like a dim, distant nightmare and not something that actually happened only weeks ago.

Thinking of it crushed her again. If everyone has one moment in life she wishes she could take back, that one was hers.

She could hear the porter bringing her things in through the side door and climbing the stairs toward the room where she would be staying. She should have followed him there, but instead she turned into the parlor, hoping to find someone. It was then that she saw Dory and Charlotte.

They were sitting together, having tea. Mrs. Delano sat on the opposite sofa. Mrs. Delano's face stiffened when Turner entered the room. She had always suspected Mrs. Delano didn't particularly care for her. Now there was no doubt. Turner Graham was the woman who had turned her town into a circus and made her only daughter a sideshow. That could not be forgiven.

Dory's face, on the other hand, was full of unexpected kindness. "Turner!" she exclaimed. She rose from the chair and embraced her old friend.

"Dory, I'm so sorry—" Turner began.

Dory pressed her finger to Turner's lips.

"Charlie and I heard all about it on the radio. We know all this hubbub wasn't your idea, and for God's sake how could you have seen it coming, with everything happening so fast?"

Mrs. Delano made an audible "harrumph" that drew a disapproving glance from her daughter, after which she bid Turner a begrudging good afternoon and left the room.

The coffee table where they were seated was covered with wedding magazines and paraphernalia. Dory and Charlotte had been picking patterns and making plans.

"I decided to hold the wedding over Labor Day weekend, the unofficial end of summer," Dory said.

Turner was amazed. "But that's less than a month

from now. Isn't that an awful rush?"

"It absolutely is. If people had told me in June that I would be planning a wedding at all, much less on a month's notice this summer, I would have said they were crazy. Too much work, too much stress. But it's different when you're in the middle of it. Now that the deed is done—I mean, now that Tripp and I have agreed to go ahead with the wedding—I just want to move on with things, to get started with our new life."

Somehow, it didn't ring true. Charlotte and Turner shared a fleeting glance that told them they were thinking the same thing. Dory spoke of her marriage as if it were a Wall Street merger. Perhaps it was.

"You know, Tripp's a great guy," Turner began, swallowing the lie as best she could in order to deflect the sting of what she was about to say, "but I honestly didn't think you were that into him. I mean, I got the sense he was sort of a take-it-or-leave-it thing with you. Obviously I was wrong, I guess, but—"

Charlotte looked from Turner to Dory, saying nothing, astonished that this question of all questions had been uttered out loud, but wanting just as much as Turner did to know the answer—to hear Dory explain how, exactly, things did accelerate from zero to matrimony with Tripp.

Dory smiled a knowing smile. She looked off into the distance, as if she were trying to decide how best to frame her answer to a question she had seen coming a long way off.

It was a question that would never have occurred to her mother or to any of her mother's friends. Of course she would marry Tripp Wallace, they would say—or wouldn't say, rather, because the subject would never come up. But if they were asked, they would be pained to explain what was self-evident. He met all the necessary criteria. He was from a well-respected family.

He had gone to the right schools, as had his father and grandfather and great-grandfather before him. He had the right friends who had gone to the same schools and traveled in the same small circles. He was accomplished at the right sports—sailing in summer and skiing in winter—and he knew how to say and do the right things at the right moment in a way that bore testament, along with his good looks, to an obvious breeding. He was tall and well formed and not overly bright or bookish or moody or sensitive. He would love Dory with fraternal affection and a benign indifference that would immunize him from the terrible angst that afflicts the lovelorn. There would be affairs, perhaps, but he could be relied upon to keep them discreet and meaningless, and there would be no brooding or melancholy or navel gazing in the wake of their discovery. New love would falter and stumble as it invariably does, but the business of marriage would march on. There would be no midlife forays into the wild unknown because he was not a curious man. His life had followed a well-worn path thus far, and he would stick to that path without the danger of navigational error that comes from needless reflection. He would lead a good life, not a well-examined life, and thereby make it possible for Dory to do the same. He and Dory would produce tall, lithe, gorgeous, towheaded children and grandchildren who, on their way to fulfilling their central role as heirs to the family's fortune and curators of its legacy, would by their laughter and playfulness banish the awful silence that would otherwise creep into their marriage, like a pestilence.

Dory knew all this, but she also knew that none of these reasons would make sense to Turner or Charlotte, nor would they suffice to answer Turner's question. It was a serious question, though, even if it was a moot issue, and she sincerely loved the friends who asked it.

They deserved a sincere answer.

"I know this seems crazy," Dory began. "It seemed pretty crazy to me, too. My mother has been pushing the two of us together for as long as I can remember. I can't tell you how many times I had promised myself to turn him down and keep turning him down. But then he showed up at the party with a ring, and something just clicked. It was suddenly clear to me that 'yes' was the obvious answer. I think I began to realize that this incredible life I had imagined for myself that was so different and so much better than the life my mother had and that her mother had—it wasn't real. It was a kind of ongoing tantrum I was having, until one day I woke up and realized that my mother and I weren't so very different, and that I was cheating myself just so I could say I had stood up to her. I don't know. Maybe I just finally decided it was time to grow up."

Turner and Charlotte nodded their heads in affirmation of this answer even as they processed the large parts of it they did not comprehend.

"And he loves me, Turner. I know that. I could see it in his eyes when he proposed."

Turner heard those words like a fist ramming into her gut. She felt a physical pain that drew her hand to her waist to fight the urge to double over. What was in Tripp's eyes when he proposed, Turner was certain, was not love but a great deal of gin. She imagined how the terrible, very different truth would sound coming from Dory's lips: *I could see it in his eyes when he proposed . . . right before he went out and tried to screw my best friend in the pool.*

"Are you all right?" Dory asked.

Turner lied, of course. "No, I'm fine. It must be something I ate on the train."

"Train food—*ugghh!*" Dory exclaimed.

CHAPTER 21

The sun was already low in the west when Charlotte woke from a nap. Dory and Turner were nowhere to be found, and the house was serenely quiet except for the tinkling sound of cups and saucers in the kitchen. Charlotte had fallen into the habit of taking naps, that summer, which was a most decadent luxury unknown to her former life. She imagined herself as a patient struggling to return to alertness after some devastating neurologic injury, but after weeks of continued sluggishness, she was failing to make progress. Her eyes refused to open now before ten in the morning.

No matter how late in the day Charlotte awoke, there was no escaping Rutla. She thought Charlotte was perishingly thin, and to remedy this deficiency became Rutla's new mission in life. She waited each morning for the sound of Charlotte's footsteps on the staircase, then frog-marched her to a table set up on the patio outside the kitchen. There, she stuffed her patient with a "brunch" that conjugated nothing but its title, consisting of an entire breakfast and an entire lunch served *ad seriatim.*

Charlotte kept up a polite but ineffectual protest for the first few days, after which she became so addicted to this daily carbohydrate high that she abandoned all resistance. At around two in the afternoon, a food coma usually overtook her reading in bed, in an armchair, or by the pool, until she awoke again around four or five, in time to go another round with Rutla.

After two weeks of this life spent hiding out from the crusaders and infidels besieging Dory's house in town, Charlotte was alternately pleased and alarmed to discover she had acquired curves. Her body was expanding at the hips and chest, while her waist, though undeniably thicker, remained proportionate to both. Inexplicably, her period had also returned five days earlier, after a two-year hiatus that she had assumed was the beginning of early menopause, just as it had been for her mother at the same age.

She rose from the bed and, on her way to the bath, noticed her naked form in the full-length mirror, stopping just long enough to swivel in front of it. "My God, I'm becoming the St. Pauli Girl," she muttered aloud, breaking out in the faintest hint of a smile.

She dressed each day in nothing but underpants and a gauzy pool cover-up for the heat, which by now had become oppressive even in New England. There was no point in dressing any more elaborately. There was usually nothing to do. They were under a kind of house arrest.

Every day she tried to get Dory or Turner or both of them to go with her in the skiff across Eel Pond to the outer beach, where Charlotte had grown accustomed to getting away from everything for large parts of the afternoon. The barrier island beyond the pond was narrow and inaccessible to all but small, shallow-draft boats, and only locals knew the water trail through the marsh. Dory almost always came along on these seaside outings. Charlotte suspected she did this out of unspoken fear that Charlotte might attempt again the slow walk into oblivion that had started the summer off with such a bang. But that night with its nearness of death seemed so distant to Charlotte now, even if the betrayal by Father Vecchio was still so near. She longed to forget him but could not banish the memory of his cloying, groping hands and stinking, hurried breaths. He had done what thirty-two years of a life filled with immeasurable tragedy and pain could not do.

He had stolen her faith.

The rite of Christian burial for her child that had once been worth everything to Charlotte—even her own life—now seemed not merely perfunctory but meaningless, even silly. That most hallowed place in her heart, where tradition and sacrament and ritual had once been so firmly anchored, with a benevolent and loving God seated upon a throne at the center of it all, was now an empty tomb.

The kitchen was filled with soothing smells that morning, as it was every morning. Baking and marinating for the evening meal had begun, and the aroma usually summoned Dory or Turner or Charlotte or all three of them for early samples. But no one was about when Charlotte walked in to find Rutla huddling over the open oven door. Dory had left, Rutla told her, on her way to an early appointment with dressmakers in Newport. A friend of the Wallaces had picked her and her mother up by boat at the yacht club pier that morning for the trip across the sound, and they weren't expected back until late in the evening. Turner had not gone with them, but she was not downstairs and was nowhere to be found on the grounds. She had eaten only toast and tea for breakfast, Rutla said, before striking out on foot in the direction of the north end of the island, near the lighthouse. Rutla had pleaded with her to go with someone from the security detail posted outside the front gate, for safety's sake, but Turner, disguised in a ball cap and sunglasses, ignored her with impunity.

Charlotte was not a boater by any stretch of the imagination, but she did not intend the absence of crew, that morning, to deter her plans to head for the outer beach and a peaceful few hours watching the waves roll in. Once she was seated in the dinghy, her gangly arms cantilevered and pivoted unevenly against the oars, pushing her vessel in little, ineffectual arcs in front of the dock, with erratic speed and progress in no direction in particular. The sun was already high in the sky, blotting out every detail against the distant, snow-white dunes with blinding light. It sparkled on the dark water of the pond like stars in a night sky.

She tried again, sitting with her back to the bow and both feet braced against the aft seat, just as Dory had taught her. Dory's lessons had mostly been just demonstrations, lasting only a few strokes until Dory took over. This morning Charlotte was alone, but like a baby bird on its first solo flight, she eventually gained command of her flailing wings. Soon both oars began to dip and pull and lift more or less in unison, and she glided on a winding, lazy path through the water.

She was still fifty yards off the beach when she heard women's voices and the sound of a guitar. Craning her neck, she could still see nothing but the whiteness of the light reflecting off the sand. Marveling at her growing competence as a pilot, she moderated her stroke to steer the bow toward the sound. It grew steadily louder until it blended with the crackling noise of the keel sliding up on the gravel.

"Ahoy there," came a young man's voice. Charlotte grabbed a dog-eared paperback, the lunch bucket Rutla had filled for her, and a towel—her provisions for the day—and stepped out. She shielded her eyes from the bright light with her hand, realizing only then that she had forgotten her sunglasses, without which it would be impossible to read.

"Hello!" she said cheerfully over her shoulder, not aware to whom she was speaking. There were several people on the beach, but those who had come down to greet her were some nervous and chatty young girls. They seemed eager to find out who, exactly, Charlotte was, and, more importantly, whether she had been sent to find them by their parents. Charlotte suddenly felt ancient, as if it were impossible that she was exactly their age only fifteen years ago. None of them looked old enough to buy the alcohol that was on their breath.

Fifty yards down the beach, a small runabout with an outboard motor was sitting high and dry. The group had taken it out to the beach late the night before for a drinking party and a bonfire, but at four in the morning the tide went out and left the keel buried deep in the sand. It was either too heavy to move, or they were too drunk to move it. The tide would be high again in an hour or so, but for now they were all delighted to imagine themselves marooned on a desert island, albeit within sight of the Delano estate.

Up the beach, where the dunes crested and formed a lookout over the ocean, coolers haphazardly surrounded a group of chairs and blankets. A charred pit of sand that had melted into bits of glass was encircled by an impressive retinue of beer cans and empty bottles of booze. Surveying the scene, Charlotte felt a wave of gratitude that she was now safely beyond what she referred to as "the stupid phase" of her youth.

"Fancy meeting you here," a deep, male voice called from the far end of the dune. Charlotte looked up, but the bright sun blocked the man's face. "You just can't stay away, can you?" he said.

At first she had no idea who this person was, what he

was trying to say, or who might fancy meeting her anywhere. She still couldn't make him out in the glare and had begun to think that forgetting her sunglasses was going to be a bigger problem than she realized.

When she circled around to put her back to the sun, she got a better look. It was a boy, and he was grinning widely. He sounded cockier now than he did that day on the ferry, fending off his girlfriend to get a word in edgewise. No wonder, Charlotte thought. An older woman who made a brazen pass at him on the ferry, two months ago, was still stalking him to the middle of nowhere. *He must be pretty impressed with himself right about now.*

Climbing up the dune, she stumbled from little avalanches of sand that slipped beneath her feet. The boy caught her and pulled her up. His hand was smooth and warm and young. It felt good to hold a boy's hand again.

At the top of the dune, the salt air swept over and around her face and hair. The ocean was shimmering, limitless. There was nothing around them but the sea and the wind and the sand—which was why she had come to this, her new favorite place on the Vineyard. Only today she was going to have to share it with a gangly skinflint of a boy who stood there still grinning at her, the wind tossing a lone, blond cowlick back and forth on top of his head like a bobble-head doll.

Perhaps he expected another kiss. She assured herself he wouldn't be getting one. After all, she had grown better at restraining her impulses in the two months since that first ferry ride.

"I thought you'd be married and off on your honeymoon by now," Charlotte said, glad finally to be back on offense after nearly rolling down the dune.

She made a point of not looking at him. Teenage boys with racehorse metabolisms and zero body fat were very fond of not wearing shirts, and while the cheerleading squad down the beach probably found that exciting, Charlotte thought it was important that she not appear to agree.

She kept looking out to sea as she spoke, as if the water were far more interesting than the boy or what he might have to say. When the silence became awkward, she turned to see if he were even paying attention. He was staring off at the horizon. She followed his gaze.

"Long story," he said, finally.

In the pause that followed, it became clear that the story, long or short, was not likely to be told. Charlotte sensed a wound that was something more than shyness. It provoked an unwanted and involuntary surge of maternalism in her.

"I'm Charlotte," she said, extending her hand. "I've been told I'm a good listener to long stories."

The boy looked at her and took her hand for the second time. He did not complete the introduction but simply held her hand in his. He wasn't coy; it just didn't occur to him that his name would be at all important to her.

In his bare feet he was not as tall as she remembered, and he seemed younger. He wasn't a child, but he couldn't have been older than twenty-two, if that. Separated from the rough girl who had been hanging on him on the ferry, he looked less like a greaser and more like a California surfer. The difference somehow mattered to Charlotte. It felt weird that it mattered.

She hadn't intended to force her company on him, nor had she asked him for his, but the top of the dune was not wide. When she wandered away the few feet it allowed and spread her towel, he followed and sat beside her. He offered a half-empty bottle of spiced rum she hadn't noticed he had been dangling from his left hand. She didn't usually drink that early in the morning—or to be more precise, she never did—but somehow she sensed this wasn't the time or the place to accentuate the differences in their ages and manners. She wanted to hear his story, and she wanted him to feel free to tell it.

Still, he said nothing. Instead, he sat next to her and peered out at the sea as if they were an old married couple, silent and content merely to have each other's company.

The voices of the others rose and fell periodically on the air, coming from fifty yards away in the direction of the skiff down the beach. That the boy's friends didn't seem in a hurry to join him suggested that they, too, knew he needed some space. Charlotte could hear them laughing and groaning and grunting, trying to pry the keel of their boat out of the sand with the help of the tide that slowly rose around it.

She leaned back on the towel and continued to follow the boy's gaze out to sea. He had an odd intensity about him, as if he were expecting something was about to happen out there—a missile launch or mermaid eruption or something. On the third pass of the rum, he turned to look at her.

"We were supposed to be having a baby," he said.

"We?"

"The girl and me—the one you saw on the ferry."

"And . . .?"

"And nothing. She lied to me. I heard about it from one of her girlfriends who called me from back home. Said she couldn't keep quiet anymore. That she felt it was wrong. She said my girlfriend wasn't pregnant—never had been. She just made that up to get me to take her away from her old man. Not that I can blame her. He used to beat her . . ."

Charlotte had not forgotten the girl's blistering right hook, and now she realized where it came from. She must have given the old man as good as she got.

"But it was a damned lie just the same."

Charlotte said nothing, which didn't seem to faze him. "A damned lie," he said again, looking back toward the sea.

"Is that why you were getting married?"

"She must have thought so, but I would have married her anyway—baby or no baby."

"And so now you're not—getting married, I mean?"

"You can't build a marriage on a lie," he said, looking at her with an expression of surprise, which she took to mean that he would have guessed someone so much older would have been a little wiser.

Charlotte let the proverb hang in the air. It was true enough, in theory, but in reality her own marriage and, she had come to believe, a great many others—perhaps even the majority—were rather elaborately built on a foundation of lies. True love was a myth, as far as she was concerned.

"'Think about it,' you said to me, back then," he continued. "Do you remember?"

"I do, but I was ..." She started to explain her bizarre conduct on the ferry that she realized, as soon as she began, made no difference to anyone now. He cut her off.

"Truth is, apart from wondering why you was such a damn lunatic and where the hell you had come from, I didn't *need* to think about it. In fact, I was pretty excited about it. That's what I guess you didn't know—and how could you. I'm sure I looked like just a punk to you."

"Still do, actually." She said this to be witty and cute, which it was not, and which alarmed her, as if her mouth had suddenly detached itself from her brain. She regretted the words as soon as they were spoken. *Another lie told to the poor boy.* He seemed rather Byronesque to her, in fact, and not at all like a punk, but

253

she didn't think he would understand why, so she left it.

"I was *excited* to be a father," he continued, indignantly. A tear rolled down. He was struggling to keep his emotions in check. She had had no idea. She suddenly felt even more mortified at her glibness a moment ago.

It was either the best or worst of all possible combinations, depending on the eye of the beholder. Here was this painfully earnest boy, wounded and still suffering at the hands of a conniving and thoughtless girlfriend. Here was this older woman, herself conflicted and out of touch with her own feelings about love and sex and marriage. Between them was a half-empty bottle of rum, and all around them was sunshine and the sea.

Had Charlotte thought in her haste as she left the house that morning that there would be anyone on this island where there had been no one all the days before, or any other reason to wear something under her cover-up, things might have turned out differently. There might have been a moment of pause to deal with some difficulty of a latch or a hook or a strap or a button—a pause into which some awkwardness might have intruded, bringing with it a sober moment of reconsideration. But there was no latch, nor any moment of pause, nor anything that intruded on Charlotte's senses but the smell of the sea, the warmth of the sand, and a blurry, disconnected idea that she would succor this boy and ennoble herself by making love to him.

Their fellow castaways waved goodbye and left, giggling annoyingly at something—Charlotte had no idea what—as they shoved off. The boy with the rum (as she would forever remember him) shouted to his friends he would return to the mainland later with "her," the unknown woman in his arms. The reason why the boy wanted to remain needed no explanation to his friends. Charlotte's reasons for staying, on the other hand, were hidden even from her.

When the others were finally out of sight, Charlotte eagerly rolled on top of the boy to administer an impromptu and—as she would have considered it even two hours earlier—utterly improbable, groping kiss. Her dress seemed to ride up of its own will and fly over her head like a kite. His lips tasted like rum. Hers tasted vaguely like coconut oil. Together they were a piña colada.

The onshore breeze, gathering warmth and speed from the rising sun, felt exquisitely clean and fresh on her bare breasts. She wondered how anyone wore clothes in a place like this—she hadn't, in fact, all summer. Her nipples swelled and firmed like ripe grapes, and the boy reached up to fondle each one gently between his fingers.

It was not that she forgot his age, but that she completely forgot her own. She let herself imagine she was eighteen again, and that he was the latest iteration of *the one she would love forever.* That pleasant fiction was the only key that could fully unlock her passion—a key she hadn't dared even imagine turning in a long, long time. Love—true love—suddenly seemed to her a thing almost real, almost possible. His skinny brown torso disappeared under the creamy-white expanse of her hips on top of him. With words unspoken, she was begging him to enter her.

How his swim trunks disappeared from his waist in those hurried moments, she later remembered hazily wondering at the time. A necessary moment of undoing had been skipped, somehow. Perhaps forgetting her own strength she had ripped them off the boy. Or perhaps what seemed like fleeting time was only relative to the speed of the alcohol running through their veins. Whatever the reason, no sooner had she kissed him than he was pushing deeper and deeper inside her. She pushed back with excruciating firmness, and she began to take control.

Her outstretched arms extended downward and pinned his shoulders on the fine sand, pulling his hands from her breasts. She rocked and rubbed herself back and forth on top of him, at first slowly and rhythmically, then faster and more erratically. As her muscles started to convulse deep inside, her hands moved from his shoulders to his chest to lift her hips higher.

She came hard—harder, that day, than she ever had before. It was a vulnerable feeling, with a hint of something almost like danger, like being caught in a breaking wave that was bigger and more powerful than her ability to swim against it, and that she ultimately would allow to carry her with its force, throwing her under and sweeping her along submerged, until she finally rolled out onto the beach, gasping for air. The first climax was followed by a succession of smaller waves that washed over her more gently but just as relentlessly.

When her hands finally relaxed their grip on his skin, he rolled on top of her and pushed her legs high in the air. Sand and laughter flew everywhere. His cerulean eyes were wild with excitement. He was smiling. She had forgotten that look of innocence. She wondered what he saw in her face, and whether he saw the same.

He began to thrust hard and fast but not for long before he cried out, arching his back, burying himself as deeply inside her as he could, and remaining there. Her legs rested, somewhat uncomfortably for her, high on his shoulders, and her feet pointed straight up to the sky. She could have stayed in that position indefinitely when she was eighteen, but now she doubted she would last another minute. Blessedly, he collapsed a moment later and rolled onto his side in an exhausted heap. She nestled her head under his chin to get closer, where she could feel the cool sweat on his skin and hear his heart still pounding in his chest. He breathed deeply and quickly for several more minutes before all was nearly quiet—all but for the softest sound of something she could hear as he stroked her hair. It was a moment before she realized what it was, and then she understood. He was gently weeping.

She never knew his name.

CHAPTER 22

Smoke's office in Edgartown would be easy to miss except for the fact that it had always been exactly where it was. Everyone in town knew it by the initials POD embossed in small gold letters on the heavily varnished entry door—"P" for "Pearon," "D" for "DeAngelo." No one ever knew what the middle initial stood for, but all three supposedly belonged to Smoke's great-great-grandfather, who first opened the office in the twenties—the 1820s. Among some readers of Milton, another theory prevailed about the origin and meaning of those initials, but few dared utter the suspicion aloud. Not many people ever came or went in that office, but those who did knew their business and didn't linger. That Smoke required no other moniker than those three letters was a testament to the power he wielded on this island, and he was about to use some of it.

The note that came sealed and addressed to Turner by hand delivery, at the Delano estate, said that Tripp Wallace wanted to see her at this address at two o'clock on Thursday. Considering what had happened in her last encounter with Tripp and the potential destructive power of the secret that lay hidden between them, Turner didn't feel it her prerogative to object to the fact that the note said nothing about the purpose of the meeting. Tripp arrived a few minutes after Turner and found her waiting in the lobby just as Smoke walked out to greet them.

"Come in, both of you. Thank you for coming—and so prompt, I might add: a courtesy too easily forgotten, these days."

Turner was wary. Tripp seemed wary, too, which unsettled her all the more. Anything coming from Smoke that was a surprise to Tripp Wallace was likely to be a surprise, indeed.

Smoke came around from behind his desk and settled into an enormous, overstuffed wingback chair, upholstered in buttery-soft brown leather that puffed out around him like a hot muffin. He was wearing his trademark bowtie and impervious smirk. Turner squirmed uncomfortably in one of two straight-backed wooden chairs offered to guests at the front of the room. She never liked the man and made no effort to hide her feelings. He made every effort to ignore them.

"I'll get right to the point," Smoke began. "I need your help, Turner."

She stiffened. He continued.

"As you may know, I am the principal source of credit for the commercial fishermen on this island. The banks long ago abandoned the industry as too cyclical, too risky. I stayed in because I believe in the culture and the heritage of this place, and we wouldn't have much of either without the fishing fleet."

Nice speech, Turner thought. If Smoke stayed in anything, it was first, last, always, and only about Smoke—and the money.

"Well, things changed this year—first with the weather, and now with this poacher everyone calls 'the fisherman.' I believe you call him Enoch. The long and short of it is, he's killing my business, and he's killing a way of life on this island. I think you know him."

"You know I know him, Smoke. I'm writing a damn

book about him. There are a hundred people picketing Dory's house on Summer Street who think I'm the Antichrist and another hundred who think I'm Mary Magdalene. What's your point? You've got enough damn money—more than enough—to float these poor shrimpers until the weather changes and the catch improves."

"That would hardly be the point, even if it were true."

"Instead you're calling their loans and crushing them. I heard a trawler was towed off to auction just this week—the fourth so far this season. There aren't that many left on the island now, anyway, and they won't be coming back. What's your goddamn hurry?"

Smoke cocked his head slightly and smiled before continuing. He knew there would be no winning an argument with her. So he went right to the terms.

"I want to meet him."

Turner laughed out loud. "He won't do it. He knows your game. He's a cagey guy. Besides, I have no way to contact him directly." That was only half-true. Simon was her way to Enoch, but she wasn't sure she even knew how to reach him anymore.

"But you do have a way to contact him," Smoke insisted.

Tripp finally spoke up. "What's this got to do with me, Smoke?" His voice sounded strangely impatient and unfriendly toward his old friend.

"In a minute," Smoke answered, waving him off.

"Even if I did have a way to contact him, why would I want to help you?"

"I would hope I wouldn't need a reason merely to ask you to arrange for me to talk with him."

"Talk? I saw the way Simon looked at you," Turner continued, "and who can blame him? You're no friend to him or Enoch. I wouldn't trust you not to turn both of them in."

Smoke's expression fell and darkened. Tripp twitched nervously in the seat beside her.

"Turner, you're not exactly in the power position, here."

"What the hell are you talking about? You have no power over me."

"Oh, I believe I do. Given your condition at the time, I don't suppose you recall that I was out by the pool when you and Tripp had your rendezvous. In fact, that was the same night I believe you proposed to Dory, isn't that right, Mr. Wallace?"

"What are you getting at, Smoke?" Tripp demanded an answer. "What has that got to do with anything?"

"Exactly nothing, as far as I'm concerned. But I'll just come right to the point. Help me in this, Turner, and your secret will forever be safe with me. Oppose me, and I'll see to it that you lose the only friend you have on this island, not to mention the gravy train you've been living on out at the Delano estate."

Turner was offended but not surprised, and she didn't take long to answer the threat. "I don't need the money anymore, asshole."

"Indeed you don't, and bravo to you for that. The Bennett & Donald imposter is now the Bennett & Donald darling. No mean feat, that. You have my utmost admiration. But as I think you'll find, Turner, money won't give you a shoulder to cry on or throw you a party for your birthday or invite you to an island for the summer when you're running from everything and everyone else in your life. You need friends for that, and at our age, well, true friends are hard to find."

"You bastard! You would tell Dory? Is that what you called me here for—to threaten me?" Tripp was shouting. He rose out of his chair and hovered over Smoke with his fists clenched at his side.

"Settle down, Tripp. Who knows? I might be saving you from a terrible mistake. Obviously you haven't finished sowing your wild oats, boy—"

Tripp cocked his right arm as if to strike him, but Smoke put up his hands in a show of surrender that was, of course, anything but.

"Yet, calmer heads will prevail, I'm sure," Smoke continued, "and I'm certain none of this will come to anything. I just want a meeting with the man where we can sit down and work out terms like reasonable people. He wants to catch shrimp. I don't want to lose my investment in the fleet. I'm sure we can work out some sort of arrangement, but I need to meet him to do that."

Tripp looked sharply at Turner, then looked away. She felt the vise squeezing around her. She would have given anything—literally—for Dory not to know.

"I'll contact you," Turner finally answered. "I'm not promising anything." Then she rose and abruptly turned, not stopping to say goodbye or notice that Tripp, who had just as much reason to be angry as she did, if not more so, didn't get up to leave with her. In fact, she would have been surprised to learn he stayed most of that morning behind the closed door of Smoke's office.

The long stretch of gravel beach at the foot of the pier on the Delano estate was a favorite place of Turner's for many things—gathering pretty stones and sea glass, hunting clams, and casting away regrets, even if they usually washed up on shore again. She walked the beach that afternoon deep in thought. She knew Smoke was a liar, and she was certain he meant to arrest Enoch—that much had been made clear in her encounter with Simon at the station. But she wondered if that were all bad. It would bring Enoch—whoever he was—out of the shadows and give him a chance to tell the world the truth about himself and what, exactly, he had done for Charlotte and Dory. Once people understood the truth, he would be vindicated, and Smoke could do him no more harm. It would also spare her truest friend the grief of her betrayal, although on this point Turner wasn't entirely sure that the larger betrayal wasn't letting her go through with a marriage to a snake and a liar like Tripp Wallace. She hadn't resolved any of these questions when a rustling in the reeds of the marsh to the east caught her attention.

She had sometimes seen deer come up this close to the estate late at night. There was a doe and a fawn, in particular, who came often to forage for food in the soft weeds close to shore, but this was midafternoon, and the sun was still too bright for wild things to wander in safety. She walked closer to see what it might be.

A few yards from the edge of the marsh, she saw him. It was Simon, hidden by the rushes in the same wooden skiff she had seen Enoch in, the night of the party. He was looking directly at her and beckoned her with his hands to come closer. He apparently didn't want to risk being seen.

Hiking up her skirt and wading in up to her knees, she climbed over the bow of the boat and sat down opposite Simon, who looked much calmer, now, than the last time she saw him.

"Me and Enoch," he said, "we're camped on the other side of the island. The police are lookin' for him everywhere, but he's smarter than them." Simon smiled as he said this, but then his face fell. "We can't do much more than feed ourselves, now. Enoch has to hide. It's caused him terrible sorrow."

"I figured as much," Turner answered. "I haven't heard anything about him for weeks, now."

"Oh, yes, and you wouldn't, you know, the way he's kept hid, but he's heard a lot about you."

"About me?"

"About you and that book you're writing."

This gave Turner pause. It was one thing to be writing a book about someone so distant and mythical that he existed as an abstraction. She rather preferred it that way. It permitted her greater liberty with the subject matter—and the facts. It was quite something else to be writing a biography of someone she knew.

"What does he say?" she asked.

"He'd like to see you, to tell you himself what he wants people to hear about him in your book. He knows they'll listen when you tell it for him. Would you agree to that, ma'am?"

It was almost too good to be true. Simon was handing him to her. She needed only to relay the time and place to Smoke, and her secret would be forever sealed. She hesitated before answering.

"Ma'am?" Simon insisted.

"Yes," she said slowly, as if convincing herself as she spoke. "Yes, I would like to meet him, but you must tell him this for me." She repositioned herself to look him squarely in the eyes. "I am not safe to be around, right now. People are watching me who want to get to Enoch, so we must be very careful about where and when we find each other. Can you help me do that?"

"That I can, and I will. You leave it to old Simon."

CHAPTER 23

Charlotte headed toward the back of the house through the kitchen, stopping along the way to grab one of Rutla's coconut-filled, dark-chocolate, walnut brownies, still warm from the oven. She got fifteen feet from the back door before she returned for seconds, then twenty feet before returning, uncontrollably, for thirds and an enormous flagon of whole milk. She scolded herself—muttering that she needed more brownies like she needed sandbags full of lard lashed to her hips. The St. Pauli Girl was about to become the Pillsbury Doughboy. But ever since Rutla had made the first batch two weeks ago, the entire household had been powerless to resist. Rutla now made them every day. Their aroma called to Charlotte from afar. She had always been a brownie fiend, but Rutla's special recipe was strangely narcotic.

Charlotte hadn't noticed Rutla standing in the pantry, where she had been putting things up and had paused to watch the running of the three-brownie relay. Her face was a mixture of bemusement and pride.

"Where are you going this evening, my dear?" Rutla glanced triumphantly at the third brownie as she spoke.

"Oh, you know, just for a walk by the beach—not far."

"And not for long, I hope. It looks like it might storm. Take an umbrella just in case you get caught."

Rutla motioned to a stand by the door filled with a superfluous number of stout, manly umbrellas, none shorter than four feet long, that had belonged to Mr. Delano. He had employed them regularly on his walks "upon the moors," as he poetically referred to his estate. Charlotte took an umbrella in her free hand—the one that wasn't holding the fourth brownie—and wielded it awkwardly.

"I won't get caught, Rutla. I promise."

She gave Rutla a sheepish smile and hurried on the path to the beach. Rutla stood by the window for a long time watching her go and noticing, not for the first time, how very young she seemed, both in manner and appearance. At thirty-two, Charlotte could still pass for twenty-two. Her alabaster complexion, laughing smile, and childish freckles betrayed nothing of the secrets of her years, or the cruelty of them.

It was as much Rutla's job to preserve secrets as it was to preserve tomatoes from the summer garden. Constance Delano knew this instinctively and trusted her implicitly—which was partly why Rutla was so troubled by one secret, in particular, of that particular summer.

Rutla was a cook and the manager of the house, not a common housekeeper. Were it not for the fact that the morning ferry that usually brought the maids and groundskeepers had broken down one day, she would have had no interest in cleaning out the upstairs bathroom that Dory, Turner, and Charlotte kept in a state of upheaval during the weeks they spent at the estate. One bathroom for three women was a minor inconvenience to them but a drudgery to the one who had to clean it. On the day that penance fell to Rutla, she was emptying a wastebasket filled to overflowing with tissues, dental floss, cotton balls, Q-tips and assorted other trash, when some debris of unusual importance fell to the floor.

It was a secret.

And not just any secret. It was that particular secret which, depending on the point of view of the keeper, was reason either for the brightest hope or the darkest dread. In actuality, it was nothing more than a thin strip of plastic. Pink, at one end.

Pregnancy is a miracle repeated three hundred thousand times a day around the planet. There would have been no mystery to the thing but for the fact that three women contributed equally and generously to the trash in that bathroom, and the trash didn't come labeled with the name of its contributor. One of them had assumed that interring this little bit of prophecy in the middle of a pile of snotty Kleenex and skin-cleansing pads would keep it well hidden. But the same lack of planning that had led to the stick led to its discovery.

Rutla's conundrum was immutable. She could not approach any of the three women without risking approaching one or both of the wrong two and revealing the secret of the right one. Her greatest dread was that it was Dory, although it would explain why she had agreed to marry Tripp Wallace—something that otherwise seemed inexplicable to Rutla. It was widely known that he was broke and hunting a fortune. But besides that, Rutla had seen enough of Tripp over the years to form an opinion of him as somewhat slippery and dishonest. That opinion was nailed down more firmly after the Delano garden party. That was the night when, after sneaking out into the garden for a forbidden cigarette at the end of a long day, she had seen Tripp and Turner together in the pool. Tripp's ever-present ally, the man they called Smoke, was waiting in the shadows like a ghoul.

Rutla could not bring herself to believe that Dory would actually marry Tripp Wallace for love, and what she saw in that pool not two hours after his proposal confirmed that love wasn't carrying him to the altar, either. An unexpected pregnancy would explain not only why Dory was marrying him at all, but why she was marrying him in a matter of weeks, depriving her mother of the satisfaction of long winter months of planning.

But Rutla knew that if Dory did love him—and perhaps even if she didn't—it would crush her to think that on the same night he proposed, he made love to another woman. The fact that this other woman was Turner, and the very real possibility that Turner was now pregnant with Tripp's child, made it clear to Rutla why she could never approach Dory. And if she could not confide in Dory, it would be a pointless and unforgivable betrayal to share her secret with Mrs. Delano.

There was, of course, the equally ominous possibility that "the stick" belonged to Charlotte. Rutla did not know why Charlotte now ventured every evening to look out over the bluff toward the outer beach on Eel Pond, but she seemed to be searching for something or someone. And then there was Charlotte's ravenous appetite for brownies, although by that logic everyone under the roof should have been pregnant, including Mrs. Delano. Rutla's discovery of the stick was, in fact, the reason for the brownies in the first place.

She now baked them every day. They were packed full of calories to ensure that a mother-to-be who didn't wish to overindulge at the dinner table could satisfy her cravings in secret and ensure that the infant who was growing in secret would be well fed. Mrs. Delano, who was far past the age of child-rearing, begged her at first to stop baking them altogether for the sake of her figure—only to return later, begging for another batch and a ten-minute head start on the others.

If it was Dory, she wasn't showing yet and likely

wouldn't be showing before the wedding. Turner was the tall, lanky, athletic type, and women like her sometimes never really showed much at all. Turner, who had practically lived in the pool all summer, had avoided it like a hot tar pit ever since the night of the party—another clue that it could be her, perhaps.

And so for Rutla, the origin of the pink stick was, and for a while longer would remain, a mystery. But like all mysteries of the kind, it would be a short story soon told.

The seas that greeted Charlotte for her walk to Eel Pond that evening were calm—calm enough for her to see all the way to the inlet, where platoons of sandpipers hopped and skittered in disorderly formations along the tide line. It had been almost three weeks since her encounter with "the boy," as she referred to him in her imagination. No one knew of her improbable tryst that day on the sandbar. She doubted anyone would guess she was capable of such a thing, and she saw no point in changing anyone's impression of her.

The boy's face and hands were clear in her mind, but much of the rest of him had become part of an impressionist rendering in her memory. He was younger, that much was certain. "At least twenty-two," she reassured herself, which was no assurance at all. Other possible numbers came to mind. Young girls making love to young boys in the sand dunes on Martha's Vineyard was hardly the stuff of news. But it would be if the girl were thirty-two and the boy were nineteen—or worse. Worse was a definite possibility.

She leaned silently at the edge of the dock, looking out over the pond like a lovelorn pirate, balancing herself on a closed umbrella. She had come there every day for the past three days looking for some sign of him. Again, he didn't come.

In the distance, by the marshes, she saw something moving. As it got closer, she recognized it was Turner. The wind had suddenly picked up, and her white tank top was fluttering in the breeze like a flag of surrender. She was stepping carefully through the marsh, attempting to stay on a path of solid ground. Charlotte called and waved to her, but Turner was looking down at her feet, and the wind carried Charlotte's voice away. Something dangled from Turner's hand.

The marsh was beautiful and a wonderful place for clamming, but it was not an especially pleasant place to explore on foot, and it would be an odd place for swimming or sunbathing. She wondered at first whether Turner going there meant something was wrong, but then she noticed the figure of a man, far off, pulling away from the opposite side of the inlet where Turner had been, in a distinctively wide and upswept skiff whose shape Charlotte would never forget.

It was him.

She ran down the beach and arrived at the far end just in time to meet Turner coming along the path to the dock. Something about the look of surprise on Turner's face, bordering on guilt, told Charlotte to be discreet.

"Exploring?"

"Hi, Charlie." Turner raised the camera dangling from her hand. "Just doing a little birding."

"Oh really? I love the birds around here. Can I see the pictures?"

Turner withdrew the camera from reach. "Heavens no! I . . . I didn't really get any good ones, and I got kind of bored and took some hideous selfies, so—no, absolutely not." She laughed unconvincingly. Charlotte wasn't buying it.

"It was him, wasn't it?" Charlotte said.

Turner stared at her without answering. Charlotte spoke again. "It was Enoch, the fisherman."

Turner relaxed in defeat. "I've been meeting him here to talk, Charlie, but no one can know—do you understand?"

"Not that I plan to tell anyone, but why?"

"Because there are some lunatics out there, and who knows what they'd do if they knew where to find him—that's why."

"How did you know where to find him?"

"The mechanic we met—Simon, you remember? He arranged it."

"Why? What for? And why you?"

Turner laughed at this and looked away, shaking her head in disbelief. She had asked herself the same questions again and again.

"Damned if I know. I wrote the blog, and now I'm supposed to be writing a book about him like he's some sort of prophet, or something." She shook her head again. "Bennett & Donald author, my ass. Here's a prophecy you can hang onto, Charlie: be careful what you wish for."

"So, is he?"

"Is he what?"

"A prophet?"

"Oh, for God's sake, Charlie. Bennett & Donald hopes to hell that everyone thinks so, and they want me to tell them so. They'll sell truckloads of books if I do, but damned if I know what a prophet looks like. This isn't first-century Palestine. The only people I hear about claiming to be prophets are on cable TV, and they're writing their own books."

"That doesn't sound like a 'no.'"

"It isn't a 'yes,' either. Look, I know what you think happened with you and this guy. And I know what Dory thinks and what her mother and probably most of their

271

friends think about what he did for Dory out on the road, and her cancer and all of it. I just don't know what I think of the guy. I don't know who the hell he is, or what he is, or why it's my job to tell the rest of the world about him."

"So why do you go to see him?"

Turner didn't answer right away. By then they had walked all the way to the base of the steep flight of stairs that led to the bluff above the beach and, beyond that, to the lights of the Delano house. Turner sat down with her elbow on one knee and her chin propped up in one hand. Charlotte asked the question again, noticing when she did that a single tear spilled from Turner's eye and began coursing a path down her face.

Turner finally answered. "Have you ever met someone you just know you could love, but at the same time you despise because he makes you think maybe your whole life and everything you've based it on has been bullshit?"

"Oh, Turner." Charlotte reached out to reassure her, caught off guard by this show of tender emotion in the friend she thought she knew better. "I'm sure he doesn't think that about you."

"That's just the thing. You're right. He doesn't think that or say that—he would never judge me. He doesn't have to. He just has this view of the world and the way things are and the way things should be that . . . that I think is either completely true, in which case it changes everything, or completely fucked up, in which case it's pretty goddammed silly for me to be writing about."

"Is that what you've been doing, coming down to the marshes? Meeting him in secret? Recording the Gospel of Enoch?"

Turner laughed painfully. It was a question that held some irony for her. "Yeah, wouldn't Bennett & Donald just *love* that. And that's exactly what they expect, but it's not there. There is no creed, no religion, no rules, no secret handshake with this guy. He talks about God the way you and I talk about the weather—we take it for granted when it's good, we bitch about it when it's bad, but we never stop believing the sun is there just 'cause we can't see it shining. For Enoch, God is not a question of whether or not, but how and when."

"That's remarkably positive."

"Yeah, I wrote that one down to make sure I got it right." She waved a small leather-bound notebook in the air.

"So, what's his angle? Is he a Christian? A Jew? A Hindu? I mean, where does he stand on abortion, gays, the death penalty—the whole shebang?"

"The whole shebang doesn't exist for him, Charlotte. That's the thing about him—there's just the here and now. He's not going to be anyone's poster boy. He doesn't seem to give a rip about rules. Whoever his God is—and I swear I don't really know—he doesn't have a local affiliate, with hours of worship you can look up in the yellow pages."

"No code of canon law, I'm guessing."

Turner looked at her friend and saw the sadness in her eyes. She knew what that reference meant to Charlotte. She brushed Charlotte's hair with one finger. "No, Charlie. No code of canon law. And he's without a doubt the most gullible man I've ever met."

"What about Dory's cancer? You know, the thing he did out on the road, and then what happened later?"

"You mean, is he a miracle worker?"

"I suppose so, yeah. Isn't that what you made everyone think? Isn't that what started this whole thing?"

"That's what Bennett & Donald is paying me to think, and to write."

"Well, is he or isn't he?"

"You won't like the answer, and I'm pretty sure neither will Bennett & Donald."

"Try me."

Turner again paused as she wound herself up to answer. She was trying to convey a meaning that she herself hardly understood.

"He lives by a simple philosophy: 'Fear not.'"

Charlotte wasn't buying it.

"Fear not what?"

"Fear not anything. Have you ever met someone who seemed completely at peace, completely present, and totally connected to the world around them—other people, laughter, joy, beauty, sorrow?"

"Well, not really, but—"

"I'll explain it to you the best way I can, which is the only way I can get it to make any sense: He goes out to sea and the fish swarm to him. He's thirsty and he doesn't have any money, but he meets Simon and—guess what—Simon has a magic no-money-needed drink machine that keeps getting refilled every month because the distributor is too busy to notice. When he needs shelter for the winter, he finds a room in an abandoned gas station with a library of great books. When he needs ice to preserve the shrimp he's catching, he finds an ice machine at the same gas station with all the free ice he can carry."

Turner seemed as amazed herself at this as she expected Charlotte to be. "The point is, Charlie, he doesn't know any of this is going to happen when he walks out the door. He just believes it will happen—for the same reason you and I didn't wonder whether our parents were going to feed us dinner, or pay the heating bill, or buy us clothes for school. We just expected those things to be there, and they were. We didn't care whether the kid we played with next door was a Muslim or a Jew or whether she'd been baptized or confirmed or what she thought about transubstantiation, we just wanted to hang out. He's the same way. Somehow—and this is the weird part—it turns out there's some cosmic kind of power in that. The man is not a prophet, Charlie, he's more like a child than anything else—a beautiful, wonderful, holy child."

Turner had been racing to the point as if she might lose it if she didn't get it out fast enough, but the harder she tried to explain Enoch, the more muddled he became to her.

"All right, all right." Charlotte signaled surrender with a raised hand. "I get it that he's completely Zen, a wise child, like you say, but how does he heal cancer? How does he save Dory just by touching her? You and I were children, and we never did that."

Slowly gathering herself, Turner responded. "The truth is, Charlie, I can't tell you if he's a genius, or some sort of wizard, or Rain Man, or a raving lunatic. I just know he's not a hustler—which says quite a lot about him, considering what he's done and what he can do. But beyond that, I don't have a clue who he is. I just know I won't ever be satisfied until I find out."

"So you *do* believe in him, then?"

"Honestly, Charlie, I don't know what to believe. But I do know one thing: he is the most beautiful soul I've ever met, and the world will devour him if it gets ahold of him. That's exactly what my book will do. It will kill him."

Charlotte sensed that a strong bond had developed between Turner and Enoch, and that she needed to respect and honor that bond. She let the conversation settle as they both stared out to the sea.

"How long have you been coming out here to meet him?"

"About three weeks now, every evening. I've got pages and pages of notes." Turner flipped through the dog-eared notebook in her hand. It was clear she had not only been writing, but also reading and rereading what she had written about him.

"Any pictures?" Charlotte asked, picking up the camera.

"Just one. It's not very good. He didn't particularly like me taking it, and I didn't feel like I could ask for another."

In the image, Charlotte immediately recognized the face—the piercing, impossibly blue eyes. She stared at his image for a long time, trying to reconstruct her jagged memory of seeing that image above the night sea.

She owed her life to him. That was an historical fact. The peripheral mysteries of how he got to that exact place in the water or even knew where to go, at precisely the right moment, and how he made it to shore miles away without a boat, did not change the central fact that he was her savior. But apart from her gratitude, she remained suspicious of his methods and motives. She did not believe.

"I have one more question about Rain Man," Charlotte said. "If he's a child of the universe and plugged into the mother lode of life as you say, why is he collecting cold hard cash for the shrimp, and what's he spending it on? Is the universe about to provide him with a cigarette boat and a duplex overlooking the harbor?"

Turner looked at her sharply and seemed ready to begin what promised to be a blistering retort when she was interrupted by a voice high up on the bluff, at the top of the stairs.

"Hey, you two need a lifeguard down there?" It was Dory, and she was standing next to Tripp. "Rutla sent us to fetch you. She's been worried."

Turner saw Dory first, then visibly stiffened when Tripp walked into view at the edge of the bluff.

Charlotte liked Tripp. He had, after all, been the second man to rescue her from the sea. He was also her friend's fiancé, which put him squarely in the club of "Good Guys," even if membership in the club could be canceled without notice.

As Turner reached the top of the stairs, the iciness in her demeanor toward Tripp was unmistakable. It was the first time they had met since that day in Smoke's office. Dory was holding Tripp's hand and had her other arm folded in his, leaning into him like he was the captain of the football team. She had become an entirely different person, it seemed, in the weeks since her engagement. She was "on" all the time, now, and in full-blown matron mode. It was remarkable to behold but still hard to believe.

Tripp was doing his level best to play the part of dashing squire, but the expression of watchful anxiety on his face was in sharp contrast to Dory's unending smile. He studied Turner closely and braced for a surprise attack.

"What have you two been doing?" Dory asked the beach wanderers, cheerily.

Charlotte looked deferentially to Turner. If there was to be a lie in the answer to that question, it would be Turner's to tell.

"I've been birding down by the marshes," Turner answered. That lie hadn't worked on Charlotte, and it wasn't working on Dory, either, but Dory was astute enough not to press the point.

Charlotte interrupted in hopes of creating a diversion. "And I've been watching the tide roll out to sea," she said, cheerily. The tide was, in fact, rolling *in from sea* at that very moment and had been for four hours.

Dory looked at them both, mystified. "Well, then," she breezily continued, "we'd better get going. Rutla's got dinner waiting for all of us."

"I'm going to have to pass," Turner said, abruptly. "I've got something I need to pick up in town before the stores close. Please ask her to save a plate for me. Oh yeah—and if either one of you eats all the brownies again, I will murder you in your sleep."

"Actually, Dory," Tripp chimed in, "I need to get back to my house to speak to one of the gardeners before the weekend. Would you mind terribly? I'll swing by after dinner for a nightcap and a kiss."

The puzzled look on Dory's face showed she clearly knew that something was up. But she also knew no one was going to tell her what it was, so she let it go.

"I'm going your way," Tripp called to Turner. "Can I walk you to the car?" He followed her down the separate path that led to the garage. Turner didn't answer him, choosing instead to wait until Dory and Charlotte were out of sight before turning and squaring on him like a lioness.

"You bastard! How dare you!" Her complexion was shot through with the blood rising in her veins. She was a blazing red sun of anger.

Tripp was wary but smooth, like a man who knew he had the upper hand. "How dare I what?"

"You know damn well what. I've been waiting to say this to your face ever since the night in the pool. I can't believe my best friend is actually going to throw her life away on such an enormous piece of shit!"

"Well then, aren't we all glad it's Dory's decision and not yours. Besides, you're being a little harsh, don't you think?"

"A little harsh," she answered, incredulously. "A little harsh? You think so, asshole?" He stepped back, warily, as she stepped forward. She looked as if she might try to hit him, but she kept shouting at him instead. "I'd say walking outside the house where you just proposed to your future wife and trying to fuck her best friend is a little harsh."

"Trying? I succeeded for my part. I can't speak for you."

Now she laughed at him contemptuously. "I could have had better sex with a dying salmon."

"Well, I do my part for the survival of the species."

Turner looked at him as if he'd lost his mind. He changed tacks.

"Fine, Turner. Why don't you tell your best friend what happened, and save her from this misery."

This was the checkmate move. He knew he had her. Not in a million years could she bear to inflict that pain and humiliation on Dory. She glared at him, searching for an out. All that occurred to her was another insult.

"Yes, that would be *so* much better. 'Your fiancé tried to fuck me in the pool right after he proposed to you, Dory, but I know he loves you 'cause he couldn't get it up for me.'"

He didn't return the insult. He was punched out and disinterested in any further sparring. Turner, though, was just getting warmed up. She switched gears to become the wise friend.

"Why bother, Tripp? I mean, really? For the money? I know you're broke, but money comes and money goes. Marriage is a long, slow burn. Do you honestly think you're going to be able to keep up this charade for the next fifty years?"

Now it was his turn to laugh. "My dear girl, every prominent family on this island has been keeping up some charade or another since before the Revolution. If you had any idea how families like the Wallaces and Delanos really work, which obviously you don't, you'd know how silly that question sounds."

She stared at him now in speechless disbelief. She had given up the fight. It was now time for him to reel her in.

"I didn't come here to argue with you, Turner. I've actually got something very important to tell you. I came over here hoping to find you. Why do you think I excused myself from dinner, just now? I need your help, and once you hear why, you're going to want *me* to help *you.*"

"Unlikely," she assured him.

"Smoke wants a meeting with the fisherman."

"Yeah. He won't get one."

"He will if you set it up."

"Tell Smoke he must be even higher than he looks."

"He'll tell Dory if you don't."

"Screw him. I'll deny it. Dory will believe me long before she'll believe Smoke, trust me."

"Not when she sees the video."

The sentence burst into the air and hung there, after the sound faded, with something like the smell of sulphur. Turner slowly pivoted away.

"What video?" she asked, cautiously.

There was a pretty white bench along the garden path near where they were standing. Turner leaned and then sat down upon it, thinking how utterly incongruous it was in that place and that moment, festooned with cherubs and winged angels, all smiling and twirling about, their images fixed and wrought in iron.

Tripp pulled out a smart phone, tapped the screen twice, and handed it to Turner. Seeing the dark but very intelligible scene in a little movie playing out before her was like watching a train wreck in slow motion. It was her and Tripp, in the pool. Taken from someplace not far away, the camera picked up the lights in the pool and magnified them, showing her bare breasts clearly in the glow as she hoisted herself onto Tripp and began writhing on top of him. It lasted much longer than she remembered. She didn't remember her bare ass coming all the way out of the water at one point, but it had. A lingering embrace that looked much more intimate and romantic than it was, followed the first kiss. There was a second kiss after that and then a third that she had forgotten. She had no memory of him fondling her breasts, but there he was doing exactly that. The audio picked up her ridiculous giggling as he did this which, perhaps mercifully, showed she was drunk. Dory would know this if she heard it. If she could bear any of it, which Turner knew she could not.

What was most remarkable in the whole sequence was something Turner could not have remembered because she could not have seen it. It was the look in Tripp's eyes when she wasn't looking at him—when her chin was on his shoulder and his chin was on hers. His head was tilted at an odd angle. He was looking directly into the camera. He had dead eyes and a lifeless expression on his face. He was watching Smoke watching her.

Turner was finding it hard to breathe. She didn't speak at first because she was afraid her voice would tremble and make her look weak. She was shot through with fear. Finally, she managed to compose herself.

"It's the money," she said. "Isn't it?"

"Of course it's the money. It's always the goddamn money. How do you think I've afforded to live the way I still do? If I marry Dory, for better or for worse, I'll be free of him forever. If we don't cooperate with him, he'll not only sabotage the wedding, he'll call my loan and take everything my family has worked to create on this island for two centuries. I'll be ruined, and you will have lost one of the few, true friends you'll ever have in this world."

Turner was not looking at him, but staring out to sea. At last she spoke, as if nothing he had just said had penetrated. In fact, she had just had a revelation—

something Enoch had not told her, but something that answered Charlotte's question and explained what Smoke was really after.

"It's the money he's giving them," she said. "That's the problem, isn't it?"

"What? Giving money to who? Smoke's not giving anybody money."

"Not Smoke—Enoch. Enoch's giving money to the fishermen." She turned to look at Tripp, an expression of wonder on her face. "He lives in poverty, and he charges nothing for his shrimp, but people have been giving him thousands upon thousands of dollars. Not just because the shrimp is so good, but because they think he's offering them something more than food— something spiritual. He's bringing in buckets of money."

"I'm not one of your readers, Turner. What do I care about this poacher or what he does with his cash? He's a distraction. I'm in real trouble, here, and so are you."

"Well, maybe he's not a distraction. Ask yourself: why in the world would Smoke be wasting his time being the fisheries police to go after one solitary poacher in a ten-foot skiff with a net?"

"Because he's putting the shrimp fleet out of business, and Smoke is losing money when they default on their loans."

"Bullshit. It doesn't add up. If the fleet was capable of catching any shrimp at all this season, what difference could one man in a rowboat off an island the size of the Vineyard possibly make to their bottom line?"

"I don't know, Turner, and I don't care. We're wasting time."

She was shouting at him, now. "He's giving them the money, you idiot!"

"Who?"

"Enoch! He's taking the money people give him and giving it to the shrimp boat captains."

"What for?"

"It may be hard for you to wrap your pointy little head around a gesture of selfless mercy, but that's *what for*. His father was a shrimper. He knows these men are losing their boats and their livelihood, and he's single-handedly feeding them and keeping them in business with the money he's earning from one small boatload of shrimp each day."

Tripp stared at her with a look of stupefaction that meant either he couldn't do the math, or he didn't understand the motive, or both.

"Don't you get it? He's feeding the multitudes from a few loaves and fishes—not the fake story I wrote about in my blog, but for real. An entire fishing fleet is being kept alive by one man with one boat and a net. It's an honest-to-God, fucking miracle, happening right before our eyes, and here I was making this shit up!"

It was apparent from the light dancing in her eyes, that to Turner this was an epiphany far more important than anything in her world at that moment. She looked at Tripp expectantly, hoping he could see it, but there was nothing but darkness in his eyes. Nothing mattered to him but one thing. It was what Smoke lorded over him.

"Is our Bible study done for the day," Tripp finally answered, "because I really need to go."

Turner exhaled a gust of exasperation and resolved to try one more time. "Let me make it stupid-simple for you. Smoke isn't worried that the shrimpers will fold. He's worried that they will succeed, and Enoch is the reason why. Smoke wants the fishermen to fail. He can more than recoup his money from the sale of their boats and equipment once he forecloses. After that, I honestly don't know what his play is, but I can tell you this: Smoke isn't the one keeping the fishing industry on this island alive—it's Enoch, and that's what Smoke wants to stop."

Tripp was a craven man, but he wasn't stupid. He had long ago caught the point of Turner's homily, but he still had no idea what to do about it, or how it affected him. Then, Turner took a different tack.

"Do you think Smoke will no longer be a threat to you once you marry Dory and her money? Would you be any more comfortable with him sharing his little story after the wedding? What about the pre-nup? If she kicks you out, you'll be flat on your back without a dime."

She could sense Tripp tightening. "No, my friend, Smoke is going to be a thorn in your side for the rest of your life, and that's exactly how long you'll be dancing to his tune if you don't find the guts to stand up for yourself now."

The logic did not escape him. He simply didn't have the courage to act. He had always taken the widest, easiest path, and that was the path on which he intended to stay. Appeasing Smoke now meant an end to the immediate threat. What came after that was beyond the power of his imagination. He decided to change the subject.

"What about you? What about your relationship with Dory? Are you ready to throw all that away?"

"To save her from your sorry ass? You bet."

He immediately regretted the question, but Turner had answered out of spite. As much as she feared Dory was headed for a lifetime of unhappiness, the pain of a friend's betrayal seemed somehow worse. Women could forgive errant husbands, not to mention errant fiancés, but there was no absolution for faithless friends. She couldn't let Smoke tell Dory the truth.

There was something else, too. Turner had seen the look on Dory's face when she held Tripp's hand, standing on the bluff over the pond. There was something different about the way she leaned into him then, like a contented kitten, with her arm folded in his, and something new in her voice. Turner didn't discount the possibility that Dory was carrying off an even bigger charade than the one Tripp was clearly engaged in, but she would have bet against it that evening. She wasn't sure exactly what could have made such a difference in Dory, but she couldn't rule out the possibility that Dory truly loved him.

Turner looked at Tripp now, severely, and began to speak with renewed purpose. "All right. I don't much care whether the shrimping industry survives on this island. But I care about Enoch, and I care about Dory. If you hurt him, I will hurt you. If you break her heart, I promise that Smoke will be the least of your worries. I will come for you, and when I have buried your name and your reputation on this island, I'll just be warming up. Do you understand? I will make your misery my mission in life."

Tripp didn't answer. He understood much more than she knew, but he feared Smoke far more than her threats.

Turner finally started to talk about terms. "How do I know he won't show her the video anyway?"

"He gave me the details. You get him a meeting with Enoch, he'll give you the video on a thumb drive."

"How do I know he won't just tell her?"

"I thought you said she'd never believe him."

"If I'm going to do this, I want a guarantee."

"You'll get one. He's having a contract drawn up with a liquidated-damages clause."

"What the hell is that?"

"It specifies that you get one million dollars in the event another copy of the video turns up or he breaks his promise not to tell Dory."

"That sounds generous."

"It isn't, and it won't be. It's meant to assure you that he'll keep his word."

"Money is what matters to Smoke. He doesn't give a damn about his word."

"Well, then, you should feel very secure."

She had no move left but to agree to Smoke's terms.

"Tell Smoke that Enoch will meet him at the end of the dirt road that leads into Deep Bottom Creek Cove at midnight on Friday—that's one minute after eleven fifty-nine Thursday night, Einstein. I'll meet you and Smoke at his office half an hour ahead of time. Tell him to bring a lantern to shine from the shore. Enoch will know to come to the light."

"You're doing the right thing, Turner."

"Somehow I don't think so. But you tell Smoke I'll have his balls on a pike if he crosses me."

"I'll let you tell him that."

"Enoch goes unharmed, Dory never sees the video or is told anything about the night in the pool."

"You have a deal."

"No, *we* have a deal," Turner insisted, "and you better hope it sticks, for your own sake."

CHAPTER 24

It was the Thursday before the wedding, in the last week of August. This was the time of year when the island started the slow lean over the precipice of fall for the deep plunge into winter. But this year the winding down of the summer season had coincided with the winding up of the wedding season. It was only one wedding, but the wedding of a Delano is a season unto itself.

There were whispers of pregnancy. Vineyard society loved nothing so much as a good scandal, and among the better families, scandals traveled like a contagion—laterally, through the servants, then upward, from one house to another.

Nothing was surer to fan the flames of rumor than scheduling, on less than a month's notice, the wedding of the sole heiress to an eight-hundred-million-dollar fortune. Far more important even than that astounding amount of money, though, was the fact that the Delanos had lived at the pinnacle of New England society for more than two hundred years. When so much effort and care has gone into the building of a family's name and fortune for so long, plans for its continuation are usually made over decades, not slapped together in a few weeks.

But Constance Delano was a force to be reckoned with, and there was no one on the Vineyard or, for that matter, in all of New England, equal to that reckoning. She had the money and the power to ignore and outlast the opinions of others. She would not let any delay—and certainly not for the sake of small notions of decorum—risk this chance to see her difficult, only daughter well married, settled, and no longer a general nuisance to herself and others.

None of which is to say that Constance Delano didn't wince at the whole hurried hubbub of it all. She, like everyone, wondered whether all the rush between Dory and Tripp meant that a child was already on the way. Mrs. Delano, like everyone, hoped to receive some reconnaissance on the subject from Rutla, who told her what she told everyone: that she had no idea. Of course, Rutla had a good many ideas but no way to be sure whether any of them was the *right* idea, so she feigned complete ignorance. Ignorance was something so utterly improbable where Rutla was concerned that Mrs. Delano knew implicitly there was some virtue at work in her silence.

The one person Mrs. Delano dared not ask was Dory herself—not because she did not wish to know, but because she did not wish, by knowing, to diminish the power of secrecy to propel her daughter to the altar. There were many ways to keep a secret, the fog of obfuscation being one of the best. People would question an eight-month pregnancy, but infants are born a month prematurely all the time. There was, in fact, a pandemic of prematurity among the broad-minded daughters of prominent New England families, and the number of these early children who arrived fully hale and hearty was a medical anomaly.

During that August in Edgartown, the caravan of bridal showers, bridal luncheons, bridal teas, and bridal parties traveled at an unusually breakneck pace. When the last of these affairs was over, Dory was awash in exquisitely rare and obscenely expensive gifts. There was a Ming vase from the Roosevelts. Lady Mary Eaton of

Dumbarton sent a gold-gilt, pearl-handled letter opener once owned by Napoleon. The king and queen of Spain sent, with their regrets, a crystal bottle from one of Magellan's ships, filled with perfume made from tropical flowers, seawater, and rum that the queen herself had collected during their latest Caribbean tour. On the table next to these gifts, and piles of others, stood a stack of stationery and envelopes. Dull with exhaustion, Dory, Turner, and Charlotte were sitting in a circle, writing thank-you notes, late into the evening.

"Does Tripp want children?" Charlotte asked out of the blue, not looking up from the page.

Dory startled at the question. "You might do better to ask whether I do."

"Well, do you?"

"We both do, yes."

"If you got pregnant before he proposed, would you have kept the baby?"

"For God's sake, Charlie, what's gotten into you? Where are these questions coming from?"

It was unclear whether Charlotte asked the question out of sheer boredom or because she had a genuine interest in the answer, but Turner immediately perked up when she heard it.

In choosing to protest rather than answer, Dory risked protesting too much. "I can't believe you asked me that! You're as bad as my mother."

"Why? Did she ask you that?" Turner wanted to know. Having smelled a bit of intrigue in the air, she was now seeking its source.

"No, but she's thinking it, and I know my mother. She can hardly contain the agony of her curiosity."

"Well?" Charlotte insisted.

"Well, what? Who on Earth knows what I would do? What would you do?"

Charlotte stiffened. She hadn't expected the question

to be thrown back at her. She wasn't getting married, after all. She didn't have a ready answer.

Turner listened and watched, mouth agape. "I can't believe you'd even hesitate with that one, Charlie! I mean, you of all people, my God!" Dory shot Turner a hot look, and Turner quickly shut up.

Charlotte waved Dory off. "I know. I'm the crazy one who nearly offed herself for the sake of Holy Mother Church. Well, what can I say? Holy Mother Church turned out to be a middle-aged loser in a Roman collar with bad breath and a hard-on."

Neither Dory nor Turner had spoken of Father Vecchio, even obliquely, since Meredith's funeral. Charlotte was well aware of that embargo and, mostly, grateful for it. The memory of him made her sick.

"I know you guys know about Vecchio," Charlotte finally said, breaking the silence that resumed along with the writing. She had stopped calling him "Father" long ago, even in the condemnations of her private thoughts. "It was written all over your faces at the funeral. Don't think I didn't appreciate it. I was just too stunned to say anything, and too afraid that one word from me would undo everything. I don't know what you did to persuade him, but I'm guessing it was an offer he couldn't refuse. It was an especially nice touch that you got the bishop over here. I mean, seriously—you guys are my heroes."

Dory glanced at Turner, looking for navigational aid—where to begin, how gently to go. "Was it just awful, Charlie?" Dory asked.

"Oh, I don't know. If you take away all the priestly bullshit, he's just another guy with a penis." Charlotte's hands were now fidgeting in her purse for something she wanted.

"It's not like I haven't met men like him before. As soon as I wrapped my head around the fact that I was dealing with a horny, overgrown altar boy and not the

vicar of Christ—and I realized that pretty damn quick—
I figured I was in control."

Charlotte shrugged, nonchalantly. "I knew what he
wanted. He knew what I wanted. He gave me a sob
story about how lonely it was to be a priest, how
underneath he was still a man—blah, blah, blah—and
after ten minutes of him burying me in that bullshit, I
finally can't take it anymore. So I say, 'Here, give it to
me.' He pulls it out, and I get him off with my hand."
She crossed herself. "Bless me, Father, for I have
sinned."

Charlotte's hands kept fidgeting. Whatever she was
looking for in her purse wasn't there. Turner suddenly
understood what it was. She pulled a pack of cigarettes
and a lighter from her own purse. Charlotte took them
both eagerly.

"I started back last month," Turner said defensively
toward Dory. "With all the crap—I couldn't help it."

"I've been dying for one of these for three months.
Don't ask me why a suicider can't bring herself to buy
her own cigarettes." Charlotte lit up and took a long,
satisfying drag before continuing.

"I mean, you have a child, and I don't care how hip
or liberal or enlightened a woman you think you are or
want to be, sooner or later you start following a script
that was written for you by your mother, and her
mother before her, because that's the script you've been
given, and it's the only one you know. That script for
me said, 'You baptize your child in the Church—period,
end of story.' I put it off for just a little while to make
peace with Meredith's father, but I didn't think . . ." She
began to cry, then stopped herself. She'd been through
this before, and she was tired of it. "I didn't think a little
while was all I had with her."

Dory moved closer and put her arm around
Charlotte's shoulder. Turner held her hand.

"It's not like I was this devout Catholic before," Charlotte continued, "or even particularly religious—I mean, you know that. It's just who you are when you're raised in it. It's just that, after she was gone, and then Mark and I fell apart, I felt like I didn't get to say goodbye. I never got to tell her, 'Don't worry, Mommy will see you in heaven, and it won't feel like you even left.'" The tears came again, harder this time. Her nose was running. She was looking for a place to put the cigarette down so she could find a tissue. Turner pulled some Kleenex out of her purse.

"Giving her the rites in the Church was how I needed to say goodbye. I tried for years with the bishop, that son of a bitch, and finally gave up. Then, once I knew what Vecchio was really after and I decided to do whatever it took, I guess I was pretty matter-of-fact about it. I mean, if he told me I had to do naked back-handstands down the center aisle at Sunday Mass, I really wouldn't have given a shit. But then it became something else."

"What do you mean?" Dory asked. She was as engrossed as she was repulsed by what Charlotte was saying.

"Well ..." Charlotte blew her nose. "It got to be something darker. I thought all along that I was in control. I mean, I thought I was in the power position. A lonely priest wants a little grab ass? *Fine.* He wants me to give him a happy ending with my hand? *Whatever.* Then one day he asks me to get down on my knees in front of him, and I suddenly realized I lacked the capacity to say 'no.' He had played me perfectly. He'd built up this relationship of trust, pretending to work with me toward 'discerning' the will of God for Meredith—whatever the hell that means—until it was like I was six years old again. And this man is in control. I'm frightened and humiliated, but disobeying him seems even more frightening and humiliating."

Her face gradually relaxed. She was reciting events as if from a dream in which she was somehow still present.

"He's in my mouth and telling me, all the while, to 'receive the body of Christ.' Only it's *his* body. Christ has nothing to do with it. He's saying it like he's offering me spiritual communion. He tells me to stick my tongue out to receive it like it was a wafer, at Mass, and I do it—why? Because I believe, in some twisted way, that he has the keys to the kingdom and my daughter's eternal happiness. Then he comes all over me, and I feel . . . I just feel like dirt, like I'm in a sewer."

"Oh my God, Charlie." Turner spoke through her own cries. Dory was weeping, too. "I'm so sorry. I'm so sorry," they both kept repeating.

Charlotte nodded. "Yeah, me too. I don't know how you guys did it—how you turned things around. But if you hadn't, I really . . . I really don't know how I would have lived with myself. You made a miracle."

"Well, Turner was the miracle worker, not me. Tell Charlotte—" Dory was about to ask Turner to regale them with the story of her coup against Father Vecchio until she saw Turner shaking her head vigorously and mouthing the word "no." Turner was glad to have saved Charlotte from that man, but she wasn't particularly proud of what she had done to make it happen.

"So, but you broke things off with him, on your own, right?" Turner interjected, changing the subject. "How did you finally decide to get out from under Vecchio's control?"

"I was at the church office, in the ladies room, you know, after," Charlotte began. She didn't need to say *after what.* "I was crying my eyes out before I got ready to leave, and all of a sudden the secretary comes in. He must have sent her in there to find me. When she sees me, she puts her arm around my shoulder, and I'm thinking she's going to comfort me—you know, say what a terrible man he is, and that he should be ashamed, and that I never should have had to go through something like that, but that's not what happens. She takes a wet paper towel, and she's blotting semen from my face and hair and dress. She's telling me how proud she is of me for the wonderful service I'm rendering to the Church."

"Oh, Jesus." Dory's hands covered her mouth.

"And I suddenly realize that she's me—or more like, I'm *her*. She's another one of his little concubines. I'm doing the same thing she used to do—or for all I know, still does for him—which is exactly what some other woman is going to do when she comes to him needing to bare her soul. She's gonna wind up baring that and a whole lot more, all in the 'service of the Church.'"

"The service of the Church, my ass," Turner mumbled, pulling hard on her own cigarette, now, and blowing the smoke high. "Women need to sue the bastards."

"That's the thing, though," Dory said. "How many women in Charlie's position are going to sue? And what with Little Miss Muffett in his office running interference for him, men like Vecchio can just deny it or claim it was consensual. Who's going to prove otherwise or want to roll in the mud trying?"

"I don't care what people say." Turner was in a rare mood now, jabbing her finger in the air. "A normal, healthy male—straight or gay—no matter how much he 'loves the Lord'"—she said it with air quotes, as if the sarcasm weren't already clear—"doesn't volunteer for a job that requires him to swear off sex for the next fifty years. I mean, whose bright recruitment idea was that? You know who really wants that job? Men who like the kind of sex they have to keep secret, anyway. It's like holding up a sign that says, 'Only seriously damaged men need apply.'"

Charlotte was nodding, but slowly. It wasn't clear whether she was agreeing with Turner or just affirming her for saying it. There was more to it than that, for Charlotte. She let Turner finish, then started to explain.

"I don't know, Turner. I hear you, and I'm honestly not really sure I disagree—not anymore, anyway. But there are creeps and weirdos and takers everywhere, and I'd be lying if I said there aren't some really kind, genuine priests out there whose hearts are truly in the right place."

"There are." Dory jumped in, carefully straddling both sides of the argument.

"It's true," Charlotte continued. "They're the ones who taught me to believe in the first place. But I'm not so sure who they are, anymore. When you're hurt and bleeding, you have to let people get close in order to get help, and when you do, it can be hard to tell the rescuers from the predators."

Dory cheered her on. "How can you, really?"

"With Vecchio, I guess it wasn't a big mystery from the start. I don't think the guy looked up from my chest once when I first met him. But I was going along with the game we all learned to play—you know—rationalizing, compartmentalizing. You tell yourself: bad priest, good Church, and you put them in different boxes. He's still a priest, so you get past it and get your ticket punched. Then that woman comes in the bathroom and starts cleaning his slime off me and talking like it's the most normal thing in the world, and suddenly I realize it's not just him—it's these people all around him who are protecting him, enabling him. I got this sick feeling that I wasn't in a church at all—I was in a butcher shop, and my ass was on the menu. That's when I knew I had to get out."

"Vecchio had a reputation as a playboy before he

entered the priesthood," Dory said, "but I guess everyone thought the collar would change all that."

"Wrong-O!" Turner said emphatically. "We're not talking about a playboy—we're talking about a predator. And men like that don't change. This is not about sex for him. It's about power and pathology."

"Obviously not. I mean—I totally agree," Dory quickly added, returning safely to Turner's side of the argument. "He's no different than a shrink who builds a relationship of trust, then abuses that trust to get off. You had no way to know that when you first went to see him, Charlie."

"You're right. I had no way to know." Charlotte let that statement hang in the air, then turned to direct her words to Turner. "I guess that's one of the things I haven't been able to work out in my mind about Enoch. You and Dory both seem so convinced that he's some sort of latter-day saint, but I'm not so sure. If he was, why would he lead me to someone like Vecchio? He actually wrote the man's name on a piece of paper, and he took Meredith's urn to St. Joseph's. He practically offered me up to Vecchio, and look what happened."

"Yeah, look what happened," Turner pounced, defensively. "The goddamn bishop himself came over to lay Meredith to rest!"

"It's not just that, either," Charlotte continued. "Think about it. The guy pulls down Dory's dress on the side of the road and puts his hands on her bare breasts. I mean, how do you explain that?"

Dory started to explain, but Charlotte cut her off. "I know what you say happened, Dory, and I respect that, but if you tell that story to someone on the street, how is that any different from what Vecchio did to me?"

"It couldn't be more different than night and day, Charlie." Dory was empathetic, but emphatic about the difference. "Like the difference between kissing your brother and kissing your lover. I don't know how else to describe it, but there was nothing frightening or aggressive or sexual about it. Maybe I should have been scared or offended, but it was different. He had this . . . gentle force."

"So it's decided, then: he's a Jedi," Charlotte quipped.

"No, listen! I didn't pass out because I swooned. I passed out because there was some kind of weird energy coming from him. He was like a human X-ray machine. He was seeing right through me."

Turner sought to add to the point. "Because of Enoch, Charlie, you are alive. You beat that bastard Vecchio, and you got exactly what you wanted for Meredith."

"You're right, you're right. I'm just a little skeptical of wise men offering healing, these days, no matter what collar they're wearing."

There was no arguing with that, and no one did. It was late, and they had written all the notes and said thank you in all the cleverest ways they could think of, for one day. The clutch in Turner's gut that had begun earlier that night, from thinking of what lay ahead, was now a Gordian knot. It actually pained her to get up. She leaned down to kiss Charlotte on the cheek. "We're in your corner, Charlie. Don't ever be skeptical of that."

It was nearly eleven o'clock. The meeting with Smoke and Tripp was only half an hour away. What she wanted to believe about herself and what she had to accept were two diverging roads. There were no easy answers—only the choice she now had to make.

CHAPTER 25

Turner thought the meeting had been canceled when she drove past the office. Everything was dark, inside and out. It seemed at first that no one was there, but then she noticed a dim light inside. It was twenty minutes to midnight. She had procrastinated as long as she could and had twice turned back on her way into town. It seemed unlikely that the plan would go well, but she was being carried along in it like a floodwater.

Despite the darkness, there were more than the usual number of cars parked on the sidewalk in this part of Edgartown on a Wednesday night. There was a Ford Explorer from the sheriff's department, a BMW, and a Mercedes. In the spot marked "reserved for clients of POD" was an antique Volvo displaying a "Choose Life" bumper sticker. Turner found herself lingering on the thought. She realized she wasn't sure whether it was life or death or something else she had come there to choose, that night.

The door was open, and as she walked in, she could hear the laughter of several men. The sound was coming from Smoke's office. As she got closer, the voices stopped. When she opened the door, she found four men standing there, all staring directly at her.

Smoke and Tripp were there, as expected. Father Vecchio and the sheriff were unexpected. The sheriff was in uniform and carrying his sidearm, which Turner at first found reassuring.

"Welcome, my dear," Smoke began.

She hated the way he spoke and always had—the false gentility that never fully covered the slime oozing underneath. Mercifully, after the conversation she had just left, Vecchio said nothing. She might have attacked him then and there if he had.

Of course, there would be introductions—as if this were an Elks meeting. "Allow me to introduce Sheriff James Tally, and I believe you know Father Vecchio and, of course, Trafalgar Wallace the Third."

Turner felt her throat closing up. If she had something to say, she needed to say it quickly, and she had no interest in any pretense of cordiality.

"What's he doing here?" She choked out the words, nodding toward the priest.

"Oh, well, Father Vecchio is a dear friend of mine, and I am a longtime supporter of St. Joseph's and the good work he does there, as you may know," said Smoke.

She did not know, nor was she surprised, nor did she care.

"So naturally he came to me with his distress about your video and extortion scheme." The words hit her like a sudden squall.

"What?" she blurted out. "Extortion scheme?" She was thrown completely off-balance. Her mind raced. She began to think she might actually be in real trouble for what she had done to threaten Vecchio, which might explain why the sheriff was there, but then she remembered Charlotte and what Vecchio had done. He would never let that come out if he could help it.

"You're crazy!" she said. "And what has he got to do with anything, anyway? I thought we were here about Enoch and your own little video extortion scheme, asshole."

"Well, name-calling really isn't necessary, Turner. We're reasonable and civilized people, here. Priests, as you know, bear the heavy burden of the confession of our sins, but often they have no one outside the church in whom they can confide, with whom they can share the load of their own burdens. I have been privileged to serve in that role for Father Vecchio, and he came to me to confess the affair he had with you."

Blindsided again, she was becoming wild with rage and fear that the situation was about to spin out of control. "Affair, my ass!" she screamed.

Smoke remained the picture of calm. "Well, actually, I understand your ass had a good deal to do with it, but that's not why we're here. We have all sinned and fallen short of the glory of the Lord, Turner, and our devoted clergy are no more immune to the temptations of the flesh than the rest of us, but rarely do they have to deal with demands for money from lovers threatening to reveal secretly recorded sex tapes."

"Money? You've got to be kidding me! Is that what he told you?" Vecchio squirmed uncomfortably in the corner as Turner's voice continued to rise. Smoke was very good at this. Vecchio was not.

"I can't believe this shit," Turner said, casting a scathing glance at Vecchio. "This man isn't a priest—he's a monster."

"So says the twice-divorced serial adulterer who entrapped, seduced, and extorted a humble, lovelorn young man who devoted himself to the service of God. Good luck with that argument in court if you choose to make it, Turner. But if you care to return to your senses and to reality, I will tell you exactly what this 'shit,' entails—specifically, the crime of unlawful surveillance within a private residence, which is a felony in the State of Massachusetts. I asked Sheriff Tally to be here to explain the particulars to you if the need arises."

The sheriff looked at her with barely concealed contempt. Turner was fuming, and scared. She had no allies in that room. Tripp stood out of the way in the corner, looking down at his shoes.

Smoke's expression hadn't changed from the thin smile he was wearing when she walked in. Vecchio's had changed considerably. His eyes were wide as saucers and darted nervously around the room, resting at last on Smoke.

"You didn't bring me here to arrest me, Smoke," Turner said more calmly, as she began to sense that she was not the prey. "What's your play? I haven't got all night, and neither does Enoch."

"Ah, yes, Brother Enoch. We'll get to him in a minute. But first I have a contract I want you to sign. I believe Trafalgar mentioned it to you." Tripp still didn't look up.

"I will explain the terms," Smoke continued, speaking as calmly as if he were at a routine closing on a three-bedroom ranch outside town. "You hand over the video of Father Vecchio and promise never to speak of your encounter with him again, and tonight you bring us to Enoch. I hand over the video of you in the pool and promise never to speak of your tryst with the fiancé of your dearest friend in the world." He said those last words slowly, with relish. "We each sign a notarized statement that there are no other copies of our respective videos. The liquidated damages for the breach of the agreement by either of us are stipulated at one million dollars."

Smoke pushed a thumb drive across the table, presumably intending to show that this was the only copy of his video of Turner with Tripp. The scene was all so neatly planned, just as she would expect from Smoke. Except for one thing: it didn't make sense that he hadn't told her about the deal for her video before she got there, that night. Damages or no damages, how could he be sure she would have the camera with her, and that she hadn't made a copy?

"I didn't know anything about his video," she said, pointing to the terrified priest. "I haven't downloaded it to a thumb drive. It's still in my camera. I have no way to give it to you, only to erase it." She pulled the camera out of her purse and laid it on the table.

"Actually, I happen to have some fairly advanced technology that does an excellent job of removing videos from cameras." Smoke opened the drawer of his desk, pulled out a large hammer, and in one motion smashed her camera to pieces.

"What the hell are you doing?" Turner screamed.

"Wiping your memory card," Smoke answered, his thin smile still unchanged, like the face of a mannequin.

"So, jackass, how do you know I haven't made a copy?"

"I don't, exactly, but that was my purpose in not telling you about this part of the deal before you got here. I didn't want to give you time to make one, which I'm certain you would have done if you hadn't done so already."

She had the feeling she was being expertly played, from start to finish, and that the performance was only just beginning.

"Then again," Smoke continued, clearly taken with the beauty of his plan, "once you sign and notarize this document, if a copy of your video shows up thirty days or thirty years from now, you will be arrested that very hour for perjury. I have a very close relationship with the office of the district attorney, and I think you'll find their prosecution of that crime to be—how do they say it—zealous."

Turner felt her options slipping away. As she read the contract that Smoke had placed in front of her, she felt her shoulders slump with defeat. But something was missing in the language that Tripp had assured her would be there. More important to her than Dory's friendship was Enoch's safety. She had nothing left to bargain with, but she didn't trust Smoke.

"One thing, before I sign," she said. "Tripp said you wanted to negotiate with Enoch—about putting a stop to the poaching. I know he's propping up the shrimp fleet and preventing you from getting your hands on those boats and their business. I know it's galling you."

A wave of emotion moved almost imperceptibly across Smoke's face, revealing the slightest unease. He had not expected this perception in Turner, and it had hit closer to the mark than he wished to let her know.

"I don't give a shit about you and your schemes," Turner said, "but I care about Enoch. If your little plan means the shrimpers have to go in order for Enoch to stay and live in peace, I'm willing to make that bargain. But you must tell me that no harm will come to him. I *must have your word.*" Even as she spoke that ultimatum, she cringed inside at the worthlessness of what she was seeking. "Tell me the truth?"

"My dear, I have told you nothing but the truth."

"Then why isn't that promise in the contract? All I have is your word that he won't be harmed. I want to be able to hit you where it hurts if you go back on that promise."

"Well, Turner, I cannot imagine what reason you think I have to harm this simple fisherman—surely you must know Sheriff Tally would never allow it—but there's no point in putting a promise *not* to harm him in a binding contract."

"Oh yeah? Why am I not surprised? Enlighten me, Mr. Webster."

"I'm not a lawyer—thank God—but I can tell you that a promise *not* to commit a crime, which is what harming Enoch certainly would be, cannot be the basis for a valid contract. The promise is illusory and unenforceable because the duty to obey the law is owed to the state, not to a private party, and therefore is not supported by consideration. It is unenforceable as a matter of civil law."

Turner's head was spinning. Contract law was not her strong suit, but underneath the mumbo-jumbo he seemed vaguely to make sense.

"So you see, my dear, in addition to having my lawyers draw this contract up at no expense to you, I've saved you the fifty thousand dollars it would have cost you for a junior legal associate in Boston to explain that same conclusion in a thirty-page letter. In simple terms, Turner, you have no need to rely on my word because you have the law on your side, and the sheriff himself here is bound to enforce it."

Turner shook her head, partly in disgust, and partly in amazement. Smoke was slick beyond imagination. How he had risen to the pinnacle of financial and political power in New England, after getting kicked out of college for a three-day bong-bender, she had not even the first clue. But it was clear he thrived on people underestimating him, and she had done exactly that.

Smoke pressed a small button on the side of his desk, and a well-dressed older woman glided into the room a few seconds later, carrying a notary seal, stamp, and pad. She presented Turner with a pen. Her expression was as indifferent and lifeless as the smile still on Smoke's face. Turner looked at him, now more with fear than amazement.

"How did you set it up, anyway?"

"Set what up, my dear?"

"The video. I get it that you're a slimy Peeping Tom and that your boy Trafalgar is a creep, but how were you in exactly the right spot, at exactly the right time to get the whole thing on camera, start to finish?"

Smoke's smile spread outward. It was the question he'd been hoping she'd ask, and here at the end of their business together, she had finally obliged him.

"Turner, for such an exceptional writer—and believe me, I'm a big fan—you're often not as perceptive as one would hope." He made her wait while he seemed to search for the simplest way to explain how the world worked, to such a rube.

"A good bird dog doesn't hunt because he likes to eat birds, Turner. He hunts to bring prey to his master's table. Because he knows and trusts his master to feed him, he doesn't need to take the birds for himself. Trafalgar is, quite simply, the finest bird dog a man could want, and he and I are old hunting pals."

Smoke's words landed like a hammer and rang in Turner's ears. It was one thing to be played—quite another to hear the quarterback reading from the playbook. She felt suddenly as naked and exposed as she was that night in the pool—drunk and putting on a show for Smoke as he watched from the shadows. She wondered now how many times that ploy had worked for him. More than once, certainly, helped along by "the finest bird dog a man could want."

When he had finished saying this, Smoke turned to Tripp, who was still standing in the corner, as if to give him due credit. He patted Tripp on the shoulder, exactly as one would pat a dog. "Isn't that right, old friend?"

Tripp didn't answer. He stood there then, as he had stood there all night, looking down at nothing.

The road to the headwaters of Deep Bottom Creek was nearly impassable from the recent rain. Turner had borrowed Charlotte's Fiat to come into town, and it did not have enough clearance to get over, much less the power to get through, the foot-deep mud. She was struggling to follow the sheriff, who was driving the Ford with Tripp and Smoke inside, when she finally bogged down for good. They didn't stop for her.

By the time she arrived on foot at the end of the road, a half hour later, she was covered in mud. Smoke, the sheriff, and Tripp were waiting at the edge of the water, where the road gave way to a sand path that led to a small landing beach in the reeds, beneath a stand of willow trees. She could tell from the sound of Smoke's voice that he was growing impatient. He saw Turner coming and walked toward her.

"Where the hell is he? It's been a half hour."

"Well, you ignorant bastards," Turner began, trying to sound as calm as she could while completely out of breath, "if you'd come back for me when I got stuck, I expect he'd have been here and gone by now. I told him not to show his face unless he saw me. He's out there, don't worry."

"All right then, get up here and call your boy." Smoke sounded much more agitated, and his language considerably less formal and genteel, than it had been back in the office. He seemed jumpy, a little nervous—a rarity for him.

Turner walked up to the edge of the road, where the light from the lantern would clearly illuminate her face, and thought for a moment about what she was about to do. The signal to Enoch was arms raised, waving in the air, as if she had seen him. Before she gave it, she felt a strange foreboding. They were out there in the dark in one of the most remote places of the island. She was leading an innocent man—ostensibly to protect him—into the clutches of a treacherous man. What had once seemed so logical and reasonable about this plan, for Enoch's sake as well as her own, now seemed anything but. Had it not been for the presence of the sheriff to ward off any violence, she would not have gone through with it.

Within a few minutes, footsteps could be heard. Enoch was coming toward them in response to the signal Turner had told him to watch for. Smoke stood between the sheriff and Tripp, legs braced, looking intently at the dark curtain of the willows, as if he were waiting for an army to charge out from underneath.

Finally, softly, he appeared, and the effect was surreal. No one spoke when they first saw him. No one moved. Turner watched Smoke carefully. His lip seemed to curl and tremble, and his face distorted to a strange appearance she at first mistook for contempt, then recognized as fear.

Turner could hardly conceal her astonishment. Smoke was afraid. This monster and bully of a man was deathly afraid of a homeless, unarmed fisherman, who was walking toward them in bare feet and rags.

"Shine the goddamned light," Smoke yelled, in exasperation, at Tripp. "I want to see his face." Smoke's trademark erudition had now fully succumbed to the brutish vulgarity of a frightened coward.

The lantern light shone round about Enoch as he stood, shoeless and alone, in the tall grass. His brown hair was shot through with streaks of yellow and gold, his skin was a honey brown, and even in the shadows of that night the crystalline blue of his eyes shone through, making the whole of him nearly indistinguishable from the sea and sand where he stood. He was guileless and defenseless as he looked at them, his hands empty and open. The world around him seemed to stop and stand suspended in a deep silence. Even Smoke did not speak in that moment of awful stillness, when everything beyond the image of this one small man, glowing in the lantern light, became an abyss of night.

Turner found herself looking at Enoch as if for the first time, not knowing it would be the last time. She saw a simple man who had spent the last weeks in their meetings together teaching her about a purer, simpler life. A man who, though he took no pride in name or place or possessions, was well fed, well loved, and in want of nothing. For all the controversy people had projected onto him—who he was, where he came from, what he expected of them, what he believed about himself—she never heard him call his God by any name or creed. Instead, he spoke of God as one would a mother, father, sister, or brother—someone present, never distant, whose love was not merely constant but irrefutable. And in this plainspoken faith his every need had been met, every grace had been given him, and his every prayer had been answered. Until that moment, when his God abandoned him.

"Who do you think you are?" Smoke bellowed at him from the darkness. Enoch made no answer. There was no fear in his eyes. He stood there looking at them in silence, as before.

"Answer me, you son of a bitch!" Smoke demanded. "Who are you? Where do you come from? What brought you here?" Still, Enoch said nothing. Turner could see Smoke's rage rising each time he spoke.

"Why are you screaming at him?" she pleaded, anxiously. "Say your piece and make your offer, and let's get out of here."

"Shut up, you whore!" Smoke shot back, delivering a stinging blow to her cheek with the palm of his hand and knocking her to one knee in the mud.

"You bastard," she cried softly. Enoch moved to help her. Smoke stepped between them.

"Now you listen, fisherman! Do you know who I am?" Smoke demanded. "Tell me, before I beat you down! Do you know what I have the power to do to you, right here, right now?"

Turner trembled in fear. She began to weep, unable to get up from the mud with Smoke standing over her. "Stop it, Smoke. Just stop, please!" she cried.

Enoch stepped again toward Turner. This time, the sheriff stepped to block him.

"You stay back, son," the sheriff finally said, "and Smoke, you'd better let this woman up. There's no call for any violence here tonight."

Smoke looked at the sheriff, now with wild, crazy eyes. "No call for any violence?" he said, laughing to himself. "Why, sheriff, you should know better. There's no call for anything *but* violence."

As Smoke said this, he reached down in one lightning motion and pulled the sheriff's sidearm from the holster, knocking him to the ground next to Turner. Enoch kept coming, but Smoke smacked him hard across the head with the side of the pistol, opening a wide gash that streamed blood over his forehead and face. Enoch staggered back.

"In fact," Smoke said, continuing to look at the sheriff on the ground and waving the now bloody gun in the air, "I'm pretty sure the scourge of gun violence on Martha's Vineyard is about to get worse." Smoke then took aim at the sheriff and pulled the trigger. The shot rang out like cannon fire.

Turner, lying two feet away from the sheriff, felt the force of the bullet as it ripped into his leg, spraying her with a warm, pink, film of blood. She screamed in shock.

"Motherfucker!" the sheriff yelled. "You just shot me! What the hell? You just shot me, you maniac!"

Smoke pulled a handkerchief from his vest pocket and threw it at the sheriff lying on the ground. "Keep steady pressure on the wound and dream of early retirement. You'll live and prosper, Sheriff—I promise you. But somehow I don't think I can say the same for Brother Enoch, here."

Smoke threw the gun at Enoch's gut as he said this. Enoch caught it reflexively, gripping the pistol stock in both hands.

"Thank you for those fingerprints, Brother Enoch," Smoke said, still laughing that strange, high-pitched laugh. "It seems you just shot the sheriff."

Enoch looked curiously at the alien thing in his hands, and at Smoke and Tripp and Turner, before letting the weapon fall to the ground. He raised one hand to touch the blood streaming down his face, with the utter bewilderment of a child, as if he had never until that moment known pain or injury. He said nothing but kept his eyes on Smoke, who remained standing astride Turner.

"Pick it up," Smoke snarled, pointing to the gun.

Turner thought the command was given to Enoch, who now looked at her with an expression of fear and disbelief, until she saw Tripp move from the place where he had, until that moment, stood like a statue. Tripp lifted the gun from the mud and pointed it at Enoch.

Turner felt her heart leap with fear. "Run! Oh God, Tripp, no! Run, Enoch!" She was almost incoherent, screaming in a frenzy of horror. Enoch remained frozen in place.

"Yes, Enoch," Smoke said, laughing. "I recommend you take our girl's advice. Our little meeting probably didn't go quite as she planned. It's about time you crawl back into the water."

"Do it," Smoke barked at Tripp. Turner heard for the second time the crisp snap of the hammer cocking back.

"You fucking lunatics!" she screamed, and threw all her weight into Smoke's leg, knocking him into Tripp. A shot rang out, but the bullet went up into the trees. Twigs and leaves came floating down.

"Run, Enoch! For Christ's sake! Run!" Turner kept screaming as she rolled under and over Smoke in the mud, trying to reach Tripp's hand on the gun.

Enoch, as if waking from a trance, staggered back a few steps before turning and starting a disoriented jog toward the water, looking over his shoulder as he went. Tripp struggled to free himself from the tangle of bodies on the ground. There was no time to get up. Enoch was soon at the edge of the marsh and partially hidden by low-hanging branches. From a prone position, with Turner landing feeble blows on his head and neck and Smoke yelling at her to get off him, Tripp took unsteady aim. He had a difficult shot at a running target, but it was a shot. When the gun fired, Turner saw the fabric of Enoch's shirt fly away from his back and his body shudder from the force of the bullet. He went down immediately, rose back into a crouch, stumbled a few yards, and fell again. No more sound or sign of movement came from where he lay.

"You bastards!" Turner yelled, digging her fingernails into Tripp's neck. He screamed in agony. She meant to get the gun, if she could, to kill them both, but the chance never came. Smoke's leaden, clenched fist came swiftly down upon the back of her skull. Her limp body collapsed into the mud.

Smoke grabbed the gun from Tripp and pointed the barrel behind Turner's ear.

"There's no need!" the sheriff grunted from the place where he had dragged himself to sit against a tree trunk, nursing his wound. "It's three witnesses against one. Who's she gonna tell, the sheriff? No one will believe her anyway."

Smoke grinned in admiration at the sheriff's prescience to declare his allegiance to Smoke at that moment, and in that way. The next bullet would have been his.

Tripp pulled himself up from the muck and shook his clothing. "Did you get him?" the sheriff asked.

"I think so," Tripp answered. "I saw him go down over there."

Smoke grabbed the lantern. Holding it out in front with one hand and the gun in the other, he and Tripp waded through the tall grass where the end of the road fanned out into a small landing on the beach. There, glistening in the sand from the lantern light, was a steady ribbon of color leading to the water, but no body.

"Dark red, almost black," Smoke observed. He tasted it with his finger. "Arterial blood. It was a good shot, Tripp."

"I'm a little out of practice with pistols. I sold my father's Grande Puissance to a collector last year for some extra cash."

Smoked laughed. "Well, stick with the plan, and in two days' time you'll have all the extra cash you'll ever need."

The two men searched the entire beach and surrounding marsh for close to an hour, poking the shallows with sticks and shining the light across the calm water, but there was no body to be found. Each man hurried to dismiss a shared, unspoken doubt.

"If he swam off, he's bled out by now," Smoke said. "He'll wash up in a day or so, another victim of a turf war between poachers. Senseless gun violence! When will it stop?"

"Oh, no question," Tripp added, with all the bravado he could muster. "He's toast."

"That would be shrimp toast, would it not?"

"Pretty goddamned lame, Smoke, even for you."

The two walked back toward the car. The sheriff was already inside. Turner's body still lay in a motionless heap in the mud.

"She's a first-rate piece of ass—always has been—but you'd never know it to look at her now," Smoke observed.

"No question," Tripp said. "I can see why Vecchio wanted some of that."

"Vecchio wants some of everything. Man, woman, or beast." Both men laughed uproariously.

Smoke observed Turner more closely, touching the bloody seam his fist had opened beneath her scalp. He eyed her curiously. "She certainly looked more appealing in the video. I think I'll watch it again when I get home."

CHAPTER 26

It was an hour before dawn when Turner was conscious enough to feel the ache behind her ear. Her fingers traced the raised welt that stretched four inches along her skull. Her hair was matted and sticky with blood. Another moment passed before she remembered where she was. She started to get up quickly to run, unsure whether she was still in danger, but her first movements were met with fiery waves of resistance from bruised muscles in her legs and back. She was still covered with mud, now crusted with a thin coating of salt and sand that, in addition to making it miserable to move, made her look like the sea-salt caramels that sold for a quarter in town. A few dozen of those and a steaming cup of black coffee—strong— would be heaven, she thought, deliriously.

But this was hell.

She was starving. And cold. Scenes from the night before rolled past her mind's eye in a disconnected jumble: Enoch running, Smoke laughing, Tripp fighting for the gun and taking aim, the shot, the spasm of the impact to Enoch's back, and a shuddering blow to her head followed by the long, deep darkness from which she was only now emerging.

Her powers of speech finally caught up with her thoughts. "Enoch!" she shouted hoarsely. Ignoring the pain, she stumbled to the place where she remembered seeing him fall.

There was blood in the sand, but no body.

She considered the possibility that Smoke and Tripp had taken the body somewhere to bury it, but she noticed the trail of bent reeds and spattered blood moving southward. The trail led to the water, where it ended. He had gone to the sea, but then—where?

The sky was already painted in pastel pinks and blues from the nearing dawn as Turner looked out over the cove. It was a long walk along the beach to Edgartown, but it was the only way that didn't risk being seen.

She moved in the direction of the open sea, picking her way in bare feet through the stubble of shells, stones, and driftwood. By the time she reached the southeast end of the island, the sun was almost coming up.

In the distance, she saw an oblong shape lying in the surf where the ocean met the cove, and her heart sank. She ran quickly now on the smooth sand of the seashore, forgetting the injuries and the stiffness, and seeing only the dark brown mass lying lifeless in the water. When she was still fifty yards away, she stopped to steady her gaze at what she thought she was seeing.

It was not him. It was a boat. It was his boat.

The skiff had swamped in the surf and dug its bow into the sand from the action of the waves. The tide was coming in, pushing it farther ashore with each wave. Turner struggled to dislodge the craft from the beach, using the force of the water to lift one side a little higher with each successive wave. When the beam finally yielded and the boat turned onto its keel, her hands slid on something slick and smooth along the gunwales. They were streaked with fresh blood.

Seeing evidence of the massacre in the hull of that boat—where Enoch had almost certainly spent his last moments on Earth—she was overwhelmed with feelings of guilt and grief. Both seemed unbearable. She had betrayed him, and she had lost him. Quietly there, by the sea, with the sun rising behind her in the false hope of a new dawn, she wept. She wept for the man who had saved Charlotte, who had saved Dory, and who had saved her just as surely from a life once devoid of meaning and purpose, but who in the end could not save himself.

The heavy wooden oars had washed ashore a few hundred yards farther to the north. Gathering first one, then the other, she fitted them to the locks of the skiff. Wading in the surf at the stern with the bow headed to sea, she used the same rhythm of the water she had used to right the vessel to push it out into the water.

It didn't take long, once she was underway, for her grief to find a mission, and for the mission to find a plan. It was pure vengeance. It would settle nothing, solve nothing, and redeem nothing, but it would cause Tripp Wallace no small amount of pain, and that was all that mattered to Turner.

Above the beach, the Edgartown Light was still sweeping faint arcs of yellow through the shadows of early dawn. She rowed steadily and deliberately for it.

One hour later, coming swiftly through the inlet on the flooding tide, Turner was too far away from the Chappaquiddick Ferry for the people on board to see the blood smeared on her hands and face. She looked instead like any other summer resident out for a brisk morning row and some exercise in the harbor.

The tide swept her steadily toward the docks of the yacht club, where she knew Tripp might be that morning. She was counting on him being elsewhere.

Once at the dock, she pulled alongside the *Victory* and tied off. There were only a few people milling about who noticed her climb up from the skiff and into the cockpit. Remembering the cardinal rule of trespassers and frauds, she acted like she knew exactly what she was doing and needed no one's permission or help to do it. Seated on *Victory's* gleaming, teak bridge deck, she removed the hatch boards from the companionway with ease. It was one of the endearing features of yacht club life on the Vineyard, and one that Tripp Wallace would soon regret, that it was considered poor form to lock boats.

"Mornin'!" A tall, well-groomed gentleman walking past on the dock called out to her. He was carrying bags of supplies toward another boat. "Mornin'," she replied, deliberately in the same vernacular, and gave him a girlish wave before remembering the mud on her face and the blood on her hand. She worried when she noticed him look a little longer and harder at her than she would have wished, but she guessed he was just curious to see Tripp Wallace's unlikely conquest, disheveled and nearly spilling out of the dress she must have been wearing when he ravished her in the mud. Then it occurred to her that it wasn't her appearance that had caught the man's attention but the fact that a strange woman was climbing around Tripp Wallace's boat at seven o'clock in the morning, the day before his wedding.

"Can you believe it? And with his wedding only a day away!" she imagined the scolds would cluck and cackle, but the man said nothing and kept walking.

Turner worked quickly. She had not been aboard the *Victory* before, but she had been aboard enough big sailboats to know their weaknesses. This one had holes drilled in the hull that were tightly sealed with bronze seacocks connected to hoses. The seacocks were opened and closed manually by levers. They allowed seawater to be pumped into or drained out of the boat for various purposes—cooling the engine, filling and flushing the head, supplying water for a deck wash-down pump.

Finding a flat-head screwdriver in the ready box at

the navigation station, she quickly unscrewed the hose clamps at each of those locations, removed the hose from the seacock, and opened the valve. Water gushed into the bilge immediately. When it did, a whirring noise could be heard deep inside the hull, followed by a noise like someone peeing into the water from the deck outside. The automatic bilge pump had been activated by the rising water level and was pumping water out as fast as it leaked in. This was not Turner's plan.

She found the pump beneath the engine and, using a flashlight kept on board, cut the wires that supplied power to the pump. All was silence, now, except for the steady whoosh of water pouring into the hull from three locations.

Before long, four feet of water had risen in the bilge and was now just inches from overflowing into the main cabin. Unless someone got on board to rescue the *Victory* in the next hour, Tripp Wallace's beloved family heirloom would be at the bottom of the harbor. But even that slim chance of rescue was too much for Turner to risk. People would surely notice the large vessel listing at the dock, before it sank, and rush to save it.

To prevent this from happening, Turner found a propane swing stove on the main bulkhead of the cabin—used mostly to heat coffee and soup for crews on race days. A bottle of propane was still attached that felt almost full. She opened the valve to "high" without lighting the flame. As the cabin filled with the noxious odor of gas, she lit one small candle lantern thirty feet away in the forward berth and hurriedly scrambled up the cabin steps, sealing the cabin shut behind her with the hatch boards. She then jumped out onto the dock to release all five of the lines that secured the *Victory* to her berth. When this was done, the *Victory* began floating steadily away from the dock in the direction of the tide.

Turner could see the faint glimmer of the candle inside the forward berth as she tied the line from the stern cleats of the skiff to the starboard bow cleat of the *Victory*. Then, with all her strength, she began to row in the direction of the anchorage, making little headway at first, then gaining speed as momentum propelled the old grande dame of Edgartown to her doom. She would tow the *Victory* out to the middle of the harbor where it would be too difficult and too dangerous for anyone to try to save her, and let her burn.

"Hey, where ya' headed?" shouted the friendly, curious man, as he watched her pass.

"Perdition, most likely." Turner answered. "You?"

Tripp Wallace stayed at Smoke's office for two hours after checking on the sheriff at the hospital. The story they had agreed to give the doctors and the media was airtight: the sheriff had been driving with Smoke and Tripp on the coast road, responding to their report of seeing poachers in the area, when shots were fired in the vicinity of Deep Cove Road. They could not see well in the dark, but they happened on what was believed to be a gun battle between rival bands. Upon arriving at the scene and getting out of his cruiser, Sheriff Tally was wounded by stray gunfire before any of the combatants could be confronted. The poachers' whereabouts were unknown, but from signs of blood in the area, it appeared that one of them was mortally wounded. Smoke and Tripp heroically applied first aid to the sheriff's wound and rushed him to the hospital for emergency treatment. Turner was never mentioned.

"Just remember," Smoke warned Tripp. "Nothing in this is to implicate this Enoch fellow in any wrongdoing. If he's dead, I want his reputation intact."

"Why? What's his reputation to you?"

"Never mind what it is to me. Robin Hood is a useful legend only if Robin Hood is dead. A live Robin Hood, on the other hand, is a pain in everyone's—"

Tripp didn't hear the last word Smoke said because it was obscured by the deafening noise of an explosion coming from the direction of the harbor. The two men stopped their conversation and looked out the east window of the office. There, above the roof line, a pillar of black smoke was rising from the water. Below the roof line, what they could not see were the final moments of the sailing vessel *Victory,* burning to the waterline as she sunk at last beneath the waves.

CHAPTER 27

Constance Delano was beside herself. "It was a miracle no one was killed—just a miracle!" She kept repeating those words as she hurried the platoons of staff along in their duties on the afternoon of the wedding.

"You don't know that, Mother," Dory protested.

"Of course I do, my dear. Miracles happen every day."

"I don't mean that, I mean—"

"I know what you mean, sweetheart, but there were no bodies among the wreckage, and we know Trafalgar"—she insisted on calling him by his full name, now—"was unharmed. What on earth are you worried about?"

"What do you think I'm worried about!" Dory yelled, and fell into tears.

"Oh, please, sweetheart. I know it's heartbreaking, but you're not marrying Turner, for God's sake. You're marrying Trafalgar, and it's a credit to him that he decided not to put the wedding off, what with all he's been through in the last two days—a shooting, vandals, murderous poachers, saboteurs . . ."

"I know, Mother, but—"

"Besides, she decided to go her own way a long time ago. When you made that girl a bridesmaid, I questioned whether she'd even show up for the wedding, but I chose to keep my own counsel. You're not a teenager anymore, Dory. You're free to choose your own friends, but what with all this nonsense about that book she's writing—my God. Ever since she showed up, you've not been able safely to enter your own home. Turner is one of those people who goes about trailing scandal and chaos in her wake."

Dory did not answer. Charlotte, sitting next to her and holding her hand, said nothing. Noticing the uncharacteristic quiet, Mrs. Delano paused to reexamine the situation.

"You're not—now don't tell me. Great Jesus, Mary, and Joseph, you're not thinking of canceling this wedding, are you? Because if that's even on your mind—"

"No, Mother," Dory answered resignedly. "You shall have me married off and safely tucked away soon enough."

"I should hope so! And so should you! I don't understand it. You speak as if you're being sent away to bonded servitude. May I remind you, young lady, that you are the heiress to the proudest family in New England." (Pride was the preferred euphuism for wealth among the wealthy, who never spoke of money in actual terms.) "And you are about to marry the scion of one of the oldest families in New England." (Longevity was the preferred euphemism among the wealthy for class, which was never to be confused with wealth.) "You have no reason to be mooning about on your wedding day."

Dory looked at her mother with a defeated smile. "Of course not, Mother. You're right, as usual." Just then, Mrs. Delano heard the sound of a large plate crashing in the kitchen and bolted out of the room toward the disaster.

It was a testament to the power of the Delano family that not only had Cardinal Dolan Flaherty interrupted his trip to Rome to officiate the wedding, he had agreed to say the nuptial Mass in the outdoor chapel on the grounds of the estate. Outdoor weddings were against Catholic teaching, which required that the sacrament of matrimony be celebrated only in a sacramental space. That meant a nuptial Mass could take place only in a Catholic church, but in characteristic fashion, Constance Delano had dispatched this obstacle with ease. The first ecclesial order of Cardinal Flaherty's visit would be to consecrate the outdoor chapel on the Delano estate as the newest church of the archdiocese, aptly named, "Our Lady of the Vineyard." This rare honor and the lightning-fast approval by the Roman Curia were abetted by Mrs. Delano's generous offer to purchase, outright, a plot of land for the Cardinal Dolan Flaherty Library to be built outside Boston. Dory's only contribution to this plan was the non-negotiable demand, which her mother found both inexplicable and in extremely poor taste, that Father Vecchio and the auxiliary bishop not be invited to the wedding. That argument raged no fewer than eight days between mother and daughter before a truce was called, with daughter refusing to budge and mother refusing to risk an impasse.

"It should be a beautiful day for a wedding," Charlotte offered, hoping to change the subject and Dory's mood. "What they've done with the garden is amazing. I never imagined I'd be part of such a fairy-tale wedding."

Dory stared out the window of the downstairs parlor into the portico, where a small army of workers were carrying pots and plants and tables and chairs back and forth in a whirlwind of purposeful movement. The sunlight illuminated one side of her face, leaving the other in shadow. Sitting there, motionless and detached from her surroundings, wearing her wedding dress for the last-minute fitting that Rutla had demanded, she looked like a painting by Vermeer.

"A fairy-tale wedding for a fairy-tale marriage," Dory replied, sardonically.

"Don't you think it is—and will be?" Charlotte asked, hopefully.

"Don't humor me, Charlie. I know you and Turner have your doubts. I mean, how could you not? Tripp and I were barely holding hands when you arrived three months ago, and now we're getting married. I'd be suspicious if you *didn't* have doubts. Hell, *I've* got doubts."

That last line was gratuitous and unexpected. Charlotte wasn't sure at first what to do with it, then decided she couldn't leave it alone.

"Then why go through with it?"

Dory laughed. It was not an appropriate moment for laughter, and that she found it to be so made the sound of it, in that still room, all the more strange. Dory didn't answer at first. Instead, she looked squarely at Charlotte with a sad smile, wondering whether to burden her with the same heavy load she carried.

"Never mind. It's a stupid question. I shouldn't have asked," Charlotte said.

"No, Charlie, not at all. I understand." Dory looked past her, dreamily, through the window overlooking the sea to the north, as if she saw something miles and miles away. She began to tell a story.

"I could almost write you a script for how it will go. It won't be like most marriages, even at first. We won't be lovebirds. We will be more like two old friends who saw they were walking in the same direction and decided they might as well walk a little closer together for safety or comfort or conversation without having to shout— something like that, I don't know—but never in each other's way, always ready with a kind word and a gentle touch, but nothing too intrusive or needy."

Charlotte listened, more confused than incredulous. "Sounds romantic," she said. "I guess I'll need to take back the sex toys I got you for the honeymoon and get you a rocking chair. And you're okay with that?"

"That's just the thing. I'm not a romantic, Charlie. I can't be. You can't grow up in a family like mine and have dreams of falling in love with Cary Grant on a Roman holiday."

She continued, making little air quotes with her hands. "I'm 'the repository of the hopes and dreams of generations,' as my mother would say, 'who have worked before you to build *all* that we have. We are born and bred to it, Eudora, like Lipizzaner stallions!'"

Dory laughed at that part. "I never got how I was supposed to see myself as a stallion, but I understood that this is the way the Delanos do marriage. I just hope my mother doesn't actually die from shock, once it finally happens."

"Hmm," Charlotte pretended to ruminate. "I've always wondered what it would be like to be a repository. I assume it's better than being a suppository?"

"Shut up, Charlie."

"Seriously, it sounds more like the way the House of Windsor does marriage."

"Haven't you figured it out? We are the goddamn House of Windsor, and Tripp Wallace has stolen the crown jewels."

In spite of Constance Delano's sneaking disbelief that it never would, the day of Eudora Delano's wedding had finally arrived. The sky to the east had dawned a crimson red that morning and swirled busily with clouds by the afternoon. Rutla stood on the bluff alone and in silence, watching the weather and daring it to rain. Directly below, the *Snow Goose*—a small, well-built, and comely ketch that Dory's father had purchased in England and sailed to the Vineyard by himself in 1933—was tied to the dock. Once brightly colored but now pleasingly faded signal flags traced the outline of her rigging and flapped halfheartedly in the light breeze. *Dress ship,* as the flag tradition was named, was reserved for the most solemn and celebratory of occasions, and the wedding of Eudora Wellesley Delano to Trafalgar Cabot Wallace III promised to be the utmost of both.

Constance Delano had planned everything to the nth degree. The reception and dance were to take place in the trellised garden. At one end, six white tents had been erected to enclose fifty dinner tables for six persons each, along with a parquet dance floor, four hundred feet square. The newlyweds would leave the reception on a caravan of rose petals leading down to the dock. There the *Snow Goose* was waiting to embark, her sails and sheets already bent on to take them out of the inlet for their honeymoon cruise to a private island along the coast of Maine. A lovely cottage was prepared for them there, with a staff of six. Rutla had overseen the loading of the *Snow Goose* that morning, with provisions for an indefinite voyage. The Delano wine cellar had contributed sixteen bottles of Dom Perignon, four bottles of 1961 Chateau Lafite Rothschild, a 1957 Glenfiddich, six bottles of rum, ten bottles of gin, six bottles of dry vermouth, and twenty cases of tonic water. There were ninety-seven limes, twenty-four oranges, eleven coconuts, three cases of olives, twenty-four tins of Beluga caviar with an accompanying set of mother-of-pearl spoons in a teak pannier, sixteen wheels of various cheeses from a dairy in Meneshma, and a generous assortment of fresh breads, rolls, pastries, chocolates, and sweets from local bakeries.

All of this fare was carefully planned for a minimum of cooking, dishwashing, and other distractions. The plan was to keep the couple well fed and continuously inebriated, the better to entice them toward their sole duty of fetching a new heir. "Dory is thirty-two, after all," Mrs. Delano kept saying, as if her daughter's marriage at such an advanced age were a moral failing to be lamented at every turn.

Through persistent striving with Dory, who had at first insisted on an intimate gathering of two dozen, Mrs. Delano had trimmed her original guest list to a scandalous minimum of three hundred. Among these were the leading families of New England, though a great many had to be omitted to keep the total within the limit. Then there were the ceremonial guests, to include three current and former senators and their wives, two bishops and their girlfriends posing as aides, the current and former governors, and the second cousin of the Queen of England.

Music for the reception was to be provided by the Tommy Dorsey Orchestra—not only because it was *the* Tommy Dorsey Orchestra, but because the late Tommy Dorsey himself had performed at the wedding of Dory's parents in 1956. The song for their first dance, "I'm in the Mood for Love," would be the song to begin Dory's and Tripp's journey together.

The endless front lawn of the Delano estate, leading to the garden chapel where the ceremony would be held, was a sea of white and blue helium balloons, streaming from a maze of flower baskets nestled in the grass. Dory hated it. It looked to her like the mother of all Easter egg hunts was about to begin. The rhythmic hissing and sucking of the helium tanks as the valves opened and closed could be heard late into the night. Lying in her bed and listening to this sound through the open window, Dory had imagined an ancient iron-lung machine, laboring to keep her alive.

Dory had, by the morning of the wedding, resigned herself to the fact that Turner was not coming home— "home" meaning Mrs. Delano's home, the place where the three of them, including Charlotte, had hid away together from the paparazzi and protesters for the past month. Dory resisted the very real fear that Turner was dead. She simply put it out of her mind. It would be ridiculous to go forward with a wedding, otherwise. It was ridiculous anyway, she thought.

The police had been searching for Turner for two days. Dory knew only that Charlotte's Fiat, which Turner had borrowed to go into town that Thursday night for reasons that were never explained, was found stuck in the mud on the Deep Cove Road. She had read the reports of the shooting incident in that location, in which the sheriff had been struck. She prayed it was not connected to Turner's disappearance, but in her heart she knew it was.

Dory and Turner had had some major battles over the years. Whenever Turner felt the need to be especially biting, she used to compare Dory to "a river a mile wide and an inch deep." It was Turner's way of telling Dory she was a poor little rich girl who lived a pleasant but meaningless life. Now, as Dory imagined herself smiling and laughing in the gaiety of a wedding while her friend and maid of honor was missing and feared dead, the insult seemed to ring true. What should have been the happiest day of her life was, in fact, a low, low tide. She wondered whether even an inch of water remained.

Then, as it comes eventually but with seeming

suddenness to every bride, the time for the wedding ceremony came at last to Dory. She was waiting at her appointed station in the bride's tent that had been erected at the back of the garden chapel, hidden from the quietly murmuring assembly of three hundred.

"Are you ready?" Charlotte asked. Dory vaguely realized it was the third time she'd asked the same question. Dory was filtering it out, waiting in the sweltering heat of the tent. Through the narrow opening in the canvas, she could see her mother seated in the second row, craning her neck tortuously to look in Dory's direction.

All brides are beautiful, but Eudora Delano was a vision. She wore her grandmother's veil of delicate silk tulle interwoven with Carrickmacross lace from Ireland. It was a brilliant white when it was new in 1923 and still nearly so when her mother had worn it, but now it was a soft ivory. She might as well have worn her mother's wedding dress, which had faded to an equal shade of ivory, but at thirty-two Dory wasn't nearly so petite as her mother was at twenty-two. And so Dory's gown was ordered and delivered in a mad rush of three weeks after the tearful pleading of her mother in a 3:00 a.m. phone call to London on the night Dory got engaged. The dress was made by the same designer in a small shop on Fleet Street whose father had made the gown for Princess Elizabeth's wedding to the Duke of Mountbatten in 1947. The design of Dory's dress borrowed heavily from British royal tradition, as befitted American royalty like the Delanos.

The lace sleeves extended fully past the wrist. The bodice was a triumph all its own. It rose close to the chin on the sides of the neck but plunged perilously deep at the bosom, which in Dory's case rose equally to the challenge. That was the difference between European and American royalty, Mr. Delano had often been heard to say in his unguarded moments, which were all those moments when the liquor cabinet was not well guarded by Mrs. Delano. He suffered from the coarseness that often accompanies the arrogance of great wealth. "The Delano women are stacked!" he would erupt, usually in the company of gentlemen married to lesser specimens. "Always have been! A testament to good breeding and the vigor of my forefathers! None of those pale, slim-hipped, English consumptives for the men of this family!"

Despite the vigor of the Delano forefathers, Dory's father had died when she was eleven. Her adolescent years were then spent in constant anxiety before mirrors, waiting for the day when she would know for certain whether she was, in fact, a Delano woman or had been left at the doorstep by wandering English consumptives.

The entire bodice, strained to its very seams that day from this Delano heritage, was delicately embroidered in a floral motif of daffodils, thistles, shamrocks, and roses. The skirt and train were of ivory and white satin gazar. The fittings for the entire dress had been hastily overseen by a dressmaker to the queen's grandniece in Newport, and shot across the Atlantic in a diplomatic cable. The result was a creation that fulfilled Constance Delano's every hope and her daughter's every fear.

It was a regal vestment, designed for empire, not entertainment—with a nine-foot train that Dory had managed only after a fit of tears, screaming, and threats to convince her mother to shorten to six feet. "It's an outdoor wedding on our front lawn, for God's sake, Mother!" Dory had protested. "A nine-foot train will make me look like I'm mowing the damn grass!" Constance Delano was devastated in the way only the mother of a bride can be. "No English girl would be seen with so short a train," she would say again and again, in response to which Dory would demand to know why her family was in constant competition with the English, two hundred years after the Revolution. "It's positively Bohemian!" her mother screamed back for the better part of an hour. In the end, Constance Delano once again accepted defeat in this, yet another skirmish, so as to survive and win the war. And from the pleased look on her face as she watched Cardinal Flaherty take his place at the altar, victory clearly was at hand.

The aisles and altar were resplendent in powder blue hydrangea blossoms, pale pink roses, white bunting, and ivory bows that matched the color of Dory's gown. Seated among the blooms, a string quartet—flown up that afternoon from Juilliard and very unhappily dressed in black—was literally melting in the afternoon heat, to the point where they had to stop after each piece to retune. They were now sprinting to get through the Bach Concerto in D major before their strings sagged again, as the last of the guests were escorted to their seats. In a few minutes they would retune and move on to the Bach Minuet in G major, the final number before the processional.

"Are you ready?" Charlotte asked again, her voice now pleading. Dory looked at her and smiled the halfhearted, halting smile reserved for true and old friends. Charlotte was the best of both. Dory knew Charlotte wasn't hurrying her along. The question was code for, "Do you want to run?"

She didn't. "Ready as I'll ever be."

The first, slow notes of Chopin's *Nocturne* sounded in soft, bell-clear tones from an old Steinway. It had been removed from the parlor of the Delano house for the first time since it arrived aboard a freighter from Hapsburg, eighty years ago. *Nocturne* was the signal for the procession to begin. Peder Albert Otteson—

Constance Delano's eternally young older brother and Dory's charming, silly, and only uncle—looked at her with a mischievous smile and gave a head fake toward the exit. He made Dory laugh for the first time that day. She had swung tirelessly from his arms as a child on his trips to the Vineyard, and he now offered his arm to escort her down the aisle.

Peering through the tent, Charlotte made sure to confirm that Tripp was at the altar before getting started, as if she had serious concerns that he might be elsewhere. Smoke was his best man—a choice of great disappointment and uneasiness for Dory, for reasons she assumed would have been clear to Tripp. Beside Smoke stood Cardinal Flaherty. He was unmistakable in a chasuble that could not have been more shockingly red amid that sea of white than if he had just butchered a lamb with his bare hands.

At last Dory began her long, slow walk. *Nocturne* was exquisitely beautiful and so perfectly suited to that moment. She had picked it herself. It was her favorite piece—the stuff of dreams. Chopin was said to have written it all at once, frantically trying to render it out of memory upon waking from sleep, without playing a single note until it was entirely committed to ink and paper. Not a single note was thereafter changed. It was thought to be divinely inspired and, therefore, a fitting accompaniment for those moments when mortal man sought to lift his gaze to something higher than the world that could be seen. Dory felt herself borne along by it as though she herself were dreaming. Waiting for her at the end of a long tunnel in that dream was one man she had said she loved and another she secretly despised. Yet, like a dreamer, she seemed to have lost control of her limbs and, with them, the ability to fight or flee. The dream led her inexorably forward.

As she came closer to the altar, in this dream there

appeared to Dory the strange, nightmarish image of another woman. She seemed to come from the direction of a grove of trees just beyond the garden. She might as well have been a nymph or a fairy, so unexpected was her sudden entrance. Yet she was no fairy. She was disheveled and dirty, a stricken creature with blood-matted hair and frightened, furtive eyes. She rushed toward Dory with purpose. Whether her purpose was malice or mercy was not immediately clear. Her dress was not quite rinsed of what had once been a great covering of mud, but she seemed utterly unconcerned with her appearance. Her whole world was Dory, to whom she now ran headlong, seeking to intercept her before she made her vows.

Turner Graham had come home.

A gasp rose up from the assembled guests, and Dory trembled upon her uncle's arm. Constance Delano stifled a scream as Charlotte ran to embrace Turner, but Turner pushed past her. Dory remained her sole focus, her only reason for being in that moment.

Smoke audibly scoffed at this intrusion and moved swiftly as if to grab Dory's arm. But Peder—that sensitive, loving, and rare man—felt Dory recoil at Smoke's approach. And so he stepped discreetly forward, his six-foot-four-inch frame presenting an unsubtle barrier between Smoke's glowering presence and the forever-little niece whom he was not overly eager to give away, in any event.

Turner wasted no time. She raced to Dory's side. All that could be heard above the rushing wind of gossip that swept over the crowd were Turner's first words, "I must speak to you, now." The rest of her speech fell to whispers in Dory's ears.

Dory, her face stricken, and Turner, with a look that spoke only of her need for absolution, joined hands. Turner refused to let go as the two sidled a few feet away to a seat on a bench in the garden. They remained separated from the astonished wedding guests by the imposing edifice of Peder, with whom Rutla now stood shoulder to shoulder and nearly equal in height. These guards, despite the disapproval on Constance Delano's face and the look of wonder on every other face, wavered not an inch until what needed to be done between the two women was done.

In that moment, when Turner had told the truth as clearly as Dory could understand it, when all that was hidden had been laid bare, the flowers Dory had been clutching in her hands fell limply to the ground. Dory looked first to Rutla, then to Charlotte, as if seeking her bearings. Finding them, she rose to her feet. Turner, her palms open and turned upward on her lap where Dory had left them, did not follow her.

Pressing her way gently between her two guardians, Dory did not look at Tripp, who only moments ago had been her only beacon and heading. Her eyes were fixed straight ahead toward the bluff in the distance, and the pond below, and the sea beyond.

Fearing the worst, Charlotte tried to speak to her friend as she passed. Dory only shook her head to acknowledge that offer of help as she refused it.

Tripp did not try to say or do anything, nor did Smoke dare further test Peder's resolve. Smoke and Tripp were both thoroughly beaten, it was already clear. From where they stood, they had not heard Turner's confession, but they could have recited every word for her. She had taken the knife Smoke had threatened to use to sever her friendship with Dory and driven it into her own breast. Both men were now riveted to the ground next to the cardinal, who anxiously glanced from one to the other, seeking some clue as to how he should proceed.

Finally, Constance could bear the outrage no longer.

Long-awaited victory was slipping from her grasp. The triumphal achievement and sole aim of her motherhood was being stolen from her before her very eyes. She rose from the second row and in a seething, hissing whisper called to her daughter. "Eudora! Eudora Delano, you stop right there, right now."

Dory was stricken, yet she retained enough presence of mind in that awful moment at least to acknowledge her mother's voice. "I cannot, Mother," she said, scarcely stopping to look in her mother's direction. But Constance Delano would not be denied. In a louder voice she made her displeasure clear to all. "You will stop right now, or I shall not speak to you again!"

For a second time, a collective gasp rushed over the assembly and spread outward like a bomb blast. Dory was stopped by this, but not felled. There was no malice or anger, only sadness in her eyes as she answered. "Yes, you will. You are my mother, and I am your child, to have and to hold. It seems we're stuck with each other, now."

By the time Dory reached the dock, she had shed the veil, the shoes, the gloves, and the better part of her dress. In a silk slip and bare feet, she stepped onto the deck of the *Snow Goose*. Rutla called to her from the dock. "Everything you need is here for you, love."

"I know," Dory answered, pushing back the companionway hatch. "Everything I've needed has always been here for me." She smiled at her loving nursemaid, first tutor, childhood taskmaster, and dear friend. "And so have you."

"Dory!" cried Charlotte, breathlessly, as she clip-clopped down the steep stairs from the bluff with one broken heel. She was trying to keep the crinoline from the bridesmaid dress from tearing on nails.

"Why I'm still bothering with this stupid dress, I have no idea."

"Neither do I, Charlie," Dory said.

The heads of a few curious guests could be seen beginning to peer out from above the pittosporum at the top of the hill, their mouths still agape. Constance Delano was not among them. Peder was standing at the fore of the group, grinning widely. He had never expected such great fun on that day, or such heroism from the little girl he once knew, and he would not abide anyone to stop her.

By the time Charlotte made it all the way down the stairs and to the end of the dock, where Rutla stood ready to cast off the lines, Dory had emerged from the cabin wearing khaki shorts, a white tank top, and dark wayfarers. Her wedding curls were pulled back into a loose ponytail. She looked healthier, more confident, and more beautiful in that moment than Charlotte had ever seen her.

"Where will you go, all by yourself? What will you do?"

"Everywhere, and anything I damn well please. You know, if I'm going to be single, and I think I rather prefer that life, I might as well embrace being rich." Dory smiled to herself as she pondered that thought for a moment. It would have been very unlike the old Dory to say such a thing, but it was clear the new Dory really didn't give a damn what anyone thought of her. "To the devil with all of them, Charlie, and God bless you and Rutla and Peder. I won't be gone forever, but I'll be gone for a good while." She waved to them both.

Dory sought to offer some instruction. "Mother may be fierce, Charlie, but Rutla runs things around here, and Mother damn well knows it. Take my room. In fact, take whatever you like, for as long as you like. I won't be needing any of it anytime soon."

Dory paused then, in her only moment of hesitation since her march from the altar. "And look after Turner, would you, Charlie? It took courage for her to do what she did. A lot has been lost between us, but she tried to give some of it back, today. I don't hate her for it."

"What happened? What was lost? What did she say?"

"I can't tell you now, but I will someday. In the meantime, look after her. She's been caught up in something terrible, and she'll need you. Promise me, Charlie."

"I promise."

A surging confidence seemed to come over Dory aboard the vessel she was preparing to make sail. She was in her element, now. She knew exactly what she was doing and where she was headed.

"But, Dory," Charlotte pleaded, "I mean, my God! How can you sail? You haven't got any help! How will you manage?"

"That's just the thing, Charlie. I haven't any help or any hindrance, either. This boat was built for freedom, and so am I."

Dory waved again and beamed a calm, self-assured smile for her two well-wishers. The diesel engine softly rumbled as the *Snow Goose* slowly made her way toward the inlet. The mizzen sail rose first, then the headsail. In a hundred feet from the dock, she escaped the wind shadow of the headland and caught a quartering southeast breeze. The *Snow Goose* lay gently onto her port shoulder and began a steady reach northward.

Rutla and Charlotte stood in silence, watching her go. "I'm so frightened for her!" Charlotte finally whimpered, still waving both hands at the friend who had long since set her hands and mind to the sea.

"Oh goodness, don't be. That child was born in a boat, and after that, we could hardly get her out of one.

She taught that fool Trafalgar how to sail when they were children, but on his best day he was never a match for her. I suppose he never will be. If it were up to me, he never would have gotten the chance in the first place. I tell you, if she had been my daughter . . ."

Rutla's words ended there. Decorum forbade her to go any further, but her thoughts wandered on as they so often did where Dory was concerned. She loved her like a daughter and always had. Looking out to sea at that little vessel and its brave captain striving against the waves, she could still see clearly the towheaded girl who was an amalgam of freckles and elbows and skinned knees and unmitigated bubblegum tangles. She had been a force of nature who was overfond of cookies and conversation and would consume both in endless quantities on early mornings in the kitchen, when she and Rutla were the only ones awake in the whole house—the child's berry-brown legs swinging freely for joy beneath the chair. Rutla remembered carrying up to bed the limp form of the sleeping girl who had forsworn sleep forever, and how many nights she had sat alone at her bedside, watching her dream, dreading this day when her dreams would come true, and she would be gone.

CHAPTER 28

The letter was unexpected. No one had heard any news of Turner until then. She was gone when Rutla and Charlotte returned to the scene of the wedding-that-never-was, and she had not returned afterwards. In the years that followed, much had been lost, and much of what remained had been changed forever.

After refusing her wedding vows and running away to sea, Dory had spent the rest of that summer and fall aboard the *Snow Goose*, wending her way around the little harbors and islands of the Maine coast. She dropped anchor at Deer Isle before the first snows of winter and savored the still, quiet season there in the cottage that had been prepared for her honeymoon. Warming her body and healing her soul beside a wood stove and a tower of books that had once been collected and left there by her father, she felt the anger and fear of the past slowly melt away and a feeling of greater peace well up inside her. A retired physician who lived on the main island and was about the age her father would have been took an interest in her, checking every other day or so to see what few things she needed. Dory suspected he was engaged in a secret correspondence with Rutla, and this was confirmed when he came one day with news from home.

Constance Delano's impetuous threat to her daughter sadly came true. Six months after Dory's disappearance, she suffered a stroke that left her bedridden and unable to speak. The words of apology she had longed to say to her daughter would be spoken instead with tears and a trembling embrace when she saw her again for the first time, the following spring. Dory gave voice to the words her mother could no longer say but so desperately wanted to hear. She loved her. She forgave her. Constance Delano left this earth one month after that, more at peace than she had dared ever hope to be in those withering days of her daughter's exile.

When Dory returned to the Vineyard that spring, she went in search of Charlotte, who was working as a waitress at the Village Ordinary, a fish-and-chippery in Oak Bluffs, and living in a rented room overlooking Vineyard Haven. It took a solid hour of teary pleading and fiery demanding before Dory could compel Charlotte to return to live at the Delano estate and find work in Edgartown. It was another full hour of tears and fire before Dory had sufficiently remonstrated Rutla for ever letting Charlotte go. The mistake would never happen again. For the remainder of her life, Rutla would dote on Charlotte like a lost daughter.

It was in the sixth year after that fateful summer on the Vineyard that the first news of Turner since the wedding reached Dory and Charlotte, and it was bad news beyond their worst fears. Turner was dead. Word arrived in a letter from a friend of the Delano family, who had learned the news from an editor at Bennett & Donald. They discovered that, after the wedding, Turner had gone to Newport and subsisted there on a series of menial jobs, working only long enough at each to earn money for her next sojourn in search of Enoch. For most of those lost six years, she had traveled the world—living in hostels and refugios and on church doorsteps and feeding herself from the kindness of strangers—as she followed every ephemeral clue to his whereabouts. Some thought she had gone mad.

That Enoch would be anywhere at all contradicted the conclusion that prevailed among most people on the island. After news reports of the gun violence by an unknown band of poachers near Deep Bottom Creek Cove, they believed he suffered a gunshot wound, then capsized and drowned while trying to escape. His empty, bloody skiff, recovered from the weeds in Katama Bay after the unexplained sabotage of the *Victory,* added to the mystery. But some believed he lived still. Turner was one of them.

She refused to complete her book in those six years, despite constant nagging from the publisher that turned, eventually, to legal action. It wasn't until Turner was diagnosed with stage-four breast cancer that the publisher called off the fight. A settlement was reached giving Bennett & Donald the right to publish the book posthumously. That gave Turner just enough time to write one final chapter. She had hoped it would be the chapter in which Enoch performed a last, unequivocal miracle for all the world to see—the one that would save her life.

But there would be no redemption for Turner Graham. She never found Enoch, and she died alone, her whereabouts and plight in the last years of her life unknown to her two dearest friends, whom she steadfastly refused to contact. She loved them more than any two people on Earth, and she never doubted that if she asked for forgiveness, she would receive it. But their unconditional love for her, after all that had happened, was for her too bright a light to look upon.

The executor of Turner's penniless estate shared all of this in a second letter Dory and Charlotte received shortly after her death. They wept in pain and sorrow for days. It was Turner's wish that she should finally return to the Vineyard to be buried. Charlotte insisted that she be buried in the churchyard next to Meredith, and Dory saw that it was so. There, Turner's old friends said goodbye to her with great sorrow but a fond farewell.

It was a Sunday afternoon, six months to the day after Turner was laid to rest, just as Dory and Charlotte were leaving to go into town to lay flowers at her grave, that a call came to the kitchen at the Delano house. Rutla handed Dory the phone.

The male voice on the other end of the line was unfamiliar. He said he was placing the call for someone else who had tried several times in the past but never found the correct number. He asked to speak to a woman named Dory, and when Dory answered, he put the caller on the line.

Her name was Martha, she said. She was Enoch's mother. She knew Turner. Turner had somehow found her in Delacroix, Louisiana, while searching for Enoch, and they had spent several days together. From there Turner had left to follow up on rumors that Enoch had left Dulac-Chavin, a nearby town, on a boat bound for the Yucatan. She planned to find him or spend her last days trying. She told Martha she would return in six months, but made her promise that if she did not, Martha would contact Dory and Charlotte and insist they come to meet Martha in person, to learn of Enoch and of Turner's travels. Dory and Charlotte flew to Boston that very evening, and to New Orleans the next day.

For all that Dory and Charlotte had heard and dreaded about the oppressive humidity of summers in the Gulf, the air rushing past the open windows on the ride from the airport was surprisingly brisk. Water surrounded and infused every inch of the soil along the Delacroix highway, which at times appeared to run directly into the bayou but then would turn and snake along some improbable, unforeseen spit of land and take them just a little farther toward the next precipice, where it would snake and turn again. They arrived at their destination just before sunset.

A gaunt, pale woman, who was neither old nor young but who moved with the unsteadiness of long sorrow, came out to meet them. She lived in a small trailer on the edge of a place that seemed less a town than a collection of unloved shacks and well-loved boats. A dock led from the edge of her property to a thin ribbon of water surrounded by rushes. Worn lines and fenders made of old tires spoke of the boat that had once berthed there, but the berth was empty. Taking their hands in hers, she warmly greeted each of them and invited them inside.

"I'm glad you came. Please sit." She did not have the speech or demeanor of an educated woman, but there was a peaceful way of wisdom in her voice. A sitting room inside the trailer was appointed with a well-worn sofa, two chairs, a lamp, and little else. No artwork hung on the walls. A candle for lighting the stove stood beside a few neatly stacked dishes and cups on the counter of a small kitchen. She put a kettle on to boil.

"I have only a little tea and some cake."

"Really, Mrs.—"

"Please, just call me Martha."

"Thank you, Martha, but I really don't need a thing," Dory protested.

"Me neither," Charlotte chimed in. They were both famished and quite thirsty, but neither was willing to take any portion of what little this woman had.

"Oh, but I insist," Martha said. "You've come such a

long way. Let me do what I can. It would please me to do for you two girls."

"You're very kind," they answered in unison. Soon there were hot slices of corn cake with butter and sweet, milky tea that was far richer than they expected.

The woman sat in a chair opposite the two of them and, saying nothing, surveyed their faces. When she had either seen what she hoped to find or had given up looking—it wasn't clear which—she started to speak.

"Your friend told me that you knew my boy Enoch."

"Yes, we did," Dory began, speaking over Charlotte. "We both did, and we're very sorry for your loss."

"My loss?"

Dory looked at Charlotte, who mirrored her expression of abject discomfort.

"Well, yes, I mean—it's terrible that he died in that way. We were all heartbroken to hear of it. I didn't— neither of us knew him well, but he was very kind to both of us."

"Died?" Martha's face had a curious expression, as if she had just realized she had welcomed the wrong guests to the wrong house and was wondering now what to do with them. Then, a wave of understanding seemed to come over her.

"You mean the gunshot wound, of course."

"Well, yes," Dory continued, "we heard reports of a gunfight, but we weren't sure Enoch was involved. We just know that his bloody—" She stopped herself. It wouldn't do to speak of gore to his mother. "His boat was found capsized, and I'm afraid we assumed—well, . . ." Dory was rambling. She decided to get to the point. "You mean to say he's alive?"

"Alive as you and me, last I saw him, and I am positive he's livin' still. But I understand you bein' confused like that. You see, I didn't know what had become of Enoch till he came back by here six years

344

ago. Said he'd been shot and needed medicine, but a kind soul had bandaged him up and took him aboard a boat to a place where he could heal. When he finally got to where he could move about, he come here. I nursed him the rest of the way 'til he was new again. New as you and me."

"But . . . but that seems impossible. There was so much blood, and the boat . . . what . . . how did he manage?"

"Enoch is a good man. He's a simple man. A man after God's own heart. He don't ask for much, and I believe 'cause of that he has always been given whatever he needs. He has always been one of God's special creatures, since the day he first entered this world."

It didn't seem to be an answer to the question, though perhaps it was, yet it was clearly something any mother might say about the son she loved. Her words had a special poignancy for Dory and Charlotte, because it had already occurred to them that they were talking to one of God's special creatures at that very moment.

She stopped their conversation long enough to refill their tea, which was made from roots she kept in a jar by the stove. Served with honey, it was unimaginably delicious.

"Tell us about Enoch, Martha," Charlotte asked. It was a request broad enough to cover every imaginable aspect of Enoch's life she might choose to share with them because it was quickly becoming apparent they knew nothing about Enoch at all.

Martha eased back in her chair and looked at them, one and then the other, while she sipped slowly from her cup. It was a story she had told others before, but its meaning was in the mind of the hearer, and she wondered what meaning her two guests would impart to the story she was about to share.

"Enoch's father, Jesse, and I came from Giles

County, Tennessee," she began. "He was twenty-one. I was seventeen, and it wouldn't do for a black man to marry a white woman down in Giles County or anywhere close to Pulaski."

"I don't understand," Charlotte interrupted, with a look of bewilderment meant as a show of indignation and support. "I mean—there are laws, now."

"Laws?" Martha laughed just a little, then patted Charlotte's knee. "No, clearly you don't see, child—but how could you, unless you was from way down South, and from the looks of you, it's clear you ain't." She laughed again at this. "But you need to understand, Pulaski isn't just in the South. It's the Old South. It's where I was born," she smiled, "and it's where Jesse was born, but," she added, her expression darkening, "it's also where the Klu Klux Klan was born, and where most of them folks in it was raised. No matter what the law says, the Klan don't smile on a black farmhand marrying a white preacher's daughter, and that goes double for a black farmhand marrying a white preacher's pregnant daughter."

Charlotte and Dory nodded silently in unison at this, more out of astonishment than understanding.

"But we were in love. So, we ran—we ran, we ran, and we ran. We didn't have no car, and there wasn't much but that we could carry, 'cause we knew we'd be walkin' most of the way wherever we was goin'. And truth was, we had no idea where that might be. But when I got to where with the baby I couldn't walk no more, Jesse stole a horse, and then they was after us for that, too. So, we cut out late one night through the woods for Alabama. It was about a dozen strong men— them that was comin' after us. They was lookin' for us high and low. We hid out for three days in an old barn watchin' them comin' past, back and forth, until they finally give up and went home. It was then we let that old mare loose and took a chance we might catch a ride with a truck, what wouldn't mind pickin' up a white woman expectin' a baby and a black man along the road. We would have taken a ride any which way out of there, but the man who stopped for us was pullin' a load of hogs to slaughter. We went with him—me and Jesse and the hogs, there in the back of that truck—all the way to the Gulf of Mexico. The bayou here is where we made our home. Ain't nobody wants to stay lost down here ever goin' to be found, and we was happy here."

Dory was squirming with discomfort for the question she had to ask. "You said your husband, Jesse, was black, but—"

"You is wantin' to ask me how is it then that Enoch is as white as you or me?" Martha grinned widely and laughed freely now—big gravy spoonfuls of a southern woman's laughter, until she could laugh no more. "Well, child, don't you know Jesse was wonderin' the same thing you're askin' me now when Enoch finally come along, though he didn't have the courage to ask it direct as you. He just kindly stayed away from me and the baby, thinkin' he knew the truth, but he didn't know the truth 'til I told him, and I'll tell you the same truth today. Jesse's the only man I've ever known, and the only man I've ever loved or will love. He was as black as the tar on that road yonder, and his boy Enoch is as white as Mississippi cotton. I can't explain it. All I know is that Enoch is his son. Whether Jesse believed me or not I didn't waste time wonderin' 'cause Jesse was a good man to me and to Enoch all the days he knowed us, and he raised that boy and loved him much as any father could."

"Why did Enoch leave?" Charlotte asked.

"And where is Jesse now?" Dory added.

The smile on her face passed over to a place of pain. She paused again before she found the words.

"Enoch was just a normal, healthy boy, you have to understand—like any other boy. But as he growed up, a change come over him. Now, I raised four younger brothers fo' I ever had a boy of my own—wild as a bag of snakes they was. Enoch was different from all of 'em. He was different from most boys. He had a gift. And as he growed, the gift got stronger in him. It was a gift for . . ." she paused again, as if trying to translate a difficult phrase into a foreign language, "for settin' things right. Takin' crooked things and makin' 'em straight. The world to you and me and to most people is full of good and evil, sickness and health, sufferin' and joy. But Enoch don't live in that world. The world to him is not what it is to you and me but what he thinks it should be. That's as near as I can explain it, 'cause that's as near as I understand it myself. He sees somethin' or he feels somethin' in this world that ain't as he thinks it should be, and he sets it right."

"But how? How does he set it right?" Charlotte sought the same answers, now, that she once demanded from Turner. Like Turner, Martha couldn't give them to her. She could tell only the story as she knew it.

"When we got down to the bayou, Jesse fell to shrimpin'. It was shrimpin' or starve. Before long, he found a boat of his own—not a fancy thing, mind you, but a broken-down old scow somebody had made into a trawler before it got stove in and washed up in the mud. Jesse dug it out, floated it off, and fixed it up. He was so proud of that boat. He painted it all white and named it *Paloma,* after his mother. I had never seen a man put so much love and care into a thing. He kept it clean and neat as a pin. All them big boats would head out every mornin', and there would be little *Paloma* right in there alongside 'em. It wasn't a real trawler, and to look at it you'd say it wasn't near big enough to hold the shrimp you'd want for a good meal, much less sell to anyone else, but somehow Jesse made a livin' out of that boat for him and Enoch and me."

Another sip of tea, and another rest before she summoned the will to continue.

"Then come the oil spill, and hard times. Wasn't nobody catchin' no shrimp. By then Enoch was old enough to go with his father, and Jesse didn't hardly have no work to do anyhow with what little they could catch in those days, so he decided he'd teach the boy." She laughed at this, as though she had said something terribly funny. "One day, he and Jesse are out early of a mornin', along with the rest of the fleet, and Enoch tells his daddy to go throw his nets down way over yonder, far from shore, in deep water. And Jesse is tellin' him, kind as he can be to a young child who don't know no better, 'Son, there ain't no shrimp out there,' and just chastisin' him gentle-like to pay better mind to what he was tryin' to teach him. But Enoch commenced to naggin' and naggin', to where Jesse couldn't hardly stand it no more. And the way Jesse told the story, there wasn't nobody catchin' nothin' noways, so he decided to teach the boy a lesson by showin' him there weren't nothing out there where he wanted him to go."

A long, slow smile came over her face. "I reckon you girls know what I'm fixin' to tell you."

"I think so, ma'am," Dory answered, "but we want to hear it all the same."

"Well, Jesse puts down his nets, and no sooner he'd drug half a mile but what the stern of that little boat comes saggin' back and swampin' like he's fouled on a wreck or a rig or somethin' like it that ain't goin' nowhere, but he knowed that couldn't be true 'cause of how deep he was, way out there in the Gulf. When he pulled up the first of that net, there come such a mess of shrimp he feared they'd founder to take it all in. So he called them other boats to come help him. It took three of them big boats and a dozen men workin' together to get that catch brought in, and don't you know there was a party in the bayou that night! All them men what came to help Jesse had food to eat and money for their boats and their families that they hadn't had in months."

"I can't say we're surprised," Charlotte said, watching Dory nod in agreement. "Your son was a remarkable fisherman in New England. Everyone had heard about him."

"It was the same here. Word got around 'bout this little ol' boy down in the bayou. People commenced to talkin' 'bout him, only not everyone who heard the news had somethin' good to say. Back then, boats was dry-docked up and down the Gulf coast. Men who had knowed nothin' but shrimpin' their whole lives couldn't make no money, the oil spill had hit so bad. And then they hear tell of this boy down in Delacroix who's got a boat can't even hold all the shrimp he's catchin', and it was hard for some of 'em to take. A lot of stubborn pride is what it was—and envy. But there started to be some bad talk about Enoch."

"What kind of talk?" Dory asked.

"Talk like he done a deal with the devil, or that he was voodoo, and that he was tryin' to ruin men's souls. Such nonsense as you never heard. But the talk got to where people started to lie in wait to see him, as if they expected him to have horns and a tail or some such. There was a cruelty about it that made my stomach turn, but Enoch never said an unkind word to nobody. He just kept goin' out with his daddy, and they would come back every day as full as they was that first day, and all the other boats what followed him was full, too."

She was tiring as she spoke, and she paused again to warm herself with tea. The farther along she got in her tale, the more winded she became, as if the mere retelling of it wore her down. Dory and Charlotte waited eagerly for her to continue.

"Before long, other boats come up from 'round places like Metairie and Mandeville—started comin' in here, watchin' Jesse out with the fleet. But when them other boats couldn't catch no shrimp, one of 'em fired a shot across Jesse's bow and told him the next one would be coming for his boy. The next day, Jesse wouldn't take Enoch with him. Enoch begged him, but Jesse said no. Told him he was goin' to work in the 'Lord's Vineyard' that day, that he didn't need no help, and that he was to stay back here with me. Well, we waited here all day long into the night, but Jesse and *Paloma* never come back. It was a week later that Enoch went out after him."

"After him?" Charlotte asked. "After him where?"

"After him the only place he knowed to go. He had done walked forty miles up to the highway to St. Bernard before the first truck picked him up. Man asked him where he was headed. Enoch said he was headed to the vineyard. He took him a little ways and let him off, and Enoch went walkin' again 'til the next truck come along. Before he knew it, he was way up north, where y'all are from. He never found the Lord's Vineyard, but someone told him where Martha's Vineyard was. You see, that's my name, and I guess Enoch figured that would surely do. He was simple like that as a child, and he stayed that way as he growed, 'til he was a man. He had a pure heart, and I never saw it steer him wrong. I reckon you girls would agree with me."

Charlotte wiped a tear streaming down her cheek. She started to speak but could not. Dory spoke instead. "Yes, ma'am. We do agree, very much. If it hadn't been for Enoch, neither Charlotte nor I would be sitting here talking to you, right now."

"But you've seen him since then, you said?"

Charlotte finally managed to ask. "Where is he now?"

"Yes," Dory added, "and where is Jesse?"

"Jesse never come back. I reckon he's gone to the Lord's Vineyard, just like he promised that boy, and I reckon that's where Enoch's gone off again to find him."

She paused again, summoning her strength. "But Enoch, now, he laid up here most of the winter that year he first come back from his travels. When he was healthy enough, he commenced to buildin' a boat with his daddy's tools out of what scraps he could find— mending old canvas thrown out down at the packin' plant, soakin' old worn-out rope he'd find around here and there, to make it soft again. It was the first of May when he said goodbye. There was twenty, thirty come to see him off—all of 'em the shrimpers 'round here he'd saved from starvin' that year of the oil spill. Them boys would have walked through fire for Enoch if he'd asked 'em. But all he said was for them to take care of me, and that's just what they done. It's been five years, now."

She could say no more of Enoch and his life there with her and Jesse. Her well of strength and memory had been spent, and in its place a lonely peace remained. She did not pine or grieve. She looked to the water, where she had watched Enoch's vessel slip over the horizon.

Finally, Dory gathered the courage to ask a hard question. "Why are you telling us this, and why did you ask us to come here?"

It was a question almost accusatorial in its directness—so much so that Charlotte felt compelled to soften it. "Because we knew Enoch, of course, and wanted to learn more about him."

"No," Dory insisted. "Turner told you to call us. She planned this meeting. Why did she want us to come here?"

The woman looked at Dory in silence for a long time. She was searching for some sign of welcome in Dory's eyes and, finding it there, finally spoke again.

"Your friend wanted you to believe."

"Believe in what?" Dory demanded to know. There was no answer.

It was late when they finished talking—too late to return over that waterlogged highway to the hotel room waiting for them in New Orleans. Martha insisted they spend the night, and with little urging, they agreed.

Enoch's room, which was the only room Martha had to offer them in her small home, was as spare and simple as Enoch himself. There was a rough wooden table on which nothing sat but a chipped saucer full of fishing hooks and odd pieces of small tackle. An open chest lying on the floor held some clothing, a little rope, a piece of netting, an old fishing reel. A pocketknife was hanging by a lanyard on the bedpost.

There was also a nightstand on which a lamp had been placed next to a wooden box with a hinged top. They debated whether to look inside. To do so seemed at first an invasion of the privacy of that most private and inscrutable man, but to Dory and Charlotte, this place was a kind of shrine to his mystery, and they were pilgrims there on a mission of discovery. The box was the only thing in the room that seemed deliberately closed to them. So they opened it.

At first they mistook the papers it contained for the kind of miscellany that finds its way onto nightstands: assorted lists and notes and reminders and directions to do this or that and go here or there to accomplish some long-finished or abandoned task. But then Charlotte thought she recognized one piece of paper. It was torn in half. The handwriting on it was hers. It was the lost half of the note she had carried in the pocket of her dress the night she waded into the sea. She read it again now in stunned silence.

. . . *Remember me for the happiness and the silliness we shared. Know that I cherished every moment. If I could live on in those moments, I would, but all that once was sweet and good and worthy in life is gone. My world is now covered in darkness, and there is no more dawn.*

I do not know what waits for me. I can only hope I will be with Meredith again someday, but my hope grows thin. Whatever I meet in death, it cannot be worse than the emptiness of this life. I am so very sorry. Please forgive me. I will miss you all. Love, Charlotte.

Reading those words now, from the distance of six years, was for Charlotte like watching the funeral rite of a primitive tribe. That she ever put so much faith in the ability of men to know the mind of God or the contours of eternity now astounded her. Her body sagged, remembering and feeling again the weight of those dark days. The page fell from her hands to the floor.

Dory, who had been turning circles in the room as she took it all in, noticed Charlotte staring blankly, then saw the note. She picked it up and began reading. As the origin of the note and meaning of those words became clear, she wrapped her arm around Charlotte's neck and pulled her closer. "Oh God, Charlotte," she whispered. "He saved you . . . He truly, truly saved us both."

"Yes," Charlotte answered. "But not Turner. Not her, of all people."

The other pieces of paper that lay scattered on the floor and on the nightstand, around the opened box, offered glimpses of a world that had passed unseen before their eyes that long-ago summer. Among these were words of prayer and penitence from dozens of nameless, faceless people who had come to the

Vineyard to see this one man. There were questions and exclamations and pleas and demands, all placed at his feet. Some called him Enoch. Some called him brother. Some called him Lord.

They sought his intercession and aid to overcome sickness, to relieve despair, to find forgiveness, to face death. Some wanted to be made whole. Others wanted merely to be fed from his hands. But he had kept their petitions and carried them with him, every one, to this place.

"This one is unopened," Dory said, as she lifted a finger gently along the seam, then pulled a letter out and unfolded it. It was from Turner.

Dear Dory and Charlotte,

You know I am not much one for the kind of superstition some people call faith, but if you should read these words, I cannot help but believe that you were meant to find them.

By the time you read this I will be gone, but of course you know that—spit-spot, my life packed up and tidied away in a banker's box somewhere, while the rest of me is stuffed into a few board-feet of cheap soft pine. (I'm sure they couldn't afford more— the money is all gone and then some.) To what place I have gone, or whether it is any place at all, or to what purpose, or whether there is still a version of a "me" able to go anywhere, I have no earthly idea. If I should have a heavenly idea, I will write again, but I rather doubt I'll find ink, paper, or stamps in that place. This letter will have to do.

You are my dearest friends. It eases my pain to say so, and I hope it heals the wounds I caused just a little for you to hear it. I repaid your friendship poorly in many respects. I took too much care for myself and too little for you both. I am forever and desperately sorry. Please forgive me.

I expect no gratitude, but I hope you will remember that I loved you enough, Dory, to save you from marrying a monster, and that I loved you enough, Charlotte, to save you from bowing down before one. If I faltered in my efforts, please do not judge me too harshly. Remember all the laughter we shared. It was so very worth it all.

I have been searching, lo these last five years—although for what I am not sure. I think I hoped to discover just who or what Enoch is and what he meant to all of us, that summer. I am no closer to the truth now than when I started.

In all the time I spent with him, Enoch never claimed to be a sage or a priest or a prophet or, for that matter, anything more than a simple fisherman. I cannot prove to you that he walked on water, or that he cured cancer, or that he is alive, or—if he is alive—how he survived the gunshot that I saw tear through his body. (Yes, I was there.) I only know what my heart tells me, which is that he lives somewhere, still, and that finding him has become the last, great purpose of my life.

Enoch is none of the things we hold high, in this world. All I truly know of his life is that he was and is a homeless vagabond. But whoever he is, and wherever he is, he has become the Lord of my doubts and the God of my choosing.

The book about Enoch will be published, now, and more's the pity. It is an unfinished work and something of a fable, much as my life has been. But Bennett & Donald is a stern master, and I no more have the power to put off the book's beginning than my own ending. Against all odds, it seems I will be remembered, at last, as a Bennett & Donald author, which should keep you laughing, Dory, for years to come. It pleases me to think so. We should all learn from this to be careful what we wish for.

I am told the book is certain to be a best seller, and for what it's worth, I have asked that the royalties be paid to the two of you. Do something fabulous with the money, girls, and think of me.

Your eternal friend,
Turner

CHAPTER 29

It was a very different island to which Charlotte returned on the ferry that July. In seven years' time, the Gulf Stream had left, and the shrimp had returned, but the fleet was now forever gone. The man named Enoch—whom she did not know when she made that first crossing but who would save her life—was also gone from that place, as was the friend who saved her life a second time that summer. But by her side on this journey was Dory, her most stalwart ally, and waiting for them was Rutla, who watched over them both with a vigilance that would shame the angels. Rutla's lengthening years had not slowed her step. She simply would not allow it.

It was a different island for Smoke, too, although that was by his design. He had afforded Tripp Wallace the rescue from his failing family fortune that Tripp had once looked to Eudora Delano to provide. In exchange, Tripp had given Smoke the deed to the derelict warehouse on the harbor owned by his family. There, Smoke—of all people—had manipulated, magnified, and promoted Enoch's legend for the purpose of erecting an improbable monument to it.

It was a rather gaudy but wildly popular restaurant named The Holy City Shrimp Emporium. Tourists and curiosity seekers flocked there in great numbers year-round to experience a taste of the wild shrimp once caught on the Vineyard by the man who, according to the newly released *Book of Enoch*, had walked on water, healed the sick, and fed the multitudes—the same man who was believed to have been shot and perhaps even murdered, yet who was said to have risen from that doom and lived again. They gathered there in that immodest monument to his modest life, expectantly waiting for his return and feasting on the food and drink that Smoke was delighted to sell them in the meantime.

After they had gorged themselves, patrons of the Emporium—pilgrims, as Smoke referred to them—could further empty their wallets in the museum that told the story of the mysterious fisherman "whom the sea obeyed" in an interactive, three-dimensional, multimedia display. The highlight of the tour was getting to touch a shard of the broken dory on which the fisherman's blood had been spilled. Tiny fragments of the wood were sold in the museum gift shop, in little cellophane packets bearing the official "Holy City" seal, alongside Holy City tee shirts printed with the only known image of the founder of Smoke's feast, recovered from the mangled camera of one Turner Graham.

Smoke was the toast of the town and a leading light in the island's civic, cultural, and religious life. The Holy City Shrimp Emporium was on its way to becoming the leading tourist attraction in New England. Plans were already underway for franchise locations in ten cities. It was Smoke's dream to spread the business to the farthest corners of the globe. Ten percent of the money that poured through its coffers was donated to the Church, in exchange for which Father Vecchio—with special dispensation from the bishop—permitted the wait staff to wear the brown robes of monastics, befitting the solemnity of the loaves and fishes being served. Martha's Vineyard and the town fathers of Edgartown, in particular, had never plumped so fully in the certainty of their favor before God. As for Smoke, although he had begun life with the wealth of Solomon, he now added to it at a pace beyond Solomon's wildest imaginings.

What patrons of the Emporium did not know and were never told was that every morsel of shrimp sold there was farmed, raised, and harvested entirely on the premises in dozens of large, aerated, and temperature-controlled stainless steel vats. With no competition or the need to pay a fleet of suppliers, Smoke controlled the price and every aspect of production. Even the wooden relics were chipped from a hoard of abandoned railroad ties from which a thousand sacred vessels could have been built.

Three faces eagerly searched the crowd coming off the Oak Bluffs ferry dock for a first look at the travelers from Louisiana. In Rutla's watchful charge were two young girls, born one month apart in the spring, six years ago. One was talkative, tall, and gangly—with shockingly red hair, bright white skin, and a blizzard of freckles on her cheeks that had ripened in the summer sun. The other was soft and shy, small and gentle as a mouse, with a buttery brown complexion, dark eyes, and shimmering brown hair. When the two girls saw Dory and Charlotte, a cry went up in unison from them, and they slipped their bonds at Rutla's side.

"Mommy! Mommy! You're back!"

"Look what Brian gave me!" screamed the red one, whose named was Elise, as she crashed into Dory with a small wooden model of a boat in her hand.

"His name is *Ryan,* not *Brian,*" the brown one replied, by way of correction. This was Maura. Pulling Charlotte down to eye level, she whispered in a slow and serious tone befitting a grave injustice, "He gave it to *me*."

"He gave it to both of us!" Elise fired back.

It was a replica of Enoch's skiff, purchased from the gift shop at the Emporium by a playmate of the girls who had been tragically unclear about which of them was meant to receive it. Or, perhaps he had not yet decided and was playing them both. In any event, into the breach of this uncertainty created by Ryan-not-Brian, discord had come between the two girls, and Rutla had striven in vain all that morning to quell it.

They were the children of that summer to remember. Elise saw Trafalgar Wallace, her father, every other week and on alternating holidays and birthdays. She understood dimly that there had been an almost-wedding, and that she had almost been part of what Dory achingly sometimes heard her describe as "a real family." But Elise was no more certain of the reasons why the wedding never happened than her father. Dory had never told him. He had never asked.

The truth Dory never uttered was that she had accepted Tripp's proposal knowing full well he wanted only a lifeboat, not someone to help row. She had also accepted that there would be affairs by one or both of them during the marriage. For that reason, his dalliance with Turner was much more intramural in Dory's eyes than Turner could ever have known at the time. Affairs were the common currency of wedded life among the well-to-do, which had little to do with love and fidelity and everything to do with money and manners— manners here meaning discretion, not courtesy.

Dory had never spoken of these things also because she hardly considered herself the innocent party. She hadn't had the courage or even the inclination to tell Tripp she was pregnant before the wedding. She had chosen, quite on her own, the course of subterfuge and entrapment her mother would have charted for her if

Dory had asked her for advice. It was to have been another remarkable premature delivery, welcomed eight months after the wedding with prayers and thanksgiving by all. The prospect of the first Delano bastard since the Melville incident was more raw honesty than Dory thought she could abide. Avoiding that scandal was the only reason she had accepted Tripp's proposal the same day the stick turned pink. Finally facing herself and refusing to build her life upon that lie was the only reason she walked away. Turner's confession was merely the catalyst, not the cause. It didn't reveal to Dory anything she didn't already know or assume about Tripp, but it showed her something she had, until that moment, refused to see in herself.

Maura was the child of passion and longing, conceived in one improbable moment on a sand dune beside the very pond where she now played each day. Charlotte had gone to that lonely place every afternoon for months before Maura was born, hoping only to tell the melancholy boy she had comforted, that day, that he did have a child after all—a daughter who would have his same sad eyes. There had been no artifice, no dishonesty, no dishonor in his passion for Charlotte, and in his ignorance of his child, he remained an honorable man. Charlotte would one day tell Maura of the boy who was her father, who had wept in Charlotte's arms for the child that never was, yet would never smile for the child who was destined to be.

For all the rude truth about how they came into the world, the world in which Elise and Maura lived was an enchanted one. Growing up on the Delano estate, they had shared a single, chronically disordered room since they were infants. Together they were allied against Rutla in her war on untidiness of any kind, and the children danced every day on a littered field of victory.

The two girls were as inseparable as their mothers

had become. Rutla was another mother to them, and she seemed to grow young again from their boundless energy. The beach on Eel Pond was perpetually strewn with the detritus of childhood summers by the seashore: bamboo poles; tangled line; dead and dying worms; shovels and buckets; wet, half-buried towels; the odd, forgotten flip-flop. It was a child's paradise, and both children would have been eager to return there that afternoon but for their excitement over the parade that was coming to town that day, as it did every year on the same day. It was the Fourth of July.

As they walked to their waiting car, Rutla remembered something she had forgotten to mention earlier. "A message came for you at the house, Dory, from a woman in Edgartown."

"Anyone I know?"

"She said she has something to give to a friend of yours from her husband. She lives behind the family's house in town."

"Did she say what it was?" Dory asked.

"I asked her that. She said she needed to explain it in person. Would you rather I go instead?"

A neighbor—that was odd enough. But "something to give to a friend" sounded intriguing.

"No, Rutla," Dory insisted. "Why don't you drop Charlotte and me off and take the girls home. We'll meet you at five outside the Old Whaling Church to get a spot for the parade."

The Delano family's old guest house in Edgartown, where that long-ago summer began and where Turner had tapped out the first blog posts that became the book that became a worldwide phenomenon, was now a tea parlor, just as Turner had predicted. The protests had faded, but a daily crush of pilgrims and curiosity seekers continued to the point where it was impractical for anyone to live there. The Delano trustees had leased the house and grounds to the town historical association, which made a handsome income selling tickets for tours and tea. The line formed at the front of the house in the morning and remained there all day long. But around the back, where the outdoor shower stood facing a slightly higher hedge of glossy abelia, the neighboring house was still private property. Walking up to the door with Charlotte, Dory saw a "for sale" sign in the yard. She had a sudden feeling of anxiety and remorse that she had never bothered to learn anything about the family who lived there.

The woman who answered the door recognized them immediately, though only Dory by name. Charlotte introduced herself. The woman held her hands warmly and smiled. She seemed genuinely glad to see Charlotte, as if she were welcoming an old friend.

The house was dark and in the process of being closed for the winter, which seemed odd so early in the season. Some of the furniture had been moved out. Large oil paintings in gilded frames were leaning up against the walls. Other pieces were covered in sheets. An airline ticket to Boston the next morning was lying on a table beneath a mirror in the foyer. Next to it was a thin white envelope.

"This is for you," the woman said, as she handed the envelope to Charlotte. "It's the money I received for your portrait. It meant a great deal to him—more than I realized. Among the papers he left, when he died, was a note asking that I sell the painting and give you the money. It's all there."

"What portrait?" Charlotte asked, incredulously.

"You will see. There's a new tavern in town—I think they call it McClatchy's. They bought the portrait at the estate auction three days ago. I believe they intend to hang it over the bar. You can probably see it if you go there now."

Charlotte opened the envelope. She thought it would be rude to ask the amount—she hadn't earned anything, after all—but inside was a thick stack of large bills. Forty thousand dollars, if she had bothered to count.

Charlotte looked up from the envelope at the woman. "I don't mean to sound ungrateful, but I don't understand." The woman's face creased with something like pain, or perhaps merely embarrassment. She had been dreading the explanation, but it was clear more would have to be said.

"My husband loved you in a way, I think. He painted many beautiful women in his lifetime. That's how we met, and that's how he made his living. But you . . . you . . ." She paused here, struggling with emotion. "You he seemed to adore."

"But I never met him. He never saw me that I know of. I didn't sit for a portrait."

"Every great painter is a voyeur," she laughed, "and Raul was a great painter. I would watch him wait for you each evening to come for your bath. You would stand there like a statute for a long time, just letting the water wash away your worries. Every night he would sketch a little more of you. He would tell me with such excitement, 'Katrina, she is exquisite.' And of course, I could see you were, but it was hard for a wife to accept that kind of adoration in her husband's eyes. You were not just a model to him. There was something very fragile and new in the way he saw you. He expressed it perfectly in the painting. I think it was perhaps his best work."

Charlotte's jaw, which had been slowly dropping as the woman spoke, was now agape.

"Oh my God!" Dory said, with genuine delight.

"It was wrong, I know—peeping on you in that way, through the hedges—but if you knew my husband, you would understand that his interest in you was purely aesthetic. You were a lovely flower to him, and he wanted to paint you in full bloom."

Charlotte finally regained her composure enough to recognize that this woman had lost the love of her life, and to realize what a lovely gesture she was making. "I'm so terribly sorry for your loss. I'm sure this—losing your husband, I mean—has been difficult for you."

"Thank you, but it was a long illness. As they say, in the end, it was a relief to see him finally at peace."

Dory was intrigued. The artist's wife was quite young—about her same age. It was entirely possible her husband had been much older, but the way she spoke of him, Dory guessed he was not. Forgetting her manners, she asked how old he was, and how he died.

"Lung cancer. A very bad way to go. He was only forty-eight. A lifetime of cigarettes, I'm afraid. He smoked them as he painted, one after another, as if it was his passion and not the cigarettes that were on fire."

The Old Whaling Church on Main Street in the heart of Edgartown had long been a gathering place for various functions, both civic and religious. On that Fourth of July, as most years, it was the center of activities spanning the entire day. Charlotte was racing at flank speed toward McClatchy's when Dory suggested they wait there, just for a moment, to see if Rutla and the children might arrive on time. Behind them and up the long steps, the great white doors of the church were open to the street. Standing on the sidewalk, they could hear a speech being given by an English professor from one of the colleges on the mainland. *The Book of Enoch* was on sale at the bookstore across the street, and the store had sponsored this lecture on a literary interpretation of the text.

It was a blessing and a curse that almost no one who had any interest in *The Book of Enoch* knew who Dory and Charlotte were or, for that matter, that the two most famous benefactors of Enoch's saving power still lived on the island. It was a blessing because Dory and Charlotte no longer had to travel in secret for fear of being accosted by protesters. It was a curse because they had to listen to their lives being described in the third person by people who had no idea what had actually happened during that notorious summer, other than what Turner had written about it.

Standing there, waiting for Rutla and the children, it became excruciating for Charlotte to listen to the speaker outline the "complex metaphorical structure" of the drowning scene in which a woman seeking God is "figuratively saved" from the sea, and how that metaphor "fits into the overall context of contemporary religious mythology."

"Have you ever heard such bullshit?" Dory finally erupted.

"Never," Charlotte replied. "Let's get out of here. Call Rutla. Tell her to find us at McClatchy's. I'm going to have a fit if I have to wait any longer to see my painting."

McClatchy's had been opened by new owners in an old tavern space in Edgartown that was blessed with fourteen-foot ceilings. They had made use of that space to fit Charlotte's larger-than-life nude portrait above the bar. Charlotte stood once again mouth agape, staring at herself from across the bar at the hostess station.

She had been exquisitely if indiscreetly rendered in a full-frontal view, gently cradling a bar of soap in one hand, and leaning slightly on one arm braced against the side of the outdoor shower. Her hair fell in rich, sensual curls over her shoulders. She had a wan expression with a youthful aura. Her skin was a pool of fresh cream floating with raspberries. Her tits were fabulous.

Dory immediately doubled over in laughter, while Charlotte went madly rummaging through her purse for a pair of Jackie-O sunglasses and promptly put them on. She could see nothing afterwards and had to be led by the hand to their table.

Dory added to Charlotte's pain by pressing the hostess for details about the painting as she seated them.

"The new owners just bought it," the very young girl told them. "I heard they paid a ton for it. It's an original Raul Bennini. He just passed away last month, so it's bound to be worth a fortune someday. Isn't it wonderful?"

"Yes, positively erotic," Dory answered.

The hostess stood there a moment, looking at the painting. "I could fast for forty days and forty nights and still not have a body like that," she finally said. Dory replied, smiling and evidently pleased with herself, "Well, you know, there are women with great brains, and women with great bodies, but very few women with both. Isn't that right, Charlotte?"

Charlotte refused to be cowed. She removed the sunglasses, gave a glowering look that failed to suppress Dory's widening grin, and told the hostess she'd have a dry gin martini, straight up. Dory ordered the same. The hostess looked at Charlotte quizzically, then at the painting, then back at Charlotte. "Remarkable! You look just like her."

"Yes, and if she had any brains, we might be twins," Charlotte replied.

By the time the hostess had taken down their drink orders and left, Dory was reaching into her purse. She pulled something out and placed it on the table. It was a hundred-dollar bill.

"What's that?" Charlotte asked.

"The bet—you win."

"What bet?"

"The Dorian Gray bet. You are victorious, Victoria." Dory laughed.

"But we're not forty yet. We've got a year to go."

"Doesn't matter," Dory conceded. "I'm calling the race early. It's a no-contest."

"Oh, shut up."

"No really, you win. No matter what I do to stay in shape from here on out, you will be ageless up there above the bar. You're like Helen Mirren. Your boobs will live on forever as an object of cult worship by strange, drunk men. In a hundred years, my boobs and I will be dust, but you'll still be the naked goddamn *Mona Lisa*. I hate you. I truly do."

When the drinks arrived, Charlotte lifted her glass. "Here's to old friends and the surprising benefits of indecent exposure."

The drinks went down with welcome smoothness. It was the first time they had truly relaxed since they had set out for Louisiana. It was as if a great divide had been laid down between the darkness of the life they once knew and the bright future that now opened before them.

The subject of Turner's royalty money came up at last for the first time since they had left Louisiana—or specifically, Dory's insistence on not taking any of it came up. She didn't need the money, she said—which was certainly true—and it would please her for Charlotte to have it. Charlotte refused and insisted that they donate the money to some worthy cause in

Turner's honor. It was at that table in McClatchy's, on a sweltering Fourth of July over dry gin martinis, that the Turner Graham School for Girls was founded.

The Delano estate, where the school would be housed, would at last find a purpose for its existence beyond an endless stream of garden parties for doddering prigs looking for new reasons to discuss why Trafalgar Wallace had been wise not to marry "that woman." Elise and Maura would be the first two students, followed in the years to come by thousands more than Dory or Charlotte or Turner could ever have dreamed.

The noise of the coming parade drew them outside the tavern. There they saw Rutla and the girls wending their way along sidewalks already lined with folding chairs, and mothers holding children holding melting ice cream cones, as they did every year. People were streaming in from all over the Vineyard, once again.

The perennial favorites passed by to cheers from all. There was the honor guard and drum corps, followed by the teetering, ancient men of the American Foreign Legion who, by the slow subtraction of old age, once more proudly fit into the uniforms they had worn as frightened boys. There was the Bay State Band and its rousing rendition of "I'm a Yankee Doodle Dandy," the town selectmen, the yacht club commodores in blue blazers and white trousers, and the lone officer of the island K9 corps, pulling along a slobbering, thirsty Labrador. There was the hand-pumped, faithful fire-hose wagon, rolled out again to deploy plumes of white water into crowds of squealing children. Elise sprinted in the direction of the spray, followed eagerly by Maura and reluctantly by Rutla.

At the end of this line in years past, for as long as anyone could remember, there would have been a large wooden cross carried by the parish council of St. Joseph's Catholic Church and the Fourth Degree Honor Guard of the Knights of Columbus in their colorful chapeaus. But this year was different. This year the church did not march. This year, instead, a small group of solemn-faced, rough men carried something altogether new.

It was a long and jagged piece of misshapen wood— the blood-spattered remnant of a broken boat—the only tangible remnant of Enoch's short life on the island. It had been recovered from a beach on Katama Bay, where it was found on the day the *Victory* sank. The men who found it and now carried it were all that was left of the fleet Enoch had kept alive and tried to save with the money he multiplied from simple baskets of shrimp sold by the roadside. Some people threw rose petals at the men's feet. Others leaned out to touch the wreck of the hull as it passed, and some pasted notes with prayers. A hush came over the crowd, and a sudden impulse came over Dory, as they passed.

She stepped into the parade, placed her hand on the wreck alongside the hands of the men, and walked with them. A muffled, twittering sound rushed through the crowd like a calling flock of birds, as some spoke the famous name *Delano,* and others repeated it down the line.

Charlotte was caught completely off guard by Dory's departure, but she instantly understood its meaning: Eudora Delano was making her profession of faith.

"I didn't know you were a believer," Charlotte called to her from the curb.

Dory looked back, her hand unmoved from the place where it rested, as she continued to walk. Her expression glowed with quiet resolve. "Seven years, cancer-free. Where else can I find a faith that can do that?"

Charlotte smiled, but she did not follow. She could not follow.

Dory and the fishermen disappeared behind the trees as the end of the parade column slowly turned toward the town commons. Charlotte saw Rutla and the children chase after Dory. They would all soon be home, where they would spread blankets and baskets of Rutla's special brownies out on the lawn and wait for the first rockets to burst in the sky over the harbor, as darkness fell.

The other parade-goers abandoned their posts along Main Street, and before long the summer sounds of folding chairs and rolling coolers, the laughter of excited children and old friends, subsided to a calming stillness. Charlotte found herself still standing where Dory had left her, and the place where she happened to be was directly across from St. Joseph's.

While there was still light, Charlotte wished to see the grave again. She walked along the familiar garden path that led to the cemetery on the church grounds. She had been there almost every day for the past seven years. She came to speak to Meredith, but she came also to sit, laugh, and wonder at the grave of an old friend. The two plots were side by side, and between them was a short bench, well suited for long thoughts.

In the cemetery that day, Charlotte found an older woman standing beside the two graves. She had not seen her there before. As Charlotte approached, the woman turned and smiled, then turned and looked at the ground without uttering a word. Charlotte hesitated to break the reverent silence, which persisted for several minutes until the woman, stooping low, spoke. It was only then that Charlotte noticed, as if scales had fallen from her eyes, that the ground covering the two graves was a seamless carpet of tiny blue flowers.

"Violets," the woman said, caressing the blossoms with her hand. "They withered and died in my garden months ago. They never last very long, but these—these are blooming still. What a good and joyful thing that is."

"Yes," Charlotte softly replied to the stranger who had come to linger over the graves of her loved ones. Charlotte stooped down beside her and reached out with her left hand to caress one of the tiny blossoms that seemed to grow right out of Meredith's headstone. As she did this, the sleeve of her blouse pulled up, revealing the nearly forgotten, thin blue line of numbers on her arm: 1183-2.

What had once been a badge of her shame was now a symbol of her freedom and a testament to her triumph. She looked over at the old woman smiling beside her, and answered again, "Yes. What a good and joyful thing, indeed."

For Dory, the faith she found in a reclusive fisherman, who once dared to touch her so deeply, never faltered from that day forward. For Turner, the quest to believe had led her into a realm of shadows and light. Some of what she found there was true; some of it was partly true; and some of it was wholly an illusion. In the end, none of it could save her. In *The Book of Enoch,* she had rendered all of it faithfully through the darkened lens of her own understanding, which is not to say accurately, but which is as close to holiness as anyone can come in this world.

Turner never revealed the names of Enoch's would-be murderers to Dory or anyone. Turner's betrayal of Enoch that night was to her a crime so great, and the memory of it a thing so hideous, that she considered the crime of his assailants a trivial failure by comparison. A longing for absolution had followed her to the grave.

As for Charlotte, the faith of her fathers on which she had once so completely relied, and for which she had stood ready to give her life, never returned to her. The very idea of faith—and along with it, the power to believe in the magic of unseen things—had been torn from her. Some scars are too deep, some wounds too painful, ever to heal. But in time she made peace with the pain, and in its midst a simple hope bloomed again—hope in the power of good and joyful things, in the smile of a stranger, and in the saving hand of a friend.

ABOUT THE AUTHOR

Born in Baltimore in 1958, Michael Hurley holds a degree in English Education from the University of Maryland and a law degree from St. Louis University. He is admitted to the bar in Texas and North Carolina.

Michael's debut novel, *The Prodigal,* won the 2013 Chanticleer Grand Prize and was shortlisted for several other literary awards. His first book, *Letters from the Woods,* is a collection of essays chosen as a finalist for the ForeWord Reviews Book of the Year Award in 2005. In 2012, Hachette Book Group published his sailing memoir, *Once Upon a Gypsy Moon,* about the 2,200-mile solo voyage that ended with the loss of his boat in the Windward Passage between Cuba and Haiti. *The Vineyard* is his second novel.

After more than thirty years in trial practice, Michael retired in 2014 to write, sail, and pursue the secret of life full-time. He lives near Charleston, South Carolina, and keeps up with readers at www.mchurley.com.